"Capta

Her voice came out sharper than she meant, and at the sound of it he turned his head, scowling nastily at being interrupted in his solitary drinking. Meg saw then that his eyes were amber-colored, gold as a wildcat's, and slightly out of focus beneath slashing black brows. There were violet shadows beneath, and he had not shaved in a while. His cheeks were prickly with a stubble as dark as those fierce eyebrows. Oh, and he was handsome. Not in the delicate, fine-boned way she had imagined—there was nothing effeminate about Gregor Grant. His was a face that had lived and suffered—a tough, masculine face, the face of a man who gave no quarter and expected none.

The Gregor Grant she had imagined had been a boy. This was a man, a man who would do no one's bidding but his own. A man who was scowling up at her with the most fascinating and yet unfriendly eyes that she had ever seen.

Meg had come to find a dream—a wispy, insubstantial girlhood dream.

Before her was solid reality.

Other **AVON ROMANCES**

Coming Soon

And Don't Miss These
ROMANTIC TREASURES
from Avon Books

ATTENTION: ORGANIZATIONS AND CORPORATIONS
Most Avon Books paperbacks are available at special quantity discounts for bulk purchases for sales promotions, premiums, or fund-raising. For information, please call or write:

Special Markets Department, HarperCollins Publishers, Inc., 10 East 53rd Street, New York, N.Y. 10022–5299.
Telephone: (212) 207–7528. Fax: (212) 207-7222.

SARA BENNETT

BELOVED HIGHLANDER

AVON BOOKS

An Imprint of HarperCollins*Publishers*

This is a work of fiction. Names, characters, places, and incidents are products of the author's imagination or are used fictitiously and are not to be construed as real. Any resemblance to actual events, locales, organizations, or persons, living or dead, is entirely coincidental.

AVON BOOKS
An Imprint of HarperCollins*Publishers*
10 East 53rd Street
New York, New York 10022-5299

Copyright © 2003 by Sara Bennett
ISBN: 0-06-051971-1
www.avonromance.com

All rights reserved. No part of this book may be used or reproduced in any manner whatsoever without written permission, except in the case of brief quotations embodied in critical articles and reviews. For information address Avon Books, an Imprint of HarperCollins Publishers.

First Avon Books paperback printing: October 2003

Avon Trademark Reg. U.S. Pat. Off. and in Other Countries, Marca Registrada, Hecho en U.S.A.
HarperCollins® is a registered trademark of HarperCollins Publishers Inc.

Printed in the U.S.A.

10 9 8 7 6 5 4 3 2 1

If you purchased this book without a cover, you should be aware that this book is stolen property. It was reported as "unsold and destroyed" to the publisher, and neither the author nor the publisher has received any payment for this "stripped book."

years since Gregor Grant was Laird of Glen Dhui. Twelve years since the Grants had come out for the Stuarts in the 1715 Rebellion, and he had ridden into battle with his father, the old Laird, and lost. Lost everything. Seventeen-year-old Gregor had been imprisoned after the Battle of Preston, along with hundreds of other men. His father had died of apoplexy in terrible conditions in the prison. And it was there, in the gaol, that Gregor had met Meg's father—a commander for the government troops—and it had been her father who saw to his release.

Free he might have been. Saved from the hangman's noose or the steamy plantations of Jamaica or Barbados, Carolina or Virginia. But Gregor had lost his home, lost Glen Dhui. His family's punishment for taking part in the Rebellion was the confiscation of their home, their estate, and with it the title of Laird. Gregor and his mother and young sister had fled Glen Dhui and never returned—they had had no choice. But the people had mourned them, him in particular—he was the young Grant Laird—and she suspected they mourned him still. She knew they had loved him, trusted him, set their hopes upon him. He had been their golden-haired boy, the light of their future.

And it seemed he still was.

"The lad will not let us down," Duncan Forbes had assured her when they had set out two days earlier.

Meg prayed his feelings were not misplaced. And yet she too was lifted by a new and vibrant hope as they rode toward their goal. If Gregor Grant was really all they said . . . if he was the sort of man who would set aside his present circumstances to return to the glen he had known as a boy . . . then Meg feared she was already more than half in love with him.

"There'll be an inn," Duncan said, noting her weariness. He had dropped back to ride at her side, and she met the gleam of his dark eyes in the growing darkness. "We'll stop there first, my lady, and ye can take your ease. Me and the men will search out Captain Grant for ye."

"Thank you, Duncan. Will you recognize him, do you think?"

"'Tis a while, but aye, I'll know him."

Meg nodded. She had never seen Gregor Grant herself, but she thought she would know him. His collection of boyhood sketches, found in the attic, and kept in a corner of her room, had drawn her attention again and again over the years. The sketches were delicate, so careful in their detail, romantic in their rendering, full of an emotion that spoke to her. The man . . . the boy who created such works must be special. From her father's memories of the seventeen-year-old Gregor and her own daydreams, she visualized him as slender and fair, with the face of a poet and the long-fingered hands of an artist. His smile would be shy and yet so sweet, it would melt her heart.

Meg was aware that such a person as she imagined did not quite fit the real Gregor Grant. For these days he was a soldier, a captain of dragoons in a Campbell regiment. The Campbells were anti-Jacobite, and it seemed ironic that a man who had fought with the Jacobites in 1715 should now keep the peace for the government in the Highlands. But that was how it was, sides were taken and then changed. The Highlander was no different from any other man in putting self-interest first. Meg could not blame Gregor Grant for switching sides, if it meant putting food in his mouth.

Her thoughts trailed off as they reached the inn. A torch flared, suddenly, illuminating a clean, tidy-looking building—which was more than Meg could say of the tavern across the cobbled square. She glanced over her shoulder into the half darkness, where the sound of rowdy voices and drunken shouts jarred the night.

Duncan strode inside the inn, his kilt swinging about his sturdy legs, and Meg followed in her trews, her jacket long enough to cover her to mid-thigh. She told herself that her appearance was perfectly respectable, and very sensible for traveling about the Highlands, and it was not her fault if the innkeeper could not seem to take his eyes off her.

"My best room is free, my lady," he informed her, cocking a stockinged leg and bowing low, his tatty brown wig threatening to slip from his head. "If my daughter, Morag, were here I'd send her to help ye . . . to . . . Ah, here she is!"

A girl with dark hair sidled into the room, glancing at her father guiltily. "I'm sorry, father, I had to—"

"Aye, well, we'll see about where ye've been later!" her father said angrily. "I've told ye not to go mooning about where the soldiers are!" He seemed to recollect the company he was in, and quickly resumed a toothy smile for Meg's benefit. "Aye, well, girls will be girls, and as I said, we'll discuss it later. Go with the lady now, and fetch her soap and water and see to her wants. 'Tis not often we have such grand folk staying at the Clashennic Inn."

Duncan Forbes gave Meg a brief bow. "I'll see ye in a wee while, my lady. After the horses are stabled, me and the lads will take a walk to the barracks and see if we canna find that matter we are seeking."

"Very well, Duncan."

Meg would have preferred to go with him and speak to Gregor Grant for herself, but such a thing was too much to hope for. Duncan wanted her safe indoors. He did not approve of women taking charge, and although he bore it at Glen Dhui, he would not allow it here in Clashennic. Since her father, General Mackintosh, had lost his sight, Meg had taken much of the running of the estate upon herself. She did the job well, she thought proudly, but there was still some resistance to overcome. Tough Highland men like Duncan were not easy with taking their orders from a woman.

Morag, the innkeeper's daughter, showed Meg to her room, and soon returned with a ewer of warm water. The room was small but as neat and clean as the inn itself, and Meg sighed with relief. She was weary, and as narrow as it was, the bed looked inviting. Sleeping in the open was something she doubted she would ever grow used to, and she admired the Highland man who could lay himself down to sleep in the heather, wrapped only in his plaid.

Quickly she splashed warm water onto her face and hands, removing the dust of travel. Not a bath, unfortunately, but good enough for now. Behind her the girl spoke. "We've mutton stew for supper, my lady, and plenty of ale to drink. My father keeps a fine table here."

Meg dried her face, and began to unpin her hair. The long, curling strands of fire fell about her back and shoulders. "I'm sure he does, Morag, but I don't know when my men will be returning. They are seeking someone in the town . . . one of the soldiers."

"Oh?" The girl's face turned curious. "Who would that be then, my lady? I know many of the soldiers," she added boldly.

Meg smiled. "His name is Captain Grant. Do you know him?"

Morag broke into an answering smile. "I do, my lady! Captain Grant is well known in Clashennic. But . . . he's at the Black Dog, the tavern across the way. Many of the soldiers drink there. I saw him but a moment ago, when I popped in to . . . that is, when I was passing by there to . . . when I was passing by."

She finished awkwardly, plainly not wanting to openly admit being anywhere near the Black Dog. Meg was inclined to think it was a place her father had forbidden her to enter, but there was no time to mull over the follies of young girls.

Gregor Grant was at the Black Dog, and Duncan Forbes might not be back for hours. It seemed meant, somehow. Predestined.

She could send someone after Duncan, and then wait for his return, but why bother when she had only to step across the way? It would give Meg an opportunity to speak to Gregor Grant first, and suddenly she knew she would far rather have her first meeting with him alone, without the distraction of Duncan Forbes hovering nearby.

"Then I must go and see him," she said firmly, more to herself than the girl. Retrieving her comb from her saddlebag, Meg began to restore some order to her tangled curls.

"Ye are going to go and see Captain Grant in the Black Dog, my lady? Like that? I mean . . . do ye not mean to change?"

Meg met the girl's eyes, wide in her round face. She glanced down at herself and for a moment saw herself as the innkeeper's daughter must. A tall, slender woman wearing trews that clung to her legs like skin, and riding boots that came up to her knees. The jacket saved her, covering as it did her hips and bottom and the fleshy part of her thigh. In truth she would not pass for a man, but nor should she draw attention to herself in the dim, smoky insides of the tavern.

"No," Meg said, "I will not change. The Black Dog does not appear to be the sort of place one would wear one's best gown."

Would Gregor Grant think it strange of her to be dressed as a man? Probably, Meg admitted wryly to herself, he will be horrified. The boy who had executed those delicate sketches must without doubt be a connoisseur of all things fine. He would like his women petite, dressed in pretty gowns, shy and sweetly mannered. Certainly not a tall, strapping lassie with fiery hair and a sharp tongue!

"Well, it cannot be helped," she told herself with her usual practicality. "I am what I am."

Perhaps it was foolish of her to feel as if she already knew the boy, and therefore the man. That she knew his mind and, perhaps more important, his heart. And yet no amount of inner discussion could persuade her differently.

Meg smoothed her jacket one last time, tugging it lower. She was ready, and her breath was only a little faster than usual, her hands were only slightly unsteady, her heart was beating only marginally swifter beneath her breast. She was ready to put her case before Gregor Grant, to ask him in her father's name to come home with her to Glen Dhui.

The square was not wide across, and yet it looked immense. It was quite dark now—only the flare of a torch on the outside wall and the glow of lamps through the open windows to draw her. Like a moth, Meg thought with wry humor. A moth to the flame.

The still-warm summer evening rippled about her as she

walked. She was twelve years old again, listening to her father recount stories of the brave Highland boy who had saved his life. A boy who had put his own safety in danger for a man who should have been his enemy. And now, at last, Meg would meet him for herself.

She stopped on the threshold of the Black Dog. It was as dim and dismal as the outside had promised. And the innkeeper's daughter had been correct; by the predominance of uniforms and men with military bearing, this was the place favored by the Clashennic garrison. Meg drew a deep breath and, ignoring the glances and nudges and rude calls for her attention, plunged within.

It was like swimming through smoke and the fumes of drink and stale food, and the pungent waft of unwashed bodies. Voices battered her senses, but the accents were beyond her anyway, so if any of them insulted her she could not take offense. Gathering her wits, Meg searched the bent heads and huddled groups for the one man she was certain she would know instantly.

Gregor Grant.

Her eye was caught by a man standing by the wall, conversing with a soldier in a red jacket and white breeches. Slim and fair-haired, he was dressed in a wide-skirted yellow brocade coat that had seen better days, knee breeches and stockings, and shoes with silver buckles. Despite the tarnish on the buckles and the stockings in need of a good scrub, he looked very fine for such a setting as this. A gentleman in a dung heap.

As he waved his slender hands in broad, artistic gestures, a voice in Meg's head chanted: *It must be him, it must be him.*

This was just as she had always imagined. . . .

She was beside him now, her face level with his, but he ignored her. "It's too bad," he was saying. "One has to travel miles to buy a decent pair of gloves!"

"Captain Grant?" She sounded strangely breathless.

Both men turned to look at her, but Meg had eyes only for one. With an aching sense of disappointment, Meg realized she no longer found his face aristocratic or refined. Instead, as he raked his gaze over her, he appeared unpleasantly sly, his eyes far too close together, his jaw far too narrow. And there was something unwholesome about him.

The chant in her head had changed.

Do not be him, it begged. *Please do not be him!*

Her wish was granted. The fop made a dismissive gesture with his artist's hand toward an even gloomier part of the tavern. Relieved, Meg moved quickly through the crowd, easily avoiding the few patrons sober enough to reach for her. She was no longer afraid, just eager for this to be over.

"Captain Grant?" she called again, a little desperately now, her voice all but lost in the hubbub.

A brute with massive shoulders and wild hair pointed out a table, his finger unerringly directing her to the only occupant. A man sat with his back to her, slouched over the drink he held cupped in his big hands. Slowing to a stop, Meg let her eyes travel over him, widening with each inch. Even the voice in her head was silenced.

He was wearing a worn green jacket that pulled taut over his wide shoulders, and a faded plaid that appeared almost gray in the poor light. His hair was unpowdered, and it was not so much golden as fair brown, the color of honey, its untidy length caught at his nape. A ribbon of shock was slowly unfurling in Meg's stomach.

This man was absolutely nothing like the Gregor Grant she had pictured in her mind for so long. His back was far too broad, his arms, resting on the table's surface, far too well muscled, and his legs, stretched out from under his kilt, were far too long. He looked careworn and scruffy and far gone from drink. He was alone, with an air about him that discouraged company.

This isn't him. This cannot be him.

"Captain Grant?"

Her voice came out sharper than she meant, and at the sound of it he turned his head, scowling nastily at being interrupted in his solitary drinking. Meg saw then that his eyes were amber coloured, gold as a wildcat's, and slightly out of focus beneath slashing black brows. There were violet shadows beneath, and he had not shaved in a while. His cheeks were prickly with a stubble as dark as those fierce eyebrows. Oh, and he was handsome. Not in the delicate, fine-boned way she had imagined—there was nothing effeminate about Gregor Grant. His was a face that had lived and suffered, a tough masculine face, the face of a man who gave no quarter and expected none.

The Gregor Grant she had imagined had been a boy. This was a man, a man who would do no one's bidding but his own. A man who was scowling up at her with the most fascinating and yet unfriendly eyes that she had ever seen.

Meg had come to find a dream, a wispy, insubstantial girlhood dream.

Before her was solid reality.

Chapter 2

A little earlier, Gregor Grant had run his fingers through his hair, lifting a swath out of his eyes and blinking about him. The light in the Black Dog was prone to be dim, could not help but be, with its low-beamed ceiling and warrenlike rooms. It literally soaked up the smells of ale, whiskey, woodsmoke, and its malodorous clientele. Gregor should know—he was a regular customer—but even so, in his present inebriated state, everything seemed worse than usual.

His body ached. Tough and fit as he was, the duel he had fought and won against Airdy Campbell in the crisp dawn had tested him. And Airdy's sword had found a way past his defenses, slashing into the soft flesh of his upper arm. He should feel bitter, because Barbara Campbell, the cause of that duel, had promptly abandoned him, her hero, and gone back to her husband. Gone back despite Airdy's defeat, despite all her declarations to the contrary.

But Gregor did not feel any more bitter than usual, just somewhat used. He had been a fool to listen to Barbara's pleas for his help, her tales of Airdy's cruelty and her own desperation. She had claimed she wanted to be free of Airdy, and Gregor had given her the opportunity. But instead of taking the chance he offered, she had promptly thrown herself back into trouble's arms.

Gregor's head throbbed.

He did not normally drink to excess; he was not the sort of man who needed to find oblivion in the bottom of his cup. Only occasionally did the past threaten to rise up and swallow him whole. Forgetfulness, however it was arrived at, was welcome then. This just happened to be one of those occasions.

The whiskey he had been drinking tonight was distilled in the hills, powerful raw stuff that singed the lining of the throat. It was very good for bringing on amnesia, to help him to forget what his life had once been and could be now, and was not. And yet for some reason, tonight, the spirit had had the opposite effect. One by one, his memories had come trooping out of the past and tapped him on the shoulder.

Glen Dhui.

In his mind he could see the turreted house, solid gray against the soft purple of the heather, keeping watch. *His* house, the house of his Grant ancestors. He still, in his heart, thought of it in that way. And it still stood watch, but the Grants were no longer Lairds of Glen Dhui. The Government had taken the estate after the 1715 Rebellion, after Gregor's father died and Gregor was imprisoned. His mother and sister had fled to Edinburgh, into the arms of his mother's family, and there they had stayed. For a time Gregor had chosen to wander, before he managed to beg himself a commission in the Duke of Argyll's regiment.

Twelve years since Gregor had been home. Twelve years since he had *had* a home.

"Captain Grant?"

He did not know the voice, but he felt he should. Quiet yet determined, tart yet with a breathlessness that caught in his chest and gripped, hard. The voice tugged at him, like a line thrown to a drowning man, bringing him up from the shadowy place where he had been dwelling all evening.

Gregor turned and looked up from the colorless swirl of liquid at the bottom of his cup. And blinked to clear his vision. A figure hovered by him. A redheaded woman in a blue jacket, her long slim legs encased in tartan trews and dusty riding boots. Briefly her image shimmered, as if she might vanish altogether, but then instead of going away it steadied. This was indeed a woman, a woman in trews. Gregor blinked again, owlishly, studying her face. White skin, pale blue eyes and flame-red hair. A flame-haired angel, risen from the sputtering candlelight.

Was such a thing likely? Or was he now having visions?

But if she was a vision, he was not alone in seeing her. The groups of men around him had fallen strangely silent. Hardened soldiers, men from his own barracks rubbing shoulders with artisans from the town and crofters from the surrounding countryside. They were staring at her, as astonished and mystified as he by her sudden appearance in their midst. Women did not normally drink at the Black Dog . . . nor did they want to.

"It *is* Captain Gregor Grant?"

The angel spoke again, in her English accent, a voice oddly precise and demanding for such a heavenly creature. Gregor frowned and looked into her eyes. They were, he thought with surprise, the exact blue of a Highland summer sky. For the first time in a very long while he had the urge to paint, to draw, to capture somehow her vibrancy. He fought it, concentrating instead on the dull, heavy throbbing in his arm where Airdy's sword had slashed deep, and the dry whiskey burn in his throat. The vision wanted conversation? Aye, then he'd give her conversation!

"*I* am Gregor Grant," he admitted at last, his voice a little slurred from the whiskey but mostly from the pain.

The angel took a deep breath, her breasts swelling under the fitted jacket in a manner that caught and held his attention. They were not large breasts, but nor were they small. Just right, he thought, plump and round. A perfect fit for his large hands. To his surprise, desire sprang to life in his groin. Would she sit on his knee, he wondered feverishly, and let him unfasten those buttons one by one?

It was the silence that recalled him from his warm imaginings. Gregor peered up into her eyes, and realized she was waiting to regain his notice. There was a wash of pink in her cheeks, and now the pale blue gaze held an edginess.

"I require your help, Captain Grant," she said, tightening her mouth. "For that I need you sober. Are you often under the influence of strong drink? It is my rule that all men in my service are sober when in my presence."

He frowned, trying to puzzle out the difference between what she was saying and what she meant. His head felt as if it were stuffed with sheep's wool. "I am in no woman's service," he said slowly, "although it is sometimes my pleasure to service women."

She did not appreciate his ribald wit. He had insulted her. The pink in her cheeks ripened and her blue eyes turned stormy.

Gregor shook his head in bewilderment. The effect of the

whiskey was almost entirely gone, and instead he had be-gun to feel sick from the relentless, agonizing, drumming in his arm. "Who are you? What'z it you want'f me? Why 'ave you sought m'out in this place?"

The words had sounded fine in his head, but his mouth had difficulty forming them. "This place," he said again, and waved at the scene around them, at the watching men. And then noticed the ugly cut on the back of his hand. Yet another reminder of his dawn duel.

The woman with the red hair had also seen the jagged slash across the back his hand. Her eyes widened and the color drained from her face. She had freckles, he thought in wonder. There was a light sprinkling of freckles across her cheeks and on her pert nose. He had the mad urge to test each one with a kiss.

"You are hurt!" she cried, and it was more of an accusa-tion than a sympathetic statement. As if he had wounded himself apurpose, to thwart her plans.

He *was* hurt. Maybe far worse than he had realized when he had tended to his wounds himself. He supposed he should have found a surgeon, but in Gregor's experience such men caused more harm than good. . . .

Gregor felt the room shift about him.

It was just like Airdy to take him by surprise, slicing up-wards when Gregor had expected him to thrust forward. Airdy knew him too well when it came to sword fighting. They had practiced together too often, playing at combat which had far too many times turned into the real thing. Airdy did not like to be beaten. He would never forgive Gregor for championing Barbara, never mind that Barbara had begged him to free her from her jealous and unstable husband. And now she had gone back to him, and Airdy would see that as his victory, just as he would see his defeat in the duel as something he must rectify.

How could they ever soldier together again? How could he ever trust Airdy at his back again?

He couldn't. That was the trouble. Gregor knew he would have to send Airdy away . . . or go himself.

"Lady Margaret!"

The exclamation shattered his wandering thoughts. Gregor focused on the small, dark-haired man pushing his way through the crowded room, his visage grim enough to scare children. With a frisson of shock, Gregor realized he knew the man. It had been a long time, aye, but despite the dizziness in his head and the poor light, he recognized him.

The flame-haired angel had spun around at the sound of her name. A sweet scent of rose and woman drifted from her clothing and the body beneath it. Familiar, and yet new and different. Gregor tried to hold on to the moment, to concentrate on what was being said, but darkness was gathering at the edges of his sight. He should have sought out Malcolm Bain after the duel, even though he had known what Malcolm would say. He had not wanted to hear the lecture about being taken in by a pretty face, being too much of a gentleman to tell her to save her own skin, being too much of a bloody hero for his own good, and did he never learn!

"Duncan." The angel spoke the name in surprise, reclaiming his wandering attention. There was something in the tilt of her head, a combination of guilt and annoyance, decided Gregor. She looked like a woman who had been caught out in a prank she knew very well Duncan would not approve of.

Duncan had already begun to admonish her in a loud

whisper. "Lady, ye should have waited at the inn for me and the lads to return and accompany ye! This is no place for quality. Ye could have been accosted. . . ."

Her sweetly freckled nose jerked up another notch. This was a woman used to getting her own way, and moreover one who did not like to be told off by her inferiors. Her voice was so cold even Gregor felt its chill.

"When I discovered Captain Grant was just across the square I thought it best to act at once, Duncan. We have little time to waste. As you know."

Duncan's jaw tightened and he visibly swallowed back a further rebuke. Just as well for him, Gregor thought with a grin. Duncan had always believed he knew what was best, but the lady did not look the type to stand being scolded in public. The two of them glared at each other, neither willing to back down.

Time Gregor intervened.

"Duncan, lad. 'S been a long time."

Duncan appeared to freeze on the spot. His eyes swiveled around to Gregor's and widened.

"The Laird," he whispered. "Dear God, 'tis you."

Gregor nodded somberly, pretending he wasn't about to slide off his chair into a puddle on the floor. "What *do* y'here, Duncan? And in s-such fine company." His gaze slid over Meg, taking in her haughty looks. "A' f-firssht I thought sh' was an angel," Gregor added in a mock whisper. "An angel in trews-s-s."

She flushed, but her voice was heavy with disgust. "He's drunk. You told me he was someone we could depend upon. Do you still think so, Duncan?"

"He is." A new voice, making them turn around. A man stood behind them, as broad as he was tall, his eyes blue and piercing. He looked as if he had worn the same clothes for a week, and slept in them too. There was a tear in the sleeve of his shirt, and a hole in his plaid where it wrapped across his shoulder.

Meg was aware of Duncan stiffening like a dog on a scent beside her, but she kept her gaze warily on the stranger.

"And you are?" she asked haughtily.

He bowed a head covered in wild fair hair. "Malcolm Bain MacGregor, my lady. I am Captain Grant's man."

Being someone's man should have sounded subservient, but when Malcolm Bain said it, it was a matter of pride.

"Malcolm Bain is from Glen Dhui," Duncan added woodenly. "He *was*."

"I see." Meg cast her eye over him. She sensed there was something unresolved between Malcolm Bain MacGregor and Duncan Forbes, but that must wait until later. At least Malcolm Bain appeared sober, which was more than she could say for his master, who had dropped his head onto his arms on the tabletop and appeared to be sleeping.

"We have come to speak to Captain Grant on a matter of great importance. Unfortunately he is . . . tipsy."

Malcolm Bain gave her a curious look, before bending over Gregor Grant, resting his hand on the other man's shoulder. "Gregor, lad? Are ye up to listening to this lady?"

With an effort, it seemed, Gregor lifted his head and scowled at his man, before his gaze shifted to Meg. She raised an eyebrow at him in mock inquiry. And waited.

Through the haze of whiskey and the savage pain in his arm, Gregor noted that she had closed her mouth in a taut line. She would be the sort, he decided, who would always need to have the last word. Unless she were kissed breathless first. What would that little mouth taste like? Would she be all fire and passion beneath her fitted coat, or would she prefer to let him do all the work?

Gregor grinned at her, and seeing her confusion and outrage, chuckled aloud. A red curl had flopped over her brow, and she brushed it away crossly and tucked it behind her ear. She was neat, apart from that curling hair. Neat as a pin. Gregor knew a desperate urge to rumple her.

"Surely," he said slowly, "you have no' come all this-s-s way just to see *me*?"

Those pale blue eyes collided with Duncan's and slid away, but Gregor had read their doubt and uncertainty. They *had* come to see him. Come all the way from Glen Dhui, the Dark Glen, tucked away in the distant hills, isolated even by Highland standards. They had come to find him after he had been twelve years adrift, and if they had come now, then the reason must be something very special indeed.

A coldness washed over him, sank into his very bones. The Glen Dhui he remembered was the one he had left behind him when he was seventeen, a little shabby from lack of money, but still grand and beautiful. He had left everything behind, taken nothing into his new life. Only his memories.

Were they, too, about to be soiled?

"What'sh 'appened to Glen Dhui?" he demanded, his words slurring into each other, making him angry that he could not make himself better understood, that he was not his usual self. He leaped up, but everything had slowed down. The floor shifted beneath his feet, like a rolling ocean wave, so that he could not find purchase. His arm hurt like the very devil where Airdy had cut him, and he caught his breath in a hiss.

The angel was so close now that he was drowning in the sweet, warm essence of her. He could see the dark pupils centering the blue of her eyes. He swayed toward her, lost his balance, and instinctively reached out for her. As he did so, he knew what he wanted. He wanted to feel her soft breasts beneath her blue jacket, the brush of her pink lips on his hot brow, the gentle touch of her fingers on his hair, the whisper of her breath against his fevered skin.

As he fell she caught him in her arms. Or tried to. He heard her gasp of shocked surprise, the little whoosh of her breath when she took his weight. For a brief, heavenly moment he was encased in her warmth, his head resting upon her bosom, just where he had wanted it to be. He tried to open his eyes against the black dots that were filling his vision, and found that her fiery hair had tumbled from its pins, covering him.

He was on fire. Burning. Maybe even dying.

If he *were* dying, then this seemed as good a place as any to do so, and better than most. With a groan, Gregor sank into unconsciousness, and wrapped in his angel's arms, tumbled to the floor.

Chapter 3

G regor Grant was so large and tough, so masculine, so much a man. Much bigger than her imaginings, much more *real* . . .

No, he was not as Meg had expected. Not as she had ever imagined in her wildest dreams.

She still felt shaky from the incident in the Black Dog. She was still reeling from the heavy weight of his much larger body pressed to hers, the hot brush of his breath on her cheek, his rough jaw rasping her soft neck. The memory of it caused a trembling feeling deep inside her that worried her.

Meg followed as the men carried the unconscious former laird across to the inn and set him down in a big, wooden chair by the fire. His head drooped low upon his chest, as if he were asleep, and his kilt had ridden up to show a large amount of muscular and hairy thigh. Meg tried not to look, but her eyes kept sliding back in that direction.

A branch of candles was brought. The light shone across his face, illuminating flesh flushed and beaded with sweat. No wonder, Meg thought, when he had fallen into her arms, it had been as if his body burned and seared hers. It wasn't so much that he was drunk; he had a fever.

But there was worse.

Blood darkened the sleeve of his green jacket. The fact had gone unnoticed in the confines of the inn, but now it was plain as the sleeve glistened wetly in the light of the candles. Meg's stomach twisted. She had never been one of those women who dealt unflinchingly with wounds; rather she was the sort of woman who instructed, directed, or gathered about her those more gifted. However, there was no way on God's earth she was leaving now, not until she had made certain that Gregor Grant would recover from whatever ailed him.

Malcolm Bain MacGregor was reviewing the sticky sleeve with a grim look, while Duncan Forbes shifted un-easily, clearly not keen to take charge. Meg sensed a ten-sion between her tacksman and Gregor Grant's man that puzzled her, but she had no time to tease out the riddle now. Whatever dark secret lay between them would have to wait.

Curiously, warily, as if she were approaching something half wild, Meg let her eyes take in the length of the man who sprawled on the chair before her. The candles flared, and his brown-gold hair gleamed in the changing light, as did the tarnished silver buttons of his green jacket. His plaid was woven in a pattern of blue and green, very faded, and a length of the woollen cloth left from the kilt section had been swept over one broad shoulder and fastened with a barbaric-looking brooch. The leather belt about his waist would be used for carrying sporran, dirk, and pistols. A thick sword belt came over his right shoulder to support the broadsword at his hip, and a narrower strap over the left held the priming flask for his pistols. It was the usual war-like fare for a Highlander, soldier or otherwise. Meg thought he looked more than capable of employing them all.

Where was her slim boy? Her pale and precious laird? This man was not he. He was too real. He made her uneasy, with his faded kilt and shiny coat. He was a Captain of a troop of Campbell dragoons who lived rough and tough, and drank desparately in gloomy taverns. This was no gentleman, no *duine-uasal*, as the people of Glen Dhui said in the Gaelic. He might be handsome enough, Meg admitted, to make some women swoon, but his high cheekbones and strong jaw and aristocratic nose did nothing for *her*. Nor did she admire his dark, slashing brows and eyes of amber that gleamed through equally dark lashes. No, Meg told herself, she was not in the least impressed by the man before her.

Why, oh why, had she allowed her imagination such free rein? Until she had fooled herself into believing she knew him? Many times she had perused the former laird's sketches, dreaming of the hand that had made them, the eyes that had seen so true, the heart that had so loved the glen. Now she was forced to admit that that man didn't exist, except in her own imagination. He wasn't real. This man, *this* man, was real. And Meg didn't know him at all.

His very maleness made her uneasy, threatened her in a way she had never felt threatened before.

"Och, Gregor lad, what have ye done to yersel'," Malcolm Bain's muttered words broke through her reverie. He turned to Meg and raised a hairy eyebrow. "I need to strip him, my lady, to properly see the damage."

Meg raised a much slimmer eyebrow back at him. "Then go ahead and do so."

Malcolm Bain and Duncan exchanged a look of resignation, their first moment of accòrd since they'd met. The two of them then proceeded to unbuckle Gregor's belts, laying aside a dirk with care. They unfastened the brooch and dropped the plaid that had looped over his shoulder down to his waist. The green jacket was more difficult. Awkwardly they unbuttoned it, removing it from the unconscious man's uninjured arm, but when Malcolm Bain attempted to ease the bloodied sleeve down his injured arm, Gregor gave a loud groan.

His lashes fluttered and lifted, the amber eyes blazing in his white face. "What are you doing to me, Malcolm, you ham-fisted oaf!" he said between clenched teeth.

"I'm doing what I always do, lad. Repairing the damage ye've done to yersel'."

"Then you'll need to cut the sleeve away," Gregor said practically, his voice growing fainter.

Malcolm fingered the once-fine stuff of the former laird's jacket and grunted his regret. Reluctantly, with the air of a man going against his deepest-held beliefs, he slipped out his dirk. The sharp blade caught on a seam and ripped through, slicing away the sleeve, while Gregor held himself rigid. It fell away at last, leaving only the white shirt now, the cloth so worn and so thin, Meg could see the warm glow of his flesh beneath it. Her throat felt a little dry, and she swallowed as Malcolm tried to unlace the ties at his master's throat, struggled for a moment, and then gave up and once again used his dirk. The shirt fell open and was quickly stripped away.

Meg held her breath.

There was something pagan about that broad sweep of naked muscle and golden flesh, furred with dark hair. A thin line of that same dark hair grew down the hard plane of his belly to vanish like an arrow beneath the folds of his kilt. Slowly Meg drew in her breath. Her eyes slid to a makeshift bandage that was fastened about his upper arm, now much bloodsoaked, with rivulets of blood dried upon his flesh.

"Good heavens, what happened?" Meg demanded of Malcolm Bain, unable to disguise her horror. "Was he in a battle?"

At the sound of her voice, Gregor stirred again. Beneath the dark veil of his lashes, his eyes were bright and restless, searching. They passed over Malcolm Bain and Duncan, and fixed upon Meg. She did not look away, although there was something in that golden gaze that made her very uneasy, just as everything about Gregor Grant seemed to make her uncomfortable.

His handsome mouth had curved up at the corners in a smile that was at once rueful and very attractive. "I fought a duel."

"A duel?" Meg repeated sharply. She had never heard of anything so ridiculous. "A duel over what?"

The smile faded, his lashes lifted on hard amber. "A woman."

Meg rolled her own eyes in disgust. Just as she had feared, he was a womanizing drunkard! So much for the boy hero. She had come all this way for nothing. Frustration and disappointment overcame caution. "Oh, a woman! And did she go off with the victor and leave you to your drink? Is that why you were lolling about in the tavern just now, Captain Grant?"

Malcolm Bain was busy unwrapping the bandage, tugging it away from the wound on Gregor's upper arm.

Gregor winced. "I *am* the victor," he said, rather breathlessly. "Sh' wen' off with the loser."

"Even *I* know that isn't supposed to happen," Meg answered him in her acerbic way. "What did you say to her to make her do that?"

Gregor laughed, grimaced again, and closed his eyes. He looked even paler. "You dinna know the half of it, lass," he said, his voice gone bitter.

"No, and I do not think I want to."

Those dark lashes lifted again, and now he seemed wary, confused. But before he could open his mouth, Malcolm tugged the last stretch of bandage free. The wound was revealed, a sword slash that looked deep and painful, a brutal incision into the hard, muscular swell of his upper arm, with the edges gaping.

They all grimaced.

Sweat trickled down Gregor's brow. Confronted with the damage to his arm, he took a deep uneven breath. Meg took a breath of her own, stilling her squeamishness.

Malcolm Bain probed at the wound with one blunt finger.

"Do you know what you're doing?" Meg demanded sharply when Gregor gasped a word in Gaelic that sounded profane.

Malcolm Bain cast her the briefest of glances. "My grandsire was a surgeon in Dundee's army in 1689," he told her matter-of-factly, as if that were an answer. "We will have to sew it up," he added. "Won't heal otherwise. The bleeding's stopped, so we dinna need to cauterize the wound. I'll clean it and then we can sew it." He looked up at her, his blue eyes intent. "Are ye a competent needle-woman, my lady?"

Meg blinked, failing to follow the change in subject. "I can sew a seam, if that's what you mean. Why?" And then, realizing exactly why, her face drained of all color. She had always had a weak stomach when it came to such things. It was an embarrassment to her, because she well knew that the lady of an estate such as Glen Dhui was looked upon as someone who would treat the illnesses and the hurts of her people. Meg did her duty, but she had never found the role easy.

"*You* are the surgeon's grandson," she said in a husky whisper.

"Aye, I am, only I'm no' so good at the sewing part, my lady. It would be better if ye did that. Now dinna fash yersel'! It's as easy as mending a rip in a petticoat."

"I doubt that," Meg retorted. "Why are you asking me? Surely there are others in Clashennic who can sew better than I."

Gregor had fixed her with mocking eyes. "Are you refusing to help a wounded man? 'Tis clear *you* have not been sliced by a sword."

"Nor would I be so foolish as to get in the way of one, Captain."

"I dinna do it on purpose," he said, a little sulkily.

Morag was sent for water and clean bandages, and a needle and thread. Malcolm Bain uncorked a bottle of whiskey and poured Gregor a large dram.

"For the pain," he said, when Meg's lips tightened.

"Surely he's had enough to numb his whole body?"

"Dinna be harsh, lass," Gregor murmured, savoring the brew. "'Tis not you who has to suffer Malcolm's tender ministrations. Last time he sewed me up it came out all crooked." He turned his uninjured arm to show her, and she gazed in dismay at a small but very puckered scar near the bend of his elbow.

Morag had returned, and Malcolm Bain set to washing the wound, trickling cold water into the gash again and again until it came out clean. When that was done, he lifted the bottle of whiskey and poured it straight onto the raw flesh. Gregor's breath hissed and he went as white as a ghostie.

Meg groaned in sympathy.

But Malcolm Bain was already taking up the needle, holding it poised in his big, blunt fingers. "Are ye ready then, lad?"

Gregor choked. His eyes lifted to Meg's. There was emotion in them, not so much a plea, but rather a request. She wanted to refuse, to turn and walk away; she wanted to pretend she didn't understand. But she had come all this way to see this man, to ask of him a favor of her own, so how could she refuse him now? And yet . . . there was more to it than that—she didn't want his smooth, hard arm to bear a scar as puckered as Malcolm Bain's last effort. And she *could* sew a seam—she had told him so.

She closed her eyes, took a breath, opened them, and gave a decisive nod. Hopefully she could do this without fainting. Without showing all these Highland men what a frail and fragile woman she really was beneath her outward show of toughness.

"I am grateful," Gregor said softly.

Malcolm Bain cleared his throat, and held out the needle. She took it with fingers that shook a little. Duncan brought a stool and placed it beside the chair, so that Meg would be sitting higher than her patient, with a better view of his arm.

Malcolm Bain stood close behind Gregor, and carefully pinched the edges of the wound together, holding it firm for her. She watched Gregor's chest rise and fall, a little quicker now, and the tightening of his mouth.

There was an expectant hush about her.

I can do this, Meg thought. *I can do this, just as I have done everything else that has been asked of me so far. . . .*

Slowly, pretending she was somewhere else, Meg pressed the point of the needle against the flesh of Gregor's arm, and pushed it through.

It wasn't as difficult as she had thought.

She took another stitch, setting them neatly, not too tight, side by side. There would still be a scar, but it should be nice and straight and narrow. She took another stitch, hardly noticing the movements of those around her: Malcolm Bain holding the wound, Gregor stiff and white beneath her hands, Duncan murmuring in sympathy, and Morag at the edge of her vision, holding the bowl of water.

Each stitch careful and precise, one by one, until there was one more stitch needed.

Meg made it, and watched Malcolm snip the thread. He took the needle from her hand. "Ye've done a bonny job, my lady. When the lad can talk again I'm sure he'll agree."

It was only then that the room began to spin slowly around Meg, turning like a top. She swayed, reaching out for purchase, and something hard and very strong gripped her hand, holding her up. She looked down and saw that Gregor had closed his large hand upon hers, fingers intertwining. She blinked and her head cleared a little, although her legs were still shaky. His amber eyes were fastened upon hers as tenaciously as his hand on her hand.

"I'm not going to swoon," she assured him, a little breathlessly.

"Neither am I," he replied.

"I've never been much good with men," she went on, and then flushed, mortified to have said such a thing. Where had that come from? Were her wits quite addled?

His mouth lifted into a smile that made her head spin all over again. "Mabbe you just have not met the right one."

"Done," Malcolm Bain announced. He had rebandaged the arm with deft twists in the clean strips of cloth supplied by the innkeeper's daughter. "There, lad, ye'll feel more comfortable now," he said with a confident air.

The 'lad' looked as if he, despite his assertion to the contrary and his charming smile, was about to pass out.

"Let's get ye to bed," Malcolm went on. "I fear we'll have to beg one here at the inn for tonight."

"Can you arrange that?" Meg asked, looking to Morag.

"I'll see to it, my lady," the girl said. "Will ye eat now, my lady, or would ye prefer a tray to your room?"

"A tray," Meg said, gratefully, and the girl hurried off to prepare a room and see to the food.

Meg looked down at the man before her, hesitant. He had said that he owed her a favor, and here was her chance to call that favor in.

"Captain Grant?"

Gregor grunted, unmoving. His fingers had begun to relax, and he had stretched his legs out toward the fire. He looked limp and helpless, not a man who had lived a brutal soldier's life, who fought duels over women and drank himself senseless. Suddenly he was much more like the gentle boy Meg had imagined sketching those portraits of glen life. The boy she had admired so much, and thought she knew so well, only . . . *bigger*.

"Captain Grant," she repeated, more loudly this time.

He opened one amber eye and glared at her indignantly. "Lass, lemme s-s-sleep now," he slurred. "I promise I'll be ready for ye again come the morning."

Color heated her face, but she supposed it was her own fault for pestering a half-conscious man, especially a man as clearly lacking in morals as this one.

Malcolm Bain hid a smile. "Talk to him in the morning, my lady."

"Aye," Duncan added, uncomfortable in agreement.

Meg gave an impatient sigh. "Very well."

"We'll get him to his bed," Duncan said, with a quick glance at Malcolm Bain, and a tightening of his lips. "Get some sleep, Lady Meg. I dinna think we'll be riding home tomorrow, but who knows? I knew a man once had his foot taken off by a blow from a claymore, and he was in the saddle again the following day. . . ."

Meg could see the sense in his advice. When Gregor woke tomorrow, sore-headed but sober, she needed to be ready. Would he do as she asked? She thought he would. Penniless and landless and lacking in morals he may be, but he was still a Highlander at heart, bound by his honor. And Meg thought that it was his honor that would bring him to heel.

And then I will have what I came for, she told herself. *Gregor Grant will be mine.*

The words echoed in her head as she made her way to her room. They gave her a warm tingle of pleasure that had nothing to do with the fire burning in her hearth. *Foolishness*, she thought impatiently. She would do well to remember that Gregor Grant was no woman's man, and certainly not hers.

Suddenly she was very weary, and missing the services of her maid, Alison, at home in Glen Dhui. Alison had wanted to come, but she was no horsewoman, and Meg knew that, as much as she valued her maid's company, Alison would only have slowed them down. So, once again tonight, Meg was her own lady's maid.

The food arrived and was as good as had been promised, but Meg had lost her appetite. She quickly undressed, slipping on her nightshift and letting the white muslin settle about her before drawing a warm wrap about her shoulders. Halfheartedly she brushed out her wildly curling hair—no easy task, for it required concentration to free the flaming mass of tangles as she sat before the crackle of the small fire in the hearth.

As Meg drew the brush slowly through her hair, she allowed her mind to drift.

The general, her father, would be wondering how she was faring. She did not like the thought of leaving him for too long. While he had been in good health he had held firm the reins of Glen Dhui, and no one had dared to threaten them. Now that he was blind and fragile in body and mind, the wolves had begun to circle, and one Highland wolf in particular had been most insistent.

It was not wise to deny powerful men, and such a man was the Duke of Abercauldy. The Duke believed he would soon be adding Glen Dhui to his sizeable estate—he already owned much of the land to the south of Glen Dhui—and Meg to his household, as his wife.

But he had underestimated Meg. Lady Margaret Mackintosh was no ordinary woman. She had never been one to be tied down by the beliefs and strictures of the society in which she lived, or by what the men of her acquaintance told her she should or shouldn't do.

Her father blamed himself for her stubbornness and her determination to do very much as she pleased. He had brought her up to value her own worth and follow her own inclinations, and often bewailed his ignorance of the consequences of doing so. No born and bred gentleman himself—coming as he did from a more humble background, he had made his money from the collieries in the north of England. That wealth had bought him power, and the rank of general in the Hanoverian forces in the late Rebellion. He had wanted but one more thing to make his rise complete, and that was for his only child, his beloved daughter, to marry a proper gentleman.

Ever since she had come of age, Meg had been tripping over gentlemen, most of them penniless and with an eye to her father's fortune. She was not the sort of woman men swooned over, or fought duels over, she thought with a wry smile. Her tongue was too sharp, her mind too intelligent, and she was not beautiful. And perhaps worst of all, she valued honesty; she was no gullible fool when it came to the motives of men. They did not want *her*, only what came *with* her, and she was not prepared to pretend otherwise.

She had determined at a very early age that she would marry for one thing only—love.

It was ironic that the general had caused the destruction of her vow. His wits, once so sharp, had been dulled by illness. He was vulnerable, and his weakness had led him to fall for the duke's subtle persuasions. By the time Meg had learned of their agreement it was too late: The papers were signed. She was officially engaged to the Duke of Abercauldy. She and her father had argued, bitterly, until Meg came to realize that he had done this thing because he had thought to protect her; because he loved her.

So, Meg had accepted her fate.

And then other matters had arisen, serious matters, that had shown her father his mistake was not just in his miscalculation of the duke's intentions, but might possibly involve Meg's life. . . .

"I'm an old fool," he'd wept, head in his hands. "What have I done to you, my Meg?"

Meg had been frightened then, for him and herself. They had sat up late into the night, and in the end the general's solution had been simple. Find Gregor Grant and bring him back to Glen Dhui, and her father would do the rest.

With a sigh, Meg climbed beneath the covers. A servant had placed a hot brick wrapped in a thick cloth just where her feet came to rest. She gave a wriggle of contentment as she warmed her toes. The journey would be a success, she assured herself. Gregor Grant would return with her to Glen Dhui and help her father stand firm against the duke. All would be well. She *must* believe that. Because, frankly, the alternative didn't bear consideration.

Chapter 4

Gregor woke in the sharp predawn air. For a moment he simply lay, wondering where he was, for this was certainly not the narrow, uncomfortable bed in his quarters at the barracks. And then he tried to move, and the sickening pain in his arm brought back his memory with a jolt.

It had begun with the duel.

He had fought Airdy Campbell and won. Except that winning had been more like defeat, for Barbara, who had begged for his help and played upon his chivalric nature, had returned to her husband, and Gregor had been left to find his own way home, wounded and alone.

There would be repercussions.

Like a pebble tossed into a still loch, the ripples would spread far.

Airdy would not let him forget this. He would have his revenge. And knowing Airdy, it would come when he least expected it. When Airdy struck it would be with a sudden savagery that would probably prove fatal. In the meantime Airdy would do his best to undermine Gregor with the men, spreading poison among them, making his life intolerable.

Gregor knew he could go to the Duke of Argyll and explain matters, but would he listen? Airdy was his nephew, while Gregor was nothing to him. And although Argyll had the reputation of a man of consideration and reason, things like blood ties were always tricky.

What should he do, then? Join one of the government regiments and go and fight in a distant country? Or leave the army altogether, and find work as some great lord's factor, haranguing tenants for their rent when they barely had enough to feed their children? Gregor felt his spirits sink even lower. He did not want that. This was not the road his life had been meant to take.

As a boy Gregor had run wild through Glen Dhui and the hills that surrounded it, sure in his heart, in his soul, that one day it would all be his. It belonged to him by right. The Grants had held Glen Dhui since Queen Mary ruled and Gregor had never dreamed it would be taken from them. Like the rising of the sun each morning, he had not thought it possible anything so fixed, so familiar, could suddenly cease to be. But it had. Glen Dhui had been lost, the sun had failed to rise, and his world had gone dark.

He moved restlessly and then bit back a groan. His head throbbed almost worse than his arm. There was a memory, something important. It proved elusive, however. Gregor shifted again in his bed, making the throbbing in his arm into a jagged ache. There had been a woman, a woman with hair like fire. She had been here, he knew it, remembered the scent of her skin. Good God, she had sewn up his arm!

Lady Margaret Mackintosh, a redheaded, acid-tongued harridan.

With skin like milk and a mouth more luscious than any ripe fruit.

A heavy knock on his door interrupted his pleasant thoughts. Gregor sighed, lifting his head to call "Come in," then wished he had not as the room swam dizzily around him. "Who is it?" he croaked.

The door opened to admit a sturdy, dark-haired man, who cautiously approached the bed. Gregor squinted up at him, his throat scratchy. Memory was returning. Duncan Forbes. This was definitely Duncan Forbes.

Duncan had been one of his father's tacksmen, and here he was, looking older, but otherwise, more or less, the same stiff-backed Duncan he had always been.

"How are ye feeling, sir?" he asked diffidently, as if Gregor were still the Laird of Glen Dhui.

Gregor swallowed and found his voice. "I've been better, Duncan. What are you doing here? I thought I dreamed you."

Duncan gave him a sickly smile.

"I have not seen you since you came to the prison, after my father died," Gregor went on, as if his head were not threatening to cleave in two halves. Duncan had not fought in the 1715—he had remained at home, to take care of Gregor's mother and sister, and estate matters. Duncan had traveled to the prison after Gregor's father's body was buried at last in the ground of his ancestors. He remembered it so well, Duncan's gloomy face, and the word picture he'd painted of Gregor's father's burial when he came to see Gregor.

He had described the black-draped bier carried in turn by the loyal Grant men, the women wailing, and the piper's lament like a shroud about them. It had been, said Duncan, a fitting end to a Highland chieftain, no matter how misguided his politics. Gregor had wept, genuinely mourning his father, even if he had never shared his Jacobite fanaticism. The Stuarts had brought greatness to the Grants—the family had been loyal to Queen Mary, who had gifted them Glen Dhui in the first place. But the Stuarts, in the form of the Pretender James, had also been their ruin.

Duncan was still watching him with quiet, dark eyes. "Do ye really not remember last evening, sir?"

Gregor rubbed the ache between his brows, trying to ease it, trying to clear his befuddled mind. "I remember it well enough, Duncan." He took a shaky breath. "Sit down, man, you make my neck hurt."

Duncan sat carefully on a sturdy chair. As the chair looked substantial enough, Gregor could only assume his caution was because he really didn't want to be there.

"Where is Malcolm Bain?"

"He said he was going to the barracks," Duncan replied, pursing his lips in the same way he had always done when something didn't please him. Some things didn't change. Gregor bit back a smile.

"We need ye to come home, Gregor Grant. We need ye to stand up for us. Lady Meg needs ye. . . ."

Gregor managed a creaky laugh. "The redheaded termagant? If it has not escaped your notice, Duncan, I am already in employment."

Though for how long, once Airdy had his way?

" 'Twas not yer fault ye lost Glen Dhui, sir."

Gregor felt his face stiffen. What Duncan said was true enough, but for all that, he didn't want to hear it. When the Stuarts had called from across the water, his father had answered, and so it was that Gregor and his father had gone out in the 1715. They had lost, and with their loss had come the staggering weight of fines and the confiscation of their lands and all personal belongings.

With his father dead, Gregor had borne the brunt of it.

Newly released from prison, seventeen years old, Gregor had had no choice but to pack up his mother and younger sister and find them lodgings in Edinburgh. His mother had landed on her feet, she always did, and his sister was young enough to adjust. But Gregor had felt as if a part of himself had been ripped out.

He was no longer Gregor Grant. He did not feel like himself, but rather he was a stranger, embittered and lost. He had only fought because it was his father's wish, because he was the Grant heir and his father was his chief, his laird. He had fought for his father, but his interests lay elsewhere. The land, that was what drew Gregor. The seasons bleeding into each other, the cycle of life and death in the glen. The constancy of it, and the comfort. He had understood it, felt a part of it. The glen had been his world; it was all he had ever wanted.

When he left . . . Well, he had survived, he had stayed alive, but he had never again been the same man.

Duncan moved, uneasily, and Gregor realized he had been silent for a long time. He scowled at the smaller man, not caring what he might think of his former Laird. It was time Duncan understood that Gregor was not the boy he had once known, the obedient, malleable boy. That in his place stood a man, toughened and hardened by circumstances, whose troops might fear his tongue and look askance at him when he smiled, but who at least knew his own mind.

"Glen Dhui is mine no longer, Duncan."

"Mabbe not, sir, but I think ye'll find it's harder than ye think to extinguish the memory of the Grants after so long in the glen. Twelve years away is but a drop of water in Loch Dhui. Ye are still the laird to us, and will be until we die. We look to ye for help, sir. Will ye no' consider it?"

The pain was quick. The memory of all he had lost. Gregor rubbed again the spot between his brows; he did not want Duncan to see his emotion. It was still too raw, too painful, even after all this time. He had thought himself over it. He should be over it! He did not want to go through the pain of loss again. His new life may not be perfect—In fact, he knew it was far from that!—but he had learned to put Glen Dhui behind him.

"I'm sorry, Duncan, but the answer is no. I am not one for retracing my steps. Whatever the trouble is, you must find another way."

Duncan looked nonplussed, as if he couldn't quite believe what he had just heard. He opened his mouth to answer, but just then a sharp, impatient tap sounded on the door. Duncan cursed under his breath. "Not now, blast the woman!"

"Captain Grant? Are you awake?" The woman in question was waiting outside, and by the tone of her voice she would not wait very long.

Bemused, Gregor looked from the door to Duncan and back again. He recognized the voice, and when the door opened a crack and a woman's face appeared, he recognized that too. Her eyes were so blue they were blinding, so that he actually blinked against their brightness.

"Captain Grant? I wish to speak with you. Are you decent?"

Gregor wondered whether it would have mattered if he weren't. He had the feeling she would still have come in. Carefully, he drew the covers farther up his chest, reminding himself that she could not see that he was naked beneath.

"Lady Meg," Duncan said loudly, "it would be better if ye waited until I am done. This is men's talk."

Lady Margaret gave this comment all the respect it deserved, by pushing open the door and marching in. "Nonsense," she said briskly. "There is no time to be lost."

Chagrined, Duncan said nothing, although Gregor could see that he really wanted to. But Duncan had old-fashioned manners, while Gregor no longer considered it necessary to have any manners at all.

Lady Meg was staring at him—she had taken up a stance at the foot of the bed. Flame-red hair, creamy, freckled skin, and those eyes of a particular pale, piercing blue. He had not imagined her. She *was* the woman of last night. Although he did not recall her as being quite so feminine. Last night she had worn trews and a jacket, and very fetching in them she had been, too; today she wore a blue gown with little taffeta bows marching invitingly down the tight-laced bodice. . . .

"Captain Grant, I wish to speak with you on an important matter," she said imperiously, autocratically. And yet, thought Gregor, there was sweetness in the curve of her mouth, and her lashes were long and thick, and under the gown her body was all woman. . . .

No! No, no, no. Had not Barbara and her pleas for his help been enough? Did he really want to go down that road again? He had been a gullible fool once this week; he did not intend to make it twice.

"Sir, this is Lady Margaret Mackintosh," Duncan interrupted. "She and her father are the owners of Glen Dhui. She has come all this way to find ye and ask ye to help us."

Lady Margaret Mackintosh gave him a speaking glance. "Thank you, Duncan, but I can introduce myself. Have you told him all?"

"Not yet, Lady Meg."

"Then I shall do so."

She opened her mouth with that intention, but Gregor did not let her speak.

"You have done me great honor then, Lady Margaret, by coming all this way to ask for my help, but you have wasted your time. I am no longer Laird of Glen Dhui, and what happens there is no longer my concern. I do not want it to be."

She looked taken aback. Her gaze slid to Duncan and she raised a brow meaningfully. No fool, Duncan, he rose to his feet.

"I will leave ye to yer talk, Lady Meg. I have matters to see to in the town," he added, and hastened from the room.

Lady Margaret waited until the door closed. The silence gathered in expectation.

"He does not approve of my being here," she said quietly, those brilliant eyes watching. "Do you remember last night at all, Captain? I sewed your wound for you and you promised me your gratitude. Is this how you repay me? By refusing my request outright, before you have even heard it?"

"I don't need to hear it. I do not *want* to hear it. I am done with Glen Dhui; my life lies elsewhere."

She narrowed her eyes at him, and then strolled gracefully around the bed. He admired the sway of her skirts, the tilt of her head. There was something compelling about her, he couldn't deny it. Not the soft pliancy of Barbara, the in-

sincerity of Barbara. This woman would not lie lightly, and
she would not be soft. She was honest fire. But that did not
mean she would not do anything in her power to get her
own way, if she were desperate enough.

She was standing beside the bed now. His amber gaze
slid down over her face, closing on her mouth. It was just as
luscious as he had remembered, and Gregor wondered what
it tasted like. Whether she would resist him if he reached up
and kissed her, or sink willingly into his embrace. The silence grew uncomfortable before he spoke again.

"You are wasting your time."

"I thought a gentleman's word meant everything to
him?" She said it sharply, leaning forward over him, her
hands planted on her hips, her jaw stubbornly set. Suddenly
he was very tempted indeed to do just as he had imagined,
to reach up and pull her down onto the bed with him, to use
his mouth and his hands on her until she gasped with need,
with want.

"But I am no longer a gentleman," he reminded her
huskily.

He watched her from beneath his lashes, wondering if
she was convinced yet of the impossibility of what she was
asking. She was watching him as well, and now her face
was a little paler. But whether it was because she was beginning to understand the futility of her journey, or her
sensing of the tension between them—him and her, alone in
his bedroom—he didn't know.

Her gaze rested on his and then, reluctantly, began to
slide down over his throat, across that part of his chest that
was exposed above the covers. As if realizing what was
happening, her eyes shot back to his, startled as a grouse
caught out of cover on the moor.

He smiled, slowly. Did she desire him, too? If so, then she was hiding it from him now, with her gaze turned watchful, cautious. Was there desire beneath that careful mask? Gregor was used to seeing desire in women's eyes; it had been there all his life. And yet this woman was different, beyond his ken.

"Will you not even hear what I have to say?" Her voice was softer now, with a note of pleading in it.

He felt himself quiver, deep inside, but did not let her see the weakness. Gregor knew very well that he was weak where women were concerned; it was a fault he had tried hard to correct. This time, he swore to himself, he would not be brought to his knees by a soft voice and a tearful gaze.

"You would be wasting your time."

There must be a way, Meg told herself desperately.

Last night she had believed Gregor Grant was hers, and now, this morning, she had made the discovery that somehow he had slipped out of her grasp, eluded her. Was it his pride that was hurt? Or was he simply too selfish to care what happened to the people who had loved him—loved him still? She had come here with the expectation that some fondness would remain in his heart, some responsibility for his former tenants and his land. That he must feel that same joining of heart and soul to the land that she felt. Evidently he didn't. The boy he had been—that she had believed him to be—did not exist.

The man who stood in his place had neither heart nor conscience. She was wasting her time.

And yet she had come so far!

Meg took a breath, opened her mouth to try again, to say . . . something. But before she could begin to form the words, there was a loud noise outside the inn. The clatter of a horse's hooves as it was drawn to an unruly halt on the uneven cobbles. And then a voice like gravel at the bottom of a pail, echoed through the building.

"Gregor Grant! Gregor Grant come out here and face me, you bloody bastard! You yellow-livered worm!"

Gregor went still. The muscles on either side of his mouth went white. He took a harsh breath and, with an obvious effort, sat up in the bed. Meg gasped and put out her hands to stop him. The skin of his chest was smooth and hot, and shocked, she quickly pulled her hands away. But he was already swinging his legs over the edge and, grasping the post of the bed as support, hauled himself up onto his bare feet. He was certainly an impressive-looking man.

If Meg had had any doubts about his state of undress, then they were answered now. He wasn't wearing a single stitch of clothing. Naked skin gleamed, the muscles in his shoulders bunched as he clung to the wooden post, his legs trembled, and what was between them . . .

Meg felt her face flame, but refused to allow her maidenly sensibilities to overcome her now. She was no shrinking violet, she had seen men before, just not quite so . . . naked. And none quite so astoundingly good-looking as this one.

"Captain Grant," she said urgently as he swayed, his head bowed, the muscles on his arms standing out like ropes. "You are not fit to go anywhere. Please, get back into bed."

"No. I will be all right." He spoke faintly but with a stubborn determination Meg couldn't mistake.

"You will not! I will handle this. Get back into bed."

She started for the door. Behind her he called out something, but she didn't stop to listen. She was already out in the corridor, moving toward the front of the inn, where all the noise was coming from.

"Gregor Grant, you bastard! Come out here and look me in the eye, if you can! I willna be beaten by you. I'll never be beaten by you. Hide if you must, but I'll have my vengeance on you!"

Meg had reached the open door now, and the glare made her blink. It was a beautiful sunny day, the only incongruous thing about it was the man atop the dun horse who was screaming out insults. His dark hair was loose and wild about his white face, a livid gash decorating one cheek. He wore the red jacket of a government dragoon, and breeches of buff yellow with black boots.

He was clearly very drunk. If Meg hadn't been able to smell the whiskey from where she stood, she would have known it by the way he was rolling about in his saddle, waving a pistol in a singularly dangerous manner.

He caught sight of her and stopped, staring, his mouth ajar.

"Who the bloody hell are you?" he demanded.

Meg straightened her back and stepped froward, out of the inn and into the cobbled courtyard. The dun horse shuffled nervously, snorting, but she ignored it. Now was certainly not the time to show fear.

"I might ask the same of you, my good man," she said in her most haughty voice. "Would you mind keeping your voice down? It doesn't seem necessary to shout when you can just as easily send a message. If you wish to communicate with Captain Grant, I will see he gets it."

He narrowed his eyes but that did not make them any more reassuring. Meg noticed, with distaste, that the gash upon his cheek had begun to bleed, a slow trickle that ran down to stain his white neckcloth.

"Barbara's run off." He said it as if that was the answer she was seeking.

"Indeed. I am sorry to hear it. Who is Barbara?"

The dun horse tried to turn, but he wrenched brutally at the reins, turning it back so that he was facing her.

"Barbara is my wife."

"Is she? Then perhaps you'd better go and find her."

"Where is that bastard Grant? She's with him, isn't she?"

"If you mean Captain Grant, then she most certainly is not!"

"I want to see him!"

"I'm afraid he is—"

"I am here."

Meg tried not to jump. He was directly behind her. Cautiously she glanced over her shoulder, and saw that he had managed to fasten the belt that kept his kilt about his waist, though the upper portion was only roughly twisted over one of his naked shoulders, hiding the bandaged arm. White-faced but steady, he was leaning hard against the doorjamb. In one hand he held his sword, point resting on the ground by his bare feet.

His eyes flicked briefly to her, as if he were aware of her perusal but did not want to be distracted. "What do you want, Airdy?" he asked reasonably. "Wasn't beating you yesterday enough? Do you want me to beat you again today, and tomorrow too?"

Airdy's eyes flared like a wild animal. "Next time I'll kill you," he bellowed, his voice breaking on the final word.

The pistol was still dangling loosely from his fingers, and now he lifted it.

Meg stepped back, forgetting her courageous poise. She bumped up against Gregor Grant, and heard his hiss of pain. Before she could move away again, his hand slipped around her waist, drawing her to one side, hard against his body. He was very hot, feverish, and as hard as iron. Despite the strength she felt in him, the hand at her waist shook, and she knew it would not take much to knock him over. He leaned against her heavily, and she bit her lip, trying not to stagger.

"You can try," he retorted calmly to Airdy's threat, and Meg marveled at his bravado.

"Barbara's gone."

"Gone?" Gregor sounded as if he was as bewildered as Meg. "Gone where? She went with you, Airdy. That was the last time I saw her."

"Well she's gone now!" he blurted, and to Meg's horror, tears began to streak down his white face. "You took her from me, you b-bastard!" The pistol swayed wildly from side to side.

Meg gasped.

"She isna here," Gregor said sharply. "I left her with you. You know this. If she's run off, then she's done it on her own. Or she's found someone else to listen to her lies. Go and find her, if you still want her, but don't waste my time."

Meg held her breath. For a moment it looked as if Airdy would fire at him—he seemed capable of anything—and then with a great shout of grief and rage, he turned and rode away.

Beside her, Gregor sagged against the jamb, his arm slipping from her waist.

His head was swimming, but he wasn't going to faint. How could he faint, when this woman had stood up to Airdy Campbell for his sake? He had staggered out here, wondering with each step whether he was going to fall down, to find her facing up to Airdy as if she were taking a stroll in the park. His heart had given a great thump of fear. She didn't know Airdy, she didn't know that he was half mad and capable of anything.

And yet her bravery was beyond question.

He blinked now, clearing the black spots from his gaze. She was looking up at him, concern making lines in her brow, her piercing eyes searching his.

"Captain Grant?" she said gently. "Can I help you back to bed now?"

Suddenly Gregor discovered that he admired her a great deal. She was brave, spirited, and generous. And he knew what he had to do. He had sworn that he would not be drawn into her problems, as he had been drawn into Barbara Campbell's, that he would not return to Glen Dhui at any price, but now . . . Now he owed her the chance to explain to him what was wrong, what she wanted from him.

He owed her that much.

Gregor let out his breath in a soft sigh, gazing down into Lady Meg Mackintosh's astonishing eyes.

"Tell me what you want," he said. "I am ready to listen now."

Chapter 5

With Meg's help, Gregor struggled to the same big wooden chair that he had occupied last night and collapsed. He looked white, and the bandages Malcolm Bain had placed about his arm were spotted with blood from his exertions. Lord, Meg thought, chewing her lip worriedly, if he fainted again there was no way she would be able to help him back to bed.

Just then Gregor gave a great shiver, despite the heat from the fire and the heat from his own body. Meg hurried to fetch a quilt from his room, calling for someone—anyone—to fetch a restorative whiskey. Was the inn entirely empty?

When she returned, Gregor was exactly as she had left him, hunched over, shaking, his hair loose and straggling about his shoulders. His obvious pain and suffering softened her heart, but more than that. There was something of her dream boy in him—perhaps in his display of weakness, no matter how unwitting.

Gently Meg tucked the warm covering around his naked shoulders.

He looked up at her, surprised. He hadn't even heard her return. "Thank you," he said, his voice low. He reached up to draw the quilt closer and his hand brushed hers.

For a moment Meg found it impossible to look away from those intriguing eyes. With an effort, she sat down on a stool close by, to compose herself. After all, she had more important things to think of right now. After his flat-out refusal to consider her request, or even to listen to it, she had not thought it possible he would change his mind so suddenly.

Why *had* he changed it?

Was it something to do with that bedlamite, Airdy Campbell?

Whatever the reason, Meg was determined to make the most of it and persuade Gregor to agree to her request, to come home with her to Glen Dhui. Striving for her usual sangfroid, she folded her hands in her lap, entwining her long, slim fingers. He had half turned in the chair and was watching her, a small, tight smile playing around the corners of his mouth. Briefly her throat went dry, and nervousness returned.

Fortunately at that moment Morag hurried in breathlessly, with a cup of whiskey. She murmured an excuse about the fishmonger's boy keeping her talking, but her flushed looks made Meg wonder whether the soldiers of the Black Dog didn't have a rival.

Gregor gulped down the whiskey, and before the girl had even left the room, some of the color returned to his face.

"Your bandages need changing," Meg said.

"Don't worry," he said, "I'll get Malcolm Bain to do it. Tell me what you have come all this way to tell me."

Meg nodded, leaning forward, her eyes fixed on his.

"After you left Glen Dhui, Captain Grant, the management of the estate was put into the hands of the government. It was . . . difficult for the people. And then my father bought it."

His smile had gone, his face turned rigid and unemotional. She could read nothing in it.

"You know my father," she said softly. "He is General Mackintosh."

Something was stirring in the depths of those amber eyes, a whirlpool of emotion he tried to keep hidden by sweeping his dark lashes over them. But she read pain in the tightening of his mouth, the stiffening of his body, the white knuckles of his clenched hand. Real pain.

"General Mackintosh is your father," he repeated, and it was not a question.

"Yes. My father is the man whose life you saved when you were in prison, Captain Grant."

Now those thick, dark lashes lifted, and she saw bewilderment. "The name was the same, but I did not think . . . Why would the General Mackintosh I knew buy Glen Dhui? He lived in the North of England."

Meg smiled wryly. "He did, and why indeed? If you think it was to repay you for your courageous action, then think again. My father is not quite so altruistic. He knew of Glen Dhui from you, presumably, and then he learned that the estate was forfeit by your family after the Rebellion. He had to travel north of the border on business that year. Glen Dhui was out of his way, but he journeyed to it anyway. There were a number of wealthy men from England who fancied themselves lairds after the 1715. They bought estates confiscated from Jacobite owners. But my father wasn't looking to increase his prestige. He fell in love with Glen Dhui, and made an immediate offer to the government. They accepted. And so we went to make our home there. He has been a good laird," she finished, lifting her chin and daring him to disagree.

Slowly he nodded his head, accepting her words. He shivered again, and pulled the quilt closer about him, his hair falling forward in thick lengths, his eyes a golden gleam through his lashes.

"Then why do you need me?" he asked quietly.

"The general is not well. Duncan helps, he is a good tacksman, and he advises us. Our tenants are loyal and reliable. But my father is no longer able to run the estate as he once did, and much falls to me. I do not mind. . . . In fact I enjoy it. I cannot foresee any problems in my taking the reins from him, when he is ready to relinquish them."

"The general isna well, but you are perfectly competent to take over. I ask again, my lady, why do you need me?"

Meg sighed, her fingers tightening upon each other. "The Duke of Abercauldy has an estate to the south of us, far larger than Glen Dhui. We have always been on good terms with him; he and the general are friends. *Were* friends."

The bitterness in her voice caught her unawares. She found those cool amber eyes once more upon her, probing her weaknesses.

"The duke came often to call, and they would sit and talk. The general . . . My father enjoyed his company—he trusted him. I trusted my father. And then one day they hatched a plot between them, that the duke and I would marry, and so join our estates together. But it wasn't the land—not in my father's mind, anyway. He has always wanted for me to marry into the aristocracy. It has always been his wish, but I have resisted. It has been a bone of contention between us since I came of age. My father has not agreed with my point of view, but he has respected it . . . until now. I . . ." but her voice failed her.

Those eyes were full of attention now, not a trace of fever. "You dinna wish to marry him?"

"I did not think to marry anyone," she replied tersely. "In the end I felt I had no choice."

"So he changed your mind?"

Meg laughed without humor. "They had signed some papers, legal documents, but that was not the reason I agreed. I am five and twenty and single, probably too old to attract another man. When my father dies I will be all alone, but again, that did not persuade me. The general is not the man he was, Captain. He forgets. His mind is fading. He did not mean to make me unhappy—the opposite in fact. I could not hate him for wanting to see me safe. When I saw what our falling out was doing to him, how it was destroying what time he has left, I capitulated."

She said it coldly, without flinching, daring him to make a comment.

He nodded, but there was a tension in him, a hardness about his face she could not read. "And now? I still dinna understand the reason you want me to go home."

Home. It was a slip. They both ignored it.

"He was married before," she said flatly. "Two years ago. To Lady Isabella Mackenzie, an heiress from the Western Isles. The marriage was unhappy. He . . . mistreated her. She died in an accident—so it was said. Tragic and sad, but unremarkable. And then . . . then I received information that it was no accident. That Isabella may well have been murdered, by the duke himself."

"And you accept this information? You trust the source it came from?"

She barely hesitated. "I do. And there is more. Once we began asking questions closer to Abercauldy's lands, we learned that he has an evil reputation where women are concerned. Cruelty and . . . and disappearances. It is just that he took care we did not know about these rumors. Until it was too late."

"Did you tell the duke what you had heard?"

"It was difficult. Stories can be denied. I simply told him I no longer wished to marry him."

"And?"

"He would not relinquish me. He is stubborn. He said he had his mind set on me. I said things. . . . I did not wish to enrage him, but I fear I have a sharp tongue, Captain Grant, and may have said things he did not like."

Humor twitched briefly at the corners of the hard line of his mouth. "I fear you are right. Does he intend to move against you?"

"I don't know. He is strange . . . unpredictable. Now I am afraid for the people of Glen Dhui as much as the general and myself. I have heard rumors that the duke is not a good landlord."

She leaned closer still, searching his face for some clue as to what he was thinking.

"My father is too ill to lead his tenants into war like a good Highland chief, even if he thought we could win against such a man as the Duke of Abercauldy. Instead he thought of you. Once *you* were the Laird of Glen Dhui, and I believe the people still think of you as such. If it comes to a fight, then you have military training. That is why my father asked me to bring you to him, to take his place at the head of his men. He says you are our only hope, Captain Grant, and maybe you are."

Gregor closed his eyes, easing himself in the chair to try and find a more comfortable position. There wasn't one. He didn't know Abercauldy. He had heard the name, of course, but nothing of the man behind it. Abercauldy wanted Meg Mackintosh, but for herself or for the land to which she was heiress? And General Mackintosh! The last time Gregor had seen him had been twelve years ago, when he had stood, bloodied and shaken, over the body of the man he had just prevented from killing the general. They had been enemies, yes, but in Gregor's mind hatred for one's enemy did not strip one of humanity. A man should be judged for what he was, not for his beliefs.

What did General Mackintosh expect him to do now? Train the people for a possible war? He could do that, but it would not make success any more likely. The duke must have considerable resources at his disposal. What did Glen Dhui have? If the general was so ill, why did he not sell Glen Dhui to the duke and be done with it, retire to Edinburgh or Inverness and give his daughter some security?

He opened his eyes.

They were watching him, those pale eyes framed by silky lashes. There was a hint of something in her face that he had seen there before. Hope? Admiration? As if she expected him to behave like a hero and was waiting to have her expectations realized.

Hero? Gregor shook himself. He was not that and never would be. What had General Mackintosh said, that Gregor had saved his life at the risk of his own? He did not want the daughter to believe he was capable of anything so heroic. He was no hero. He had done things to survive that made him ache inside. He was nobody's hero.

"So you want me to come with you to Glen Dhui, to help defend it against the Duke of Abercauldy?" he said coolly.

Her eyes flickered, as if she was surprised by his emotionless voice, but she nodded. "That is right, Captain."

"And in return? What do I get in return?"

He could see his question had startled her. Good. She blinked, looked away, then back again. The expectation had gone from her face now, wiped clean. She looked a little shocked.

"What do you get?"

He nodded. "Did you expect me to do this from the generosity of my heart, my lady? I have nothing, I am nothing, but I do not risk my life for nothing."

Slowly she nodded, but he thought he caught a flicker of disgust in her face. She was thinking he had no honor, that an honorable man would do this for the sake of the people of Glen Dhui and his family's long tradition there. She did not know what it was to lose everything, then. She did not know how it felt to be dispossessed, with no hope of a future. He wasn't that honorable fool anymore, he was a soldier who fought for whichever side offered him the most.

Better she learn it now and have no false ideas about his motives. And he was twice a fool, if such a thought caused him any concern. Gregor waited for her answer, ignoring the sense of regret gnawing at him for the change in her manner.

"We will pay you," she said stiffly. "What is the rate for a mercenary these days?"

Those cool, hard eyes examined her again, and although

she saw no expression in them she sensed he was darkly amused by her disapproval and disappointment.

"I'll take what Argyll was paying me, that will do for a start," he said. "I will get Malcolm Bain to fetch my belongings from the barracks, and take a letter resigning my commission."

She wanted to ask him what he would do in the future if he was not a soldier, but he did not look like the sort of man to take her into his confidence. He had closed himself off from her, shutting her out as effectively as closing a door. Anyway, Meg was not sure she wanted it open. Did she really want to know what made him what he was? She had thought he would agree as soon as he heard what was happening at Glen Dhui. Not for her sake, but for the sake of the people who had once been his people. Instead he had asked about payment.

Meg supposed she could not blame him for his selfishness. He had to think of himself first, how else had he survived in this harsh world? And yet, still she had harbored some of her dreams. She had believed him to be a certain kind of man, and to discover he wasn't had been a dissapointment. She would not be fooled again.

They were interrupted by Morag bringing food, and soon afterward by the return of Duncan Forbes. Duncan looked very relieved to hear Gregor would be returning with them, and was eager to carry the letter to the barracks.

"Will ye be fit to ride tomorrow morning?" he asked, looking Gregor over with a professional eye.

"Of course," Gregor said coolly, his expression daring a dispute. "Wait, and I will write the letter."

Paper and ink were found, and Gregor set to work. Meg sent for clean water and bandages, and when he had done, began without a word to unwrap his wound.

Duncan, with a glance at Meg, left with the letter.

"Malcolm Bain can do this," Gregor said, tight about the mouth. "There is no need—"

"Now you are in my employ, Captain, I need to know you can deliver on your promises."

He grunted, but said no more as Meg inspected his wound, bathed it, and carefully rewrapped it. The flesh looked a little swollen about her neat stitches, a little hot to touch, but in Meg's experience fever was a normal part of recovery. The strong survived, the weak didn't, and Gregor Grant was definitely one of the former.

When Gregor went to his room, he was walking as carefully as a man crossing hot coals. Meg hoped that he would spend the day in sleep, and regain some of his strength. She did not look forward to riding such a distance with an injured man, especially one so stubborn he would not admit he was too ill to ride until he fell off his horse.

"Lady Meg?"

Meg looked up from her seat by the fire. Duncan had returned, and he looked like he had been carved out of stone. For a moment her heart beat faster as she wondered what new disaster was about to befall them.

"Duncan? Is all well?"

"I have given the letter to the man in charge, and I have brought back the Captain's baggage and his horse." But he said it stiffly, with resentment.

"There is something wrong. What is it? Do tell me, Duncan, I am not in the mood to guess."

Duncan pursed his lips, but before he could answer her, Malcolm Bain appeared behind him. His fair hair—the characteristic that gave him his appendage *Bain*, or "fair

Malcolm"—was as wild and windblown as it had been last night. His face looked even more rugged this morning, the creases in it making Meg wonder if he had had any sleep at all.

"My lady," he said with a bow, a twinkle in his eyes. "I hope ye dinna mind me tagging along with ye. I am Captain Grant's man and he canna manage without me."

Duncan sniffed repressively.

Meg hid a smile, puzzled by the tension between the two of them; they had been the same last night. Like two dogs coveting the same bone. It was Malcolm Bain himself who explained matters.

"I am a Glen Dhui man myself," he said blithely. "When the lad lost the land, I went with him. My father was his father's man, and my grandsire's his grandsire's, and so it goes. I had a sworn duty to care for him."

"Tell that to Alison," Duncan muttered darkly.

Malcolm Bain looked at him and sighed. "Ah, Duncan, I tried to. She dinna understand."

"She still doesna understand," was Duncan's grim reply.

Meg looked from one to the other. "What do you mean, Duncan? Alison, my maid? Alison, your sister?"

Duncan answered readily enough. "My sister was to wed this . . . this creature, my lady. But then he left her and she hasna heard from him in twelve long years! He broke her heart."

Meg thought of dark-haired, dark-eyed Alison, plump and full of zeal. In Meg's opinion she did not appear to be suffering from a broken heart, but neither had she ever mentioned a desire to wed or an interest in any of the local men. Meg had presumed that was because Alison had never found the right man to give her heart to. Was she herself not in similar straits? Besides—and yes, she was selfish in this—a single Alison suited her own needs just fine. But now suddenly, she could see that Alison's aloneness may well be because she had loved and been hurt and therefore had given up on men entirely.

This was clearly what Duncan believed.

Malcolm Bain made a sound closely resembling a snort. "I never asked her to wait for me," he said in a harsh voice. "There were plenty of others would have been hers for the taking, if she'd said the word. If she's still single, then 'twas because she was content to remain so!"

Duncan took a step closer to him, pushing his face aggressively into the other man's. "Mabbe she dinna want any of the others. Mabbe she wanted ye, ye selfish—"

"Will you both stop it!" Meg grabbed Duncan's arm, pressing a warning with her fingers. "I am quite sure, Duncan, that Alison will not thank you, for making her the subject of a brawl. And as for you, Malcolm Bain, your master is resting. Go and see if he needs anything, and take his luggage with you."

Malcolm Bain shot her an uncertain glance, but went to do her bidding. Duncan glowered after him, and Meg squeezed his arm again, more kindly this time.

"I am sure Alison can handle her own affairs, Duncan," she said gently. "You are a good brother to her, but truly I think these matters would be better left to her and Malcolm Bain MacGregor."

Duncan's nod was brief and clearly dissenting.

Dear Lord, Meg thought when he had gone, *if there are not complications enough!* Now she must play King Solomon to her maid and Gregor Grant's man. She only hoped that she was right, and that Alison had long since recovered from any pain she may once have felt over Malcolm Bain's leaving her.

"Gregor lad?"

The familiar voice brought Gregor up from the faintly unpleasant dream he was struggling through, where women with red hair clung to him and men with wild, dark eyes waved pistols in his face. He blinked and then focused on the worn, lined face that he knew as well as his own.

"Malcolm Bain," he said, and his mouth twitched into the smile that was not seen by many people. Captain Grant was sober and taciturn; Gregor Grant was another matter entirely. "Where were you?" he asked. "What do you mean by leaving me here in the hornet's nest?"

Malcolm Bain chuckled. "Ye wouldna by any chance be meaning a red-haired hornet? What does she want of ye? I have a feeling that one is used to getting her own way."

Gregor shrugged. "She's no match for me," he said smugly.

Malcolm Bain's eyes slid over his face but he said nothing, keeping his thoughts to himself. "Did ye know Airdy's wife has run away from him?" he asked instead. "He's been ranting and raving the whole day, swearing one moment to kill her and the next that he canna live without her. 'Tis a pitiful sight, mon!"

"Then it's one I'm glad to forego. Does he know I've resigned my captaincy?"

"That pleasure yet awaits him."

Gregor nodded, shivering, and carefully pulled the covers around himself with a sigh. "You're not surprised by the news, then?"

Malcolm Bain shrugged. "It was only a matter of time, lad. Ye've been restless for months now. I think the Camp-bell dragoons doesna have the same flavor for ye that it once did. As long as ye're certain 'tis the right thing to do . . . ?"

"Aye," Gregor said softly, "I'm certain. She's offered to pay me, Malcolm Bain. Pay me to go home." He laughed, but there was sorrow and bitterness in it, emotions he rarely showed to anyone else. "If she pays me enough, I'll use the money to buy myself some land, enough to live on."

"No life for a Grant laird," Malcolm Bain murmured.

"I am no longer a Grant laird," was the retort. "Tell me, what do you know of the Duke of Abercauldy?"

Gregor was determined to change the subject. Malcolm Bain contented himself with straightening aspects of the room that displeased him and stoking up the fire. "I know little enough of him. I know he fought for the English dur-ing the 1715 and made himself rich on the estates and fines of those who dinna. He's a clever man, but as far as I know that is not a crime."

"No, it isn't. Did you ever hear that he had a wife?"

"No. Has he a wife?"

"She's dead. Rumor has it he did away with her. Now he has set his eyes on Glen Dhui and flame-haired Meg. That is why I am to go home, Malcolm, to see that our clever duke does not take what is not his."

"The land, or the lady?" Malcolm asked, with a sly glance up from the fire.

"Both, Malcolm, both."

"Then ye will need to build yer strength for the ride south, and the fight when ye get there," was the reply. "I'll fetch ye some food and some ale, and then I'll take a peek at yer arm."

Gregor grimaced, clearly disliking the thought of his arm being touched again. "As you say, Malcolm."

Malcolm paused on his way out of the door, looking back. Gregor lay still and pale, no doubt in some pain and with a fever. But that would not stop him from riding all day tomorrow and the day after that to reach Glen Dhui. Strange that a twist of fate had seen to it that he must return to the one place he had denied himself for twelve years. Gregor Grant had made another life for himself, he had no option—he was no longer the boy he had been when he fought the English and was imprisoned for it. That boy had watched others around him die in the filthy gaol, and then barely escaped transportation to the plantations. He was a man who had known much pain and hardship, and it showed.

Malcolm wondered now how Gregor would cope with returning to a place he had loved, a place which was now no longer his own. And how would he manage to obey orders from a woman who was clearly used to giving them? It would be . . . interesting, to say the least. And Malcolm would be there, he *must* be there, for Gregor's sake. He could hardly abandon him now, although he was sorely tempted.

For there was an ache in Malcolm Bain's heart that had nothing to do with Glen Dhui and Gregor Grant. Waiting at Glen Dhui, as she had, according to Duncan, waited all these years, was Alison Forbes. His sweetheart, the woman he had planned to marry and grow old with, the woman he had put from his mind when he left.

Did she still hate him, as she had hated him the day he rode away from her? Or was she indifferent to him, having long ago shut his memory away? Duncan might be wrong—the Alison he had loved and remembered could well be so changed now that he would not recognize her.

Malcolm Bain didn't know what he hoped for. One choice felt as dismal as the other.

Chapter 6

M eg drew her mare up from a gallop. While it stood blowing and tossing its head, she turned to look back. The men were following in the distance at a steady pace, although that seemed to be more for Gregor Grant's sake than any wish to tarry. The former Laird of Glen Dhui rode stiffly, as if any sudden movement pained him, but he had not asked for them to stop. Nor would he, Meg suspected.

As she watched, he turned his head, gazing to the high mountains that lay before them, their jagged, snowy peaks gleaming in the sun. They would have to cross those mountains tomorrow, traversing the narrow pass that cut through their towering mass. For Glen Dhui lay beyond.

This morning Gregor had sat down to breakfast with a pale face and a determined expression. He wore a fresh shirt beneath a brown jacket, and his kilted plaid, as well as all his weapons. He had spoken little and eaten less. His only reply, when Duncan questioned him as to whether he was fit to ride, was a long, unsmiling stare. "Of course," he had said at last, coldly, as if Duncan was impertinent to suggest otherwise.

Duncan's ears had gone pink.

Meg hid her smile. To put taciturn Duncan out of countenance was no mean feat, but Gregor Grant had managed it. She imagined he would be a formidable master. Despite his assertions that he was a landless, penniless nobody, he still wore the arrogance of his birth around him like a cloak. He was a leader of men who expected his orders to be carried out without question.

And he was hers.

Meg took another swallow of the cold air, and calmed her jittery mare with a soft word. She had not slept well last night. Like the mare, she had been restless and restive; she had wondered if she was doing the right thing. Her father had told her to bring Gregor Grant back to Glen Dhui, and she was doing that. He had said nothing of payment, but then he had not expected the man who had grown from the boy he remembered to ask for recompense. The general believed that inside the man Gregor Grant lived the same young, heroic, idealistic boy he had been then. He would realize for himself, when they reached Glen Dhui, that that was not the case.

Assuming Gregor Grant made it that far.

Meg lifted her head to gaze at the sky, wondering if the fine weather would hold until they found shelter tonight. Late summer in the Highlands was unpredictable, with showers one moment and sunshine the next. She knew they would be lucky if they reached their beds without a drenching, and that was the last thing Gregor Grant needed. He still had a fever, and when Malcolm Bain had unwrapped his wound this morning it had looked even more reddened and swollen about the stitches that she had so carefully set into his flesh.

"We will wait another day," she had said firmly.

Gregor had shot her a narrowed look. "No, we will not. We go today."

"But your arm—"

"Is not the issue here. We ride today."

Their gazes had clashed, each seeking to dominate. It was Malcolm Bain's voice that had poured reason onto the situation.

"I will keep a watch on him," he had said. "Captain Grant is a strong and healthy man, even if he is pigheaded."

Gregor had shot him a look of disgust, but the comment had reassured Meg. For a while. Now the worry had returned. There was so much dependent on this one man, so much dependent on her getting him home. The thought of anything happening to him on the way, of him *dying* . . . well, it didn't bear thinking. Indeed she felt quite light-headed when she did, as if some vital part of herself had come adrift.

Of course it was because his returning to Glen Dhui was so important to her father. There could be no other reason for his possible demise to affect her so. She didn't know him—he was a stranger, and any belief she may have had that he was that heroic dream she had carried with her since she was twelve years old had been effectively banished with her first glimpse of him in the Black Dog.

Some of the going would be rough. And they must take the new military road through the pass and brave the suspicious eyes of the government soldiers who stood guard there at the military post. The soldiers were mainly Englishmen, and they considered the Highlanders to be savages—half-civilized beasts that might at any moment decide to turn on them. They despised these people whom they had come to subdue. Meg saw it in their faces and it worried her. It also made her angry. She knew the Highlanders, and although they spoke Gaelic and their lives were very different from those of the English soldiers, they were not the animals the soldiers thought them.

Despite the attitude of his men, Meg was on good terms with the officer in charge of the military post. After the 1715 Rebellion it had been decided by the anti-Jacobite victors that roads must be forced through the Highlands, roads that could be used by soldiers in the event of any further uprisings. Government soldiers were posted to strategic trouble spots, to keep watch on the people and dispense English justice. Many of those soldiers were resentful, felt alienated, and took out their feelings on the people they were supposed to be in charge of.

But not all the English officers were to be hated or feared. There were some, like Major Litchfield, who was well educated and broad-minded enough to find his current posting interesting rather than bemoan it as exile to the end of the civilized world.

Meg turned her head again, and noted that her men were almost upon her. Gregor Grant, sitting as stiffly in the saddle as before, was at least still astride his horse. She eyed him narrowly, just as he looked up. Their gazes held, clashed. Something close to a smile lifted the corner of his mouth.

"Lost your way?"

Impatiently, Meg dug her heels into her restive mare's sides and set off again in the lead.

There she was. Ahead of them. Her red hair burned against the blue sky as she rode off on her mare. She was wearing her trews and jacket again, with long boots of soft leather. Her hair was fashioned into a long, thick plait that hung down her slim back. She rode well, without fear, as if she had been born to the saddle. But despite the masculine attire, there was no way Meg Mackintosh could be mistaken for a man. Everything about her was most definitely feminine: the curve of her breasts beneath the tight jacket, the swell of her hips, the tender curve of her jaw, the full shape of her lips . . .

Gregor felt his body respond despite his discomfort. A sort of miracle, considering the way he was feeling, and the fact that he had just been used by beautiful Barbara Campbell for her own selfish ends.

Meg wasn't even his type. Freckles on her nose, tart tongue, bossy manners—nothing there to attract him. And yet it did, all of it. He didn't just find her interesting, he actively lusted after her. Last night he had slept fitfully, only to wake from hot, feverish dreams in which Meg Mackintosh played a prominent part.

What would she think if she knew? If she knew exactly what he had been imagining her doing, in those sweaty, frantic fantasies? Would she be horrified and disgusted? Would she withdraw from him?

Possibly.

Probably.

Better she never know, then. . . .

"Lady Meg has a mind of her own."

Duncan Forbes's toneless voice interrupted his thoughts. Gregor met those dark eyes, wondering what the tacksman had seen in his expression that made him aware Gregor was thinking of his lady.

"Doesn't the general keep her reined in?" he asked.

Duncan smiled—it looked as if it hurt his face to assume such an unfamiliar expression. "The general indulges her."

"In all things?"

"Aye. Well, almost." Now Duncan appeared troubled. "It was her impending marriage that they were at odds over. She has refused to wed any of the men her father put before her. She was . . . *is* fussy. There is always some reason . . . some excuse why they are unsuitable."

"She is hard to please, then?"

"Aye, she is difficult when it comes to suitors."

"Until the Duke of Abercauldy."

Duncan looked worried. "He came calling often, but we thought 'twas more to see the general than Lady Meg. The duke would spend hours with the general, flattering him by listening to his stories. A man like the general, who all his life has been busy and important, whom people have looked to for advice—such a man finds it more difficult than most to grow old and feeble, to be set aside. When the duke flattered him, he believed him. They made the marriage deal between them and the general signed the papers. When he told Lady Meg, she was verra angry. She wept, too. But in the end I think she would have accepted the arrangement, for the general's sake, if they hadna found out the Duke wasna the man they had thought him. But by then it was too late. The Duke seems set on her and he isna a man to change his mind."

Gregor believed the story as Duncan told it; it tallied with Meg's, and sadly, it sounded all too plausible. "So, tell me, is it the land he wants? Or the lady?"

"I dinna know that, Captain. There is a look in his eyes when he gazes upon her. He wants her, aye. He . . . he covets her, I think. But then there is the land, too. With Glen Dhui added to his estate it will stretch far. He will be thought an even greater man than he already is."

"Do you trust him, Duncan?"

Duncan's sour expression soured even more. "He has the manners of a London gent, and no, I dinna trust him an inch."

Gregor nodded. If the Duke was not to be trusted, then Lady Meg must not wed him. Therefore they must find a way of extracting themselves from this mess without bringing his wrath down upon their heads, and without starting a war they would be sure to lose. The general was the man for that—strategy had always been his strong point. Gregor wondered why his own presence was so necessary, but he was content to wait. Soon enough he would be able to ask the general that question for himself.

It would be strange to see him again.

He moved in the saddle, forgetting. The throb in his arm was an agonizing reminder that all was not well. Gregor bit his lip and sought to distract himself. He looked to Duncan again.

"I remember when we fought in the 1715, the Glen Dhui men were armed . . . in a manner of speaking. What happened to those arms, Duncan? Were they confiscated by the English?"

"No, they were set aside for a rainy day."

Gregor smiled. "I thought that might have been the case."

He supposed the guns would be rusty by now; they had already been old when they were used last time around. The Duke of Abercauldy would probably have a small army of his own: well-trained men and up-to-date equipment. Glen Dhui had never been modern; it was out of step, isolated, a place where time seemed to stand still, or where it moved along at a very slow amble.

Gregor had always believed the glen could be improved without being spoiled. During his school years in Edinburgh, he had looked into new methods of agriculture, of managing the land. He knew there were better ways than those presently in use. But his father had sneered at his ideas and called them "Sassenach foolishness."

"There will be nay changes here while I live!" he had declared.

Gregor had tried to persuade him differently, but he had been a boy and his father would not listen to him. So he had put aside his sense of restlessness and dissatisfaction, telling himself that there would come a time when he would be able to do as he wanted, when the estate would be all his.

Instead the Stuarts had come, the Rebellion had happened, and they had lost everything.

Again Gregor fixed his eyes bleakly on the woman riding at the head of the little troop. He was going home. It was true, it was real. He was going home, and with that knowledge came all the painful emotions he had been avoiding. Suddenly he didn't know whether to hate her for obliging him to return to something that could never now be his. Or to love her, because he was going home to Glen Dhui.

* * *

The day was fading fast. Long shadows were draped across the glen between shards of gentle light. The mountains were dark monoliths against the rose sky, where high upon one onyx cliff, a tiny spume of white water arced downward, catching the last of the sun in a spray of diamonds.

Not far now to the croft where they would spend the night, thought Meg gratefully. She cast a glance at the grim, tired little group at her back. Gregor Grant was riding as if he were asleep, his face a white blur in the muted light, swaying in the saddle. As she watched, Malcolm Bain reached out to steady him, murmuring encouragement.

Ahead of them, down the shadowy glen, she saw the flicker of a lantern. Relief flooded her. Shona was there, waiting. Meg needed to speak to her friend, the village healer, to hear again the stories that had first turned her and her father against an alliance with the Duke of Abercauldy. To hear the reasons she should not wed such a man, and in refusing to do so must put at risk herself, her father, and all her people.

Meg thought of Shona's croft as cozy, though she supposed some would call it crowded and close. But for Meg, Shona's greeting was always so warm that she never noticed aught else.

Shona came from her doorway, lantern held high, to bid them welcome. "My lady!" she cried gladly. "Come in, come in all of ye. Kenneth will see to the horses." With her classic Highland coloring of dark hair and blue eyes, Shona was a lovely woman, with a smile that encompassed them all.

"I have but two hands, wife," Kenneth grumbled.

Shona clicked her tongue at her man. "Away with ye,"

she said, gently scolding. "How often do we have guests? What is a little bother, when the sight of Lady Meg cheers me so?"

Kenneth smiled. Their eyes met in a moment of perfect understanding, in a manner that made everyone else feel slightly left out. Meg experienced a catch in her throat and wondered, as she always did in their presence, whether she would ever find a man who loved her and whom she could love, as Shona and Kenneth loved each other.

Anything less than that was not to be contemplated.

It was a stance she had taken long ago, and one her father did not understand. For him, prestige, family ties, and important bloodlines meant more than his only daughter's fancy for love.

They began to dismount, and it was only when Shona's eyes widened that Meg realized something was wrong. She turned swiftly, just in time to see Gregor sink limply into Malcolm Bain's meaty arms. He was on his feet again in an instant, pushing himself upright, but his face was ghostly in the pale light and the sweat shone on his skin like dew.

"What is wrong with this one?" Shona demanded sharply. "Is he sick with some malaise?"

Meg found her voice, for she seemed to have lost it in the moments when Gregor fainted. "No, no, nothing like that. He was wounded, his arm cut open. We . . . I sewed it up, but it is not good."

Shona was watching her, a glint of amusement in her blue eyes. "Ye sewed it up, Lady Meg? When 'tis known up and down the glens that Lady Margaret Mackintosh faints at the sight of blood?"

"I am ashamed to say that I do, usually, but on this occasion I managed to stay on my feet. Shona, can you look at Captain Grant's wound? You are skilled with such things, and I would count it a special favor."

Shona searched her face a moment, as if she saw something interesting there, and then she nodded her head. "Of course I will, my lady."

Meg felt such utter relief she hardly heard the rest of what Shona said. And her relief confused her, because it seemed more concerned with the man himself than bringing him home safe to her father.

"Come inside now, my lady, and settle him by the fire, and I will take a wee look. Kenneth! We need whiskey for these men, and see to their horses, won't ye?"

With Malcolm Bain supporting him on one side, Gregor staggered into the cottage. Meg followed, helping to ease him down onto the bench by the fire, and then holding the cup of whiskey that Shona poured to his lips. He took a deep swallow and seemed to revive, for his dark lashes lifted and he looked at her with fever-bright eyes.

"I am all right," he insisted.

Meg shook her head. "Anyone can see you are not all right, Captain."

Shona laughed, glancing from one to the other. "Ye should know better than to argue with Lady Meg. Now, let me see yer arm, Captain! Anything I don't know about healing is not worth the learning."

He hesitated, but only for an instant. To Meg's relief, he began to shrug off his jacket as best he could. The process was a painful one. Meg and Malcolm helped ease down the sleeve, and then the shirt was unlaced and pulled down from the bandages. The wound looked even more swollen and inflamed than it had that morning, the stitches tugging into the flesh in a manner that must be very painful.

Meg shuddered and leaned back against the wall in case she fulfilled Shona's prophecy and fell over. She watched, silent, as Shona pressed and prodded, ignoring her patient's swift intake of breath and his alarming pallor.

"Well," she said at last, "'tis clear Lady Meg and yer Malcolm here did their best, but I can do better. I'll need to snip some of these fine stitches, Captain. Bear with me, and believe me, ye'll feel better when 'tis all done."

With deft, practiced fingers, Shona set about snipping some of the tight stitches at the very edge of the wound. Pressing firmly but gently, Shona began to clean it thoroughly with clean water. Finally she set about preparing a poultice, crushing some herbs into a paste and smearing it upon the wound. Then she heated up a greasy mixture in a cup and pressed it to his lips with some whiskey added. Gregor drank it with a grimace, while Shona found fresh, clean bandages and busily rewrapped his wound.

It was all done quickly and competently.

"I will look again come the morning," Shona said, "but I think ye will heal now."

Meg's legs quivered and she held herself up through sheer effort of will. When her vision cleared, she met Shona's bright, piercing gaze.

"Never fear, Lady Meg," the other woman murmured gently, the words meant for her ears alone. "He will be as good as new again. No part of him will be lacking vigor."

Meg felt the color rush to her face. She heard Malcolm snort his laughter and knew Shona's voice had not been as discreet as she had thought. She prayed that Gregor had not heard. She cleared her throat in a manner she hoped showed her authority.

"Captain Grant is coming to Glen Dhui to help my father and me, Shona. That is all. There is nothing of a . . . a personal nature between us."

"Oh?" Shona raised her eyebrows.

"I want you to tell him now what you told me and my father," Meg went on, gathering up her confidence and position. "Tell him what the Duke of Abercauldy did to his first wife."

•

Chapter 7

Meg's men had found places to sleep—some in the stable and barn, others in the cottage itself. Now Kenneth sat beside his wife in the front room, his hand holding hers, while Meg and Gregor sat on the settle opposite, anxious for her to speak. Since Meg's asking Shona to tell her story, there had necessarily been a waiting time, during which Shona insisted her guests be fed and made comfortable before she would talk. At last all was quiet and she was ready to begin.

"Are you going to help Lady Meg?" she asked Gregor now, in the proud Highland manner which gave favor to no man.

He met her eyes without resentment. In the hours since Shona had redressed his wound and given her her tincture, he had seemed much better. The fever had left him and there was color in his cheeks that had nothing to do with the whiskey he had drunk and everything to do with returning

80

good health. Shona was something of a miracle worker when it came to healing, and Meg was grateful enough not to question her ways.

"I am going to help her, Shona," his deep voice broke into Meg's thoughts. "Why don't you tell me what you know?"

Shona searched his face a moment, as if she would draw the truth out of him, and then at last she nodded. A glance at Meg, accompanied by a smile, and she settled back beside her husband.

"My Kenneth was away," she began simply. "He was taken from me after the 1715, and sent to Virginia. I dinna know if I would ever see him again. There was no money, so I took work as kitchen maid in the house of the Duke of Abercauldy. Because I was clean and clever, I rose above that station quickly. When he brought his bride home, I was given the task of keeping her room tidy. Lady Isabella had auburn hair and a temper, and I dinna believe she was much in awe of the duke, her husband. She laughed in his face, and she made a fool of him with her sharp tongue, in front of his tenants, in front of his servants.

"Mabbe that was why he found her so fascinating. Most women, I had heard, feared the duke. Isabella dinna. And yet she should have feared him. There were stories of other women, whispers of women who had come to the duke's castle and then vanished. 'Twas said that one of them screamed for hours, locked away in some hidden place. The next morning she was found dead, below the north tower."

"The same tower where Isabella fell," Kenneth murmured.

"Or was pushed," Shona returned grimly. "Aye, she should have feared him. Isabella walked a narrow and dangerous path by flouting such a man. I saw him strike her once, when she had pushed him too far. Another time, he locked her in her room for a week. And even then she could no' see the danger she was in. Too strong-willed by far, do ye see? She laughed in his face, driving him on, making him wild with rage. Sometimes I thought it gave her pleasure, to see him lose control. It was as if she had won the battle."

"Did he love her? Or was it all about winning?"

Shona's fingers entwined with those of her man. "He watched her. She frustrated him, and yet she fascinated him. It was as if he was trying to discover her secrets, so that he could own her entirely. Is that love, Captain Grant? If so, 'tis no' the kind of love I know. The more he showed himself desirous of winning her affection, the more she resisted him. She was perverse in that way—manipulating. But then, so was he. They seemed to enjoy inflicting pain upon each other."

"So it was a game between them?"

"Aye, a strange, unhealthy game."

"And she died . . . how?"

Meg shifted uneasily, and Gregor looked at her. She appeared tired, there were shadows beneath her brilliant eyes, and her skin was chalky with exhaustion. He wanted to brush his finger along her cheek, cup that delicate curve with his calloused palm. He wanted to lean in to her and close his mouth on hers. He wanted to kiss her until they had both forgotten about the Duke of Abercauldy and his difficult wife. . . .

"Captain?"

"Hmm?" He glanced up into Shona's knowing blue gaze. She smiled, just enough to let him know she had guessed what he had been thinking.

"Do you want to hear how Lady Isabella died?"

Gregor frowned, carefully shifting his arm. "Go on."

Shona's smile slowly faded. "She fell from the north tower. There was talk that she had jumped, through homesickness and unhappiness, but I know neither to be true. She was no' homesick, and she was no' the sort to kill herself. She had too much to live for. And she and the duke enjoyed their strange games, so although her marriage was no' what I would call ordinary, it was no' the sort of marriage that would cause a woman to kill hersel' to escape it. 'Tis my belief Lady Isabella could have left anytime she wished—she had powerful relations—but she dinna choose to. Why would she kill herself?"

Gregor thought a moment, considering her words. "So what do you think happened, Shona?"

Shona straightened her shoulders and took a deep breath. "I think she was pushed, Captain," she said firmly. "It just so happened that that day I was in the vicinity of the north tower mysel'. I had been to see the cook's child, who was feverish, and was coming back that way. I . . . dinna wish to be seen. Some of the duke's people dinna like it that I was a healer. So I came by way of the north tower, where I knew it would be quiet and deserted."

Her blue eyes became distant, shadowy in the light of the lantern, as she returned to the past.

"I saw the duke coming down the stairs. He moved slowly, in a dream, as if he had a heavy weight upon his mind. His face was white, whiter than I had ever seen it. I dinna know whether to step out from the tapestry where I stood, to make myself known. Just then a cry went up from outside. The Duke lifted his head and went perfectly still. There was such a look on his face . . . A wild look, like an animal caught in a snare. A look of guilt and regret."

Meg shivered as if she were cold, although it was warm in the room with the smouldering peat fire. Gregor sensed her tension. His foot brushed hers, and she did not draw back. Instead she inched closer, as if she found comfort in his presence.

"He knew she was dead," Shona said with certainty. "Even before word was brought to him, he knew. Why would he keep such news to himself, unless it was due to a guilty conscience? Unless he had killed her with his own hands?"

"But why would he do such a thing?" Gregor asked impatiently. "If he married Lady Isabella for her money, why kill her when he already had what he wanted? Or if, as you say, he was fascinated by her, why dispose of her in such a way?"

Shona pulled a face. "Ah, Captain, you dinna see them together. She taunted him, teased him, kept him on edge. A man like that, a cold, controlled man . . . Once he lost his temper it could be verra dangerous. He might do such a thing without being able to stop himself, not until it was over, and too late. And as I said, 'twas often whispered about the castle that he had killed before."

Gregor raised a dark eyebrow. "So he killed her in a rage, and then kept quiet about it?"

"Aye," Shona said softly. "He pretended to mourn. He *did* mourn. I think he had loved Lady Isabella, in his way. And then one day he rode to Glen Dhui to visit the general and saw Lady Meg. She is much like his wife, in looks as well as manner, although of course Lady Meg is far, far sweeter." She smiled at Meg, but her eyes were serious. "But the duke wouldna see the differences, Captain. He is the sort of man who would see only what he wanted to see: another Isabella. A second chance to master Lady Isabella.

In his mind he isna marrying Lady Meg. He is marrying Lady Isabella . . . again!"

The pause that followed her words was a tribute to the telling, and to Shona's utter sincerity.

"I came home soon after the Lady Isabella died," Kenneth said, his deep voice breaking through the tense silence. "Shona came away home with me. We dinna talk of this thing very often, it isna safe. The duke is a powerful man, with a long reach. But when Shona heard of his betrothal to Lady Meg, she felt she had to tell. If the duke could do such a thing to one wife, then he could do it to another."

Shona's blue eyes shone with tears. "When I heard that the duke had set his sights on another woman, I went to see her for mysel'. And as soon as I saw Lady Meg, I understood why he wished to wed her. I couldna let such a thing happen again, and I couldna let Lady Meg wed herself to a murderer. I had to warn her, even if I risked my own life to tell her my story."

"For which I am forever grateful," Meg assured her, leaning forward to take her hand. "I do not relish being such a man's next victim."

Shona nodded, took a shaky breath, and glanced up at her husband. "I'm sure Captain Grant willna let that happen. I can rest easy with the burden passing to him."

Gregor wondered if she was right. Could he keep Meg safe? It sounded like no easy task. And yet there was a determination inside him, burning slow and hot, just like the peat fire in the hearth. And it was not something that would be easily extinguished.

"I will deal with the Duke of Abercauldy," he said softly. Meg turned her face toward him, surprised at his grim tone. Briefly her eyes searched his. "We will deal with him together," she reminded him quietly.

He nodded assent.

Her gaze returned to the firelight. Her hair was brighter and warmer than any fire. Again Gregor had the urge to take her in his arms and kiss her, and he smiled at the thought. She would fight like a hellcat, and he would probably pass out from the pain inflicted to his wound. Not the ideal passionate scene, then.

"'Tis late." Shona rose. "There is our bed, my lady, if ye—"

"No," Meg replied swiftly. "I would not take your bed, Shona. I will be quite all right here, by the fire."

Shona smiled, and something in her face made Meg suddenly suspicious that this had been her plan all along. "Verra well. I will fetch blankets for when the fire cools. I'm afraid there is so little room left in my home tonight that here is as comfortable as anywhere else. What of ye, Captain? Do ye mind sleeping here? I know ye are a gentleman and completely to be trusted."

He laughed. "Thank you, Shona. Aye, I am both a gentleman and to be trusted—tonight, at any rate."

Meg forced a smile in return. She still felt rather breathless from being held captive by Gregor Grant's eyes, and she wasn't sure she wanted to spend the night here, alone with him, but she would not take Shona's bed. "We will be fine. Thank you."

Kenneth followed his wife into the shadows.

Silence crept over the cottage, broken only by the faint sound of voices and the cry of an owl outside in the glen.

Meg glanced sideways at the man beside her, and decided his closeness was disturbing her more than it should.

He had been staring into the fire, but now his gaze shifted and found hers. Something in those amber depths questioned her, and once again drew her in. She wanted to back away, and yet at the same time she had the definite urge to lean forward until she was pressed close up to him, until his breath whispered in her hair and his arms enfolded her.

Sheer need for human contact, she told herself firmly. She was feeling uncertain, afraid, and he was a strong and confident man. She was drawn to him, yes, but it was a natural reaction.

"Meg? If you wish it, I will go and find other quarters."

Startled at the sound of her name on his lips, Meg was surprised once more into meeting his gaze. Lines creased his brow, experience hardened his face, weariness clouded his eyes.

He was not the man she had believed she was going to find in Clashennic. He was nothing like the dream she had believed in since she was twelve years old. He was more than that, frighteningly, stomach-clenchingly more.

"You are not as I expected."

She had spoken the words before she thought to stop them.

His brow quirked down into a frown. "What did you expect?"

Why not be honest? Meg thought. He already knew a great deal about her; he might as well know this as well.

"There was a man at the Black Dog, wearing yellow brocade and buckled shoes. He looked as if he would be more comfortable holding a snuff box than a pistol. I imagined you would be like him."

His frown deepened. "Good God. I wouldna lasted five minutes if I had been like that. I am a man made by circumstance, Meg. If I am taciturn, then my life has made me so. I became what I had to to survive."

He was right, of course he was! And yet, in her heart, Meg regretted the boy who had drawn those precise, intimate sketches she so treasured.

A chuckle brought her back from her thoughts. Meg raised her eyebrows as Gregor laughed softly again.

"I amuse you?" she asked in a sharp tone. Perhaps honesty was not the best option after all.

His eyes glinted with mocking humor. "I was wondering how my men would have reacted if I had given them an order in the outfit you just described. I have a feeling it was Georgie Moncreith you saw at the tavern. He's the only son of a factor and believes himself almost gentry."

His tone was filled with scorn—an insult from a man who did not have to play at being a gentleman. A man who, despite his worn clothing and lowered circumstances, still carried himself like the proud laird.

Yes, he was very different from the boy she had dreamed of, but much more intriguing. Not a disappointment, Meg realized, with some surprise. Whatever Gregor was or wasn't, he had not disappointed her.

Shona chose that moment to return with the bedding, and the next few minutes were spent making up a couple of comfortable spots by the fire.

"Good night," she said, turning down the lantern and leaving them alone in the firelight.

Gregor stood, hesitant.

"You should sleep," Meg said at last. "Tomorrow will be another long day. How are you feeling now?"

He smiled ruefully. "Remarkably well, considering how I felt before. Your Shona must be a witch."

"I don't know if she is mine, but yes, I have heard her called so."

"You didn't answer my question, Meg. Should I go elsewhere to sleep?"

Meg didn't look at him, busying herself arranging her own bed to her liking. "Of course not, Captain Grant. I will trust you, if you will trust me."

He hesitated a moment longer, and then removed his boots and lay down, pulling a blanket over him. Meg followed suit, taking off her boots and leaving on her stockings and other clothing. She would have enjoyed a long, hot bath, but such a luxury seemed unlikely in the present circumstances.

Meg closed her eyes. She was uncomfortable, tired, and dirty. She could hear Gregor Grant's breathing gradually slowing. He was falling asleep already. Meg supposed it was a vital requisite for a man in his position, to sleep whenever and wherever he could. She squeezed her eyes tighter shut and tried to pretend she was at home in her own comfortable bed.

It didn't help.

An hour later, Meg was still awake. She turned over for the dozenth time, shaking the bolster to try and make it softer beneath her head.

"It will be more comfortable if you lean on me."

His voice startled her; tingles ran over her skin. He sounded practical, even kind. Why then did Meg feel so uneasy at the thought of being so much closer to him?

"Then *you* will not be able to sleep," she said at last.

"I have no trouble sleeping, Meg. Come here, and we will arrange ourselves so that we are both more comfortable."

Was he right? Suddenly Meg was so frustrated and tired

she was willing to try anything. She shuffled closer, and settled in at his side. He had turned slightly onto his back, his wounded arm on the other side, out of harm's way. He slid his good arm under her, snuggling her in to his chest. The sensation of warmth and comfort was immediate, like one of Shona's sleeping tinctures. Meg felt quite dizzy with bliss.

She gave up on her objections with a sigh of sheer pleasure.

Gregor smiled into the darkness. Her hair brushed his nose, the scent of it filling his head with a dramatic intensity that set his pulses racing. He slowed them down, reminding himself she was now his employer. She owned him, in a way. He was here to look after her, certainly not to seduce her.

It was a pity his body didn't seem to realize that.

Meg sighed again. She tucked her feet up, and cuddled closer, clearly trying to relax, although she had started out as tense as he. Maybe she felt it too, this thing between them? Physical need. The attraction of two people to each other that had nothing to do with their minds or ideals or anything else in their heads and hearts. This was a need of the flesh, Gregor told himself, and he could control it. If he had to.

"Good night," he murmured firmly, and smiled when she yawned.

"Good night," she whispered back.

After a short time she went limp, her breathing slowing to sleep. But by then Gregor was already himself asleep.

Chapter 8

It was dawn. Here, outside, the air was cool and sharp, removing any lingering webs of sleep from Gregor's mind. Mist clothed the surrounding mountains and pooled in the glen. The loch lay still and glassy, shining in its cradle of dark hills.

Gregor stripped off his shirt and bent to splash the cold water over his chest and shoulders, ducking his head into it until his hair was plastered to his head like a dark cap. He avoided the bandage about his arm as much as possible, but the wound felt more comfortable this morning and his fever was gone. Whatever magic Shona had worked on him was still doing its job.

Shaking his head so that water sprayed outwards, Gregor straightened, stretching out the muscles of his back and legs, rolling his arms—carefully in the case of his injury. He breathed deeply of the cold mountain air and felt glad to be alive.

Home was over there. Beyond that cluster of dark peaks. He could almost smell it. Suddenly he felt dizzy with longing. Gregor wiped his face with his hands, sluicing off the dripping water. *Don't be stupid*, he thought. *Don't let yourself feel like that again.* Life was so much simpler if one did not care. For twelve years he had worked at pushing away the memories, the caring, and now they were back, resonating in his head. But he couldn't let them in. Losing Glen Dhui had hurt him in a way that was physical as well as mental. He had been like a boat whose ropes were cut, let loose, drifting with nowhere to go.

Gregor had hated Edinburgh: the tall tenements, or "lands," as they were known there, home to numerous, pale-faced families. The twisting, narrow streets with their cargo of refuse and noise. Everything felt so close and dirty, it was as if he were choking, as if he couldn't breathe. Within an hour of arriving, he had known he didn't want to live there, couldn't live there.

But his mother and sister had taken up residence, and his mother had soon re-formed old friendships and made new ones, and had settled into the rich social life to be found in the city. She was happy, and he suspected it was for the same reasons he was miserable. She was glad to be away from the isolated wilds of Glen Dhui; she had been born and bred in Edinburgh and she had never transplanted well to the Highlands, when she was wed to Gregor's father.

Gregor's sister was morose about her change in circumstances, but she made the best of it, following her mother about, somewhat mollified when she was decked out in the latest fashions. She was young, Gregor had told himself to ease his conscience when he left her. She would soon learn to forget the past, to fit in to her new life. Young enough to set aside the memories, as Gregor could not seem to.

He had known then that Glen Dhui was a part of him, his flesh and blood. Aye, he could live without it—the fact was, he had no choice—but that did not mean it did not hurt. It hurt so much that it ached. And it very nearly destroyed him. In twelve years he had built a new life for himself, but the old one had never left him. It had been waiting, biding its time, until now.

Gregor realized he had been standing as still as a rock, wearing only his kilt, and up to his knees in the freezing loch, staring into the past.

With a shake of his head, he bent down again, cupping his hands in the water and splashing it over his face, letting it trickle over his chest. The chill made him gasp and catch his breath, but at least it cleared his head. This was not a time to be regretting what was, what could not be changed. This was not a time to be keening for what was long ago lost. . . .

The sound that came from behind him was slight, but his hearing was acute. Gregor turned his head sharply, wishing he had strapped on his weapons, and found Lady Meg standing some paces behind him. She was on the rocky shore, a shawl wrapped about her shoulders and her red hair loose and streaming down her back. She was pale, her skin almost translucent in the early light, and her breath was a misty cloud.

"I'm sorry," she said, her voice sounding more tentative than he had ever heard it. "I wasn't spying on you, Captain. I thought to take some air. It is stuffy inside, and Shona and Kenneth need their privacy."

Gregor nodded. "I am finished now, anyway," he offered,

watching her as he slowly waded out of the loch. He reached down to pick up his shirt, and began to dry his naked arms and chest with it, mopping up the water with the fine but worn cloth.

Meg Mackintosh was a puzzle to him. He expected women to behave in a certain way, to be manipulative like his mother and Barbara Campbell, or kind and motherly like Shona. And yet this woman was different. She could be cool and formal, an icicle, and then in the next breath she could be authoritative and tough, very much in charge. And then again, she could be achingly vulnerable, bringing to the fore all his protective instincts.

She unsettled him.

And she was blushing.

Surprised, Gregor watched the color burning in her cheeks, and rising in a tide from her throat, where she was clutching at the shawl with stiff fingers. Why on earth was she blushing? And pretending she wasn't? Was she embarrassed by his presence? She cleared her throat, and stared out across the loch behind him, as if there were something other than empty water on view.

He understood then. It was the sight of him, half naked, that had made her blush. It was Gregor Grant himself who had disturbed Meg Mackintosh's equilibrium.

Did his informality offend her? Because she was not used to men being half naked around her? Or was it because she found herself as drawn to him as he was to her?

The last thought stilled him, opened a door on new and interesting possibilities. He didn't know whether to laugh at her maidenly modesty, or fumble on his wet shirt like a callow youth. Women found him attractive, it was something he knew and accepted. He had never felt self-conscious about his body, although he was not a man who naturally displayed his wares to all and sundry.

Why then, quite suddenly, did Gregor have the urge to walk over to where she stood, so particularly not looking at him. To force her to look up at him, to really *look*. To place her palms upon his skin and make her touch him, press them to him, make her aware of each contour, each muscle. To bend his head and take her pink lips with his cold ones, and see how warm she was inside. To slide his hands down over her body and see if all those warm curves were as soft and inviting as they had felt last night, when she slept in his arms.

As if in a dream, Gregor took a step toward her.

Just then, maybe drawn by his long silence, she turned to face him. Something in his expression must have hinted at his intentions. Her eyes widened, her lips parted. Meg shivered, desperately wrapping the shawl closer about her body. Her voice was a husky whisper.

"What do you think of Shona's tale?"

Gregor was confused. Who was Shona? And then the world righted itself, tipped back onto its proper axis, and he knew he couldn't kiss her, couldn't touch her, couldn't do any of the things that were clamoring in his head. She was no lightskirt, but a born-and-bred lady. She had asked for his help, and that brought with it certain responsibilities. He had no rights to her, whereas she had every right to order him.

Briskly, hands shaking only slightly, Gregor pulled his shirt on over his head, leaving the wet cloth to flap loosely about his damp, cold torso. He smoothed his hair back from his face with both palms, twisting the ends to wring out the water, taking his time. Giving *her* time to regain her natural composure. When at last he shot a sideways glance at her, he noted that she had lost her bright color and was now regarding him with her usual pale, clear gaze.

"You asked me what I thought of Shona's tale?" he repeated. "I think it sounds possible. You say there are other rumors? Stories of Abercauldy's evildoing?"

"Yes, there are stories. Many of them told by good and honest people. Too many, I think, for us to disregard them."

"No, we canna afford to disregard them."

"So the Duke of Abercauldy is a murderer? He did kill his wife?"

Gregor believed just that. He opened his mouth to tell her so, and then hesitated as another thought struck him. His eyes narrowed. She was very tense, watching him anxiously. Did she want him to say aye or nay? Did she—and the idea that had come into his brain made it burn, made his eyes flare—did she *love* the Duke of Abercauldy? Was she hoping to hear that he was innocent, so that she could go ahead and wed him with a clear conscience?

As soon as the thought occurred to him, he knew it was not so. Could not be so. Had the cold seeped into his brain? Of course she did not love Abercauldy! She had told Gregor herself that she had fought against the marriage and only given in for her father's sake, because she was worried about his health. She had loved no man in such a way, nor did she wish to love one—he could see that, he *had* seen that. She was the sort of independent woman who very much preferred to be in charge of her own life. Where had this sudden surge of jealousy come from? Why had he imagined, even for a moment, that it was otherwise? And why had it made him so angry?

Best not to think of that.

"It is a distinct possibility that Abercauldy killed his wife, aye."

She nodded, swallowed, glanced at him uneasily, her shawl still wrapped tightly about her. Did she think that piece of woollen cloth would protect her from whatever threat she believed he posed? And what threat was that? Did he make her nervous? Suddenly Gregor wanted to know exactly what it was about him that made her as restive as a filly in the spring. Was it a woman's natural fear of a man she did not know well? Was it maidenly modesty? Or was it the fact that she was as attracted to him as Gregor was to her?

He wanted to know, he *needed* to know, and he didn't stop to ask himself why.

Gregor took a lithe step toward her. Her body stiffened, her mouth tightened, her eyes widened. And yet even as he saw the signs of her tension, she tried to disguise them, easing her stance, tossing back her long hair, playing a game he knew only too well. *I'm not really interested in you*, she was saying, when everything about her told him otherwise.

He hid a smile. Och no, she was not as unmoved by him as she would like him to believe. What would she do if he reached for her now? Kissed her now? Would she jump like a scalded cat? Would she run screaming into the cottage, calling for dour Duncan Forbes? Or would she capitulate, melt into his arms and beg him for more?

And what would that accomplish, he asked himself wryly, other than to prove his point? What would he do with a screaming woman, or for that matter, a compliant one? Better to keep the status quo; after all, there was no room in his life for these sorts of complications. And had he not sworn, after Barbara, that he had had enough of women and the troubles they always seemed to bring to him?

She needed his help, and she was willing to pay him for it. He was performing a job for her. And that was all.

Why then did the way in which the cool morning breeze played with her hair fascinate him to the point where his fingers actually twitched with the need to touch those long, silky strands?

"I will keep you safe, Lady Meg," he told her reassuringly, knowing that the heat in his eyes was anything but reassuring.

Meg's eyes slid to his and just as quickly away again. "I–I can keep myself safe, thank you, Captain."

Her color was back, and brighter than ever. His smile broadened—he couldn't help it. He took the few remaining steps and came to a stop immediately before her. Very close—too close—until he could feel the warmth from her body. Her pale eyes were lifted to his, fixed there unblinkingly. He saw the pupils dilate, while the pulse in her throat fluttered like butterfly wings, begging for him to touch his lips just there. Aye, there was some great emotion inside her, something tumultuous. If things were different, he would have liked to discover what it was.

But things weren't different, so Gregor pulled back from the brink, and instead of kissing her, made his voice playful and teasing, made himself into something she could dismiss and despise.

"Och, but you are paying me to do the looking after, Meg. I wouldna want you not to get your money's worth, now, would I?"

Meg could have said she had had her money's worth from him last night, when she had lain comfortably, asleep, in his arms. She could not have said what it was she dreamed, but it had been a sweet dream. Gregor Grant was not a man to give any woman nightmares. When she had awoken this morning, refreshed, her first thought had been: *Where is he?* He already seemed so much a part of her life. . . .

So she had come looking for him, and seen far more than was good for her peace of mind.

He was still smiling at her—that crooked, rueful smile that twisted something in her chest, until she wanted to reach out with her fingers and trace his mouth, very slowly. The full lower lip, the arch of the upper lip, and on from there.

As if he had read her mind, he moved, and believing he meant to touch her, Meg jumped back. But he only chuckled and walked on past her, lengthening his stride until he had vanished around the corner of the building.

Meg closed her eyes. Her heart was pounding furiously and she felt breathless and lightheaded. Utterly ridiculous! she told herself. How could she be so affected by seeing a man bathing? Was she such a child? She had seen men bathe before, she had seen men *naked* before and taken such things in her stride. If one lived beyond the civilized boundaries, then one learned to accept such awkward moments.

And yet, when she had seen Gregor, the water running in rivulets over the firm, golden skin of his back, spearing through the crisp hair that grew on his chest and down his belly, vanishing into the waist of his kilt . . . Oh yes, she had been dizzy! Dizzy with desire! Lightheaded with lust!

Meg laughed at her own flowery prose, but her humor had a bitter edge to it. She chewed her lip to regain control. Was she going mad? She was a woman grown, a sensible spinster who had never yet had the urge to wed. Why did this tough man affect her so? Did she still believe that somewhere, beneath his hardened exterior, dwelt her artistic hero?

Whatever the truth of that, she had learned something new today. She had learned that the longing to find love, and the feeling of desire, were two separate entities. She may not love Gregor Grant, but she certainly desired him. It did not matter that such feelings were completely inappropriate; they could no more be denied than the sun rising up now, shining over the glen before her.

"You are paying him," she murmured crossly to herself. "He may be the former Laird of Glen Dhui, but he is your employee. You must not compromise him, or yourself."

Meg nodded to herself. She would have to keep a tight rein on her feelings. Not just for the sake of propriety, but because she would simply die of embarrassment if Gregor Grant ever discovered that Lady Meg Mackintosh was mad with lust for him.

If he didn't know it already . . .

Of course he did! Why else had he smiled at her just now? And looked at her just so? Because her feelings amused him. A man like that, he must have known countless women, fought duels over hundreds of them! What was Meg Mackintosh to him but an amusing moment? Best, for her own dignity, that it go no further.

With a sigh that was half regret and half wistful thinking, Meg turned back toward the cottage.

Chapter 9

B y afternoon they had reached the pass through the mountains.

Once this narrow and treacherous road had been open to everyone, but since the 1715 Rebellion, military roads had begun to be built throughout the Highlands under the supervision of General Wade. This was to enable government troops access to the seething, rebellious clansmen in their isolated glens, and to keep order where it was considered trouble was most likely to occur. A small garrison of soldiers now manned the way through the pass, and anyone travelling through was sure to be questioned closely before being allowed to move on.

Meg and her band of men were no different.

"Madam!" The private on guard, well turned out in his red jacket and breeches and white, spotless stockings, straightened himself as Meg rode forward. That was one thing Meg always noticed about Major Litchfield's men, they looked like proper soldiers, not the ragtag bands that sometimes terrorized the Highlands for no better reason than that they could.

"I am returning home, Private," she said now. "May we pass through?"

The soldier opened his mouth to answer, but before he could do so, a second voice interrupted them.

"Lady Margaret!"

An older man, wiry, with a thin, intelligent face strode from the direction of the soldiers' quarters. He wore his red coat and waistcoat embellished with gold trimmings, but it was quite plain in comparison to some of the officers Meg had encountered. He had doffed his hat, and was beaming at her from beneath his plain, brown wig.

"Back so soon, Lady Meg? Did your journey go well?"

Meg returned his smile. She genuinely liked Major Litchfield. He was not the sort of biased, narrow-minded Englishman she had met before and abhorred—the type of Englishman who believed civilized life began and ended at the Thames. Glen Dhui was only a half day's ride from here, and if the soldiers had been inclined to, they could have made life very difficult for the people. Meg felt they were fortunate indeed with Major Litchfield in charge of his men.

"I am very well, thank you, Major," she said now. "I did not expect to see you here."

"I am on my weekly inspection. Have to keep the men on their toes. You are on your way home?"

"Yes, and looking forward to getting there and seeing my father."

"The General." The Major shook his head sadly. "'Tis a rum thing to see such a great man brought so low. Tell him

I will call on him soon, before I leave the Highlands." He glanced up at her as he spoke the last words, something speculative in his gaze.

Meg's smile faded. "Before you leave? Are you leaving, Major Litchfield?"

"Sadly, yes," he said, and there was real regret in his voice, and something more, that suddenly Meg preferred not to delve into too deeply. As with the Duke of Aber-cauldy, she had always considered Major Litchfield to be her father's friend. She enjoyed his company and was ap-preciative of his attitude toward the Highland people, but she had no romantic inclinations toward him.

"I am being ordered to join a regiment in Ireland. As you know, Lady Margaret, I have been kicking my heels here for over two years. That's not to say I haven't enjoyed my stay in Scotland, for I have found it most interesting, but it is time to move on. As soon as my replacement arrives I will go. If I may, I will call at Glen Dhui beforehand. Tell your father I look forward to a last game of chess with him, if he is well enough."

Meg smiled. "Of course you may! And I'm sure he will be well enough for that, Major." She held out her hand to him. "I will be sorry to see you go, sir. Take care in Ireland, and we hope to see you back here again, one day."

His eyes lit up and as if it were made of glass, he took the hand she stretched down to him. "I pray that will be so," he said, and raised it to his lips.

His fervency was a little too much for her. Meg felt her face color as she turned hastily away. She caught Gregor Grant's eye without meaning to, not realizing he was so close behind her. And found she could not look away.

There was something in his very stillness, the rigid set of

his shoulders, the glint of his eyes through his dark lashes, that spoke of danger. He simmered with it. Startled, Meg searched her mind as to why that should be so. Major Litchfield had been perfectly friendly to them, and yet Gregor was acting as if they were under threat.

Now the Major was greeting the other men by name. He knew them all, because upon his arrival here he had made a point of meeting and learning about the people who lived on the estates nearby. It was one of the reasons Meg liked him. When he came to Gregor's large figure upon his horse, the Major paused and arched a graying eyebrow.

"Why, it's Captain Grant, isn't it? I am not mistaken, am I, Captain?"

Gregor nodded once, not returning the smile. "Major Litchfield."

"What do you in Lady Meg's train, Captain?" he asked politely, but curiosity was alive in his eyes and a glint of something more.

Gregor smiled without humor, as if he accepted the other man's right to ask the question, but he didn't have to like it. "I know General Mackintosh. He and I are old friends."

"I see." There was doubt in his face now, and a trace of suspicion. "I heard you had left Glen Dhui after the 1715, Captain." Major Litchfield spoke politely, and yet it was clear he wanted answers, and as the superior officer he expected to get them. "Why have you returned now? You are stationed to the north, are you not? Have you leave?"

Gregor shifted slightly on his horse, but not enough to give away emotion. Meg searched his face, but whatever he had been feeling before was gone. Wiped clean, as if it had never existed. "Northwest, at Clashennic. I was there with the Duke of Argyll's dragoons."

Major Litchfield's face cleared. "Of course, I remember now. I have heard good things about you, Captain, from His Grace, the Duke of Argyll, and the people of Glen Dhui. But that still does not explain what you are doing here, now, with Lady Margaret. I really do need an answer."

He glanced at Meg as he said it, and suddenly she had the inkling that perhaps the Major was being so insistent because of her. He was being protective of *her*.

"We have traveled a long way, and Captain Grant is weary. Is this really necessary . . . ?" Meg began, in turn finding herself protective of Gregor. There was surely no need to interrogate him for her sake.

Gregor turned his head and looked at her in surprise. His amber eyes searched hers thoroughly in less time than it took for her to draw a sharp breath, and they seemed to like whatever it was they found. Meg felt the color in her cheeks again; she couldn't help it. Clearly her urge to protect him was misplaced; he could well look after himself.

"I have resigned my commission," Gregor was speaking to the major, and suddenly he sounded almost cheerful. "I am visiting the general while I decide upon my future. We met after the 1715," he added, with a rueful grin. "But I was a Jacobite in those days, Major."

Gregor was baiting him. Meg bit her lip, and waited.

But the corners of Major Litchfield's mouth lifted. "I remember. You are not a Jacobite now, I comprehend?"

Gregor laughed. "Och, no! I do not think it worth my life to set a man upon Scotland's throne who will care no more for its people than the English king in London. They are much of a muchness, these great men. I prefer to leave them to their work, and for them to leave me to mine."

The major must have agreed with those sentiments, for

he nodded. Satisfied his questions had been answered, he turned again to Meg. "I will call, my lady."

Meg nodded and smiled, and urged her horse onward, down the steep road that led into the glens, her men behind her. An osprey flew high overhead, drifting on the air currents. Meg tilted her head back to gaze up at it, and at the same time breathed a sigh of relief. For a reason she didn't properly understand, there had been tension between Gregor Grant and Major Litchfield. She told herself it was to do with their pasts and their politics, but that wasn't entirely true.

She had the oddest feeling that it was to do with her.

•

As the road wound lower they found themselves in a land of more hills, covered with a forest of great pines and firs, and the finer, silvery birches. Above them, to the northeast, Liath Mhor lifted its somber head, while Cragan Dhui peeped around its shoulder. A bitter little wind reminded them that summer would soon be done, and in a few months all this would be under snow. Despite the long shadows of evening, the landmarks of home were visible all around them, and one by one the men fell silent. They were all weary, longing for their loved ones and other familiar faces.

Just as was she.

The general would be pleased. She had done exactly as he had asked. She had sought out Gregor Grant and brought him home with her. She still did not understand just how he could help them, apart from the more obvious ways of training and leading the men of Glen Dhui. But it was what her father had wanted.

The general wasn't well enough to travel, so it had been left to Meg to make the journey. Now it was nearly over, and they were nearly home.

Duncan Forbes galloped forward and drew rein beside her.

"I'll go on ahead, if ye'll allow me, Lady Meg. Let them know yer coming, so things can be readied."

"Of course, Duncan."

He nodded without smiling and rode off into the deep shadows of the trees. The sun was a mere blur of gold above the horizon, streaking the sky with crimson. The long gloaming was about to begin.

Meg felt someone move up close beside her and turned her head, thinking it must be one of the other men, homesick, and wanting to ask permission to accompany Duncan. But it was Gregor. He was staring after Duncan, his face paler than it had been all day. In fact he had seemed remarkably well for a man whom she had feared at one point would not survive the journey. His arm had regained some of its movement, and when they stopped at midday, he had eaten quite heartily. If he had been quiet, keeping his thoughts to himself, then Meg did not mind that. In fact, she admitted, she preferred it. After this morning, when she had seen him bathing half naked in the loch, it had been a relief not to speak to him at all.

It was safer so.

Safer for her own peace of mind.

Meg knew that there was some feeling inside herself for him, some need for him that she had not experienced for any other man. But there was also a sense of danger, a need for self-preservation. Meg had decided, after the incident with Major Litchfield, that she must take a big step back. If she stayed away from him, then whatever this emotion was inside her might melt away, might vanish like ice in the sun.

But now, as she looked upon his profile, her gaze drawn to the straight slash of his brows, the steep line of his nose, the strong set of his jaw, and the sensuous curve of his bottom lip . . . Meg realized in dismay that her feelings might not be so easily dismissed. It rose up, a great rushing tide, filling her head and body, making her want to gasp for breath. It was only through a sheer effort of will that she prevented herself from actually reaching out and touching him. . . .

"Duncan has gone ahead," she said abruptly into the silence. Her voice was strange and stilted, held in check, because she feared herself too much to allow the slightest warmth to creep in.

He nodded brusquely, and they rode on together. Cragan Dhui was closer now, peering down at them, but Glen Dhui was still out of sight due to the rise in the road. As they came out of the forest and reached the final crest, they stopped as one. And there it was below them, the narrow head of Glen Dhui.

The rest of the glen followed the silver line of the burn to the southeast, widening out as it went, the rich green haughland lying flat either side of the broadening stream. In the gloaming, it looked secretive and shadowy, the mauve of the heather turning to brown, the slatey rock reflecting the sky, and the surrounding hills gathering their forested slopes about them. Down in the glen, heather-thatched crofters' cottages were gray smudges, the brown shapes of cattle dotted about them. At the place where the gray stone bridge crossed the burn, an avenue of yew trees marched down a long driveway to Glen Dhui Castle. From this distance it was no more than a solid gray rectangle, decorated with four pointed towers, one at each corner.

The home of the Grants.

As always, the view took Meg's breath away, but at this

moment there was even more emotion than usual charging
through her. And if she felt like this, then how must the man
beside her feel? His stillness was so intense, it was painful.
His hand was clenching and unclenching on his reins, and
his face was set. Meg had already sensed his mixed feelings
when it came to his return to Glen Dhui, and now she realized just how hard he was working to keep them contained.
Suddenly her own need to put distance between them took
second place.

"All is well," she said gently.

He turned sharply at the sound of her voice, as if he had
forgotten she was there. He was frowning, those dark brows
lowered over his brilliant eyes.

Meg smiled. "Whenever I've been away, and I come
home to see Glen Dhui like this, laid out before me like a
tapestry, it's as if I'm seeing all the peaceful lives being
lived out within it, all the familiar faces, everything in its
place and as it should be. I know then that all is well with
my world."

The frown had gone, though his face was still drawn tight
by emotion, his slashing brows and the stubble on his jaw
dark against his pale skin. He could easily be an outlaw,
thought Meg, and a desperate one at that!

"Has it changed in twelve years?" something prompted
her to ask.

He shook his head, not taking his eyes from hers.

"I pray . . . I trust this homecoming will not be too
painful for you, Captain."

He hesitated briefly, and then turned back to the glen. In
that moment all his protective barricades were down. He
gazed at it with the savage hunger of a man who has not had
a proper meal in a very long time; he looked at his former

home with a deep and agonizing longing that Meg could
barely imagine.

"Och, no," he said, his voice gruff and raw, " 'tis not too
painful for me, my lady. I can bear it. Shall we go, before
Duncan comes to fetch us?"

Meg hesitated. The former Laird of Glen Dhui was sick
with longing for his home, but he did not want her to feel
sorry for him. Instead he meant to ride sedately beside her,
all the way down the glen to his former home, every step
full of heart-wrenching, squirming agony for them both.

Meg knew she couldn't do it. Not like that. His homecoming should be a joyous thing, or at least it should be
gotten over with quickly.

Her mind made up, Meg gave a sudden whoop, and dug
her heels into her mare's sides. The tired animal reared, and
then put her head down and flew. Down the turning road,
down the steep hill, down into the glen.

She heard his shout behind her—anger, surprise or sheer
wild excitement? She wasn't certain which, only that the
thud of his horse's hooves was quickly following. When
she glanced back, she saw the shape of him against the fading sky. Pursuing her.

Her blood drummed in her veins, her body tightened, and
Meg found herself laughing aloud.

Home.

The sense of it filled him, completed him, and overflowed. His head was spinning, and not just because of his
wound. He felt so alive, so much a part of this place, that he
tingled. He was Grant of Glen Dhui, and to have denied it
all these years seemed like the worst sort of foolishness.

But what had coming back here done to him? He had opened himself to pain, to the longing for something that was his home no longer. It belonged to *her*, to the woman riding in front of him. Just as *he* now belonged to her.

Pride and anger rose up in him, threatening to make him do something foolish—like turn around and ride all the way back to Clashennic. He stifled the impulse, just as he had learned long ago to stifle any impetuous impulses. He could not afford them, not anymore.

She rode low on her mare, her plaited hair spearing out behind her, her slim body at one with the animal. The two of them sped through the night like a shot from his gun. And suddenly he had the feeling that she, too, belonged to this place, that she had the same sense of belonging as he did.

His horse stumbled. He held it up, despite the wrenching pain in his arm, and they were in pursuit again. But it was enough to bring him to his senses. He was behaving wildly, foolishly, more like the lad he had been than the man he had become. Captain Gregor Grant was not likely to race a lady down a dangerously narrow road in the near dark. It was the sort of impetuous behaviour he had just been telling himself he no longer indulged in.

He came abreast of her.

Her face, what he could see of it, was ablaze with excitement. She meant to best him. She was that sort of woman. Best him, or die in the attempt.

He was tempted—the subtle lure was thrown to him again—but he ignored it. He was a responsible man, a tough and practical man. *This* was madness. If one of them should fall and be hurt—if *she* should be hurt . . . In that instant, he snatched her reins from her and dragged at her mare. Both horses began to slow, not putting up much of a fight. They were weary, they had had enough.

They came to a halt. The silence was broken only by the blowing of the horses and the thud of Gregor's heart. Startled, still in the grip of the race, Meg spun around to face him, her breasts heaving under her jacket, her eyes wild. She pushed back a curl of red hair, tucking it behind her ear, and he could see the flush on her skin in the pearly light. She looked hot and mad with excitement, and he wanted her.

It wasn't the same sort of want as he had felt at the pass, when Major Litchfield had kissed her hand. That had been the kind of jealous feeling that any man might have, when another threatens the thing he has been secretly coveting. He had seen the way the major looked at her, and he knew he had a rival.

This was different. This was a simple, basic, earthy need. Gregor saw her, and he wanted her in his arms. He wanted to taste her skin, to thrust his tongue deep into her mouth. He wanted her under him, her naked skin against his, and he wanted to hear the sound she would make when he pushed himself inside her.

"I would have won."

He blinked, thrust away his own madness, and leaned closer. She didn't pull back, but he saw the question in her eyes.

"Do you think it quite proper for the Lady of Glen Dhui to arrive at her doorstep looking like she has been rolling in the heather?"

Anger flared in her pale eyes. "You only say that because I would have beaten you."

He stiffened. "No."

Her mouth tightened, but she made it smile. "We shall see, Captain. There is always another day."

So saying, she straightened her back proudly, tugged the reins from his fingers, and put some space between them.

"Are you ready, then?" she asked him. There was a flicker in her eyes, an uncertainty, that had not been there before.

It made him wonder, briefly, if the whole thing had been a ruse, a distraction, to take away his pain at returning home. He dismissed it. Why should she care? Besides, she had been as caught up in the race as he.

"Of course," he said coldly, and she rode off at a more sedate pace, with him following. He did not watch the way her hips swayed in the saddle, or the long line of her legs in their tight trews. He stared ahead, to the gray bridge and the avenue of yews, to the place he had loved and lost.

Glen Dhui belonged to her now. Once more he gave himself the grim reminder.

And so did he.

Chapter 10

Glen Dhui Castle sat solid against the last faint glow of the sky. With its rectangular base and stiff turrets and gables, it was more like a fortified home than a castle, but what it lacked in fairytale prettiness, it more than made up for in solidity and security. There were many stories of raids by other clans upon Grant territory, of battles fought and enemies slain, and of womenfolk safe within these walls, while a ferocious foe waited outside.

Gregor had been brought up on these tales.

His throat felt dry. *This is no longer my home*, he reminded himself yet again. *No longer mine*. Then why did it *feel* like home? His heart, which he had fortified as strongly as this house, was swelling with regret, with longing, but he would not let the emotion spill free.

He dared not.

The main door was open. A plump, dark-haired woman stood hesitantly in the light from the lantern she held. Beside her hovered a lad who was nearly as tall as she, his fair hair like a halo. Gregor recognized the woman—it was Duncan Forbes's sister, Alison. The woman Malcolm Bain had planned to marry, until the 1715 Rebellion interrupted their dreams of bliss. It would be their first meeting since then, and as Gregor recalled, Alison had always had a fiery temper.

"Lady Meg!" Alison came down the steps, her voice trembling with concern and relief. Behind her, the lad remained on the step and peered suspiciously at the new arrivals. "Thank the Lord ye are all right. I expected to see ye back yesterday."

"We were delayed." Meg dismounted and reached out to give Alison a hug, adding a smile for the fair-haired lad Angus.

Alison might be her maid, but she was also her friend, and had been since Meg first arrived in Glen Dhui. And Meg was concerned for her. She had not known about Malcolm Bain, although of course she knew there had been a man. But she didn't know the details, and she had never pried into Alison's personal life, unless Alison broached the subject first.

This situation would be difficult.

"Ye must be famished," Alison was saying. There was strain in her eyes, so dark, like her brother's. Her gaze strayed beyond Meg, toward the troop of horsemen waiting a little behind her, and quickly slipped past the familiar faces she knew from the glen. She found Gregor's tall shape, hesitated, then seemed to set him aside for later consideration. Finally, she found and settled on the stranger with the broad shoulders, whose face was in deep shadow.

Meg felt Alison's sudden rigidity; it was as if the other woman had simply turned to stone.

"Alison?" Meg said gently, giving her a little shake.

"Malcolm Bain . . . Duncan spoke true. It *is* ye. . . ." Alison's whisper was no more than a sigh.

Malcolm Bain could not have heard her, but it was as if he had, because he was looking directly at her. A torch held by one of the grooms sputtered and flared brightly, briefly illuminating his face. He was pale, and the lines about his mouth were carved deep. Meg thought he looked like a man who had been visited by a spirit.

Abruptly, Alison turned away, staring at Meg, waiting for her instructions. Her usually full lips had gone straight and hard.

"Please make up a room for Captain Grant, Alison," Meg said gently. "We will sup together, in the little parlor, I think. Is the general awake?"

"He's in his room, Lady Meg. I will let him know ye are here. He will want to see you."

"Tell him I will be up directly, Alison. And thank you."

Alison whirled about and vanished inside, shooing the fair-headed Angus before her. The men were dismounting—Meg heard the clank and creak of harness and saddle, and glanced around for Gregor. He was gingerly extracting himself from his horse, holding his hurt arm and shoulder unnaturally still. For a long moment he stood, head bowed, while the other men, riders and grooms, went about their tasks. Meg waited for him to gather himself, to lift his head and find her. His eyes gleamed yellow in the flickering light, like a wounded animal. Out in the darkness, above the rush of the burn, a curlew called him a mournful welcome home.

"My father may want to see us straight away," Meg said.

"Of course."

Whatever feelings had gripped him on the road above the glen were gone, wiped clean. *Very well, if that is how he wants it . . .* Meg turned briskly toward the door and stepped into the Great Hall of Glen Dhui Castle with the former laird close behind her.

Gregor felt distinctly odd as he strode into Glen Dhui Castle and back in time. As if the past had shifted into the present.

The Great Hall reared up about him, chilly and shadowy despite the tall candles and the fire in the big granite hearth. The arched ceiling was in darkness above his head, but the stone walls gleamed with weapons and the heads of stags and other beasties captured in various hunts. The wavering light caught a glassy eye here and a claymore there. In the place of honor, in a walled case directly before him, was a hunting horn carved in ivory—a gift from Queen Mary herself.

Gregor felt his heart stop beating, and then restart like a drum. Nothing had changed. It was as if he had stepped out for a breath of air, rather than been gone for twelve long years.

"Captain Grant?"

Her voice steadied him. Held him safe from the maelstrom that he felt he was very close to tumbling down into. Gregor turned his head, blindly, and found her. She was standing in the door of the room his mother had always called the Blue Saloon. The candles on the table beside her bathed her in their warm light, shining on the buttons of her jacket and the glory of her hair. There was compassion in her gaze, a watchful sympathy. It turned him cold. He did not want her pity, he didn't want anybody's pity.

"When my father came he bought everything just as it stood," she explained quietly. "It seemed wrong to replace what was already here—the past, the memories, the history . . ."

She waved her hand awkwardly, indicating the Great Hall with its stone and dark-paneled walls and gleaming weapons. "So he kept what was yours, Captain. He paid your mother, all was settled between them. It gave my father pleasure and it did no harm. I am sorry if it distresses you."

He shrugged as if it didn't matter. And it shouldn't. She was right, better her father make use of the history of the Grants than it be lost, forgotten. And yet it hurt, it felt as if something had been stolen from him. "You and the general are more than welcome to my disreputable ancestors and their spurious histories," he said coldly.

Her eyes flashed but she didn't respond as he expected. "We can talk in here," she said with a polite smile, and gestured for him to follow her into the Blue Saloon.

It was no longer blue.

With a huge sense of relief, Gregor strode farther into the room. His emotions had taken enough of a battering for one evening, and the changes were very welcome. There were still a number of objects he recognized, but others were foreign, and the softly ticking clock that sat upon the mantel was not something he remembered. With a sigh he turned and found Meg behind him, standing perfectly still, watching him.

He wondered what she saw in his face. He was not foolish enough to think she did not see something in him to concern her. He was not made of stone, although there had been times when he wished it were so. But whatever she saw and felt, she was not going to let him read it in her slightly wary blue eyes again.

"Meg," he began quietly, meaning to try and explain—a little—but before he could go on, a third voice interrupted them.

"Lady Meg?"

Alison hovered in the doorway, her dark eyes anxious. "The general says he will see ye now. He will see Captain Grant after ye have both had supper."

"Thank you, Alison." Meg glanced over at Gregor with a faint smile. "I won't be long. Please, warm yourself by the fire and remove your . . . ah, your knives and pistols."

He felt himself smile in response. His knives, huh? Well, he wouldn't remove all his weapons, but he would warm himself by the fire. A moment alone would be welcome, and he could gather his wits for his meeting with the general. And more important, for supper with Lady Meg.

The door closed behind her. Beyond the window, he could hear voices. The men he had ridden with from Clashennic, he thought. Where was Malcolm Bain? Well, no doubt he would find himself a bed—he was no stranger to Glen Dhui either. With a smothered groan, Gregor sank down in the chair by the fire, absently rubbing his arm and letting the comfort of Glen Dhui seep into him at last.

Meg hurried up the staircase with light running steps toward her father's room. She tapped briefly on the door panel, and opened it.

The general was seated by the window, his back to her,

staring out as if he could see the dark sweep of the glen beyond. He must have heard her, for when he turned his head, an expectant look in his cloudy blue eyes, he was smiling.

"Meg?"

"Father."

She came to him, quickly kneeling by his chair and taking his hands in hers. His smile showed a mixture of relief and anticipation. "Is he here?" he demanded. "Did you bring him?"

"Yes, he is here."

The general took a deep breath and his eyelids dropped down over his sightless eyes. "You have done well, Meg. Thank you."

" 'Twas not such a chore, father. He came like a . . . a lamb."

He smiled again, but wryly now, for by her tone he had guessed otherwise. "I will speak with him when he has eaten," he said, with a quiet and grim determination.

Meg looked into his face, seeing the deep lines and folds of age and illness. Her father seemed to have grown more feeble even in the short time she had been away. "Are you sure the morning wouldn't do as well?"

"No, Meg, we have no time to lose. There was a message from Abercauldy yesterday, asking after you. He says he wants a firm date for the wedding, so arrangements can be made. He wants to bring his servants here to Glen Dhui, to oversee it, to be sure that 'all is in order,' as he puts it! The man is intolerable, Meg. Read it yourself. Now, where did Alison put the letter after she'd read it to me . . . ?"

Meg felt herself pale. Dear God, after she had tried her best to explain to the duke that she had no intention of marrying him, he was carrying on as if everything were to go

ahead as normal! Meg fumbled for the letter in the pile on
the table beside her father. She remembered when she had
spoken to the duke upon their last meeting, when she had
told him she did not want to marry him. He had cocked his
head to one side, as though listening to a voice she could
not hear. And then he had smiled at her. A humoring smile.
At the time Meg had feared he didn't believe her, or simply
chose not to. Now here was the proof!

The letter was just as her father had said, a request for a
firm date, the tone gently scolding rather than demanding.
Why, Meg thought, *is that velvet glove so much more frightening than a bare fist?* Why was the duke's studied, blind
patience with his bride-to-be so much more terrifying than
a show of rage? And why did the look in his eyes frighten
her so—as if she were already his?

"Gregor Grant," her father's murmur drew her back to
the shadowy room.

Carefully she laid the letter, with its emblazoned crest,
aside. "I will send him up after supper, father, but I do not
understand what—"

"Leave it to me, Meg. I created this mess, I will clean it
up. With Gregor's help."

His tone reminded her of the old days, when he gave orders to his men. Meg was sorely tempted to remind him that
the mess had been created because he had gone against her
wishes in the first place, made a decision without consult-
ing her—and now he seemed to be about to repeat the same
mistake. But he was old and sick. Besides, she had already
made up her mind that she would be present at this meeting
with Gregor, so she held her tongue.

"Very well, father," she said with uncharacteristic
meekness.

She had reached the door again before the sound of his voice made her turn.

"I am so glad you are back safe, Meg. You mean more to me than I can say. I . . ." But the words failed him, or the tremble in his voice threatened to stifle it, and he shook his head and fell silent.

"Things will come around, father," Meg said gently. "I *know* they will."

Gregor was still by the fire, but now he stood leaning against the mantel, his arm resting along its edge, while he gazed into the flames. The General Mackintosh he had known had never been one to do anything without a purpose. Why had he wanted Gregor back? What did he have planned for him? Why was his presence so crucial?

Gregor found himself watching Meg's face, trying to guess from her expression what might have been said between father and daughter. He thought she looked as if she had something on her mind, but whatever it was, she was not sharing it with him. She had changed from her riding attire into a green silk gown with lace falling from the tight, elbow-length sleeves. The low, square neckline was made more modest by a fine gauze scarf. It suited her vivid coloring and creamy skin, making him think of mermaids on sunlit shores. *Morvoren.*

If he had any doubts about his need for her, after their encounter by the loch, he was certain now. He felt every muscle in his body tighten, instantly, every sinew harden.

She came to stand beside him, her skirts rustling, and held out her hands to the heat. Maybe he looked as stunned as he felt, for she cast him a quick, searching glance before she turned away again, and concentrated on the fire. But

Gregor didn't turn away, couldn't turn away. Instead, he noted how the light sparkled and shone in the glory of her hair, the tilt of her nose, and the pensive set of her mouth.

"Your father is well?" He broke the silence.

"Thank you, yes. He says he will see you once you have eaten and rested. He does not sleep much these days, so it will not matter to him if the hour is late."

He nodded, and his eye caught a small box beside the mantel clock. Frowning, he stretched out one long finger to touch it. The lid was inlaid with an oval-shaped painting, the delicate likeness of a beautiful, smiling woman with a cloud of fair hair.

Meg had seen the direction of his gaze. "'Tis an exquisite thing," she ventured. "*She* is exquisite."

"My mother," he replied without inflection.

Meg bit her lip, dismayed. "This is very awkward," she went on after a moment, her voice low. "I feel I should apologize, Captain Grant, but my father did write to your mother. He thought the box valuable, and that perhaps she may wish it to be sent on to her in Edinburgh. She did not, but she informed him of the price she wanted for it. He paid it."

"You have no need to apologize," he said abruptly. "What happened isna your fault. My mother is an unsentimental woman. She has a small income and probably lives beyond her means. She clearly needed the money more than the box."

"You speak as if you do not see her."

"Not in years."

Meg worried her lip again. "This is still . . . awkward. Us being here, in your family home."

He looked at her bent head, the delicate pallor of her

nape uncovered where her hair was pinned up. "I do not feel awkward," he replied quietly. "I do not covet these things, Meg. When I left Glen Dhui I had nowhere to live, certainly nowhere to keep such possessions as this. I was adrift. I am glad that someone had the use of them."

Meg tilted her head to look up at him. Her eyes were pale and clear, and he felt their touch like a warm breeze.

"You are a strange man," she said at last.

He laughed despite himself. Whatever he had expected her to say, it was not this.

"I am . . . resigned to my life as it is, Meg."

Was he? Meg asked herself. Or was he simply trying to put her at ease in the home that had once been his, to deflect her attention? He was still watching her, his amber eyes intent.

"Will we be dining here alone?" he asked her abruptly.

"Yes."

He smiled, a secret amusement tugging at his lips. "And is that proper?"

Meg frowned and said sharply, "Why would it not be? I am no sheltered miss. I am my own woman, Captain, and I do not dance to anyone's tune but my own."

Now his smile grew broader. Her sharp answer had evidently amused him. He leaned down to her, as if to share a secret, and suddenly they were very close. She felt his soft breath against her face, and she could see the texture of his skin, the dark stubble on his jaw, the mauve shadows under his eyes that spoke of weariness and recent illness. The moment was intimate; took her by surprise. Her heartbeat seemed to quicken, and her breath.

"Does Abercauldy know that?" he asked her in a quiet, deep voice.

Meg raised her eyebrows, refusing to step away, refusing to let him see how uncomfortable his closeness was making her.

"I informed him of it in no uncertain terms, Captain! But he cannot know me well, because I do not think he believed me. He accused me of being over-modest in believing I did not deserve him!" She spoke acerbically, leaving him in no doubt of her true character and opinions.

He laughed.

Meg was stunned. Was there a gleam in his eyes? Did she really delight him? What could it be about her tart tongue that pleased him, when so many other men preferred sweeter fruit?

Meg was not naturally bitter. Her sharp manner was a defense, a way of keeping others at bay, or keeping herself inviolate. She had never been beautiful, though any disappointment she had felt in her looks as a young girl was long past. She was different, unusual, a strong-willed woman who knew her own mind. Did he see something in that that pleased him? His evident enjoyment of Meg made her uneasy, suspicious, and yet . . . and yet it gave her a sense of wonder.

Captain Gregor Grant delighted in her—he enjoyed her. *What does it mean?*

Gregor, too, was busy considering his feelings.

At Clashennic he had had the inkling that if he did not climb out of his sickbed, mount his horse, and ride for Glen Dhui, then Meg Mackintosh would have carried him home upon her own slim back. She would nag at him to turn back from death itself, if she wanted to accomplish her task strongly enough. His mouth twitched at the thought of Meg telling the grim reaper off. What was it about her that piqued his interest? She was certainly no great beauty, like Barbara Campbell, and she had nothing of the languid looks of his mother, who in her day had set the standard. Meg was no beauty, although with her red hair and blue eyes she certainly attracted glances. Apart from that, her manner was abrupt, her speech sharp, and her tongue bitter. She said what she thought, and smiled when she meant it— both refreshing traits. She did not seem to care if anyone should notice that her two front teeth were separated by a small gap.

A small, enchanting gap.

And the way in which she looked him in the eye . . . not coyly, not with a coquette's vapid stare, but honestly, openly, without guile. He found that he liked that about her, liked it very much. And he liked her hair. That flame-red, curling glory forever falling into her eyes. He wondered what it would be like to loose it about her shoulders with his hands, send it tumbling down. To have her enchanting smile beaming up at him as she watched him with her pale blue eyes. And if he bent to kiss her, opened her lips, would her tart tongue mate sweetly with his?

Gregor all but groaned aloud.

In an instant, a mere moment, he was out of control— teetering on the verge of pulling her hard against him and devouring her mouth with his, of running his hands down her body and making her aware, all too clearly aware, of what she did to him.

How had this happened so quickly? So completely? It was not like him to allow a situation to slip beyond the tight grasp he kept upon his emotions, especially when that situation involved a woman like Meg.

It was almost a relief when Alison, accompanied by a couple of serving maids, chose that moment to enter the room with their supper.

Meg seemed relieved, too, eagerly turning to the women to exchange some chatter. They spoke easily of household matters, friendly with each other.

Gregor half listened, still reeling from his need to hold her, to kiss her, to make her his. It must not be. It could not be. He must abide by these strictures. He knew this! Why then did he ache to be a rebel again?

Chapter 11

∽◦◯◦∽

Meg's mouth was watering. She had always been blessed with a good appetite, and now as she moved toward the table where Alison had set out the dishes, she was very glad of the distraction of her stomach. She sat down quickly, saying, "Please, help yourself, Captain. We can be informal tonight, and I am sure you must be as hungry as I."

After a moment, almost reluctantly, he came and sat down opposite her. Meg was already helping herself to cold game pie and stewed kale and seethed fish, ignoring him as much as possible. She swallowed a sip of claret, and closed her eyes with a sigh. When she opened them again, he was watching her with a wry smile.

"You really are hungry."

"I cannot think straight until I eat," Meg admitted, returning the smile.

He held her gaze across the steaming dishes, and his amber eyes were straight and frank. "I prefer a lass with an appetite."

"*Do* you?"

He nodded, and suddenly he was so handsome he took her breath away. "I do."

And then he smiled, a broad curl of his mouth that she experienced down to her very toes. If, Meg thought, she did not know better, if she did not know herself very well, and the complete lack of attraction she held for handsome men like this, then she would almost think he was trying to . . . that he was . . . Meg felt the blush rise slowly up from her neck, turning her face hot and uncomfortable. Anger followed, anger with herself for allowing her feelings to control her, and with him for whatever game he was playing.

They may be man and woman, but that did not mean they must necessarily flirt! Was that how he expected her to behave? Well, he would be disappointed. Meg had no intention of allowing the former Laird of Glen Dhui to be anything more to her than a man she expected to take her orders. And obey them. A man like . . . well, like Duncan Forbes . . .

She opened her mouth to tell him so, but he had already turned away. He seemed to have lost interest in her, and was twirling the pewter goblet between his long fingers, watching the metal change color in the candlelight. For a time they ate in silence.

"How is your arm, Captain?" That seemed a safe subject.

He flexed it a little, winced. "It will heal. I have had worse. My trade as a soldier ensures I am set upon on a regular basis."

"But not usually by your own men?" she responded dryly.

He laughed at the barb. She had amused him again, delighted him again. But this time he did not flirt. Instead his amber eyes grew cool and watchful, as if he too were prepared to keep his distance.

"No, not often by my own men. Airdy is an exception. He is also a fool. A fool with a beautiful wife. Barbara wanted to leave him but Airdy would not allow it, so she came to me for help. Airdy misconstrued our . . . association. We fought a duel, and I won, but Barbara returned to Airdy. I can't pretend to understand her reasons; I fear a woman's mind is a puzzle to me."

"And now she has run off and left Airdy, and Airdy blames you?"

"Aye, that is about it."

"I heard him swear revenge on you for what he perceives to be your betrayal."

"Airdy is a vengeful wee bastard."

"Do you think he really means it? Or will he forget, given time and distance?"

"Airdy is the sort of man who would follow me to the edge of the world, Lady Meg. He is the sort of man who never forgets."

Meg picked thoughtfully at a bowl of wild strawberries. So would he find Airdy first, and take action against him? Or wait until the moment of confrontation came, as he seemed to think it would? She was tempted to ask him, but when she looked up, he had that amused look on his face, as if he knew exactly what she was thinking, and perversely, she didn't want him to have the satisfaction of being right.

"Do you think we can turn the Duke of Abercauldy from his chosen course?" she asked instead, setting aside her empty plate. The food had warmed and filled her; she was nicely replete. It was a shame that Gregor Grant's presence made her so edgy.

He took a sip of his claret, biding his time in answering. After a moment he looked up at her and sighed. "Abercauldy and your father have signed papers, and that means that legally your life is already bound to his. The next step is the priest's blessing."

Meg echoed his sigh. "I feared it was so. I should tell you that Abercauldy sent a message while I was away. It was couched in polite terms but there was iron behind the pretty phrases. He wants a firm date, so that he can set our marriage in motion."

He was still watching her, but she could read little in his steady gaze.

"You have nothing to say to that, sir?" she asked with irritation.

"I have much to say, my lady, but none of it good."

Her chin went up, her pale blue eyes sparkled, and a flush colored her pale cheeks. "I would prefer to hear it anyway, Captain Grant."

"Very well. If your father has signed his agreement for you to wed the Duke, then there is now little room in which to move. It would help if you could persuade Abercauldy he has made a mistake, get him to agree to revoke the terms. But I have to say, it does not seem as though he will. He *can* insist upon a marriage between you. You will refuse, Lady Meg. Of course, you *will* refuse," he said it clearly, his eyes insistent. "But when you do refuse, there is no reason for him to be a gentleman about accepting it. He can demand recompense."

"Recompense? Do you mean he will ask us for money?"

"He can claim you have damaged his reputation."

Meg snorted in disgust.

"That is as may be, but he has the right. He can ask for money, or he can ask for something in lieu of money. If he wants Glen Dhui, then he will ask for that . . . or part thereof."

"No," Meg whispered, shocked, "he cannot have it!"

"He may try and take it. He has the means."

"Then we must stop him. *You* must stop him!"

"I have promised to help you, madam," he said impatiently, "but even I cannot make a miracle."

"I am paying you!"

"Can you pay enough for a miracle?"

"If I must."

He laughed, half in frustration, half amused.

Meg leaned forward, intent upon his eyes beneath their slashing black brows. His eyes narrowed on her own, and the smile faded from his lips. A long, red curl slipped from its pins and fell, soft against her cheek. She ignored it, her fingers clasped tightly together, as she concentrated upon his face and what she was saying.

"I do not *want* to marry him. He may be urbane and charming on the outside, but there is something cold inside him. Something brittle. Something . . . menacing. I think it is true, what Shona says—he feels a need to break a woman's spirit. I do not like him. I do not trust him. He frightens me. Surely in such circumstances any agreement would be rendered invalid?"

"Only if you can prove he really did murder his wife."

"But we cannot prove that, unless Shona speaks out!"

"I know, 'tis the word of a common Highland woman

against a duke. The odds on believing her are not high, Lady Meg."

"And to put her in such danger . . ."

"Even so, it may be the only way."

"But—"

"Of course, if you were to—" *If you were to marry someone else, the Duke would no' be able to force his own marriage on you.*

Gregor stopped abruptly, shocked, staring at her. *Marry someone else?* He cleared his throat, and his gaze dropped away, unable to meet any longer the confused questions in her own. He reached for his claret and took a sip, and cleared his throat again. What in God's name had possessed him even to *think* such a thing? Marry someone else? Who? Who could they find to stand against a man like Abercauldy? And would Meg, so finicky when it came to a bridegroom, marry someone else anyway?

And who was this "someone else"?

He took another sip, his hand shaking. He was playing a game with himself. Because he knew who it was, aye, Gregor knew very well who this hypothetical man was. . . .

Meg was still staring, bemused, though she had drawn back, and tucked the loose curl behind her ear. "What?" she demanded. "What is it? What were you going to say?"

He shook his head, but then, as if he could not help it, he looked at her once more. The intensity of his stare seemed to catch and hold her fast. Her lips, reddened by the strawberries, parted, and for a moment he struggled with the mad urge to kiss them.

"I had a thought, but it will not do," he said with quiet and deadly seriousness. "It will not do at all, my lady."

Meg hesitated, clearly still curious as to what he had been thinking to make him react so, and then reluctantly she let it go. Her green silk gown shimmered in the candlelight, the gauze scarf slipping to show the full swell of her breasts above the square bodice. He wanted her to straighten it, to cover herself modestly again, but she seemed lost in her own thoughts.

Gregor finished his wine with a gulp. At least he had not spoken the words aloud. At least he did not have to worry about extricating himself from such a blunder as that. It wouldn't have surprised him if she had laughed in his face, or ordered him from the house. . . .

She picked up another strawberry.

Suddenly Gregor couldn't take any more. He rose abruptly to his feet.

"I would like to see the general now."

Meg rose with a noisy rustle of silk, obviously startled by his haste. "Oh. Yes. Of course."

He strode to the door, opened it, and waited for her.

Glancing at him nervously, she passed through into the Great Hall, hurrying to the staircase. "Follow me, Captain Grant. We will go together. I, too, would very much like to hear what my father has to say to you."

He hardly heard her. He was in the past again, sinking back in time with each step he climbed. The general. There were memories in those two words, painful memories he had held prisoner for many years, just as the young Gregor had been a prisoner. But now those memories had broken free. . . .

"And how is young Gregor Grant today?"
Gregor lifted his head. The other men in the cell shifted

to make way for the general, most of them good-naturedly, one or two grumbling. The general was a regular visitor to the gaol, taking an interest in the prisoners, speaking with them, offering to get news home to their loved ones. He did a fair job of it, in Gregor's opinion, even if some of the others said he was not worth spitting upon, because he had fought on the side of the English king in the 1715 Rebellion.

No, Gregor decided, the general was a just and fair man, which was more than the Jacobites had expected to find when they were led here in chains after the Battle of Preston. The general may have fought against them, but it was their ideals he disliked, their politics he disagreed with, not the men themselves.

The general seemed to have a particular fondness for Gregor. It stemmed from the fact that Gregor's father, who had come to the prison with his son, had died here. Apoplexy. He had died in Gregor's arms, unable to speak, staring wildly, hardly aware of those around him. Gregor had been distraught; the general had stepped neatly into the shoes of surrogate father.

"Will you have a game of chess with me this evening, young Gregor?" The general stood on his heels, rocking back and forth in the small space allowed him by the men who sat and crouched and knelt. He was beaming down into Gregor's wan and dirty face, as if there were nothing odd in such a scene.

Gregor knew he had lice, but everyone else had them too. The conditions in the prison were worse than anything he had seen in a Highland hovel. Indeed, most Highland hovels were palaces compared to this. The General had commented adversely on the state of the place, he had complained to the governor, he had even written to parlia-

ment. No one cared. They were Jacobites after all, rebels, and in the eyes of most of the population, they deserved what they got.

Gregor had grown used to living within sight and hearing of twenty other men, but he enjoyed the general's visits. His only other escape was within his own mind. He could take himself off to Glen Dhui whenever he wanted to. His memories of his home were so clear that he could recall every curve in the hills, every patch of heather, every stone.

He took himself off to Glen Dhui often.

"Thank you, sir, I would like to play chess this evening," he said now, politely, but without any real warmth. He did not like to be singled out like this, but neither would he give up his chess evenings with the general because some of the others didn't like it.

"Remember what he and his like stand for! A friend of German George who calls himself our king, that's what he is, Gregor. Spit in his eye, laddie!"

"Aye, he's German Georgie's man."

"Mabbe he likes 'em young, huh? Has he ever tried to kiss you, laddie?"

They all said things like that, although MacIlvrey was probably the worst. MacIlvrey was bitter, turned half mad by what had happened to his wife and child when they were left behind, after the beaten Jacobite army fled into the north.

Their words made Gregor feel angry and sick, but he would not be drawn into a fight. He pretended to listen to their arguments and the coarse jokes, and after a time they let him be, allowed him to go off without further trouble. Sometimes he pretended to grumble, as if he didn't really want to go and play chess, but it was just a ruse. The evenings away from this crowded, smelly cell were like paradise, the peace and warmth of the room the general used as his chamber on such occasions were almost as good as dreaming of Glen Dhui.

Sometimes the general would pour him a glass of Rhenish, and expound on the state of Scotland. Sometimes he would try and persuade Gregor to his point of view, never realizing that his protégé had made up his own mind, long before he was taken prisoner, that the Stuart cause was not for him.

But loyalty to his father and the other prisoners kept him silent.

"Good, good!" The general beamed now at his acceptance, his genial smile making the creases in his face sink deeper. He had the bluest, most direct gaze Gregor had ever encountered. It seemed to see straight into his soul, and yet it was not invasive. It was comforting.

The general was looking down at him. They didn't see it coming. Suddenly MacIlvrey rose up behind him like a man-mountain, all six foot five of him, and put his hands around the general's throat.

"I'll kill ye, ye Sassenach bastard!" he shouted, and began to squeeze.

The guards were at ease outside the door. There had never been trouble before, everyone seemed to accept the general. The men in the cell were either too startled to do much, or ambivalent about the whole thing. Gregor saw what was about to happen, and only Gregor acted.

He came around the general like a whirlwind, fists flying, feet kicking. Through sheer luck he landed a blow to the unhealed wound on MacIlvrey's leg, and the man gave a keen-

ing sound and let the general go. The general fell, gasping, choking into Gregor's arms, his face the color of a pomegranate, just as the guards came running.

For a time there was confusion. Gregor was thought to be the attacker, and he was taken to another cell, jostled and struck, his eye blackened and his lip bloodied. It was only some time later that the General, able at last to speak, had explained how Gregor had saved his life, not threatened it, and came himself to see the boy released from his confinement.

"I thank you," he had said, taking Gregor's hands in his, with eyes a mixture of pity for the boy's state and anger that it was so. "I'll not forget this, Gregor lad."

Gregor ducked his head, and felt the tears in his eyes. He would not cry. He had not cried since his father died in his arms.

But the general seemed to understand. "Don't worry, lad," he said quietly, "I'll get you out of here."

And so he had.

When Gregor's sentence was read, stating he be sent to the American plantations as indentured labor, the general moved heaven and earth, and somehow found a sympathetic ear. Gregor was pardoned and released. He was free. Even if freedom hadn't meant very much to him then, with time he came to realize that the general might well have saved his life.

A fair exchange.

"Captain?"

Gregor blinked, looked down at the curious face turned to his. Meg was watching him, and he wondered how long he had been standing here in the shadows, lost in the past.

Her green silk gown shivered with color and light, as though she were under the ocean. With her hair and her strange, pale eyes, she was even more like a mermaid than before.

"Morvoren."

"Captain Grant?"

He had not realized he said it aloud. Embarrassed, bemused, he shook his head. He was tired, that was all. It had been a long, long day and his arm was aching. He needed to get this over with so that he could sleep. Tomorrow did not promise to be any easier, but it may feel so if he was rested.

"My father awaits within," she was reminding him. "Are you ready?"

Gregor nodded, and she reached for the door and opened it, and led him quietly into the room.

Chapter 12

Inside the general's room it was dim, with only a single branch of candles. There was a meager fire in the hearth, and the window was ajar, the smell of the glen wafting in. The man who sat by the sill was not stooped; he sat straight as a poker, his gray head turned slightly toward the sound of their entry.

"Meg?" he said, and his voice was so familiar Gregor felt dizzy. As if he were walking on some uneven, unsafe surface that might at any moment give way and plummet him down into darkness.

"Yes, father. I have Captain Grant with me."

"Good, good. Bring him here to me."

Meg glanced back at Gregor, where he stood just inside the door, and raised a questioning eyebrow. "Captain Grant?" He realized then that he was behaving strangely, and followed her down the long room.

"Your daughter tells me you haven't been well, sir," he spoke as he drew closer. "I am sorry to hear that."

The face turned to his went still with shock, and then all its creases and grooves deepened in a broad, beautiful smile. "Gregor! I'd know your voice, even now."

"I hope it's deepened a wee bit, sir."

He had reached the general now, and looking down into his face realized he might be more worn—older certainly—but he was still the same man he had been twelve years ago. The blue eyes turned up to his were staring directly at him.

"I am grateful that you have come back to Glen Dhui with my daughter. Meg? Have you informed him of our problems?"

He turned, head cocked to one side, listening rather than looking for Meg. The action was unusual and Gregor frowned, suddenly watchful.

Meg took a step forward, brushing her fingers against her father's shoulder in a reassuring gesture. "I am here, father. And yes, I have told him."

"Good, good." The general nodded and then sighed. He looked up at Gregor again, but now his gaze was slightly to one side of Gregor, aimed beyond him, into the corner of the room.

"I dinna realize," Gregor said hoarsely. "I am so sorry, sir. I dinna realize you could not see. . . ."

The general lifted a hand to stop him. "A foolish complaint, Gregor. It began as a cloudiness, a fine mist across my sight, but as time passed it grew thicker. I am in a permanent fog now, but I have my memories, and they are as clear to me as they ever were."

"Father," Meg began gently, "what is it you have to say

to Captain Grant? It is very late, and the day has been a long one."

The general nodded. "Very well, Meg, very well. Do not be impatient, girl. I will speak to Gregor alone."

Her pale eyes narrowed. "I think it is my right to hear what you have to say," she said woodenly.

The general snorted. "Right? You are my daughter, Meg, and therefore you obey me. I will speak to Gregor alone. You have brought him to me, and for that I thank you, but now what must be said is between us men."

Color whipped into her cheeks, anger flared in her eyes, her mouth trembled on the verge of harsh words, or sobs, Gregor wasn't sure which. He felt an acute sympathy for her, a sense of fellow feeling. It seemed most ungenerous of her father to send her from the room like a child, after all she had been through to please him.

"Perhaps Lady Meg might stay," he ventured.

"No." The general's mouth closed in a stubborn line, and suddenly he looked very much like his daughter.

Meg flashed him a look, but Gregor shrugged his shoulders. What could he do? He had no rights here, not over the general and certainly not over Meg.

Meg didn't value such lukewarm support. With a final glare in his direction, she strode from the room, slamming the door behind her. They heard her footsteps moving away at a rapid pace.

The general chuckled softly, admiring of his daughter's temper. "Meg is a termagant. A fighter. No wishy-washy miss, my girl, eh, Gregor?"

"I would not call her a wishy-washy miss, sir, no."

The general chuckled again at the dry note in Gregor's voice. "You like a bit of spirit, do you not? I cannot imagine you wanting a woman who jumped to your every word, Gregor. Might as well marry one of your soldiers, eh?"

"You're right, General Mackintosh." Gregor pulled a chair closer. He was bone weary, his arm was throbbing, and he felt dizzy in the head. If the general did not get to the point soon it was quite likely he would fall over, and they would have to call the servants to drag him, feet-first, to his bed.

The general said, with the uncanny perception of a blind man, "Before you sit down, Gregor, there is some whiskey there that isn't too bad. They have been making it in a still near Cragan Dhui from the dawn of time, but you would know that. Pour us both a dram, would you? Meg waters it down; she thinks I don't know. She thinks I drink too much of it. She tries to make me drink that devilish tea that is becoming all the fashion now—*psst*! Well, maybe it's true, maybe I do drink too much whiskey, but what else is there to do to help pass the long nights?"

Gregor poured the drinks, and then sat down in a chair facing the old man. The whiskey was raw and strong, and its warmth coursed through him, reawakening his tired brain. He watched the general drink his own, seeming to manage with ease despite his lack of sight. For a moment they sat companionably by the window, as if they hadn't just met after so long apart.

"So you know about the Duke of Abercauldy?" The general's voice was weary, resigned, repentant.

"I know as much as Meg has told me."

"Ah, *Meg* is it?" A smile curled his mouth, but soon faded again. His head bowed gloomily, his straight back slumped. "I believed he was a fine fellow; I realize now that was what he wanted me to believe. I was easy meat for that crow, Gregor! Feeling sorry for myself, feeling old and worn out. He puffed me up with tales of my own vanity and self-importance, and in return I agreed to let him marry my daughter! Even knowing she would be furious with me for doing so. I told myself I had her best interests at heart, that eventually she would thank me for it."

He shook his head mournfully and continued. "I *do* worry for her. That is my excuse, though it is a poor one. I worry what will become of her when I am gone. She will be alone, a little lamb surrounded by the circling wolves. I convinced myself that the duke would protect her, cherish her, and give her everything she deserved. I wanted to see her happy and content, Gregor. Is that so terrible?"

"I can understand that, sir."

"Can you?" the old man demanded eagerly.

"Aye, 'tis not such an outlandish wish for a father to make."

"Meg was so angry I don't think she spoke to me for a fortnight," he went on, the misery seeping back into his face and voice. "And she wept in her room night after night. It broke my heart, Gregor, I can tell you. If I ever thought to be a strict and stern father to her, then that was my un-doing. . . .

"But she came around. For my sake, rather than the Duke's. She knew she was trapped, we were trapped, and she faced it like the courageous girl she is. I thought . . . I hoped all would be well then. But shortly afterward we heard the story from Shona, and although I told myself it was a lie, that I didn't believe it—I didn't *want* to believe it . . ." He pounded his fist against the arm of the chair with each word, "It . . . was . . . truth."

"Shona is an honest woman."

"She is. The truth was there in her voice, and I knew it. And soon we found that it was not only Shona who had a tale to tell concerning the Duke of Abercauldy. Then it was I who wept in my room, Gregor. For I realized I had signed my daughter's life into the hands of a murderer, and I did not know what to do about it."

"You told him you had changed your mind?"

"Of course. He would not hear of it. Meg gave him one of her tongue-lashings, but I think it just fascinated him the more. He is in thrall with her. I do not understand it, but Meg says he watches her every move when they are in the same room. He dotes upon her, Gregor. Nothing I say, or she says, will persuade him to stop this marriage. He goes about it as if everyone is in agreement, as if nothing is wrong. There is something unnatural in it."

Gregor had not realized just how strong Abercauldy's feelings were, and it gave him a jolt. The frustration and misery in the old man's voice gave Gregor some idea of what he and Meg had suffered. He knew the general was slow in getting to the point, but Gregor was content to wait, to let him reach it in his own time and in his own way. Gregor took another swallow of the whiskey, enjoying the sensation of it slipping down. The ache in his arm had almost gone, and what was left didn't matter.

"I saved you from being sent in chains to the plantations, Gregor."

Gregor looked up, surprised at the change in subject. "Aye, and I am grateful for it, sir."

"Are you?" Those cloudy eyes met his as if they would pierce the veil between them. "I wondered, sometimes, long afterward, whether you really were glad to remain in Scotland. You had nothing to go back to when they freed you from prison. You were just another landless laird. You might have preferred to go to the Americas, where others have made new lives for themselves. Fortunes, too!"

Gregor thought for a moment. General Mackintosh was right, there had been times when he'd wished himself elsewhere—even dead! But he had survived, and now there was a kind of pride in that fact. "Whatever I thought then, I am grateful now. My life has not been too unbearable."

The general sighed. "Maybe, maybe. Do you know, you were the reason I came to Glen Dhui? I heard it was taken from you, and I was close by, on another matter, and I had an urge to see it. So I came." He smiled. "I do not pretend I thought of you when I bought it, Gregor. As soon as I saw it, I knew I wanted to live here. I told myself that it was far better I had the Glen Dhui estate than someone who would not care for it and its people beyond the money to be made. I'm sure you've heard the stories of tenants being turned from their crofts to make way for black-faced sheep? But the real reason was entirely selfish. I fell in love with your glen, lad." Gregor went to speak but the general did not let him. "Well, I have been a good master, I think. I have been a better master than I have been a father."

"Why am I here?"

There, the question was spoken. The general hesitated, his fingers restlessly tapping now on the chair arm. Gregor leaned forward and covered them with his own hand, surprised by the other man's bony fragility. The answer stopped his breath.

"I need you to marry Meg. I want you to wed her and protect her with your name. Abercauldy will be angry, but if

Meg is wed to another he will no longer be able to pretend everything will go on as he wishes. He will have to open his eyes to the truth. And I hope, with time, he will accept matters and turn his dangerous sights elsewhere."

It was so like his own thought, earlier, in the Blue Saloon. Wed Meg? Marry Meg Mackintosh? What would that make him? Laird of Glen Dhui, again?

The blood drummed in his ears, the lightheadedness returning. Laird of Glen Dhui. Home, home again for good. Or at least until Abercauldy sent his army in to drive him off. Or kill him.

"Gregor?"

He felt the general's fingers turn and clasp his, squeezing hard, bringing him back to the dim room and the scents of the glen through the open window.

"Gregor?"

"I am all right. Just . . . I am tired. There was a fight in Clashennic. My arm . . ."

The general frowned, leaning forward. "You were hurt, lad? Meg did not tell me this!"

"I . . . 'Tis nothing. Are you serious in this proposal, sir?"

"Of course. I never say anything if I do not mean it."

Gregor laughed despite himself. "No, ye never did! Sir, I . . . I dinna think I am the man for this. Your daughter wouldna wish . . ."

"She has to marry *someone*, Gregor. It is the only way out of this mess. If she is wed, then Abercauldy cannot have her. It is not a perfect solution, I know, and there will be problems and likely repercussions, but Meg will be safe and that is all that matters to me now. I did not want her to wed someone from the glen, a Duncan Forbes or Jamie Farquharson. I did not want her to wed a finely tailored gentleman from Edinburgh, or some Highland chieftain with more hair than wit. I have thought of it long and hard, and it seemed that you were the only one. I am thinking of Meg, Gregor, but it is also the fact that you lost Glen Dhui twelve years ago, and now you can have it back."

So Glen Dhui was the bait. Not Meg. Not Meg with her flaming hair and blue eyes and sweet lips. And her delicious curves. The general thought to tempt him with the glen, so that he would not mind if he had to wed Meg. Strangely, it wasn't Glen Dhui that was in the forefront of his thoughts at the moment.

It was the general's daughter.

"I could not marry her if she dinna wish it," he said, and marveled that he was even contemplating it. Did that mean he was willing to do it? That he was agreeable?

"She *will* wish it." The general said it grimly.

"From her own mouth, sir. I willna wed an unwilling woman. I dinna know if I will wed *any* woman, but in the circumstances I . . . I need to speak to Lady Meg."

The general gripped his hand harder. "Not yet, Gregor lad. Not until I have spoken to her. Let me talk with her, reason with her," he ignored Gregor's laugh, "and then you can broach the subject. Is it agreed then? Will you do this? Will you wed Meg and regain your lost lands?"

Gregor closed his eyes. Madness, it was all madness, and yet he heard himself saying, "Aye, sir, I will. *If* she is agreeable."

Meg sat, staring into nothing, as Alison brushed her hair. The flaming tresses tumbled and curled about her, clean again from the bath Meg had taken earlier. Alison's care helped take some of the sting out of her father's stubborn

refusal to share with her his reasons for bringing Gregor
Grant to Glen Dhui.

"Lady?"

She blinked, looking up to meet the other woman's dark
gaze. Alison's face seemed very pale. Meg remembered,
uncomfortably, that there was more than herself suffering
here.

"I am sorry about Malcolm Bain," she said gently. "Why
didn't you tell me? You never spoke of him. It was not until
Duncan told me that I—"

"Duncan had no right."

"I thought we were friends."

Alison twitched uncomfortably.

"Does he . . . does he know about Angus?" Meg asked.

Alison's eyes flew, horrified, to Meg's. "Nooo, he doesna
know, and he must not! I dinna want him to know, Lady
Meg! Promise me ye willna tell him!"

Meg shushed her gently. "I won't tell him, never fear.
But he will find out, Alison, he can't help but discover it, in
time. You should tell him first, before that happens."

Alison looked away, blinking fast to stop the tears.

Meg sighed and rose, wrapping her shawl about her plain
white nightgown. Once she stepped off the thick rug, the
floor was cold beneath her bare feet, and she quickly
climbed into her bed. Alison bustled about, tidying up
clothing and folding it away.

"My lady," she said at last, "I dinna wish to speak out of
turn."

"Of course not. You can say whatever you wish to me,
Alison."

"The laird . . . the Captain. He will bring trouble to the
glen."

Meg narrowed her gaze, trying to see into the other woman's mind. "How do you know that, Alison?"

Alison shrugged uncomfortably. "I feel it, Lady."

Alison's "feelings" were well known in the glen and not to be taken lightly; she was one of those with the second sight. Meg nodded soberly and thanked her. "I will take care. I will be watchful."

Alison gazed at her a moment longer, and then nodded her satisfaction with her mistress's answer. "Verra well. Good night, my lady."

"Good night, Alison. . . ."

The door closed and Meg was finally alone. Alone in the darkness with a single candle. Alone to wonder what it was her father and Gregor Grant were discussing, and why it was she could not hear it.

Chapter 13

Malcolm Bain strode along the upper corridor, his mind preoccupied. He had spent the night in the stables, sleeping in a pile of less-than-sweet straw, while horses snorted and farted all around him. Now his back ached and even the cold water he had pumped over his head in the yard had failed to put a dent in his weariness.

I am too old for this, he thought to himself. I should have stayed at the barracks in Clashennic.

If ye had never left Glen Dhui, a voice whispered in his head, *ye'd have a house of yer own now, with a family to welcome ye to it.*

He'd made a choice between family and duty. At the time he had felt he had had *no* choice. He still did.

And now he must find Gregor Grant and rouse him for the long day ahead. There were men coming from all corners of the glen, carrying a motley collection of arms. Meg's tacksman, Duncan Forbes, in his usual high-handed manner, had sent out word without waiting for instructions.

Malcolm Bain did not see the plump, dark-haired woman step out of the doorway into his path. Not until he collided with her and all but sent her flying.

"What the—" she began, turning to glare. Black hair and black eyes, big and round, and getting rounder. Alison Forbes actually quivered with anger.

"I dinna see ye," Malcolm Bain spoke cautiously.

"Then ye're blind as well as stupid!" she screeched back. "Ye great poopnoddy! What do ye mean by crashing about without looking where ye are going? I could have fallen and broken something!"

He had meant to be unfailingly polite to her, to answer her with gravity and respect. But now her words had made him smile. He caught it before it could grow into a grin, but it was too late.

"Wipe that smirk off yer face, Malcolm Bain," she hissed. "Do ye think this is funny? Do ye?"

"I . . . 'tis just that if ye did fall, Alison Forbes, ye would bounce before ye broke. Ye are so delightfully soft."

Her black eyes flared like wildfire, her mouth pinched white at the corners, and he knew she meant to mortally wound him. In a flash, he was past her, and hammering desperately on Gregor's door. A sleepy voice within bade him enter, and he did so, gladly.

"Was that you shouting out there?" Gregor asked, yawning, and blinking in the early light.

"Not me," Malcolm Bain said grimly. "I bumped into Alison Forbes."

"Oh." Gregor Grant hesitated, questions in his eyes, and then carried on. " 'Tis barely dawn. What do you want?"

"Aye, and there are already some men down in the yard

awaiting ye. Duncan spread the word that ye were back, and that we mabbe in for a fight. They've brought their weapons to show ye, as ye requested."

Gregor groaned and ran his hands over his face. "I dinna mean at first light! Verra well, I'll be down in a moment. Fetch me some water to wash in, Malcolm, so I can feel half alive."

"There's always the pump in the yard," Malcolm suggested slyly.

His master eyed him uneasily. "I prefer my water warmed, if I can get it. Find a maid and send her for a ewer."

But Malcolm Bain lingered, shifting from foot to foot and glancing furtively at the door. Gregor's mouth kicked up at the corner. "Are you afraid, Malcolm Bain?"

"No!"

"I think you are. You're afraid wee Alison Forbes might be waiting for you out there. With a big carving knife."

Malcolm shuddered. "I wouldna put it past her."

"She's not forgotten your leaving her then?"

Malcolm's shoulders slumped in defeat. "No, she hasna forgotten. She has it in her head that I wronged her."

"You should have stayed. I should have *made* you stay. If I'd been thinking straight at the time, I would have."

Malcolm eyed him in surprise. "Ye were but seventeen years old, Gregor, and I was your man. I was your father's man before that. I couldna leave ye to face matters alone, I wouldna been able to live with mysel', to sleep sound at night, if I had."

"So you put my welfare before your happiness?" Gregor sighed and sat up, rubbing his arm where the bandage encompassed it. "I *am* grateful, Malcolm—don't let yourself be persuaded otherwise—but I'm sorry you had to make such a choice. If I'd thought . . . If I'd been capable of thinking at the time, I would have sent you home. Can I help smooth matters over between you and Alison?"

Malcolm scratched the stubble on his jaw. "I dinna know," he said moodily. "She hates me now. She'd like me dead, lad. I can see it in her eyes."

"Give her time. She'll get over it."

Malcolm nodded, but it was clear he didn't believe it. He took a deep breath, cracked open the door to check all was clear, and left the room.

Gregor sank back against the pillows, gathering his strength and ordering his thoughts for the day ahead.

Had the general really asked him to marry Meg? For her sake and the sake of Glen Dhui? Had he really offered Gregor the one thing he had longed for these twelve endless years? The one thing he had never in his wildest dreams thought to possess again?

But to *marry* Meg . . . *Meg!*

Gregor doubted she would be very pleased with her father's grand plan. Would she *want* to marry him? She had told him she did not want to marry anyone, had only agreed to Abercauldy because her father had placed her in an impossible position. Her love for the general had driven her to accept something she would not otherwise have contemplated, let alone have agreed to. And what would her marriage to Gregor give her that she didn't already have? Freedom from the duke's attentions, for a time, but who knew what would come after? In this way were Highland feuds begun. . . .

But maybe there was more than the prospect of her own safety, and the safety of the glen, to sway her. Gregor remembered now the manner in which she had looked at him, when he had stood knee-deep in the cold loch outside Shona's cottage. Looked at him as if he were her whole world. There had been desire in her eyes then, he had not been mistaken about that. She had wanted him, needed him, but her feelings had frightened her. He had frightened her. Could desire bind two people together, for a time? Could desire make a marriage, and hold it firm? Gregor didn't know, but it was a temptation.

She was a temptation.

Could he persuade her to say yes? Did he want her to say yes? Did he want what the general had offered him? With an uncomfortable feeling in his belly, Gregor knew that the opportunity was too good to resist.

Meg peeped out of the upper window at the wide lawn on the side of the castle. There were men everywhere. She recognized them, for they were all Glen Dhui men, some dressed in their best Sunday clothes, others in their everyday kilts. They had come to see Gregor Grant, and they had brought their weapons with them.

Old, rusty claymores and swords, ancient muskets and pistols, pikes and dirks that had seen better days. They had brought whatever they had, and they were eager to show Gregor what they were capable of. As Meg watched, hand over her mouth, eyes brimming with laughter, old Jamie Farquharson did a stumbling run with his broadsword, shouting fit to wake the dead.

If enthusiasm could win a battle against the Duke of Abercauldy, then surely Glen Dhui would be victorious.

The laughter faded from her eyes and she sat down on the window seat with a sigh. This was no laughing matter. When she arose this morning she had intended to go and see her father, to demand he tell her whatever it was he had told Gregor. She had meant to insist, to force him to tell her. Instead she was here, lurking in the small room she used for adding up the accounts and interviewing the tenants. And for hiding. This was her sanctuary, her retreat.

Meg was afraid, and she was angry.

She admitted it to herself. She was afraid of what her father had said to Gregor, of what they had said together. She was angry that he had felt able to discuss things with a near stranger, and yet he could not speak of them to her, his own daughter. She had done all he asked of her and more! She had found Gregor and brought him here, no easy task, and then he had sent her from the room like a child. It would not do.

It would not!

Meg glanced down at the bundle of thick pages she held in her hands. Old, faded sketches of the glen, some grand, sweeping vistas of mountains and cloud, others small, intimate portraits of a flower or a deer grazing on the hillside, or rain striking the burn's surface. All of them beautiful, original, the product—or so she had always believed—of an exceptional soul. He had captured all that was special about this place, he had laid his heart bare with every line, every stroke.

Meg did not believe that someone who had once drawn so exquisitely was entirely devoid of feeling. After all, she had seen his pain last evening, as they waited upon the crest of the road that overlooked the glen. She could understand why he had resisted returning, why he had not wanted to come home to the place he had loved. The glen was no longer his, he was no longer the laird, and that must hurt.

"Although you would not know he was no longer the

laird," she murmured to herself, glancing from the casement again and even cracking it open a fraction. "Look at them! They still think of him as their chief."

Meg knew she would be a fool to believe there was anything of the boy who had drawn these pictures in the grim, warlike man Gregor had become. She would be a fool to allow the slightest part of her to soften toward him. And she was all the more determined to remain aloof because she knew it would be so easy to succumb to him. That moment by the loch had shown her that, and then last night in the parlor had reinforced it.

He found her company amusing and enjoyable, he looked at her with eyes that told her she was attractive to him. For Meg, who believed she was not, the longing to take that step closer was very tempting.

"Remember, you are no more than a thorn in his side," she reminded herself sharply. "You have prodded him into doing something he really didn't want to do."

"A thorn in whose side?"

Meg jumped, and then laughed when she turned and saw Alison standing in the open doorway, her black eyes wide with curiosity.

"I was talking to myself, Alison. It is a bad habit and one I should learn to curb."

"Aye, ye are aright there. The Captain asks ye to come down to him, Lady Meg."

Meg's slim eyebrows descended and her eyes narrowed suspiciously. "Come down to him? Why is that?"

"Ye'd best ask him yersel'. I am but passing on the message."

The request was innocent enough, but Meg could not

help but wonder what was afoot. If she came down, she would only be displaying her ignorance of the matters of war. But would anyone expect otherwise? Meg had never pretended to be an Amazon. If anyone would lead the men into a battle—if it came to that—then it would be Captain Grant. That was the reason he was here, wasn't it?

Unless her father had another . . .

"Why dinna ye go down and ask him?" Alison said dryly into the long silence.

Meg laughed, wondering if her thoughts were so plainly to be read on her face, or whether Alison just knew her too well. "I will do that, then." She glanced out of the window again.

There were even more men down there now, and young lads scampering on the hillside like lambs in the spring.

"Donald, is that your grandsire's musket?"

She could hear Gregor's voice, floating up to her in the stillness. He had picked up a large, long-barreled weapon, turning it over in his hands, and then sighting it down the glen.

Young Donald puffed himself up. "He was oot with Bonny Dundee, sir," he offered the information with great pride.

"I remember. He was a braw man."

Meg observed the two men with wonder. Gregor had spoken the words easily, honestly, with hardly more than a glance at Donald. And yet the effect was profound. Donald had loved Gregor before he spoke—they all did—and now he worshiped him.

Gregor handed the musket back to Donald and turned, glancing up at her window. Did he know she was up here, spying? Quickly Meg moved back, feeling suddenly breathless. It would not do for Gregor Grant to know how curious she was about him, how interested she was in him. How dangerously fascinated.

"I will be down in a moment, Alison," she said quietly. "Just let me tidy my hair."

"As ye say, my lady."

And something in Alison's smile made her blush.

Gregor realized he had been well and truly spoiled by his troop of Campbell dragoons.

They were proper soldiers, well trained and well equipped. It was a pity he could not have brought more of them with him. Still, he knew the men of the glen had their good points, too. They lived here in Glen Dhui, this was their home, and they would fight all the harder if the Duke of Abercauldy decided he wanted to take it from them.

"Captain," Malcolm Bain alerted him, and nodded his head in the direction of the house.

Gregor's gaze followed.

She was there, watching him, wearing the blue dress with the taffeta bows down the front. Small, neat bows in a long, straight line. His fingers itched to pull them apart, every one of them, and find what was hidden beneath. To unpin her hair and lay it about her. To kiss her pink mouth until she sighed and gasped and wound her arms about his neck.

He looked down at the ground, where the men had scuffed and trampled the grass to mud. He took a deep breath. He told himself he was mad or sick, or both. He carefully, methodically gathered his thoughts, and put on his mask. But when he looked up again it had made no difference. She was still there, and he still felt the same.

"I received your message," she told him coolly when she reached him. "You wanted to see me, Captain?"

She didn't like being sent for like a lackey. He had not intended it so; he hadn't thought of couching his request in more palatable terms. He was a direct man, not used to games, and sometimes he forgot to be polite.

Gregor tried a smile. "I thought it would be useful if you were here with me, to look over the men as they drill. To show we are in accord over the matter of the duke."

Meg raised an eyebrow. "I see. But I know nothing of weapons."

"That is not the point of the exercise, Meg."

She took a step forward, until she stood beside him. He could smell her, a light and fresh, womanly scent, overlaid with the sweetness of her hair. He could hear the rustle of her blue skirts, and beneath them, her petticoats. He closed his eyes and wondered if he could send her away again without making her even more suspicious and wary of him. Without making himself look like a halfwit.

"Captain?" Malcolm Bain stood before him, hair windblown, blue eyes narrowed. Malcolm knew him too well. He would be aware that something was wrong. "Do ye want me to drill the men now? I'll set up some targets, to see how good their aim is, but it would be best if we dinna waste too much of our ammunition."

Gregor pretended to look about him, consideringly, as if he had been thinking of that all along. "Verra well, Malcolm, you see to it. Lady Meg and I will watch."

Malcolm Bain nodded, pleased, and went off to do as he was told.

The air was warming, the scents of late summer drifted on the breeze. It was a day for lying in the grass and looking at the clouds, as he had as a boy. It felt like home. He *was* home. His skin tingled, his blood coursed through his veins. He was home, and suddenly he felt more alive in this moment than he had in any of the past twelve years.

"They are a motley lot." Meg sounded doubtful at his side.

"They fought well in the 1715. They may well have won at Preston, if our leaders hadn't decided to surrender. Don't be deceived, Lady Meg. Courage and determination means a lot in a battle; it could tip it our way." Did he really believe that? The Duke of Abercauldy probably had an army at his disposal, and if it came to a fight he would slaughter them all. But he hoped it wouldn't come to that. If the general had his way, if Meg married him, maybe they could avert any bloodshed.

If . . .

She stood beside him for a long time, watching the men of Glen Dhui form a ragged line that gradually grew straighter, watching them learn to shoulder their weapons, to aim and fire. Watching them grow into a more military-like band. She didn't say much to Gregor, but she spoke to the individual men, offering praise, laughing at a joke, and showing her pride for what they were doing.

Malcolm Bain bawled out orders, striding through the groups of men, pausing here and there for more specific instructions. Meg's heart almost stopped when he paused by young Angus, bending to help the boy with a powder flask. The sun reflected off their untidy, fair hair, blending it perfectly. Uneasily she glanced sideways at Gregor, wondering if he would see the resemblance, but he was looking elsewhere.

Alison's secret was safe then, for a little while longer.

The men really seemed to appreciate her being here—

she sensed their pride in their accomplishments—but their hearts were Gregor's.

"It does us good to see ye here again, Gregor Grant," old Jamie Farquharson said as he shuffled into line once more, the suspicion of tears in his eyes. Others murmured their agreement—tough Highland men who were close to weeping because a Grant was among them again.

"I am glad to see you too, Jamie," Gregor replied evenly. "Now straighten your back, man!"

Jamie straightened his back without protest, his wrinkled face beaming.

Jamie and the others believed that Gregor returned to Glen Dhui because he was, still, at heart, their laird. And it just wasn't so.

When Gregor turned toward Meg, her eyes were on him. He met them directly, expecting her to look away, but she didn't. There was accusation in her pale blue gaze, as well as condemnation. Clearly she had something on her mind and she meant to share it with him.

"Do your devotees know we have to pay you to be here, Captain? Do they know you are come only for the money? Have you told my father that yet?"

He managed a smile, as if her words did not strike hard. She had a right to be annoyed with him, to feel put out, but she didn't know the half of it and he wasn't about to tell her. "You'd be better off asking the general himself what he knows, Meg. I am sworn to silence."

"Oh, I will," she said at last, in the same cold voice she had arrived with. "Don't worry, Captain, I will!"

Meg went upstairs again to her sanctuary. There was plenty to do. It was she who ran the estate now, and she was meticulous in her notes and bookwork. Throughout the long afternoon she worked. Sometimes the voices from outside disturbed her, but mostly she managed to block them out. Once, when she happened to glance out of the window, she saw that Gregor had stripped off his shirt, leaving just his kilt slung low on his hips. Most of the other men had done the same, the sweat shining on their bodies, their chests heaving with effort.

But it was Gregor who drew her gaze.

He was just a man, she told herself crossly. And not even the man she had dreamed of, the boy artist she had half fallen in love with. He was a stranger. Why did she find him so fascinating? Why did she want to stroke his skin and gaze into his eyes like some lovesick wee lassie? She was a grown woman, alert to the ways of men, aware that her attractiveness was in her inheritance rather than her face and figure and what she had to say. She accepted that . . . or she had.

Why did she now wish it all different?

Outside the window, Gregor captured a young lad who had run in front of a man with a sword, putting himself in danger. He swung the young boy up onto his hip, holding the child while he issued more orders.

It was the strangest thing. . . .

Meg felt so dizzy she had to sit down. She knew what she was thinking, but she hardly dared admit it to herself. If Gregor Grant was hers, then they could have a child together. A child to grow up and run free in Glen Dhui, just as he had done. But this child would never be sent away, would never be outcast, as Gregor was. It . . . they would live here, happily, forever.

She groaned and put her face down onto her books, un-

caring if she got ink on her cheek. She was mad. Gregor
Grant would not want her, he would have too much pride to
sell himself for Glen Dhui.

Wouldn't he?

Chapter 14

Alison Forbes had laid out the meal in the upstairs dining room. The heavy rectangular table glowed with a sheen that reflected a great many years of polishing. It was set with the usual pewter, some more valuable silver, and even glassware, rarely seen in the Highlands. Lighted candelabra fluttered in the draft from the open window; the air brought with it the rush of the burn and the rustle of the yew leaves. Portraits, shadowy and faintly menacing, glowered from the walls, Jacobite Grants mingling with Mackintoshes as if they would never have been deadly enemies in life.

The irony was not lost upon Meg as she entered the room in her green silk gown, nor the awkwardness of the situation. Gregor Grant was there already, waiting, a glass of claret in his hand. He turned to face her, his expression giving away little, his well-worn but elegant clothing doing nothing to disguise what he was.

165

Meg had had plenty of time during the long afternoon to take stock of her reactions to him, and to tamp them down. The cool smile she presented him with, as he politely drew out her chair, was exactly as she had planned it. Distant and untouched.

"A productive afternoon, Captain?" she asked him, as she sat down.

He paused, leaning over her chair, so that she had to look up into his face. It put her in an exposed and vulnerable position, and suddenly her confident mask wavered. His gaze wandered down, lingering on her lips, down the arch of her throat, pausing on a curl of hair that lay against her shoulder, to the soft swell of her breasts above the neckline of her gown. There was no gauze scarf tonight, but the décolletage was modest enough—Meg would never have worn it otherwise. Yet, the way he looked . . . as if the silk was transparent, or torn. As if she were entirely naked before him.

She should have felt angry, and in a way she did, but her feelings were more confused than that, more complex. The way he looked at her stirred a response deep inside her, something that shivered and resonated. Meg tingled all over. If he were to bend a little lower, his lips would be close enough to . . . to . . . Just as she thought she was about to reach up to him, wind her arms about his neck and draw him down to her, doubt engulfed her.

He was a stranger, a man she hardly knew, and a man she was paying to be here! He had no right to be looking at her as if he were about to gobble her up.

Meg opened her mouth to voice her protest, but just then his gaze locked with hers. "We made some headway," he said quietly, in answer to her question.

Meg forced the fluttering in her stomach to subside through sheer effort of will, making her face impassive.

"They are pleased that you are back in Glen Dhui, whatever your true reason."

He laughed abruptly. "Thank you . . . I think."

"It wasn't a compliment, Captain," she replied sharply.

He let it go, merely smiling and moving to his own chair at her right side. Relieved by his retreat, Meg took a breath, and helped herself to hare soup. For a time they were quiet, with only the sounds from beyond the window to disturb them and the occasional mournful cry of a curlew out in the darkness. Their silence might even have been companionable, thought Meg, if there wasn't this over-stretched tension between them.

Anticipation.

As if something were about to happen, and she didn't know whether she wanted it to, or not.

"I noticed you have the American potato in your garden." He poured them each a glass of wine. "They are rare enough in England, but this far north . . . Was it the general's idea to grow them?"

Meg looked up, surprised by the change of subject. "No, it was mine. Major Litchfield spoke of them to me, and I had some sent north to me here, because I was interested and it seemed they might be helpful to the people. They do seem to grow well in our soil. Do you know much about the potato, Captain Grant?"

"Only that one eats the root rather than the leaves. I have tasted them, though."

"They are an exotic—or so they are treated. A few of the great houses grow them in their gardens as a curiosity, and although they do not have much taste, they fill the stomach. It is my belief that they will help to feed the people here, something to fall back on when the oat crop fails, or there is famine. As you know, there is always the fear of famine in the Highlands. I have been trying to persuade some of our tenants to grow them in their kaleyards, though they are resistant to change. But I have hopes of changing their minds—I have managed to bring them to the point of growing carrots and turnips, so why not potatoes?"

Meg smiled at him, but although he responded, he said nothing. She thought that she knew what he was thinking: What does she know of crops and the tenants of Glen Dhui? What does she know of hardship and famine, and why does she care? Such things should be left to men, as Duncan Forbes was always hinting to her. Men who understood the ways of the land and its people, and had done so since Adam.

"The old ways are not always the best," she said abruptly, helping herself to some mutton pie, annoyed that his opinion mattered to her. "Sometimes the old ways need changing, for the good of us all. Sometimes, to survive, we need to look forward instead of backward."

Gregor looked up with surprise, and swallowed his mouthful of oatcake. "Och, don't tear strips off me, Lady Meg! I agree with you."

Meg blinked. He *agreed* with her?

He set down his fork and leaned forward, closing the space between them until she felt that familiar tingle of excitement. "You have an open and innovative mind, my lady. The general is the same. You look to improve, and you are not afraid of new ideas. Things were not so . . . so forward thinking, as you say, when my father was Laird of Glen

Dhui. I tried to change his mind, but he would not listen to me. Sassenach foolishness, he called it."

Meg took a moment to grasp that he was not scoffing at her at all. He admired her! He was envious of her success when he himself had failed to affect any change with his own father. He was not Duncan Forbes; he was nothing like Duncan Forbes.

"I . . . Thank you," she said, a little breathlessly. "Unfortunately there are many like your father, who will not listen. Anything new is open to suspicion and superstition. I have heard that some of the men of the church are calling tea the devil's brew! I drink tea with my breakfast, and I believe in Edinburgh they take it at four in the afternoon, and make a party of it. Tea is very fashionable, and there is nothing wrong in it, that I can see. They said the same of coffee, when it first arrived in this country, but now no one thinks it anything other than a pleasant beverage. Perhaps your father would have come around in time. . . ."

His smile held bitterness. "I doubt it. In those days I was young and I told myself it dinna matter what my father said, that I would do as I wished, when it came my time to be Laird of Glen Dhui. Unfortunately, that time never came."

Meg set down her fork with a clatter. "I am sorry for your troubles, Captain Grant, I really am. But it is not *my* fault you lost Glen Dhui. I cannot feel guilty for something that is not my fault. And I *won't*!"

"I don't expect you to," he said, raising his dark brows. "I don't want you to. It was an explanation, not a plea for pity. Pity is the last thing I want from you, Lady Meg. Don't you know that yet?"

What did he mean? What was he saying? What was it

she could see in his eyes, looking so directly into hers. "Gregor—"

"Meg, I want—"

But whatever it was he wanted, she would have to wait to find out. He had stopped and was looking toward the door, and Meg herself was suddenly aware of the raised voices coming from the Great Hall. At that very moment they were lifted another notch, and she realized it was a man and a woman. Arguing.

Gregor jumped to his feet, spilling his wine across the table, and went to the door. Meg was not far behind, but when she made to move past him, he placed a large, warm hand on her shoulder.

"Stay behind me, Meg."

She might have laughed at his concern, or simply refused to obey, but she was stopped by the seriousness of his still, clear gaze. Meg was used to being in charge of her own life, she preferred it that way, and yet she found herself stepping back and allowing him to open the door.

The noise from the Great Hall drifted up the stairs, and they moved down, Gregor still in front, to find its source.

"Yer boots are dirty!"

Alison was standing in the middle of the high-ceilinged Great Hall, her hands on her plump hips, looking pointedly down at Malcolm Bain's feet. Malcolm was before her, his fair hair straggling around his shoulders, his expression dismayed. For all his large and tough bulk, at the moment he looked like a child.

"Well, they are, aren't they, ye canna deny it?"

"Och, I've been working, what do ye expect?" was his reply, as he cast his eyes to heaven.

"Then ye should have taken them off outside the door."

"If I did that, my feet would be cold."

"Better ye have cold feet than I have mud on my floor!"

"*Yer* floor!"

Gregor turned to look up at Meg on the step behind him, and his expression was bemused. Meg smiled; clearly her brave protector needed help in dealing with this particular situation.

"Malcolm! Alison!" Meg spoke loudly and authoritatively, brushing by Gregor and hurrying down the remaining stairs. Her voice rang out in the shadowy space.

The pair turned, startled, a little guilty.

"Enough," Meg went on, before either one could mount a counterattack. "I want no more of this. Malcolm, what are you doing here?"

Malcolm Bain stood stiffly, as if he were under attack. "I wanted to speak with Captain Grant, my lady."

Gregor came to put his arm about the other man's shoulders, leading him firmly toward the door, saying, "Then come outside, Malcolm, and we will speak there."

Meg waited until they had gone, then gave Alison a long, stern look. "You are making a fool of yourself."

Alison bristled. "I am not, my lady! I speak as I see fit."

"I think it is time you put the past in its place."

"I will never forget the past," Alison retorted in a low, thrumming voice. "*He* abandoned me."

"He had a duty to his laird."

"He had a duty to *me*!"

There was pain in the other woman's voice, a great deal of pain. Clearly Alison had loved Malcolm Bain, had expected to spend her life with him. Gently, Meg touched her hand. "He did, Alison. He did have a duty to you. But he made his choice. He cannot change what has been, and neither can you. You must put it behind you and move on. 'Tis the only way."

"Is it? Well, I want him to suffer as I suffered."

"Have you told him?"

Alison's eyes widened, and she didn't pretend to misunderstand the question. "Nooo! And I won't, and neither will anyone else, if they know what's good for them."

"Alison, you know that someone will tell him, eventually. Or he will simply realize the truth. They are very alike, you know, Malcolm and Angus. Wouldn't such a thing be better coming from you?"

"I dinna want him to know. Angus is *my* son!"

Meg spoke gently. "He's Malcolm's son too, and sooner or later Malcolm will discover it."

Alison shot her a look of mingled rage and fear, and bolted toward the kitchen.

Meg stood alone in the Great Hall.

Alison's child had already been born when Meg came to Glen Dhui. She had told Meg the father had died in the Rebellion, but gradually Meg had come to understand, through overheard remarks and chance snippets of chatter, that the father had been Alison's sweetheart, and that he had left Glen Dhui years ago.

Duncan would not speak of it, but it was obvious he believed his sister had been cruelly deserted, and his animosity toward Malcolm Bain had been made abundantly clear upon their first meeting in Clashennic. There was no hope of a cool head then, in that quarter—the Forbeses were renowned for their tempers.

Still, Meg hoped that something could be sorted out of the mess. It would have to be, if they were to live peacefully together once more. And yet it was doubtful any progress could be made, if Alison and Malcolm did nothing more than shout and argue.

Meg smiled wryly to herself. She was a fine one to give advice! She had not spoken to her own father since the evening before, when he had sent her from the room. How could she ever win him to her point of view, if she did not speak to him? It was time to go upstairs and sit down and put an end to this nonsense. Whatever had been said to Gregor, and Gregor had said to him, was something she had a right to know. Meg meant to make a determined attempt to discover exactly what was going on between them. . . .

In that moment she realized Gregor was standing in the shadows by the main door, watching her.

Tonight he had caught his hair back in its habitual black ribbon, the fair strands shining in the flare of a torch set in a sconce on the wall. His piercing eyes were hollows, and the hard planes of his face were etched in dark and light. In his old, faded kilt and brown jacket he looked like the ghost of some ancient Highlander, some handsome Grant chief, come to reclaim his home.

How long had he been there? She felt herself shiver at the idea of him observing her without her knowledge, of his gaze examining her, minutely, inch by inch, while she stood in the Great Hall in her green silk dress. Such a thought made her squirm with discomfort . . . and something else that was suspiciously like pleasure.

"Is Malcolm gone?" she asked abruptly, more to still her own discomfiting thoughts than to break the long silence between them.

"Aye." His voice echoed in the room, a whisper of sound. "Alison?"

"She, too." She smiled ruefully. "But I fear their battle is far from over."

"I think you are right, Meg."

He stepped forward, and now the gold in his hair caught the candlelight, the silver buttons of his jacket glinted against the dark cloth, and the red stones in the ancient-looking brooch that fastened his kilt at his shoulder gleamed.

"Are you still hungry?" he asked her in a quiet, deep voice.

Meg thought of their half-eaten meal. Whether because of Malcolm and Alison, or Gregor himself, there was a fluttering in her stomach now, an edginess, that would not let her eat. She did not want to eat.

"No, I am not hungry."

"Then will you walk with me? The night is fine and I have questions I wish to ask. And I feel . . . awkward in this place."

Awkward? Well, he probably did. She could not blame him for something that was perfectly natural. She had felt awkward herself, having him here. Outside they could be themselves, and the darkness would give her a certain sense of freedom that the candlelight denied her.

"I should go up and see my father," she began, even knowing she would say yes. The thought of walking with Gregor in the gardens at night was far too tempting for her to resist. Even her former resolution to be cool and distant was rapidly crumbling.

"Och, please? A verra little stroll, Meg."

Meg nodded, pretending to be reluctant, as she moved toward him. He held out his arm, and she laid her hand upon it, feeling the coarse stuff of his sleeve and the warmth of his flesh beneath. He bent his head close to hers, almost touching, and said, "I feel as if I had never left this place. It is like one drawing upon another, almost matching but not quite, the lines just a wee bit out of kilter."

"I understand, Captain Grant."

"Call me Gregor. I am not a Captain of dragoons now. I am . . . I am nothing much."

"I think the people of Glen Dhui would disagree with you."

"But as you reminded me so properly, they dinna know me, not anymore."

Best not to answer that, Meg thought. He had a way of filling her heart with the need to take him into her arms and hold him, to offer comfort, even though it was something he had told her he did not want.

They were outside, their shoes crunching on the gravel path that led to the herb garden set within its sheltering gray stone walls. Away down in the glen, lights flickered where people were going about their lives, and the smell of peat smoke was strong on the summer breeze. Gregor pushed open the wooden gate and they stepped through.

Meg drew a deep breath, trying to sort out the different aromas, the different plants, enjoying all those heady scents. Lavender, of course. It brushed her skirts, drifting about her, clearing her head. And roses, white and red, some of them long past their spring flowering, others abundant with blossom. And there was rosemary, fennel, thyme, honeysuckle and sweet lilies. Pale moths hovered over them, gorging themselves, and night insects buzzed. On the far side of the stone wall the burn rushed by, under the old bridge, and down the glen.

"This was overgrown in my day," Gregor told her, looking about.

"So it was when we came here. But I have always had an interest in gardening, so I set about repairing the damage and replanting what was old or dead. Shona comes here to replenish her stocks for her medicines."

There was a silence while they walked slowly between the beds, pausing by a round pond. "I have been thinking of the Duke of Abercauldy," she said quietly. "Should I write him a reply to his letter? I can tell him again that I will not marry him, but I warn you now he will dismiss it. He tells me I am full of foolish fears and doubts, and I must disregard them, just as he does. He will then set about persuading me just how happy we will be, *when* we are wed."

Gregor was watching her, and although she could not see all of his face properly, she felt as if she could. He would be frowning, looking down at her with that intensity that made her so uncomfortable and yet conveyed so clearly that, unlike the duke, he really was listening.

"He is determined to have you, then, Meg?" he murmured.

"I think he must be," her voice was a whisper.

He nodded. "Aye, the general said as much. Your father is suffering for what he did, Meg. He will not rest until all is made well again."

Meg turned her face away. "But how can it be? Oh, I know he suffers, and I am sorry for it. I have forgiven him. But how can it be?"

She felt his fingers on her cheek, and stiffened. His skin was rough and callused, and yet so gentle. His hand cupped her jaw, his thumb caressing back and forth as though he wanted to remember the feel of her. He bent his head and whispered in her ear.

"I can make it well again, Meg."

His breath was warm, and she shivered. He slid his fingers into her hair, dislodging a curl, twining it around and around his forefinger.

"You dinna have to do everything on your own, Meg."

And she couldn't think. When he stood this close to her, when he touched her, she couldn't think. She needed to escape, to be alone, to gather her thoughts. She needed . . .

His lips brushed her cheekbone, soft as a petal from one of her roses. Once, twice, and again, moving inexorably toward her lips. Meg gasped, and turned to face him, to . . . what? Tell him to stop? That was what she made herself believe, but as she opened her mouth to speak, his lips reached hers and, with a sigh, closed over them in the sweetest, most gentle kiss she had ever been given.

For Meg had been kissed before, many times. Sometimes she had kissed reluctantly, sometimes out of curiosity, sometimes because she wanted to be kissed. But never like this. There was something different about this kiss. Something she had never felt in all the embraces and kisses she had received from all the men who had come to secure her hand, and her inheritance, since she had grown to be of age. When Gregor Grant kissed her, it was as if she had been waiting all her life for his lips to find hers.

Her heart gave a great lurch. She leaned into him, into his arms as they reached to enfolded her. And she was there, held fast against his chest, his silver buttons pressing against her breasts, the lace at his cuffs tickling her skin.

His mouth was no longer soft. Any illusions of sweet gentleness had vanished, and he was kissing her with a rough and desperate intensity. For a moment he paused, taking time to trace the shape of her upper lip with his tongue, and then the shape of the bottom one. His mouth was hot and moist, as it closed again on hers, and it sent a spear of sensation straight down into her belly.

Her legs went to water. She felt as if she had drunk several drams of Cragan Dhui whiskey, directly from the still. Her fingers found his hair, held by the black ribbon, and she tugged upon it as if it would hold her upright. His mouth was hot on her throat now, in the hollow there, and he let it trail down to the gentle rise of her breasts.

"*Morvoren*," he murmured, the word unfamiliar to her but sounding very much like an endearment.

His ribbon came loose in her fingers, his hair falling forward, and she tangled her hands through it, enjoying the sensation. His mouth was still upon her, teasing, promising, making her wild for him to go further. And the spear of sensation in her belly had lodged between her legs.

With a gasp, Meg pulled away.

He did not let her go, instead giving her enough room to lean back from him but not break the contact entirely. She heard his breath, as hard and fast as hers, and wondered if his heart was beating as wildly.

From somewhere, she found a laugh. The same brittle laugh she had used on all those suitors who came to her door when she was younger, those men who had had an eye to her fortune and pretended they were drawn by her person. When she spoke it was in the voice she had always used on such occasions, the voice that was designed to make the suitor feel like a fool.

"Captain Grant, I can only think you have lost your mind."

He let her go. She took a couple of clumsy steps back,

away from him, out of danger, and felt the loss of him like a bereavement. Now he was a dark shape against the stars, big and angular with his wide shoulders, and his head tilted toward her.

"Mabbe I have," he said at last, his voice deep and somber. "Lost my mind, that is."

"Then you had better find it again before the morning," she advised him a little breathlessly. "I am no young lassie to be flattered with your kisses, you should know that. If you want a . . . that is, if you require some feminine company, then you'd better go and look for it elsewhere."

Gregor made a sound suspiciously like a snort. "I dinna want a trollop, if that's what you're asking. I had a strong need to kiss you, Meg. I find you desirable. I *like* you. 'Twas as simple as that."

But it wasn't simple, not at all. It was very, very complicated.

"I must go in," she said, sounding flustered. Where had the sophisticated lady gone? The woman who was going to hold herself distant? She had been sent into flight. "Good night, Captain Grant."

And Meg turned for safety, only noticing when it was too late that she still held his ribbon between her fingers.

Her footsteps hurried away, and the gate creaked shut. Gregor stood and looked into the darkness and wondered what on earth had possessed him. He had not meant to kiss her. He had not meant to frighten her or make her angry or wary of him. She was a virgin, that much was clear, but she was no young and frightened miss. She was a woman who had lived in the world and knew her own mind.

And he wanted her.

He had wanted her from the moment he saw her, in the Black Dog, when she had stood over him and demanded to know if he were drunk. He had fought it, told himself he was a fool, told himself he could not have her. And then— when he had stood watching her in the Great Hall, standing in her green dress with her hair afire, lost in her thoughts, her mouth sad, her eyes dreamy—he knew. The taste of her, the feel of her, had only heightened that knowledge. He wanted her, he had to have her, and he would do just about anything to achieve his aim.

Chapter 15

Meg tapped lightly on the general's door. She felt flushed and agitated after her encounter with Gregor Grant. Not at all the cool, calm woman she had planned on. Her lips were bruised and swollen from his; he had kissed her as she had never been kissed before.

I had a strong need to kiss you, Meg. I find you desirable. I like you. 'Twas as simple as that.

Had he meant what he said? How could she believe him when she knew there was nothing in her face or figure to attract such a man as this? She had known men like Gregor Grant before. Tough, handsome Highlanders who had no difficulty catching the eye of any woman who took their fancy. They rarely looked at her, and if they did it was with the thought of her father's land and money uppermost in their minds.

If he could have any woman he wanted, thought Meg, why choose her? Well, he would not, and there was an end to it.

Her father's call of "Enter" brought her into the room. The single candle tried hard to hold back the shadows, but even so, it was not a cheerful scene. The general sat silent, gazing into the darkness that was now his world. Guilty that she had taken so long to return, Meg came forward. The fact that he had hurt her should not make her react in like. He was her father, ill and old, and who knew how much longer they had together? Meg wished she was able to set aside her anger and wounded feelings, but she found it difficult. First the Duke of Abercauldy and now Gregor, they had both come between father and daughter.

"Father?"

His face lit up as he turned toward her. "Meg? Is that you at last? I thought you had sent me to Coventry."

"Well, if I did, you deserved it."

"No! I have only your happiness and safety in mind, Meg. You know that, and if you don't, then you should."

"Oh, Father . . ." He still didn't see that he had done wrong by her. He never would. He believed he had her best interests at heart and that she should sit quietly and accept his judgment. It was a pity Meg had never been the sort to either sit quietly or blindly accept her fate. She was bossy, she was a fighter, and she could no more be meek and mild than the sun could stop rising each morning over the glen.

"Alison told me that Gregor had the men drilling this morning?"

"He did," Meg agreed, glad to find neutral ground. Putting aside her fears and frustrations, she came to sit on the stool at his feet. "He certainly worked them long and hard, but not one complaint."

The general chuckled, slapping the arm of his chair. "I wish I could have seen it." Briefly, self-pity swamped him, but it was only for a moment. Next thing he was reaching out his hand toward her, folding her slim fingers in his gnarled ones.

"Have you spoken to Gregor Grant?"

He kissed me in the garden, Meg wanted to say. *And when his mouth pressed to mine, I wanted to wrap my arms around him, so tight, and never let go.* But she couldn't say that; how could she say that? Gregor was here to give them the benefit of his soldierly expertise, and to carry out her father's orders. Stand in her father's stead as the leader of his men. How Meg felt about him was a secondary matter.

"We ate supper together and made polite conversation, if that is what you mean."

Oh, more than that, much more than that . . .

The general smiled and cast her a look that was almost cunning. "You want to know what we spoke of last evening?"

"Yes."

"You are cross with me again, Meg. Aye, I know it. I am not quite as senile as you think me. But I have a solution to our troubles, and I want you to listen to me. Only promise me this: Don't speak until I am done, no matter how sorely you are tempted."

"You make it sound as if I will *want* to speak, Father."

His fingers squeezed hers, and his expression turned long-suffering. "Oh, you will, Daughter, you will."

Meg couldn't help but smile. "Very well, I will hold my tongue. Now, tell me."

For a moment there was silence as he gathered his thoughts. Meg waited, content to watch him, to soothe her uneasiness in the quiet of the room. Her lips still felt swollen from Gregor Grant's kisses, her skin felt raw and sensitive. He had made her feel as she had never felt before, he had made her think things she had never thought before. Want things she had never wanted.

It was frightening, and it was wonderful.

All these years she had held herself apart from her suitors, telling herself it was love or nothing. And now she was wondering whether love really mattered. If Gregor Grant could make her feel this strongly, then wasn't that enough?

"I think I have a way out of this mess, Meg."

Meg blinked away her thoughts, and looked up at him.

"A way in which you can be protected from Abercauldy—an escape from this marriage I have thrust upon you. If my plan succeeds, he will be unable to force you into a wedding with him, and you can remain here, at Glen Dhui. You want to stay here, don't you, Meg?"

"You know I do, Father. This is my home. It would break my heart to leave it."

"Very well." He took a breath and, leaning forward as if he could see her, smiled at his own cleverness. "Instead of marrying Abercauldy, I want you to marry Gregor Grant!"

For a moment Meg wondered if she had dreamed his words. Was it a dream? She looked about, but nothing had changed in the room. The peaceful air, the muted light of the candle, her father's expectant and smiling face. And then reality struck her hard—as if she had run into a stone wall—sending her reeling.

The general thought he had solved all of their problems—she could see the smug satisfaction in his expression. He wanted her to marry someone else, so that the duke could not have her, and at the same time he was soothing his own sense of justice and fair play. Because, if Meg married Gregor Grant, the boy who had saved his life all those years ago could at last return to his home.

Two birds with one stone, as the saying went. Brilliant.

The perfect, fairy-tale ending.

It was wonderful . . . or it would be, if it was not so utterly preposterous.

"Oh, Father," she said, not knowing whether to scream or cry. She pulled her hand from his, her fingers suddenly chilled by the contact. "Marry Gregor Grant? I cannot believe you are asking such a thing . . . that you think I will agree to marry *anyone* after the last . . . No, and no, and no! It is ridiculous, and how you can suggest such a thing is beyond me. Even *I*, who know you well, cannot believe you would even begin to imagine this is a solution to our problems!"

"Meg!" His voice was filled with irritation and pleading, the lines in his face deepening until he looked like the old man he was. "Just think for a moment, before you fly off in a miff! *Think*, girl! What else is there for you when I am dead? You are five and twenty, not a young lassie anymore. When I die, you will be alone here, and even if you are fortunate enough to rid yourself of Abercauldy, there will be other wolves at your door! They will hunt you down, and they will not be as easily persuaded as me, Meg. You need a strong man at your side. If you will not face the facts, then I must face them for you. You need someone to protect you—"

"I can protect myself, Father!"

"You can't, Meg! You are a strong woman, and I am proud of you, but you cannot survive against such men as these. They will hunt you down, and when they have you cornered, they will take what they want." His voice broke, and that he was so upset and genuine in his concerns only made the whole thing worse.

Meg's chest was tight; she didn't feel as if she could get enough air. Why would he not listen to her? Why would he not believe she was perfectly able to run her own life?

"Meg," he began again, shaking his head, and to her horror, she saw that his eyes were wet with tears. "You think I do this for Gregor, don't you? I admit it would give me pleasure to see the lad returned to Glen Dhui. He never followed the white cockade, 'twas his father who did that, and Gregor lost the estate through love and loyalty to his Jacobite father, when such should have won him high praise. Aye, he deserves to have his lands returned to him. But I am thinking of you. I need to know you are safe, Meg, before I die. *Think*, Meg! It is such a perfect answer, it is *right*. A Grant and a Mackintosh founding a dynasty at Glen Dhui. And most important of all, you would be safe. . . ."

Safe from everyone but Gregor Grant, Meg thought bleakly.

The appalling realization struck her that her father had already spoken of his plan to Gregor, and that Gregor had known all last night. He had known, and said nothing.

She replayed their moments together, until she came to the scene in the herb garden, and each word and each touch suddenly took on an entirely new meaning. What had seemed magical and special now had a darker significance. Had he been manipulating her? Laughing at her? All of Meg's feelings of inadequacy came to the fore, her sense of not being beautiful enough, of being pursued for her money alone. He could not possibly want to marry her, not really, so why had he held her so tight?

Glen Dhui.

Of course. Meg had learned already that he was mercenary, that he had little honor remaining. The answer was simple. His need for Glen Dhui was so great that he would do anything to get it back.

"What did Captain Grant say when you put this monstrous idea to him?" she asked, her voice trembling with emotion. "What did he say, Father?"

The general appeared puzzled. "He said yes. Of course he did. Gregor's no fool. But he made the condition that you agreed to it with your own mouth. Gregor can see that the offer is a good one, for both of you, Meg."

The breathless feeling was choking her. Meg stood up, walking to the other side of the room, and then back again. There didn't seem to be enough air in the room, and she pressed a hand to her chest.

"Father, I cannot . . . I cannot . . ."

"Meg, my dear daughter, calm yourself! If you have a dislike of Gregor I would not expect you to . . . we will think of something else."

The casement was open. Meg leaned upon it, thrusting her face into the cool evening air. She drew in a deep breath, and then another. Marry Gregor Grant?

The idea was preposterous.

Marry the former Laird of Glen Dhui, to protect herself from Abercauldy, to return to Gregor what he had lost twelve years ago?

It was . . .

Be Gregor Grant's wife and wake up with him every

morning? Have the child she had dreamed of only this afternoon, the child who would never be forced from his home by circumstance? Live out her life here, in the place she loved, with the man she . . .

Dear God, she was considering it.

She was actually considering it!

"Meg?" Her father sounded uncertain, unlike himself. Meg took another deep breath and turned to face him. He had stretched his hand out toward her, and now she came to take it. "Meg." He sighed.

"Have I done the wrong thing again? I thought only to . . . I wanted to help . . ."

Meg knelt by his chair and pressed his hand to her cheek. "I know. I know that's why you did it, Father. And I will think on it. I promise you, I will think on it before I make my decision."

He nodded. He looked very tired. Meg felt the familiar guilt, that her headstrong behavior had done this, her selfish desire for her own way. Why could she not be like other daughters, content to follow their fathers' advice, content to travel the path that was laid out for them, to marry men they didn't know and to live in their shadow? Why did she have to be different?

"Sleep now," she said gently. "I will send one of the servants up to help you to bed, Father. Do you want a hot posset? Shona has left one of her special powders for you to take to help you sleep."

He nodded wearily. "Aye, that would be very nice, Meg. I need to sleep. I have been thinking and thinking, trying to discover a way out of our maze of troubles. I do not think I have slept properly since Shona came to tell us the truth about Abercauldy's wife."

"Well, you can rest easy," Meg told him firmly. "It is up to me to decide what will be done now. You have done all you can, Father. Will you promise me you will sleep, and you will not worry?"

"Very well, Meg." He reached out and patted her face.

There was no doubt in Meg's mind that her father had acted with her interests at heart—he had found a strong man to protect her, now and when he was gone. He had solved all their problems to his own satisfaction.

It was a shame Meg could not rejoice.

Gregor climbed the staircase. He felt indescribably fatigued. His wound was only just healing, and the long day had taken its toll, but it wasn't only that.

Being here, being home, was battering at his defenses.

He hadn't realized it would be so difficult to keep aloof from the memories. They encircled him, surrounded him, demanded he pay heed to them, and filled his mind with the past. He had thought himself toughened, hardened, by his years away. He *was* tough, else he could not have survived, but the memories had a way of sliding under his barricades.

This staircase, for instance. He remembered, as a lad, running down here, the steps almost too big for his little legs. He remembered, when he was older, attempting to slide down the banister and almost coming to grief on the flagstone floor below. His mother had had hysterics, but his father had laughed.

"He's a braw lad!" he had declared. "A proper Grant!"

There would be no proper Grants here, not anymore. The hall felt empty, ghostly, as if he himself was the ghost. . . .

"Gregor?"

She was standing at the head of the stairs, her hand on the

newel post, her hair a brilliant halo in the light from the candle in the sconce on the wall behind her. He couldn't see her face—only the shape of her, the curves of her, against the candle glow.

He heard his own breath suck in, as every inch of him went on alert.

They stood a long moment, unmoving, she looking down and he up. And then she turned her face to the side, and the light shone on her cheeks and the glitter of tears.

"Meg? What is it? What's happened?"

She shook her head, holding out her hand to prevent him from touching her as he came halfway up the stairs toward her. "I have just spoken to my father, and he has told me what you discussed. I don't know whether to rage or weep."

Spoken to her father? Then she knew! And she was crying? It did not bode well for her answer. Gregor stood and waited, uncertainly, while she found a plain handkerchief in her sleeve and used it to mop at her wet face. She sniffed, and then gave a bitter, shaky laugh.

"Well, say something! I want to hear what you have to say, Gregor. My father says you are willing to participate in this . . . this *farce*. If that is so, then tell me why. Although I think I already know your reason."

Gregor could imagine her thoughts. He had made that road for her to follow, after all, with his request to be paid for returning to Glen Dhui. She would think he was marrying her to get his home back again, and yes, that was part of it. But there was more. He wanted her. He wanted her as he had never wanted another woman in all his life, and the thought of giving her up, or of someone else having her, was almost more than he could bear.

Gregor's fingers twitched, longing to touch her. To rest

his hand on the curve of her shoulder, to brush his fingers against her lips, to smooth back the wild tangle of her hair. But he was aware she would not like that. She did not want his touch. She could hardly stand to look at him! Gregor knew he would not win her through emotional pleas, through appeals to her heart and her desire, so he kept his hands to himself. He made his voice sensible and calm, and appealed to her sense of what was practical.

"I am willing, aye. If you stand back, Meg, and view this thing pragmatically, you will see that it is a way to stop the duke from forcing a marriage upon you that you dinna want under any circumstances. And I think you will agree that he is far more dangerous than I can ever be."

Meg lifted her nose a notch, as if she disagreed with him, but she said nothing. She was listening, and Gregor meant to make the most of it.

"To marry me is to put you beyond Abercauldy's reach, and mabbe that will be enough to stop him. If it is not, then we are no worse off than we were before. He will still demand some sort of recompense, and perhaps he will come to try and take what is not his. But, if he is inclined to act in that way, then he was likely to have done so, whatever we did to try and stop him. And I will be here to lead the men, to rouse them up as Laird of Glen Dhui, with my Lady at my side. I do not mean to take over, Meg. I am not here to usurp your place, or your father's . . ."

"Are you not?" She was still half turned from him, and he could only see her profile, but it did not look as if she were softening to his arguments. "I am more than capable of running the estate, of seeing to the people, of taking care of them."

"And leading them into battle, Meg? Fighting at their

side? Wielding a claymore at the enemy? Do ye think ye can do that, and if ye did, do ye think the likes of Duncan Forbes would follow ye?" His accent had broadened in his passion, but he hardly noticed. He was fighting to win more than a simple argument here.

Meg sighed. "You and my father have put me into a corner."

"Mabbe it's a corner that was there all along, you have just been avoiding it. I can see that your father has his own reasons for wanting you to marry me, Meg, but that need not sway you. There are others who would be just as willing to be your groom. I know for a fact that old Jamie Farquharson is on the lookout for a new wife."

She turned and looked at him, her eyes agleam in the candlelight. "You are joking?"

His mouth quirked up despite his intention to be serious. "Aye."

She took a breath, put her hand to her mouth to hide the fact she was smiling, then dropped it again. She looked tired and beaten, and Gregor didn't like that at all.

"So you have said yes to my father's proposal?"

"Aye, I have, but only if you agree to it."

"I can see your reasoning," she went on, smoothing her skirts meticulously, inspecting the cloth so that she did not have to look at him. "You want Glen Dhui, and in this way you can have it. A painless exchange of land ownership. No fighting, no bloodshed. A stroke of the pen, and you are laird again. And my father will be happy. This eases his conscience, and he is fond of you. You are like the son he never had. So, you can be the Laird of Glen Dhui once more. All sewn up very neatly, all the loose threads tied off. Everyone will be happy."

"You, too, Meg. You will be safe from Abercauldy, and if he decides to fight, then I will protect you. That is part of the bargain, and I will honor it, I will fight for you, be in no doubt."

"Do you really think that is all that concerns me?" she murmured, smoothing, stroking the cloth of her skirt. "How can I trust you, or anything you say? Can you not see that everything is open to question, now that I know your true aim?"

"My true aim?"

"To have Glen Dhui back. All your words, all your . . . your kisses. You are no different from the others, Captain Grant."

Ah, so her sensibilities were hurt. She believed he had attempted to seduce her for his own ends. He remembered how she had spoken once of the suitors who had been making the journey to her door since she came of age. They had swarmed about her money, playing at love. No wonder she was suspicious. No wonder she found it almost impossible to believe that any man could want her for herself. That any man could see past her father's money to the woman that was Meg Mackintosh.

And she believed him no better than those other men. He read it in her tense shoulders. She thought him a predatory creature who kissed her for no other reason than to gain her trust, and manipulate her to his own ends.

Her pain reached out to him. All his chivalrous and heroic instincts rose up, drowning out what caution was left.

"Tell your father that I will sign a document denying myself Glen Dhui. The estate is yours, Meg. If I marry you, the land stays with you."

He blurted the words out. Even as he spoke them he was

wondering at himself. Was he mad? Glen Dhui was *his*, it belonged to *him*. How could he give away all that should be his, just to soothe Meg's feelings?

At least he had made her look up.

Shock caused her freckles to stand out on her white face, and her lips parted to show that enchanting gap between her teeth. In another moment she had masked it, her pale eyes full of a fierce concentration, as if she were trying very hard not to let him see inside.

"The people would still believe you their laird, whatever documents you signed."

"But you and I would know the truth, Meg," he insisted. "Isna that what counts?"

He had her. He could see the wavering in her eyes now, the confusion. She had never expected him to do this. How could she, when he had not expected it himself? What was it about him, Gregor wondered bitterly, that he could not resist playing the hero? It seemed he would do, say anything to turn a quivering feminine lip into a smile, and to dry a woman's tears. But this wasn't just any woman—it was Meg, and she was special.

Meg had turned away. She stood a moment, as if gathering her thoughts. "I must think," she whispered shakily. "This isn't fair. You must give me time to think."

Gregor bowed. "Of course, my lady."

Before he had even finished the courtly movement, Meg was fleeing along the upper corridor. Her door slammed after her.

Gregor stood alone. What had he done? Malcolm Bain, if he knew, would call him every kind of fool. He had played the part of the bloody hero. *Again.* Into the silence of the house crept the soft sound of a woman weeping.

Meg.

Gregor groaned and covered his face with his hands. He had meant to reassure her, and instead he had made it worse. Suddenly it mattered very much that Meg trust him, that Meg believe in him, that she want him.

As much as he wanted her.

Chapter 16

⟨~⟩◯◯⟨~⟩

This morning Meg rose early, as she had risen early for the last three mornings. She had spent hours tossing and turning, but so she had tossed and turned for the last three nights. For days now, she had locked herself away in her room, while the house tiptoed about her and Gregor Grant drilled his men. She felt like an animal in a snare, and this morning she wanted to be free.

Quickly Meg dressed in her usual riding outfit of trews and jacket and, ordering her mare saddled, set out at a wild gallop down the glen.

For a time she hardly noticed what she was doing. Her mind and heart were so full. But gradually the sensation of the wind tangling her long hair, the sting of it against her cheeks, the feel of the mare beneath her, began to overcome her tired confusion. Her thoughts cleared, ordered themselves. When finally she drew up at the edge of Loch Dhui, a narrow and long body of water set between high hills to the south, Meg was ready at last to properly consider her position.

The fact that she thought she had anything to consider at all told its own story. When her father had put the Duke of Abercauldy before her as a possible bridegroom, Meg had rebelled instantly, refusing even to contemplate him. This time it was Gregor who stood before her, and instead of ranting and raving, here she was, staring into the black waters of the loch, reviewing his case as if she were seriously thinking of marrying him.

And so she was! Meg admitted it to herself. She was seriously contemplating Gregor, but *why*, that was the question. Why had she been brought to this point, when the thought of Abercauldy had given her hysterics?

His kisses. The way in which he held her. The heat of his mouth on her skin. He had made her heart beat faster, as if she were more alive than she had ever been. For the first time since she was a naïve young girl, who had yet to be taught the hard lesson that her handsome suitor was wooing her not for herself but for her property, Meg felt the urge to throw aside caution. Her skin tingled, her blood stirred, everything that made her a woman cried out to him. . . .

And there was her big difficulty.

Whatever Gregor's real motives, he held a physical attraction for her she simply could not deny. Meg was aware that, clever and practical as she was, she had never really had a passionate love. She had realized early on that the men arriving at her door all had their eye on her inheritance and not her person, and so she had kept her feelings locked away. She had not allowed herself to engage them, certainly not allowed herself the possibility of being hurt by falling in love with any of them.

Only the dream of the young Gregor had stolen her heart, and he hadn't been real. Maybe that was why she had allowed herself that one indulgence, because it *was* a figment of her imagination. A pretend passion, a safe love.

The real Gregor was very different.

She should have found him as unattractive as the rest, and yet he had been the one to crack her hard, protective shell. He did indeed make her feel as she had never felt before, as if there were new directions her life could take, that the things she had only previously experienced in dreams might actually be possible in real life.

He is only wooing you because he wants Glen Dhui. The voice was coldly insistent, but Meg shook her head. "Then why did he say he would sign away his rights to the glen?" she asked aloud, her voice a little wild. "Why do that, if all he wants from me is Glen Dhui?"

Meg could speculate as to the answer. Was it simply enough for him to live here? To be here? Or did he hope to persuade her to negate such a document later on? Did he think that he could work on her, make her so besotted with him that she would eventually change her mind?

An osprey flew above the loch, floating on air currents, a dark shadow against the blue of the sky. Meg watched it dip and soar, wishing she could so easily escape her own problems. She had heard that some birds mated for life, remaining together till one of them died. Did they concern themselves with such things as land and property, and trying to guess at each other's thoughts, when the mere fact of survival was difficult enough?

The stark truth was that Gregor had promised to protect her.

In these uncertain times, in this dangerous place, it was more than many brides were promised by their husbands-to-be.

Meg slid down from the mare's back, her boots crunching on the smooth, brown stones. She twisted the reins around a convenient fallen tree branch that had been washed up on the shore, and walked to the water's edge, gazing out over the loch. Wild duck floated on the glassy surface, keeping a wary eye on her. Glen Dhui dozed beneath the summer sun, looking perfectly peaceful, as if nothing bad could ever happen here.

The general had asked her if she wanted to stay, to live in Glen Dhui all her life. Of course she did! But Meg knew many women did not have that option. They wed, and they moved away. So it would have been with Abercauldy. And yet if she wed Gregor, she would remain in Glen Dhui. Nothing would change; it could all go on as before.

Of course it would change! she told herself impatiently. She would be his wife, and he would always be there. He would be a part of the glen, and of her, just as she would be a part of him. Things *must* change, if she wed Gregor.

You could marry him in name only. A marriage of convenience! What of that?

In name only, when her body heated and hummed whenever he was close? Suddenly, standing here alone on the loch's edge, Meg knew it was important to be honest with herself. Even if she kept her own counsel with her father and Gregor, she must not keep the truth from herself.

She wanted him.

And if he was to be believed—and she wasn't at all certain about that!—he wanted her. Her heart beat harder in her chest, and caused an ache that refused to go away. Meg knew that she would find it very difficult to go through with such a proposition as a marriage in name only.

Besides, if she wed, she wanted a child. Children were important. There were many women who gained solace in their marriages from their children; children balanced the books against unhappiness.

And what if you don't marry him? What then?

Meg stooped and picked up a smooth pebble, throwing it far out across the still water. The wild ducks took fright and flapped away, their wings beating against the cloudless blue sky.

"Life would go on." Meg answered her own question. If Abercauldy did not insist upon marrying her—and she had no intention of allowing him to win—then she would go on as before. The Lady of Glen Dhui. Years would pass, and she would have her small victories, overcoming the prejudice of men like Duncan Forbes, helping her people to carry on with their difficult and precarious lives. She would grow older, keeping her own company—but solitude had never been a concern to her. She would simply be happy remembering her achievements and being loved by her people.

That was how she had always imagined it to be, for how likely was it that she would find love at her age? No, she had thought she would grow old at Glen Dhui, content and at peace with her decision to be alone.

Except now, Meg realized with dismay, she no longer felt satisfied with that version of her future. *They* had spoiled it for her, the general and Gregor. They had put thoughts and hopes into her mind that had not been there before. They had allowed her to dream of what may be. She wanted more, and now she could not be satisfied with less. Now it would be twice as difficult to go back to being the solitary Meg Mackintosh she had been.

"And what if you *do* wed him?" she asked herself softly, gazing into the cold, dark water. "What if you wed him and then turn out to be miserable with him?"

Not a pleasant prospect, perhaps, but suddenly, *not* to wed him—not to take the risk—seemed a far worse option. Cautious Meg wondered how she had come to such a pass as this, to be willing to take such a chance, such a leap. For once she did make that leap, there would be no turning back. Not even if she wished to. . . .

Meg had walked back to her tethered mare, when the voice called out to her, echoing over the water. She saw the riders fast approaching from the south, galloping along the side of the loch. They had come upon her so swiftly and quietly, she had been unaware. Or maybe, dangerously, she had simply been too enmeshed in her own thoughts to notice their arrival.

It was then, standing at the edge of the water, quite alone, that suddenly Meg realized how isolated she was. And remembered that Glen Dhui was no longer safe, not since the Duke of Abercauldy had turned his cold and acquisitive gaze in her direction. She could not ride out alone as she used to. She should have brought a manservant or two with her, to watch over her, and if she had been thinking clearly, if she had been thinking at all, then she would have done so.

Now it was too late. Even if she had set off down the glen for home, they would have overtaken her. Nothing to do but stand and wait.

They wore white. All white, as did the Duke of Abercauldy's men. Nervously, her mind registered the fact that she was about to be surrounded by the duke's soldiers.

"Lady Margaret!"

She recognized that voice. Turning her head she stared up at the Duke of Abercauldy's favorite servant. Lorenzo wore all black, a startling contrast to the other men, but Lorenzo was the sort who liked to be noticed.

And feared.

According to Lorenzo he had been born in Italy, to a rich and aristocratic family fallen on hard times who sold him to a wealthy Englishman. Through various cunning ploys—according to Lorenzo—he had found his way into the duke's service. Meg wasn't sure how much of the story to believe, and her father insisted there was a hint of Glasgow in Lorenzo's Italian. But the Duke of Abercauldy found him amusing and held him high in his estimation, so much so that sometimes Meg thought he treated him more like a friend than someone paid to serve him. And Lorenzo served him slavishly.

With an effort, Meg stilled the fear in her heart and made her voice calm. "Lorenzo, you are far from home."

The other riders had drawn up at a distance, but Lorenzo came close, gazing down at her with the smile that never quite reached his doe-brown eyes. His eyes flicked scornfully over her windblown hair and man's attire, as if she were beneath his contempt. He certainly thought her beneath the contempt of a man like the duke. Lorenzo's insolent manner spoke the words for him, words that he did not need to utter aloud.

"We are on a mission for His Grace."

Meg smiled back and waited, for it was clear that Lorenzo was big with some news. She knew him well enough to know he would not be able to keep it to himself.

Lorenzo was a gossip, sometimes amusing but usually malicious. He used his tongue as other men used their swords, to wound and inflict pain.

"As we passed south of the loch we stopped at the croft of Fiona MacGregor, my lady. She told us that you have a guest at Glen Dhui Castle, a man who used to be the laird before he went out for the Jacobite James Stuart. It seemed so strange, I hardly knew whether to believe her. Why would General Mackintosh offer his hospitality to a traitor? Lah, 'tis beyond *my* comprehension, and I don't know what His Grace will say."

Meg spoke pleasantly, trying not to grit her teeth. "I do not know if it is either the duke's or your business, but if you mean Captain Grant, then, yes, he is here. He and the general are old friends."

"Old friends?"

Meg smiled.

Lorenzo's smile back was just as false as hers. "Fiona MacGregor says he is young. Young and very handsome, she says. A man to turn the head of any woman, no matter how discerning. And we all know how very discerning *you* are, my lady."

Meg frowned. "Fiona MacGregor is so old that any man under half a century is young to her, Lorenzo. Have you a message for me from your master? Is that why you are here? If so, please deliver it and be done."

Lorenzo bowed very slightly, giving the impression that he only did so because good manners meant he was obliged to. "His Grace says you are yet to answer his last letter, Lady Margaret. He is in need of a date for your wedding. He has great plans, you know. A fantastical celebration. His

Grace works day and night to make this wedding something that will be remembered in the Highlands for many years to come. An occasion!"

Despite the sun and the fine day, Meg felt completely chilled. Suddenly it seemed remarkably foolish of her to be dallying over a proposal from Gregor Grant when the implacable Duke of Abercauldy believed her to be his.

"I have spoken to His Grace, Lorenzo, and he knows my thoughts on the matter of our wedding." Meg's voice sounded strained.

Lorenzo waved a hand dismissively, in a manner very reminiscent of the duke himself. "Ah, you play games with him, my lady. He understands that; it is what ladies do to tease and make the chase more enjoyable. But now the time for games is past, and His Grace *must* have a date."

"I do not have a date," Meg said stubbornly, her eyes fixed on his.

"You do not have a date." Lorenzo sighed dramatically. "Then I will tell him you will decide on one very soon, my lady. He is impatient. Such plans he has! Do you think this Captain Grant will come to your wedding?"

The question startled her, and the look that accompanied it was sly and knowing. Meg moved closer to her mare, running the reins through her fingers as she considered her answer. Even though she had no intention of marrying Abercauldy, it was better he did not see Gregor as a threat. "I do not know. He may be gone by then. In fact I am certain he will be. How many people does His Grace mean to have at this wedding?"

"Five at last count, my lady."

"Five?" Meg laughed.

"Five hundred."

If Meg had been chilled before, she was frozen now. Her fingers and toes were icy and her skin rose in goose flesh. Five hundred! It was an enormous number of guests. Of course Lorenzo might be telling lies, but she did not think so. His words had the shocking ring of truth. This was worse than she had thought, far worse, for how could Abercauldy back down without losing face, if he was inviting so many guests to a wedding that would never happen?

"You must feel privileged to have stirred such powerful emotions in the bosom of such a great man," Lorenzo murmured, dripping with insincerity.

"You cannot possibly guess my feelings on the matter."

Lorenzo bowed again, but his smirk told her he was pleased with his troublemaking. "I am instructed to deliver my message to your *father*, my lady. It is for him alone."

"Then give it to me and I will be sure he gets it."

Lorenzo shook his head in mock playfulness. "No, no, Lady Margaret, I have my orders. Will you ride with us to Glen Dhui Castle?"

"No!" Her anger betrayed her, and Meg swallowed it down. "No, I . . . I have something more to do first."

"Then I bid you adieu. Lady." Yet another bow, another false smile, and Lorenzo was gone, waving cheerfully at the others to follow him.

Meg stood and watched them go—a thin white spear with a dark tip, heading down the green glen. Her stomach fluttered. She had fooled herself into believing that Abercauldy would release her, that he would give up. Now she must face the fact that that was most unlikely to ever happen. He wanted her; he meant to have her. And nothing she had said so far, no argument she had come up with, had had any effect upon changing his mind or his plans for their future together.

And now he would hear about Gregor—Lorenzo would make certain of that. Had she given herself away? Had he seen by her demeanour that she was enamored of this man? She did not think so, but Lorenzo had sharp eyes. Meg climbed upon her mare, using the tree branch as a mounting block, and slowly turned her head for home. She had lied to Lorenzo, she had nothing else to do, but she had had no intention of riding with him and being subjected to more of his stinging comments.

He was false and sly, he was a mountebank, but such men were often weak. Did that make them any less dangerous? Like a slender snake, Lorenzo lay in the shadows, ready to strike when one least expected it. Together, Lorenzo and Abercauldy made a formidable enemy. How could Meg continue to live peacefully here in Glen Dhui if she did not agree to Abercauldy's demands?

"So how will I escape him?" she whispered to herself. "How will I rid myself of this menace?"

But she already knew the answer. There was only one way that she could be free from Abercauldy, and that was to bind herself to another.

To give up her own freedom, and marry Gregor Grant.

Glen Dhui Castle looked peaceful, and apart from the men in white clothing waiting with their horses, nothing might have been different. Lorenzo had gone in alone then, Meg thought, to deliver whatever message he had for the general. Another veiled threat, probably. Another of the duke's demands to make a sick, old man even more frantic for his daughter's safety than he already was.

If she had not hated Abercauldy for her own sake, then Meg could readily have hated him for what he was doing to her father.

At the stables, Meg dismounted and stood, stroking the mare's nose, making much of her before the groom led her away. She had no other option but to dawdle reluctantly while she headed for the castle.

The Great Hall was empty, and cold even during the day. The grim antique weapons fixed to the walls reminded her that the Grants were used to fighting, to holding on to what was theirs. That knowledge was somehow comforting, she thought, as she moved toward the stairs. Lorenzo was probably still with her father, his slim, black-clothed figure quivering with malice. The general could hold his own with Lorenzo, but even he would grow weary of the Italian. It was time she put an end to his unwelcome visit.

Meg placed her booted foot on the first step, and looked up, straight at Gregor Grant.

He was descending, and his face was thoughtful. Not quite the taciturn Captain Grant, but something close. He saw her a moment after she saw him, and stopped. They stayed, gazing at each other in a reversal of their places of the other night. He seemed bigger, stronger, in his old faded kilt and worn linen shirt. His hair was tied back—Meg remembered she still had his black ribbon in her room—and he was freshly shaved.

His dark brows came down. "Meg. You look . . . What is it?"

"I was out riding."

His mouth quirked up at one corner. "I can see that."

Suddenly, like sinking into a warm bath, Meg felt a tremendous sense of relief. Her mind had been made up for her, and she would do it. She would! It was the right and proper thing to do. And beyond that, it was what she *wanted* to do.

But first he must be warned. Meg could no longer pretend that what she was about to embark upon was not without its dangers. To herself. To her father.

And to Gregor Grant.

"Lorenzo is here," she said, her voice trembling.

"Abercauldy's Italian servant? Aye, I know." He was watching her intently, as if he were trying to make her out. "He said he had a message for the general."

"He has already heard about you from someone in the glen. I do not trust him, Gregor. He will carry news of you back to Abercauldy."

Gregor frowned, and with a measured tread descended the last few steps to stand before her. "Is there anything wrong in that?"

"I told him you were visiting my father, but . . ." She bit her lip and shook her head. "He has seen you. He will describe you to Abercauldy. He will let him believe the worst—Lorenzo enjoys making mischief. He hates me. He doesn't believe me good enough for his master."

Gregor appeared to sort through this. "The man is a fool." His dark brows rose suddenly. "Why will he believe the worst, simply through a description of me?"

Meg gave him a wry smile, and moved closer, she couldn't help it. Apart from the feel of his warmth in the big, cold room, there was something that drew her to him, and for a moment she gave up on resisting it. "If you did not know it already, you are too handsome, Gregor," she said boldly. "He will think you have swept me off my feet. He will demand I wed him at once."

Momentarily, Gregor looked taken aback. A faint flush colored his thin cheeks. Didn't he really know how handsome he was? Didn't he realize how women must covet him? Or did the truth annoy him, rather than puff him up with pride?

"You aren't such a fool, Meg, as to be swept off your feet by me, or anyone else," he answered her crossly. "Are you?" he added, uncertainty creasing his brow.

Meg had wondered that herself, but she wasn't about to let him know how much he affected her.

Gregor's face had cleared, and he took her hand in his, his fingers closing hard. "If he will think that, if that is so, then we must act at once! We must wed as soon as possible, Meg. If Abercauldy is as determined as you say, and he discovers our plans, he will move to stop us. We cannot risk that."

That was true, Meg knew it was true.

She took a deep breath. "Gregor . . . I do not think you realize how much danger you will be placing yourself in by marrying me. No, listen! If you . . . if we wed, then it is possible Abercauldy will see you as an object in his path, that he will seek to remove you. Destroy you. If he has murdered before, then it will hardly matter to him."

Gregor's smile grew irritatingly smug, even a little patronizing. "I am not afraid of the Duke of Abercauldy. Dinna let that influence your decision, Meg. I have survived worse than him. But whatever your decision is, you must make it verra soon."

Meg knew she was in danger and her choices were limited. She could face Abercauldy alone, or she could wed Gregor and they could face him together. For three days she had been agonizing over her decision, and now it was simple.

"I will keep you safe, Meg," Gregor's voice was soft and low. He had moved closer, his chest brushing her shoulder, his breath in her hair. "I will protect you. That is part of my vow, and be in no doubt, I will honor it."

They were words she had wanted to hear, and yet they were all about honor and protection. There was nothing about holding her, kissing her, taking her to his bed. Meg's face flamed at her own thoughts, and the sudden realization that maybe Gregor did not want her in that way. Why should he? She was plain, tart-tongued Meg Mackintosh. Why should he desire her? How humiliating, if he were to feel obliged to bed her!

The words spilled from her lips.

"I . . . A marriage does not mean we must share other than our vows. It could be in name only. We are near enough to strangers, after all. I do not mind if . . ."

His amber eyes stared into hers, and then he shook his head slightly, as though clearing it. "We are no more strangers than many other husbands and wives when they first wed. And you forget, Meg, if a marriage is not properly done, it can be turned aside. Do you want that?"

She gazed up into his face, trying to read him.

It was impossible.

"What are you saying?" she asked in a low voice. "That you think it would be wiser to . . . to consummate it? That it is in our best interests to do so?" Her breath was quick and fast, but she controlled it. Was this his reasoning? That they must sleep in the same bed to make their union legal? Was that all that mattered to him?

"Aye, it would be sensible. Don't you agree?"

Sensible.

His amber eyes were still searching hers, as if he sought

to read something in them that wasn't there. Meg closed her own eyes a moment, trying to gather her thoughts. What had she wanted? A passionate avowal of lust and desire? She was a fool, and thus she was bound to be disappointed. This was a business arrangement between two strangers, not a love match. As Gregor had said, *sensible* . . .

"Meg?" His voice had an edge to it. And suddenly his hand closed on her arm, and her eyes opened, finding his face very close to hers. His breath brushed her skin like a caress.

Impatience tightened his lips and made a frowning crease between his brows. "Och, if you marry me, Meg, then I want all of you! I dinna do things by half measures!"

Well, that was plain enough! And somehow comforting, even if it wasn't the speech she had dreamed of since she was a girl. Meg nodded, once, then twice. "Very well then, very well. I will wed you, Gregor. But you must be laird in fact as well as name. You must have the authority of Glen Dhui behind any orders you give. In such circumstances I cannot hold Glen Dhui alone. We will hold it together."

She had made that decision on her ride home. As much as his rejection of his rights as laird had pleased her and shocked her, she could not allow him to have his way. If he was to fight for her and Glen Dhui, maybe give his life, then he deserved to be laird in fact as well as name.

He was watching her, gauging her, and then he too nodded his head. "Verra well, Meg, it will be as you say. We will hold Glen Dhui together. The Grants and the Mackintoshes, there's a combination to strike fear into the hearts of our enemies! Abercauldy won't stand a chance against us."

So easy, Meg thought. After all, it was such a simple thing. And if she were not quite as ecstatically happy as she had hoped to be at this moment in her life, if it had not gone quite as she had always dreamed, then she must learn to live with disappointment.

"So it is yes, Meg?"

Meg managed a serious little smile. "It is yes. Yes, I will wed you, Gregor, and it will be as you say. I will tell my father when Lorenzo is gone and—"

"I am finished with your father, my lady."

The voice came from above them.

They looked up.

Meg was shocked to see that thin, smiling face at the head of the stairs. *Lorenzo.* He was standing, hidden in the shadows, spying on them. It was impossible to know how much he had heard, or whether it had been enough to give their secret away, but Meg was quite certain of one thing. Lorenzo would make whatever mischief with Abercauldy it was in his power to make.

Chapter 17

There above them on the stairs, Lorenzo smiled down,
like the black devil he was. Meg had stiffened her
shoulders, preparing to bluff it out, but Gregor spoke first,
his voice calm and commanding, as befitted a Captain of
dragoons. The moment was a dangerous one, and he did not
intend to relinquish control to this smirking assassin.

"Signor Lorenzo. Are you done already?"

Lorenzo came down the stairs to join them, stopping a
couple of steps above, so that he would not have to look up
at the taller Gregor. Lorenzo was observing him, but Gregor
was secure in the knowledge that Lorenzo could not read
his face. Gregor had long ago learned to hide his feelings
from his enemies, and he had known from the first moment
he saw him that Lorenzo was his enemy.

"My message was brief and to the point."

Meg frowned. "You have not upset my father?"

Lorenzo bowed with pretend concern, playing her like

the master he was. "Of course not, my lady. Why should I do such a thing to a man who will soon be my master's father-by-marriage? Or . . . perhaps not?" Lorenzo gave his famous smirk.

Meg met Gregor's eyes, a look that spoke of caution and doubt and fear, all the things she could not say to him aloud. He read her easily, and felt a burning anger at the sudden turn of events. The man before them threatened all he had worked for, all he had just believed he had won.

Meg had agreed to wed him, agreed to be his wife in fact as well as name. Gregor wasn't quite certain of her reasons, other than that she needed his help in the matter of Abercauldy, but he intended to make sure that before too long she forgot those practical considerations. He had had enough women to know he enjoyed them, and they enjoyed him. He was arrogant enough to think that Meg would find what they did in bed similarly enjoyable.

And this grinning creature before him was not about to ruin his one chance for a real and proper life.

"He knows," he said quietly to Meg, not taking his eyes from Lorenzo.

Lorenzo gave a startled laugh, but he was too sure of himself, he was enjoying his moment too much, to play games. "My hearing is acute," he agreed. "And even if it were not, my eyes see very well. My lady gazes at you as if she would ravish you entirely, Captain. A woman like her is not worthy of His Grace, and so I will tell him when I return to—"

"I don't think so, lad," Gregor interrupted grimly.

Lorenzo's brown eyes flashed, and he struck a dramatic pose. "You would not dare to lay a hand on the Duke of Abercauldy's man!"

"Wouldn't I?" Gregor reached up and caught the front of the other man's shirt, tearing it a little, and pulled. Lorenzo came down the last remaining steps with a clumsy clatter and fell against him. He struggled like a fish on a hook, but he could not wriggle out of Gregor's powerful grip. When Lorenzo opened his mouth to shout, Gregor swiftly drew his dirk from its place on his belt, and held the blade against Lorenzo's throat.

Lorenzo went suddenly very still, in contrast his eyes rolling and wild in his white face.

"Gregor!" Meg gasped, and he noticed that her blue eyes shone with a mixture of horror and glee. The glee won. She was enjoying this. Lorenzo had taunted her for too long, and she would not be human if she was not keen to have her revenge on him.

"We will lock him up nice and safely," Gregor told her in a quiet, matter-of-fact voice.

"No, no, ye dinna understand! The duke canna be left alone, he needs me!" Lorenzo shrieked, his accent slipping into Scots. "He is . . . he is no' well, sometimes. Fools, fools, let me go!"

Gregor gave him a shake, and when he was still again, went on. "Send someone out to the duke's men to tell them Lorenzo-lad will be staying on for a day or two, and they're to go home without him."

Meg thought a moment. "I'll tell them I need Lorenzo to help me with preparations for the wedding."

"There will be no wedding!" Lorenzo hissed, spitting hate despite the sharp blade pressed to his throat.

Gregor leaned closer, his mouth very close to Lorenzo's ear. "Oh, but there will be a wedding," he whispered. "As soon as your men are on their way home, lad, we'll send for the priest. There will indeed be a wedding, but it just will not involve the duke. *I* am the fortunate man who is going to marry Lady Meg."

Lorenzo went rigid with fury, but this time, wisely, he said nothing. His gaze slid to Meg, piercing her with his contempt and loathing.

She ignored him. "I'll go and see to the men," she said, and hurried away to do Gregor's bidding. Gregor gave Lorenzo another little shake. "Come along, laddie," he said cheerfully. "I know a nice, warm cell that is just your size."

He didn't listen to Lorenzo's angry reply, a garble of Italian and Scottish swear words. He was thinking about Meg.

He was to be wed. Wed to Lady Meg Mackintosh, his redheaded termagant. She had said him yes, given him his answer right under the nose of the duke's servant! He might have laughed if the matter were not so serious.

Gregor had sworn he had had enough of playing the hero after Barbara Campbell, and here he was again, playing champion to a lady against the odds. And the odds this time were formidable.

But there was another reason why this time was different. Why, this time, he could not afford to lose.

This lady was *his* lady.

He felt it in his very bones. She was the one. And if he did not catch her now, and hold on to her, he would regret it all the rest of his days.

Duncan Forbes stood behind him. Malcolm Bain could *feel* him, feel the disapproval, like pin-prickles on his flesh. And he didn't need to turn and look to know what expression would be on the other man's face. A sneer. Because he considered Malcolm Bain had betrayed and deserted his sister, all those long years ago.

And desert her he had, but it had not been an easy choice, and if he were to make it again . . . Well, such things as that were best not thought of when it was too late to do anything about them, and Malcolm Bain was never one to be crippled by regrets. In his opinion, life was there to be lived, and one had to just get on with it.

Malcolm Bain and Gregor had chosen a core of twenty men, to train up to the standards Gregor considered necessary. The rest of their small army could manage well enough, given orders to follow, but these twenty men had to be precisely taught and well drilled. It was Malcolm Bain's job to see that they reached that standard in as short a time as possible.

Duncan had been watching, that sneer on his face, as if he could do better. He was almost as big a nuisance as the lad with the fair hair, who, whenever his work permitted him, hovered about on the edges of the training ground. As far as Malcolm Bain could tell, the lad was a servant in the big house, carrying wood and seeing to the horses. He was young, too young to grow a beard, but tall for his age, and with a keen eye. He was desperately keen to be one of the elite men Malcolm Bain was training, and desperately disappointed that he was too young.

Each of them was as big a nuisance as the other, thought Malcolm Bain, but at least the lad didn't sneer. He just looked sort of wistful.

If Gregor were here, he'd have gone over to the lad, made him smile, made his eyes light up with hero worship. But Malcolm Bain wasn't much good with children. He was used to shouting at tough, hardened old soldiers, and putting the fear of the devil into them to make them do as they were told. Children didn't take much to being bawled at.

Malcolm Bain wasn't certain what had gone on this morning—he had had other things on his mind—but after the duke's men had come and gone, several of the Glen Dhui men had been sent off to fetch the priest, with instructions to bring him back, willing or no, and as quickly as possible.

At first Malcolm Bain thought the old man—the general— must be ill, possibly close to death for there to be such urgency. But shortly thereafter, he had been passing through the Great Hall and seen the general himself, descending the stairs on Gregor's arm, looking as spry as a two-year-old.

It was Gregor who looked edgy. Pale and serious, his eyes shadowed. In Malcolm Bain's opinion he had hardly slept a wink the past few days. Something was certainly up. And Lady Meg, following along behind the two men and hovering like a demented moth, looked as if sleep had been eluding her, too.

"We will have a banquet!" General Mackintosh's voice had risen with excitement and echoed about them. "It's been a long time since we've had something to celebrate at Glen Dhui Castle!"

Malcolm Bain thought it was interesting, how Gregor and Meg had, after one brief glance, worked hard at avoiding each other's eyes. He suspected Gregor was playing the bloody hero again—dinna the man ever learn!

And now here was Duncan Forbes, creeping around behind him like the grim reaper himself. Suddenly it was all too much. Malcolm Bain spun around and strode quickly toward the other man. Taken by surprise, Duncan stumbled back a step, almost tripping himself over, before he regained his balance and stopped. The two men came face to face, barely an inch between them. Malcolm Bain was pleased to see Duncan's eyes flicker.

"Have ye no' something better to do, mon?" he asked in a low, tight voice. "If ye want to join in, then come and stand in line and I'll see what ye are made of. Otherwise, get lost."

"Ye are the one should get lost," Duncan growled, pushing against Malcolm's chest. "We dinna want ye here. Ye are no' welcome."

"Who are ye to say so, Duncan Forbes? Ye dinna own this place. I was asked to come here by Lady Meg, and I willna go until she tells me to!"

"Have ye no sense, mon! Go now, before ye ruin Alison's life entirely!"

There was passion and anger in his voice, and something more, that stopped Malcolm Bain when he may well have punched Duncan in the nose.

"What is it?" he asked quietly. "There is something. Tell me, Duncan, tell me!" And he caught Duncan by the front of his shirt and shook him the way a terrier shakes a rat.

"Let me go—"

"Tell me! Or I'll go to Alison now and ask her mysel'."

Duncan's eyes swiveled in his head.

"Be a mon and tell me to my face."

The dark Forbes eyes flashed, and Duncan pulled away from the other man's grip. "I'll tell ye then," he hissed. "Ye've ruined my sister, that's what ye've done! Left her without a backward glance when ye had promised to marry her. Left her with a child in her belly, and no one to care for her or it but her own kin. No wonder she hates ye, Malcolm Bain! No wonder!"

Malcolm Bain was stunned, shocked into stillness. He did not feel Duncan pull away, did not see him walk away, shaking his head in disgust. He was adrift in a sea of memories. Alison's smiling dark eyes and long hair, loose about her pale shoulders. Her body, soft and warm beneath his, and her cries of pleasure. He had loved her, thought to be forever with her, promised to care for her . . .

And instead he had left her.

Duncan was right. He had abandoned her, never thinking, never imagining she was carrying a child. *His* child. Why hadn't she told him? Why hadn't she got word to him? Didn't she know he would have come straight back to her? Nothing in this world would have stopped him, if he'd known.

And where was the child now? Was the boy here, at Glen Dhui? Perhaps he had seen him, smiled at him, spoken to him. All the while unknowing that this stranger was his son . . .

Malcolm Bain put his head in his hands and groaned.

He had thought to at least make amends with Alison, to try and patch over the past. Now he knew for certain he could never do that. She hated him, and she must have hated him all that time ago, if she had not told him. Aye, and her hate had only grown with each year since.

She had kept his son from him.

Anger built within him. It was like a peat fire, sullen, smoldering, but gradually getting hotter. Until the heart of it was as fiery a red as Lady Meg's hair.

* * *

"Will the priest be here tomorrow?"

The general's voice was querulous as he asked the question for the dozenth time. Meg glanced at Gregor, wondering if he felt as tense and anxious as she did. He certainly looked grim, but he had looked that way since this morning, since he had put Lorenzo in the cell with the iron grating set in the floor beneath the storeroom. In a way she was glad her father could not see their faces—he would not find much to celebrate if he could.

"The priest will come with all haste, father. He will surely be here tomorrow."

"He had better! I have my heart set on a banquet tomorrow evening. A wedding feast, Meg! Why has it taken you so long to find a husband, eh? Well, well, I won't complain. I am happy with your choice."

He held her hand in one of his, and with his other, reached out toward where he sensed Gregor stood. Gregor glanced questioningly at Meg and then clasped the general's hand in his. The old man smiled enigmatically and, with the air of one performing a wondrous act, pressed their two hands together.

Gregor hesitated, and then his fingers closed on hers, warm and strong. Meg knew she was blushing, looking anywhere but at Gregor, wishing herself anywhere but here. They were not an ordinary couple—this was not an ordinary situation. They were marrying because of desperate circumstances—why did her father have to pretend it was otherwise?

"Father, please!"

And yet she could not really begrudge him his joy. She supposed it was a great thing, to bring Gregor Grant home again, to have him back where he belonged, and to join her name to his. It was a cause for celebration. If it had been anyone else but herself playing one of the central roles, Meg would probably have been cheering along with the general.

"I am a happy man," her father went on a little petulantly. "Why should I not be? Out of catastrophe has come joy. I am glad Abercauldy set his sights upon you, Meg. Otherwise you would not have gone to fetch Gregor home. There, I have said it!"

"Father, do not say such things."

"General, I do not think—"

But it was no use, the general did not wish to hear their objections, or perhaps he could not. Gregor had begun to wonder whether the old man's health was failing more swiftly than Meg had believed. Over the past days, his conversation had been a mixture of rambling memories and complete fabrication. He had many lucid moments, yes, but there were just as many that were worryingly vague. It was clearly distressing for Meg, who had enough to contend with just now.

Gregor conquered the urge to take her in his arms and hold her. She would not thank him for it. Ever since their decision, she had withdrawn into her own world, within her own strong self-contained walls. Gregor knew that breaching them would not be an easy task.

"The priest must hurry," the general was saying now, nodding to himself, unheeding of the feelings of his daughter. "If Lorenzo were to carry word back to Abercauldy . . ."

"He will not," Gregor swiftly assured him, but his attention was still upon Meg. His words might be directed to the old man, but they were actually meant for Meg, to reassure Meg. "The deed will be done before the duke can prevent it.

And once we are wed, then all will be well." His fingers tightened on hers, trying to channel some of his own confidence into her.

She purposely did not look at him. Meg Mackintosh may be marrying him, he thought, but she did not trust him and she did not believe in him. She was a strong and independent woman, and she probably told herself that, apart from this minor problem with Abercauldy, she didn't actually need him.

Gregor wondered what he would have to do to win her over. She may be able to live in a world of her own devising, but he did not want to. Not anymore. He had learned since he met Meg that he did not want to be alone anymore. He wanted a wife with whom to share his future, someone to whom he was everything, and who was everything to him.

He had believed that Meg might be that woman. Now he was not so sure.

Meg had heard his words, but all she could think was: *It's a lie.* He could not know that all would be well. How could he know it? Meg was fairly sure that all would not be well at all! Lorenzo would be released, a whirlwind of fury, and if he did not whip the duke into a frenzy of revenge, then the duke's own pride would ensure he took action against them.

And yet, despite knowing all that, she was almost convinced by the overwhelming confidence and sincerity in his voice. As if he were mesmerizing her with the sheer force of his personality. *All will be well.* Why would he say that, when he must know it wasn't true? In his own life *all* had rarely been *well*!

For your sake, of course. Her inner voice mocked her obtuseness. *He wants to make you feel secure, he wants you to trust him.*

Gregor's grip on her fingers tightened, but she pulled

away. It was her father she should be thinking of now, her father she should be comforting. Her father, who seemed to grow frailer every day.

"I am sure Gregor is right," she told him now, striving for that same confident note in her voice as Gregor's. "Abercauldy will simply give up when he hears I have wed another. What man would wish to fight for a woman in such circumstances? A woman who showed him all too clearly that she didn't want him."

Gregor's mouth curled in a thin smile. He knew and she knew that the duke would be more likely than ever to fight. His pride would be dented, and his pride would demand he make some sort of effort to save face. Five hundred guests invited to a wedding that would not now take place! If he sent his men into Glen Dhui for some pillaging and burning, he could say he had made them sorry for causing him to look like a fool. But would that be enough? Or would he feel it necessary to take out his anger on the couple themselves? Would he believe it was necessary to actually *hurt* Gregor?

Kill Gregor?

Meg did not want to think of such things. She did not want to imagine them. Gregor dead and gone? Gregor taken from her before she had had a chance to live her life with him?

At the thought of Gregor hurt or dead, something within her twisted, like a breaking bone. Agony, pain, heartbreak. She caught her breath sharply, fighting it back. Now was not the time for emotion. She must be strong and calm. She must be the practical Lady of Glen Dhui, ready to lead her people.

"Meg?" But Gregor had heard her sharp breath and

moved closer, peering down into her face. "What is it? What's wrong?"

"I just thought of . . . I . . ." She bit her lip. To feel such pain, and for a man she hardly knew! As if she were dying herself at the very thought of losing him. How could she possibly explain that to Gregor, without seeming to be as vulnerable and confused as she felt? Meg did not want him to see that in her, she did not want him to know her weakness. He would use it against her, just as all those other men had searched her smile and her conversation for a chink, a crevice, a way inside her. So that they could strip her of all she owned—money, land, and self-respect.

Meg would not let Gregor do that to her, no matter how much she craved his arms around her. To him she must remain the sharp-tongued and autocratic Lady Meg.

" 'Tis nothing," she said at last. "I have not slept well, that is all."

Gregor searched her face a moment more and then he lapsed into a smile. "Neither have I."

Meg only managed a faint smile in return. "We will sleep better when this is all over," she assured him, in what was meant to be a coolly comforting tone. "After we are wed."

Gregor blinked at her, and then he laughed: a low, suggestive chuckle. "Do ye think so, lassie?"

Meg felt her face flame. There was no mistaking his meaning, despite her own words being completely innocent. It was there in the hot amber of his eyes, the tension in his broad shoulders and muscular body. She could smell him, the smell of soap and leather and wool, and male. Without meaning to, the memory of their last kiss flashed into her mind. Heat—raw, sensuous heat—filled her. Her body turned to fluid, her breasts ached, and the very air around her seemed to shimmer with need.

She wanted him. She wanted him so much that it honestly hurt.

Abruptly Gregor had turned his head, removing that intent gaze from her. Whatever the interruption, it was welcome. Meg was filled with dizzy relief, in the moment before she heard the loud footsteps.

Malcolm Bain, his face an angry blur, swung his fair head back and forth, as if searching the room for someone. Even before he spoke, Meg had a very good idea who that someone might be.

"Where is she? Where is Alison Forbes? Alison! Show yersel'."

Not again! Meg shook off her own concerns, and started toward the man, ready to intervene.

But Gregor was before her. "Malcolm! What do you mean coming in here shouting like this! This is no barracks, man!"

Malcolm's eyes were as wild as his demeanour, but he lowered his voice and spoke with a raw intensity. "I need to find her, Gregor. I need to speak with her."

"Then you can do so when you have quietened yourself down. Come with me now." And when Malcolm Bain appeared stubbornly frozen to the spot: "I said NOW!"

Meg jumped, as did everyone else within earshot. If that was how Gregor gave orders, how could anyone refuse to obey him? She knew she wouldn't dare! She had never seen Gregor like this—an officer in command. It came as a revelation to her.

And yet still Malcolm Bain hesitated, holding out, until

with a low groan of frustration, he spun around and led his captain from the room.

"Meg? What is going on?" Her father was peering toward her, his cloudy eyes uncertain.

"They have run mad," she said, letting go a shaky breath, trying to make a joke out of it. "'Tis Malcolm Bain and Alison—ever since they set eyes on each other, they have been like two cats in a basket." She touched his shoulder gently. "Perhaps you should rest, Father. It will be a long day tomorrow, and a long night, if we are to celebrate this wedding as hard as you wish."

"I am not tired. I am too happy to be tired."

At least someone knew how they felt! thought Meg. For herself, after that moment of wild emotion just now, she preferred to focus on domestic matters, on the mundane. It seemed safer, somehow.

Alison was in the kitchen, dealing with the enormous task of planning the banquet. Meg wondered what Malcolm Bain had wanted her for, but she had a fair idea. He must have discovered the truth about Angus. Only the discovery of his son could have put him into such a wild state. As if matters weren't complicated enough! She only hoped Gregor could talk sense into the man, for Alison would not thank him for confronting her in such a public manner.

"Should we have music, Meg?" her father was asking her. "Will we have Geordie the piper? Or Annie with her pure, sweet voice? Or both! Aye, I think it appropriate we have both for such an occasion. The Great Hall will not have been so full of happy people since Queen Mary's day."

"Both Geordie and Annie sound fine," Meg replied. "I will see to it. And we will have dancing, too. How long since you have danced, Father?"

She listened to her father's rambling answer. It wasn't simply her own state of mind, she was certain. He really had deteriorated over the past few days. The man she had looked to all her life for advice and comfort was fading. Was that because Gregor was here? Had her father been clinging on until he found someone to take over from him, to protect and care for her, as he would do? Was he releasing his once-tenacious grip on life because Gregor was able to step in and take charge?

Despite their differences, Meg loved her father. He had been her hero, more like a father *and* a mother to her, since her mother had died when Meg was a baby. How could she live if her father was not there? And yet she would, she knew she must. Gregor was here now. And Meg suspected Gregor was someone she could trust and rely on, as she had the general. It was just that she was so used to protecting her own heart, she didn't want to risk breaking it.

"You're certain?" Gregor asked doubtfully, hoping it was not so.

"Of course I'm certain, Gregor! She had a son and he's mine. Why dinna she send word? Why dinna she write and ask for me to come home? She never did. What sort of woman is she, to keep that to hersel'?"

He sounded as if the pain were almost too much for him to bear, a strong man like Malcolm Bain, reduced to wiping the moisture from his eyes. Gregor felt sick with compassion for his friend and companion.

"Alison is a proud lassie," he said at last, trying to comfort.

"Pigheaded, ye mean!"

"Mabbe. A little." There was an understatement! Gregor bit his lip. Dear God, what would happen next? Malcolm

Bain MacGregor had a son he hadn't known about for twelve years, a son Alison had kept from him—aye, hidden from him. He had abandoned her for the sake of duty, but she had had her revenge.

"Leave it for a wee while, Malcolm," he said quietly. "She will not thank you for forcing an answer from her now. And any answer she gives under pressure will be hasty and full of anger. Leave this matter for now, let it bide. At least until after the banquet."

Malcolm Bain shook his head, his hair waving about him, making him look even more crazed. "Banquet? What the hell are ye talking about, Gregor Grant? What banquet?"

"The banquet tomorrow night, for the wedding feast." A smile kicked up the corner of his mouth, as he realized Malcolm didn't have a clue what he was talking about. Here was a way to turn his mind elsewhere. "The fact is, I'm to be wed, Malcolm. Lady Meg and I are to be wed."

Malcolm Bain looked dazed; he blinked several times. "Lady Meg? Ye and Lady Meg?"

"That's it. I'm to be the Laird of Glen Dhui again, and she my lady. What do you say to that, Malcolm?"

"I should congratulate ye, I suppose," he replied gloomily.

Gregor gave a crack of laughter. "You dinna sound too sure about it, man! I am to wed Lady Meg and have back what I lost twelve years ago. I have a duke to fight and lands to protect, and I am marrying a woman whom I dinna even know, who has a tongue like a sword. And I dinna care. I'm happy. *Now* say your piece, Malcolm Bain."

Malcolm Bain hesitated, and then his hand closed on Gregor's shoulder, fingers squeezing painfully. "Are ye sure about this, Gregor? Ye know we can ride away now, go

back to Clashennic? We can even go to France, if ye wish it!
Just say the word, man, and we'll be gone from here before
the deed is done."

Gregor smiled, a broad, genuine smile. "Och, Malcolm,
you're a loyal friend to me. But no, I dinna want to ride
away from all this. I want to wed Meg. I . . . I feel as if it is
right. Dinna ask me how or why, but my heart tells me it is
the right thing to do. As you know, I havena been listening
to my heart of late, and mabbe it's time I did."

Malcolm Bain nodded, still looking more than a little bemused. "Then if that is so, ye must do what you feel to be
right. Dinna do what I did, Gregor, and ride away without a
backward glance. I have a son," he added bitterly, "and I
never even knew it!"

Gregor patted his back in a gesture of comfort, and they
fell silent. After a moment they glanced guiltily towards the
door that led into the Great Hall. "Should we return then?"
Gregor asked.

"I dinna think I can face it," Malcolm Bain groaned. "I
think I'd rather get back to training the men. At least I can
shout at them without them taking offense. At least I dinna
have to try and guess what they're thinking."

Gregor hesitated and then nodded decisively. "Aye, I'll
come with you."

Chapter 18

All day, people had been arriving at Glen Dhui Castle. Lassies barefoot but in their best dresses, come to help cook and serve. Lads come to help fetch and carry. Alison set them their tasks, and they joined in with the rest. The place hummed with antlike activity.

Meg had wished they could perform the ceremony quietly, but when she saw how much pleasure the people of Glen Dhui were deriving from the thought of a grand occasion like this—not to mention the general—she decided it was better not to complain. This was a celebration for them, something for them to remember and tell their children, and their children's children. One of those tales that makes grown men cry. How the Laird of Glen Dhui was cast out, and then returned to marry the Lady and live there happily, forevermore . . .

But would it end so neatly? Could it?

Deep in her heart Meg didn't think so. Abercauldy would

not let it be so. And Lorenzo, when he was released, would be fit for any mischief. Meg had taken food to his cell, and seen him glaring up at her through the black grill, his face full of a sullen fury.

"Ah, Lady Deceitful!" he had called to her. "Do you mean to poison me now?"

Meg had set down the food basket, nodding to the guard to open the grating so that it could be lowered down. "Don't be ridiculous, Lorenzo," she had said mildly. "And do not talk as though I have done something wrong. I have told your duke many times that I will not wed him; he just refuses to listen."

"So you will marry a handsome face instead!" Lorenzo had sneered. "I wish you happy of your pretty soldier, Lady Meg, and hope he will not break your heart when his eyes stray elsewhere."

Meg had felt a shiver run over her as Lorenzo's sword tip found its mark. He knew it, too, for his smile widened. "Enjoy your meal," she had called, and then, in a pretended whisper, "but do not eat the mutton pie. You are right, Lorenzo, it is poisoned!"

She had turned her back on him then, but she had seen the doubt flicker in his eyes. Lorenzo probably knew she would not poison him, but there would still be a question hanging over him, as he sat in his cell and contemplated that succulent slice of mutton pie . . .

She shouldn't have done that, Meg thought now. But she had wanted to give him something to worry about, just as he had done for her. She wished she could take a gallop on her mare, to blow these worries from her head, to forget her troubles in the sheer joy of riding through the place she loved best in all the world. But apart from her allotted tasks, it was too dangerous just now, and chafe though it might, she had to accept that, and stay put.

Gregor was busy with the men, he and Malcolm Bain keeping well out of the way of the preparations and— thought Meg—Alison Forbes. Not that Alison had gone looking for Malcolm Bain. Meg had spied her talking with her brother Duncan, and her face had been as white as the oatmeal coating her hands, so she must know that Malcolm knew about Angus. As for Angus himself, the lad was kept busy with the rest, and as far as Meg was aware, he didn't know a thing of what was happening around him.

Meg had taken a tray in her room the previous evening, pleading a headache, but really she had been unwilling to sit with Gregor, alone, in the dining room. The reasons for their wedding were clear enough, and they were good and practical reasons. Yes, she accepted them. But paradoxically, those same very good and practical reasons caused a sense of disappointment in Meg that just kept growing.

She had dreamed of all-consuming love, of wild passion, of tears and joy, with all the highs and lows such a love would bring her. Loving so fiercely might make her cry, sometimes, but at least she would feel alive. She would *be* alive.

Instead, the motto for her marriage was to be convenience and necessity.

The priest arrived in the late afternoon. Meg happened to be passing the windows that looked out upon the yew tree avenue. She watched as the old man on his ancient horse, surrounded by the men of Glen Dhui, made his way toward the castle. Except there was an unexpected visitor among them. A straight-backed man in a red coat and buff breeches was riding with them. It took only a moment for Meg to recognize Major Litchfield.

During his stay at the military post, the major had come often to Glen Dhui to visit her father. At least, she had always believed it was her father he had come to visit—now she was not so sure. She hesitated, watching the men approach, wondering why the major was here now. But there was too much else to occupy her. The food was almost ready, the Great Hall had been made up into a bower of leaves and branches and flowers. Her father had donned his best clothes and had found a wig to wear that he had bought once in London, and she had chosen, with Alison's help, her wedding gown.

Now that the priest had arrived, all was ready.

The moment had come for her convenient marriage.

"Ye look beautiful," Alison assured Meg, surveying her with a satisfied smile.

With her long auburn hair loose down her back, and simply caught up from her face at the sides with narrow green ribbons, and her favorite green silk gown rustling about her as she walked, Meg did look beautiful. Though she didn't feel it. She felt . . . well, she felt like herself. Plain Meg Mackintosh—the same as always. Alison had dusted powder over her face, but the freckles were still there. It seemed like a sign, a reminder that no matter how she tried to deck herself up in her finery, she was the same woman, the same Meg—and she always would be.

Downstairs the noise was deafening. People from up and down Glen Dhui were arriving, eager to participate. The general had sent a messenger on horseback through the glen, spreading the news and inviting all to come to the laird's house for the celebration. Even at such short notice, they had dropped everything and come, wearing their best clothes, and with a determination to enjoy themselves.

In the Great Hall, children squealed, women chattered and men laughed, spilling out into the balmy evening, taking up every available space. The general had had his chair placed in the very center of the hall, so that he could greet the guests as they arrived and converse with the rest. So that he would not miss a single moment.

Meg knew she should go down now, and see that all was well. There were probably some last minute problems, and she was the one that everyone looked to to do the solving. And besides, she should show the people her face; they would be expecting a smiling bride. The fairy tale could not be complete without a happy bride.

Meg took a deep, steadying breath.

She was about to wed Gregor Grant. The priest was awaiting her, her father was awaiting her, the guests were awaiting her.

And Gregor, her bridegroom, was waiting, too.

"Are ye ready now, my lady?" Alison sounded slightly anxious.

"Almost, Alison. Just a moment." Meg fiddled with the ribbons in her hair. "You have had no more 'feelings,' Alison?" she asked, more to delay leaving the room than because she really wanted to know. Alison had not mentioned any forebodings of late.

Alison's brow had furrowed at the question, but her eyes were clear. "I think there is a shadow ahead, my lady, though 'tis not clear. Ye must make merry tonight."

"You told me that Captain Grant would bring trouble to us, do you remember?"

Alison nodded. "Aye, that I did. And I do see trouble, now he is here, but I dinna believe anymore that he is the cause of it. The shadow has been coming for a while, Lady Meg."

"What is this shadow then? Is it Abercauldy?"

"I dinna know, but I do know this: There is light through the shadow, on the other side. Ye must look through it, toward the light, my lady."

All very well, thought Meg in frustration, but how did one do that?

Alison touched her hand, her eyes warm, her mouth wide in a smile. "Dinna be afeared. If I see more I will tell ye soon enough. For tonight be merry, my lady. Be happy! That is my advice."

"Thank you, Alison." Meg returned her smile, still hesitating.

Alison gave her a little push. "Go!"

That made Meg laugh. What was she afraid of? They were all her friends, after all. Picking up her skirts, Meg took her courage in her hands and left the sanctuary of her room for her future.

"It seems I must congratulate you."

Gregor turned and met Major Litchfield's direct gaze. The other man appeared sincere, but there was a forced look to his smile that spoke of a personal disappointment. Perhaps he had had hopes of winning Meg for himself— Gregor had thought so, when he had seen the major speaking to Meg at the pass. There had been something eager in Major Litchfield's eyes that had dumped a thick wave of jealousy on Gregor, despite the fact that he knew he had no rights to Meg. No, she hadn't belonged to him then, but nei- ther had he wanted anyone else to have her.

Did Meg realize the major was interested in her? Surely, if she did, she would have turned in his direction rather than Gregor's? It was clear she trusted him, leaned upon him, and the general liked him, too.

A perfect match, Gregor thought dryly.

Well, perfect or not, it was too late now. The die was cast; Meg was his.

The knowledge sent a shiver of relief through him, as if he had secured something far greater than a woman's hand.

"I was planning to visit Glen Dhui Castle in the next weeks in any case," Major Litchfield was saying. "When the priest told me his mission, it seemed a good idea to come now. My replacement is due. It has happened sooner than I planned. He is some relative of a great man, who has to be put somewhere quiet for a time. A troublesome rela- tive, by the sound of it. I do not like to leave such a one in charge of the place and people I have grown to like—very much—but I am afraid it is beyond my control."

"And I say again, I'm sorry to hear you are going, Ma- jor," the general called, turning in their direction. "I'll miss our conversation, and thrashing you at chess!"

Major Litchfield laughed. "I'll not regret that, sir. You are a master of the game."

"He played a fine game when I first met him," Gregor added with a smile. "I never did win against him."

"The trick is to put yourself into the mind of the other man," the general instructed him. "To . . . to . . ." He seemed to lose the thread of his thought, and turned away, diverted by some new arrivals.

After watching the old man for a moment, the major said

in an undertone, "I do not like to say so, Grant, but the general isn't the man he was when last I was here. Time seems to be catching him up rather swiftly."

Gregor knew it was so. Since his own arrival the general was fading, but despite that, tonight it was clear he meant to enjoy himself. And he was right; it would be soon enough tomorrow, to face their myriad of problems.

"You will have a monumental task before you," the major went on, eyeing a plate of crisp oatcakes. "Stepping into the general's shoes, I mean."

"Och, and I know it, Major."

Major Litchfield turned his gaze to Gregor, and suddenly he gave him a more genuine smile. "Oh, I think you will manage it, Captain Grant. You have the look of one who can manage most things."

Gregor was still pondering this unexpected compliment, when a movement at the top of the stairs caught his eye. He looked up, and all thought left his head.

A *morvoren*—that was what she was. A mermaid in a green silk ocean, her long curling hair streaming about her like fire. Something to be desired from afar, unobtainable, a mystical creature.

And yet Gregor both desired and meant to obtain this mystical creature. He swallowed. Desire had turned his body hard, and the blood was rushing through every inch of it. Beside him, Major Litchfield murmured his approval, while the crowd in the hall smiled and nodded, and gave of their opinions in hushed whispers. This may be a surprise wedding, a rushed marriage, but Meg was no disappointing bride. It was clear they loved her, had taken her to their hearts, and that this moment was one they would never forget.

Certainly not Gregor.

But unlike the others, he wasn't content to admire from afar. He had never been a man to sit and gaze at a woman across a room, or to pen a poem to her untouchable beauty. And right now he wanted to do desperate things to Meg, ungentlemanly things, things he should not even be allowing himself to think, before all these good people.

Gregor groaned softly.

In short, he was dreaming of bounding up the stairs, grabbing her, and finding an empty bedchamber so that he could satisfy his lust on her. Hardly the way to soothe the fears of a virgin, for he had no doubt that so she was. How in God's name was he to hold himself in check, with such thoughts as these writhing through his fevered brain?

"Meg?" The general had risen to his feet, supported by Duncan Forbes. "Meg, are you ready? Gregor?"

The spell was broken. Gregor watched as Meg came down the stairs, careful of her skirts, Alison hovering behind her. He stepped forward to meet her, his hand outstretched to take hers. Her eyes were wide in her pale face, and she seemed to be trying to read his expression as she placed her fingers lightly in his. He hoped to God he had his thoughts well hidden.

"You look very beautiful, Meg," he said with quiet sincerity.

She smiled, shyly lowering her head and at the same time running her gaze over him. Gregor was wearing his best dark blue jacket, its sleeves slashed in the popular Scottish manner, his best white shirt, and a kilt that had been lent him by the general. It was woven of dark cloth with a yellow stripe, and when he walked, it swung jauntily.

"So do you," Meg murmured.

He chuckled.

Cheeks burning with color, Meg realized what she had said. She looked up at him in dismay, her blue eyes wide and her lips parted. Gregor found her confusion completely adorable.

"Meg?" The general said again, impatient for the wedding to begin.

It gave her an excuse to turn away, smiling at the people who smiled at her as she passed, making her way to her father's side. Gregor followed in her wake.

"I'm here, Father."

The old priest stepped forward, his face rosy from the whiskey and the company, his somber clothes still a little dusty from the long ride. "Lady Meg, this is a wee bit unusual!" He tried to look stern, but there was a gleam in his eyes.

"The circumstances are a wee bit unusual," the general retorted sternly, more like his old self. "We are prepared for a wedding here, Father. I hope you do not mean to disappoint us?"

Receiving this stern interrogation, the priest replied in the only manner he could. "No, no, I do not mean to disappoint you, General Mackintosh. I am here and ready to do God's work."

The general nodded, pleased with his answer. "Then let us begin!"

It was a dream, Meg thought. The familiar faces of the people of Glen Dhui and her father's bright smile, the priest's voice droning on, Major Litchfield looking as if he was determined to enjoy himself. Meg could not look at any of them, and especially not at Gregor Grant, her groom.

He took her hand as they stood before the old priest, his fingers hard and warm. Meg wanted to cling to them—perhaps he expected her to—but she resisted. He was a stranger, and she did not want to lean on him—she dare not. In all her life Meg had only ever leaned on one man, and that was her father—and even he had let her down.

She did not know Gregor—she had thought she did. Visions of him had filled her girlhood, and she had ridden about the glen with dreams of him in her head. The man at her side was not the boy she had dreamed of, and yet in a strange way he was. She'd had glimpses of that boy. As if Gregor Grant had built a stout wall about himself but occasionally, very occasionally, a brick came loose and left a gap, and through that gap she caught a glimpse of the boy.

"Meg? Come, come, what is your answer?" Her father sounded impatient.

Meg realized with a start that they were all waiting for her response, their expressions amused and knowing. Quickly she gave it, feeling her face color yet again. Gregor spoke then, sounding more like a soldier than ever. No hesitation from him, and probably no doubts. And then it was done. They were joined as man and wife.

A cheer went up from the gathering, lifting in joyous echoes to the roof above. Glen Dhui had given its approval.

Malcolm Bain stepped around a pair of children who were mock-fighting. "I am the Laird of Glen Dhui," one of them insisted. "Nay, *I* am," the other retorted. "I will fight ye for the right!" "Nay, I will fight ye!"

"Ye are neither of ye the laird, ye wee devils," Malcolm said with mock sternness, setting them apart. "Now off with ye both."

The two boys took to their heels, weaving around startled guests and groaning tables. Malcolm smiled after them, hands on his hips.

He sensed her before he turned—a warm, wary presence at his back. And then he was looking into Alison Forbes's dark eyes.

For a moment time retraced its steps. It was twelve years ago, and Alison was his woman, his future. And then the Rebellion had happened and he had gone off with Gregor and his father, and everything had changed. Changed so completely that when Gregor had lost his lands and ridden away, Malcolm Bain had gone with him as easily as if there was nothing to keep him.

How could that have happened? Why had it happened? What had changed him into a man who no longer believed he had a future at Glen Dhui with Alison? That he must flee and suffer among strangers, for the sake of his young laird? Had he done the right thing, all those years ago?

How could he know?

If he had not gone with Gregor, the lad might now be dead. If he had stayed . . . he and Alison might have ended up fighting like cat and dog. How could anyone truly read the future, although Alison tried? Malcolm Bain had never paid much heed to her gift—he believed a man made his own future.

The words came from his mouth without conscious thought, his pain turned into sound. "Why didn't ye tell me I had a son?"

Alison's dark eyes flashed, and the famous Forbes temper shone in their depths. "Because ye left me."

"I had no choice!"

"Ye *did* have a choice, Malcolm. But it wasna even

that. . . . It was the *way* ye left me, without a backward glance. Why should I have told ye, after that? I was on my own and ye made certain I knew it."

"If ye had told me—"

"What? Ye never would have gone? I dinna want ye to stay because ye thought ye should!"

"I have a son!"

"Alison!" Duncan stepped warily between them. It was only then that Alison realized, from the silence about them, that they were now the center of attention for some twenty or so guests. Luckily, outside that circle, the noise and joviality went on. She had meant to stay away from Malcolm Bain tonight, not to spoil Lady Meg's wedding day with her own problems.

"I am sorry," she said, to no one in particular, and walked away.

Duncan glared at Malcolm Bain. "See what ye've done," he hissed. "Stay away from her, ye bastard."

"I'll do what I think is right, Duncan, now will ye leave me alone!"

And he too turned, and walked away.

The fiddler struck up, the drummer close behind. Their lively music thrummed through the room, until all feet were tapping and all hands clapping. Gregor led his bride into a dance, her hands in his, her silken skirts brushing his kilt. Her eyes were sparkling and her cheeks were pink, for she had already danced many times, with many men.

Major Litchfield had taken a turn, smiling like a besotted fool, while Gregor had watched. He had been conversing with another of the guests, trying not to let the sight of his wife and the major concern him, but the jealousy had simmered inside. Gregor had imagined he was hiding it well, until the guest he was conversing with suddenly stopped talking and gave him a very uneasy glance.

Had there really been murder in his eyes? Gregor hoped not. He was not a jealous man—not normally—but something about Meg made him want to grab hold of her and never let her go.

Now the fiddler quickened his pace, his fingers flying, and Gregor spun Meg around and around. Her head fell back and she laughed. He spun her again and she laughed again, her eyes shining, her hair bouncing about her in a cascade of flame curls. Suddenly it didn't matter what had been before this moment. The music, the dance was to be enjoyed for its own sake. And Gregor meant to enjoy it.

He pulled her forward into his arms, feeling the sway of her slender but curvaceous body, the scent of her skin in his nostrils, the soft brush of her hair as she turned her head.

The moment was as heady as Cragan Dhui whiskey. He was home, back in the place he loved above all others. He was home, and Meg had made that possible.

Now he wanted to move on to the next part of this special night. He wanted to make Meg his wife in truth.

"It grows late," Gregor said softly, and knew by the sudden tension in her that she understood exactly what he meant.

Meg couldn't stop her eyes from flying to his. She wondered if he saw the anxiety in them, and the doubt. He must have, for his mouth curved into what was meant to be a comforting smile.

"They are expecting us to leave very soon," he went on. "They are waiting, Meg."

Meg glanced about her. Half of their guests had nodded

off, the priest among them, but the other half were watching them closely, alert, and waiting for the happy couple to retire. The general was slumped in his chair, while beside him Major Litchfield's eyes were rather glazed from claret and good food. Gregor was right, it was time to face the ribald remarks, along with the laughter and good wishes.

With a quick nod, Meg assented.

Gregor slipped his arm about her waist, his hand resting naturally on her hip. "Are you ready then?" he asked her, as if he wanted to be absolutely sure.

Was she ready? Meg shivered with apprehension, and something else that curled in her belly and quickened her breath. His hand on her hip burned; no man had ever touched her there, so familiarly, so possessively. Meg had never lain with a man before, and yet she wanted to, if it was Gregor. She wanted Gregor. It was the truth, and she had told herself that day at Loch Dhui that she would admit the truth to herself, even if she told no one else.

"I'm ready," she whispered.

With a brisk nod of his head, Gregor took her at her word. But for a moment longer, his golden eyes looked into hers. Meg was surprised to see, deep within them, a flicker of doubt. Was Gregor Grant uncertain, perhaps a little afraid, for all that he was a ladies' man and a hardened soldier? And as he reached to hold her hand, Meg was surprised to feel his fingers tremble.

Just as her fingers were trembling.

Chapter 19

Candles, their flames dipping gently in the sweet breeze from the open windows, softly lit the room. It was Gregor's room he had led her to, the big room that she supposed had once belonged to his parents. Rather ornate and formal, it had never appealed to Meg. She had always preferred the smaller bedroom, with its faded walls and larger windows and the view of Cragan Dhui.

Meg paused now on the threshold, suddenly doubtful. Perhaps, after all, she had been too quick to agree to a proper marriage to him. Perhaps she needed time to reconsider. She turned her face to his, meaning to tell him she wasn't certain this was the right thing to do. Just as Gregor bent down and closed his mouth on hers.

Startled, Meg froze and her eyes grew big. His, she couldn't help but notice, were closed. And he made a sound like a groan, as though the feel of her lips on his was more than he could bear. His mouth moved, sliding over hers, tasting her, enjoying her. Meg wondered whether she should pull away, or lean in closer. What was it he was feeling? What was it that had him in its hot grip?

And then the sensation reached her, too.

Heat, trickling down her spine, into her belly and in the secret place between her thighs. Abruptly she realized the bodice of her gown was too tight across her breasts, abrading her nipples. Her skin was hot, wanting to be stroked. She felt dizzy, lightheaded, and wonderfully pliant.

Naturally cautious, Meg felt the need to pull back, to take a breath. But Gregor's mouth was warm, so warm, his lips softer than she could have imagined, and they were teasing hers. She was drowning, drowning in desire.

Lost in lust?

Meg smiled, and felt his mouth curve in response. And she knew then that she couldn't pull back now. She was an explorer in a foreign land. A Sir Francis Drake or a Sir Walter Raleigh, setting out for unknown seas and a distant horizon. Only this exploration was one that would involve much touching and stroking, and such disturbing actions as kissing Gregor Grant's hard, golden body and having him kiss hers. . . .

His fingers were on the fastenings at the back of her green gown. He had turned her about, so he stood behind her, his warm breath on her nape. He bent and kissed the soft, tender skin there, his mouth trailing down so that she shivered in delight and expectation.

"Should I call Alison to help me?" she asked, her voice husky and unfamiliar.

"I can manage," he said, and true to his word he had soon unfastened her gown enough so that he could slip it from her shoulders and halfway down her arms.

The décolletage slid down, and he eased the sleeves further, dragging the front of the gown with them. Slowly, slowly he lowered it. Discovering, inch by inch, her rounded, ivory flesh, not quite disclosing her naked breasts to his eager gaze. His breath was uneven—she could feel his chest rising and falling—and his body hot and close against her back. Meg swallowed, and looking down, watched her own body be revealed. But instead of being embarrassed or apprehensive, she tried to see herself through his eyes.

It was difficult, for all she saw was Meg Mackintosh. Her breasts were largish, it was true, and an annoyance to her whenever she wished to ride like a man. Did he see something else in them entirely that she had been missing all these years? He seemed . . . spellbound.

"Gregor," she whispered, uncertainly.

"You are so beautiful," he breathed, astonishing her, and let go of one sleeve to rest his hand briefly on the fleshy curve of her upper breast, trailing his fingers into the shadowy niche between them. She found herself watching his hand, his fingers, on her skin. The darker color of his flesh, the scars and marks upon him that came from many years of fighting and living in the Highlands. The sight of his male skin against her white breasts was suddenly, marvelously, exciting.

Her heart beat faster.

Gregor lowered the décolletage a little more, slowly, so slowly. They were both breathing fast now. And then the green silk caught on the very tips of her breasts, giving a teasing glimpse of the darker circles around her nipples, now barely hidden from view.

"Ah, *morvoren*," he said, his voice low and ragged. "Let me just . . ."

His fingers trembling, he freed her from the constraints of her bodice, and the cloth fell to her waist, catching on the swell of her hips. Now at last her breasts were bared to his gaze, and in wonder she let him take his fill. And watched, hardly daring to breath, as he brought his hands up beneath them and gently took them, one in each palm, until the bountiful, creamy flesh spilled over his fingers.

Meg's head fell back against his shoulder and she gasped with a pleasure almost too much to bear. His fingers stroked, caressed, his thumbs finding her nipples and rubbing at them until Meg was squirming against him. Wanting, needing . . . When she could stand it no more, she turned about, facing him. Her lashes lifted on blue eyes that were dreamy and sensual.

Gregor smiled. He knew he had stirred passion in her, but there was a long way to go yet, until she was entirely his. Somehow he had to control his own passion, hold back, and let her gain the most pleasure. He bent his head and took the tip of one breast in his mouth.

Instantly the heat surrounded her aching nipple, the moist sweep of his tongue causing her to cry out. Meg reached up to find something to hold on to, just as her trembling legs gave way. She grasped his shoulders, and then his hair, her fingers tangling in the silky length, drawing him even closer.

He placed one last kiss upon her breast, and then turned to the other one, giving it the same treatment. Meg moaned deep in her throat. The heat was gathering in her belly and her chest, and between her legs. She didn't know if she could take much more without her body shattering with pleasure. In desperation, she forced his head up, kissing his chin, his jaw, the corner of his mouth, before he reached to still her frantic movements, a hand either side of her face.

As if he understood completely how she was feeling, Gregor smiled down at her. But it wasn't a gentle smile. His handsome face was hard, his eyes glittered. He looked as if he wanted to devour her whole. She might have been afraid of what she saw then, in his expression, if she had not wanted above all things to be devoured.

His mouth closed on hers, opening her lips with his, and she felt his tongue. The sensation was new and strange, but she bided her time, allowing him to guide her. Soon she was playing with his tongue, using her own to follow and explore. Her breasts were pressed to his chest, the buttons on his jacket slightly painful, and he had slid his hands over the bare flesh of her back and shoulders, down to the curve of her bottom. Cupping her through her gown, he pressed her urgently against his body. And she felt the hard length of his desire.

For the first time since he had drawn her into his room, Meg's dreamy state threatened to unravel. She knew what that hard rod was, she knew what it meant, and she knew where it was made to go. Suddenly, she was less than keen that he use it on her.

As if sensing her change of heart, Gregor shifted her in his arms, bringing a hand up to her breasts, fondling them until she was once more gasping and pliant in his arms. She slid her own arms about his neck, once again using his strength to support her weakened legs. And then, before she could do more than squeak in protest, he was lifting her, holding her to his chest, and in two long strides had reached the bed and placed her upon it.

Meg found herself sinking into the feather ticking; her hair in her eyes, her gown still caught about her hips and hampering her movements. She struggled up onto her elbows, complaining, only to stop when she realized that Gregor was hastily disrobing. He had already removed his jacket and was now pulling the fine linen shirt over his head and tossing it aside.

Suddenly the memory of him, by the loch near Shona's cottage, returned to her. His body, half naked, in the cold dawn. She had stood upon the shore, spellbound, her fingers itching to touch him, to tame him. And yet she had not dared; she had told herself it would not be proper. Well, now she could touch him as much as she wished.

If she were brave enough.

His kilt fell to the floor, and, naked, he came toward her. He was just the same as he had been, when he dragged himself wounded from his bed at the Clashennic Inn—not that she had dared more than a glance or two! But he was different, too, for then he had been weak and shaking with fever, barely able to stand. Now he was fit and strong, a man in his prime. And he was aroused. Oh, yes, he was very aroused indeed.

Meg swallowed nervously as she ran her eye over the great length of him. He was surely far too large for a normal man? How could he possibly put . . . how could she . . .

"It will not fit," Meg told him with characteristic bluntness.

Gregor's eyes narrowed and he gave her a slow, entirely wicked smile. "Would you place a wager on that, lass?" he asked her gently.

Meg chewed her lip, her eyes still fixed on that part of him. She seemed completely unable to drag her gaze away. "I don't want to place a wager, and I certainly don't want—"

"There will be pleasure in it," he interrupted roughly. "For us both."

"I have heard that it can be painful for the woman," Meg blurted out. "I have heard stories."

He was her husband; he could force her if he wished, and no one would dare question him. How could she have forgotten that small fact?

There was a silence, apart from the beating of Meg's heart, as she held herself ready to flee. Or fight.

"Sweet Meg," he whispered.

Now she did look at him, and saw such tenderness and understanding in his eyes that her own filled with tears.

He went on in that same enticing voice, and Meg felt her fear begin to ease. "I willna hurt you beyond a wee bit, *morvoren*. That I swear. I will be slow, so slow, and when it is time for us to join, you will want me to. You will beg me to, my Meg."

She watched him approach her, not relaxing as he rested one knee upon the mattress right beside her. With an eye on that part of him that appeared to have grown even bigger— or maybe she was just closer to it—Meg shrank back as he leaned over her. But he ignored her fear, and began to remove the gown from her, tugging it carefully over the soft curve of her belly, down to her thighs. He murmured something in Gaelic, as his eyes swept over the curls of auburn hair at the juncture of her thighs, and then he slipped the gown all the way off.

She wore her good silk stockings, that came to above her knees. With great care, he rolled them down, and as he did, he kissed her skin, from her knees right down to the curved arch of each foot.

Meg watched him, caught between wonder and suspicion, wriggling a little as his hair tickled her skin. She reached out her hand, smoothing it over the muscle of his shoulder, feeling it bunch as he moved. He didn't stop her. Growing bolder, she ran her fingertips down his arm, testing the firm flesh there, seeing whether she could close her hand about his muscular upper arm. She could not. He was strong and hard, and just as fascinating as she had always thought him.

He was kissing her belly, now; hot open-mouthed kisses that made her squirm. His tongue trailed lazily through her damp curls, down to the cleft that seemed to open of its own accord at his touch. She should stop him, Meg supposed distractedly, for now he was tracing the fleshy folds between her thighs, as if he had all the time in the world.

"Gregor," she said, "I feel silly like this."

"Do you?" he asked, and began to suck at her, pulling and nibbling, and after that Meg couldn't say any more. She couldn't do anything much at all, because she had gone still.

Very still.

She felt as if something was pending, a great wave of pleasure building, driving at her. Meg gasped and shuddered as his wicked tongue found a particularly pleasurable spot, but before he could do any good, he had moved on again, lazily kissing her inner thighs, reaching up with his hand to tweak at her aching breasts.

Playing with her.

The great wave of pleasure smoothed out, almost went away. Was this all there was to it? Meg asked herself in frustration. And then Gregor found the spot again, sucking hotly now with his mouth, and suddenly she was bucking beneath him, keening and pleading. Meg heard her own voice, and even as she wondered at herself, she knew she could not help it. He had stripped her caution and control from her as easily as her green silk gown.

"Do ye want me, Meg? Will I take ye now?" His voice was harsh, a command rather than a question.

She opened her eyes—she had not realized she had closed them—and found him above her. His body was resting over hers, not quite touching, for he held himself away, but near enough to feel the waves of heat pouring off him. Meg shivered, and her gaze slid over his broad chest with its covering of dark hair, down to his hard belly and narrow hips. To the part of him that seemed to have a life of its own. As she looked, he pressed a knee between her thighs, opening them, and lowered himself between them, where she still throbbed from his mouth.

It felt a little strange, but pleasant enough. Still, she could not expect him to lie like this all night. He would want to do other things.

"I am still uncertain," she told him.

"Och, Meg, you're never uncertain about anything," he retorted, kissing her cheek, tiny, hot kisses that ran down her jaw to her throat. Between her thighs, she felt his erection jutting against her soft, swollen flesh, rubbing against her very like his hand and tongue had done, only different.

She found herself concentrating on that friction, losing herself, even moving against him a little, enjoying the sensation. Until he groaned and took a ragged breath, his shoulders shaking slightly with laughter. "Oh God, Meg, ye'll be the death of me," he said. He lifted his head and looked down at her, his amber eyes aglitter with passion and heat, and something very like pleading.

"I'm only a man," he reminded her. "Let me take ye, Meg. I am burning up."

She eyed him uneasily, but then he moved against her, the head of his rod finding her moist cleft and sliding a little way in. The sensation was not . . . unpleasant, oh, not at all. And when he groaned again, moving on her, his big body sliding against hers so that all his hairy bits abraded her soft skin, it was rather nice.

"Just be careful," she told him breathlessly.

He laughed as if he, too, was finding it difficult to catch his breath. His mouth came down on hers, tasting of her, and his kiss was as thorough and insistent as he was in all the things he did. His rod slid deeper, finding resistance, and out again. Her hips urged him forward, her mouth clung to his. She was so hot and damp and ready, it was easy when he gave one hard thrust and broke through the thin veil that kept her virginity intact.

Meg arched and gasped, feeling the tearing like a burn, a stinging inside her. And then he was kissing her face, gentle kisses, apologetic kisses, hushing her with Gaelic words that she didn't understand and yet which soothed her to stillness again. His fingers were busy caressing her, and he sucked at her nipples, causing her breasts to ache all over again. But all the while, between her legs, he was still. Waiting. Patient. When at last he lifted his head again to look into her eyes, he must have seen that she was afire with need, for he smiled, slowly and with a certain male smugness.

"Ye want me now, Meg Mackintosh." It wasn't a question.

Still watching her, still reading her eyes, he thrust his hips and slid deep inside her. It didn't hurt now, only that he was so big and she felt stretched, but even that wasn't unpleasant. Straightaway he withdrew, only to sink into her again, filling her, stretching her, causing little tingles and quivers throughout every inch of her body. She slid her arms about him, holding him close, her hips lifting against

him so that he slid deeper inside her still. That felt nice.
That made him groan. He reached down to cup her hips in
his big hands, adjusting her, tilting her, so that when next he
thrust into her he was brushing against that spot. That special, achy spot.

Now it was Meg who groaned. She felt the wave catch
her, suddenly, unawares. It rolled her, out of control, while
her body clenched and grasped upon his, and she tossed her
head from side to side upon the mattress. And then he had
opened her legs wider, moving hard against her, driving
himself deeper and deeper as her body welcomed him in.
Into her very core, and there he spilled his seed.

Tremors ran through her, lessening as the pleasure wave
receded. Her breath gradually slowed, and her heartbeat returned to normal. Lazily, Meg opened her eyes, becoming
aware that she was lying on her side, pressed along the
length of him. Both of them were quite bare, without even a
quilt to cover them, but it didn't seem to matter.

He was tracing her smooth skin, running his callused fingers down into the slender dip of her waist, before climbing
the curve of her hip. Then back again, over and over, as if he
could never get enough of the feel of her. She liked the sensation of his hand on her, the sense of being his. Not owned
by him—never that, for Meg was not the sort of woman
who could be owned by any man. But being by his side, a
part of him, his other half.

As Meg ran a proprietary gaze over him, she noticed that
his rod was standing to attention again. Did she dare?
Could she be so bold with a man who was near enough to a
stranger? But this was Gregor Grant, and just now she
dared anything.

With a little smile, Meg sat up, her bright, curling hair

cascading about her. Surprised, Gregor leaned on his elbow, his movements fluid and easy.

"I thought you were asleep," he said, eyeing her carefully.

Did he think she might run screaming? Meg had no intention of going anywhere.

"I am awake, Gregor," she said, "and now it is my turn."

His eyes narrowed as if he doubted his hearing. "Your turn?"

"That's right. The wife is allowed to take a turn, isn't she?"

He understood, and he wasn't laughing at her. In fact he looked as if he was about to swoon. "Aye, Meg," he said in a husky, breathless voice, "the wife is allowed to take a turn."

Taking her time, Meg leaned over him, and began to taste his skin, swirling her tongue over his chest and the rough hairs that covered it. She decided he tasted of man, and of her, and she liked it very well. By the time she had worked her way down over his belly, exploring him with her fingers and her mouth, he was shaking beneath her like a tree in a gale.

That was good, and it served him right after what he had done to her, but she had yet to reach the most important part. The most interesting and fascinating part.

"Now," she said, eyeing his rod. "I wonder. Maybe if I were to . . ." Her tongue licked delicately along the length of him. He cursed and bucked beneath her. "Interesting," she murmured. "What if I were to put my mouth over—"

He caught her up and tossed her ungently onto her back. With a gasp, Meg found herself pinned beneath a savage Highlander, his glittering amber eyes fixed on hers.

"You are tormenting me, Meg."

"No," she laughed, "truly I am not. I am . . . I am curious, I suppose. I have never had a man in my bed before, Gregor. There is much for me to learn about you. I don't want to waste a moment."

"We have all our lives to learn about each other," he reminded her quietly.

Meg wished she could believe him, but she feared that, even if Abercauldy did not destroy them, Gregor would eventually tire of her and find someone else. Someone prettier and more interesting. No, much as she wanted to trust him, she knew he was wrong. Their time together was short and precious, and therefore she meant to make the most of it.

"Gregor, let me just—"

"Och, Meg," he groaned, and bent to ply his mouth on hers, kissing her until she'd forgotten what it was she had meant to do. Then he slid gently inside her, carefully, making sure she was not hurting from the last time. But Meg was not hurting, apart from a desperate ache to have him back inside her. She arched beneath him, seeking to have more of him, but he held back, smiling at her frustration.

"You are cruel," she gasped, as he stooped to suckle on her breasts.

"Aye, verra, verra cruel."

He moved suddenly, pushing inside her deeply, then further again, resting there. Meg's lips parted as she gasped, and with trembling fingers she stroked his cheek. "You were right, Gregor. You've made me want you. Is it always so?"

"Like this, do ye mean? No, lassie. You and I have something rare; our bodies fit together verra well. Never take it for granted." He turned his head to capture her fingers, kissing them, sucking them.

Meg watched his mouth avidly, knowing that the reason she felt like this was simple. She wanted Gregor Grant. It was Gregor Grant who made her feel as if she was on fire, as if she never wanted him to stop.

Pleasure swept through her as he drove deep again, and she cried out and clutched at him. He thrust with a measured, controlled motion, building her pleasure, and in such a way, he brought her to another shuddering, breathless release. And then his control slipped and his breathing grew ragged, and Gregor found his own wave.

Glen Dhui Castle was still at last. Gregor felt it close about him like a mother's arms—though not *his* mother, it had to be said—sheltering him, holding him safe, just as it always had when he was a wee lad. Such things were an illusion, he knew that now. A house could not keep him safe. He was not safe. But despite his loss of innocence, the sensation was worth savoring.

Meg lay pliant, asleep in his arms, her soft curves pressed to his hard lines. She had turned over, so that her back was spooned into his chest, and his arm was wrapped tight about her, beneath her full breasts. Her hair tickled his nose, the sweet scent of it filling his head. Her soft bottom was pressed enticingly against his groin, her long thighs resting against his more muscular ones.

He could not get enough of her.

It was a fact.

He had taken her twice now, and still he wanted her. Despite the fact that she had been a virgin and he must have hurt her. Gregor was not a man who hurt women—but he knew he'd have to have her again, soon. It was like a force of nature, a storm or a drought. There was no stopping it.

This insatiable need was not something he was used to. A woman was a woman, or so he had always thought. When Gregor was lucky enough to have one in his bed, they made love, they sated themselves with each other, and then they parted. He did not hunger after his partners like this, as if he were starving and without any hope of a meal!

He remembered now the way in which she had licked her delicate tongue over his skin, down over his belly to his cock. He hadn't believed she would do it; he'd hoped she would, but he hadn't really believed . . . but she had. Oh God, the feel of her tongue on him—he almost groaned aloud at the memory.

Who would have thought his bossy wife would use her sharp tongue to such effect? Or those luscious pink lips?

Gregor nuzzled against her, breathing in the scent of her, trying not to sneeze when her hair made his nose twitch. She stirred a little, wriggling closer against him, causing his cock to harden even more, nudging against her bottom.

How long before Abercauldy came? As soon as that creature Lorenzo was released, he would ride for home and spill his poison into the duke's ear. *Unless Lorenzo doesn't go home.* Gregor mentally shook his head. That would be murder, and Gregor was not a man who would stick a knife in another's back. He preferred to face his enemies and look into their eyes. And then if he had to kill them, the fight was fair and equal.

Meg murmured in her dreams, as if his grim thoughts had disturbed her sweet slumber. He drew her closer still, delicately circling one nipple with his thumb. It perked up instantly, the dark rose flesh begging for the attention of his mouth. Gregor had known his bride was sensual—he had known it since the morning at Shona's cottage—but he had not imagined she would be so quick to find pleasure in their marriage bed. Apart from her initial, natural caution, she had been eager to learn, and partake in what he could give her.

He would like to draw her.

The urge to draw came upon him at times—a tingling sense of anticipation when he discovered something that inspired him. It had been rare enough these days, and when did he have time to sketch the scenery or the faces about him? But now Gregor longed to capture the tilt of Meg's chin, the fall of her hair, the sweep of her lashes over those brilliant eyes. And her lips, lush and full, their sensuality disguised by that straight line she ordered them into.

Aye, he must capture all that.

"You are not asleep, Gregor Grant."

Her accusing tone surprised him from his thoughts, and he raised himself a little to look down on her. She was smiling, her mouth reddened from his kisses, a flush along her cheekbones, her eyes dark beneath their shielding lashes, and with violet shadows beneath from weariness.

He should let her be—Gregor knew it, but he also knew that he could not.

He wanted her. And once Lorenzo was freed, who knew how much longer they would have to enjoy such delights?

Meg cuddled closer to him. "I am so glad I decided not to be a wife in name only," she sighed.

Gregor stared at her, and then he began to laugh. "Och, Meg, so am I!"

Chapter 20

⁓⁓◦◦⁓⁓

"My lady?"

Meg opened her eyes. It was morning and the room was still and quiet, as it should have been. Except that someone else was in it with her; someone else's breathing sounded by her side. She knew if she were to turn her head, then she would see Gregor Grant, his hair unbound, his strong, handsome face relaxed in sleep.

Her husband, her man, her lover, her love . . .

"My lady?" Alison was standing by the bed, peering anxiously into her face.

Her love?

Meg blinked, feeling disorientated and different. Not just in her body, which was stiff and sore in places she hadn't known she had—as she realized when she tried to sit up—but different, too, in her mind and her heart. She felt a sense of foreboding. Something fundamental had changed within her, as if her eyes had gone brown overnight, but she did not as yet understand quite what it was.

"Alison?"

"'Tis Major Litchfield, my lady. He is to leave this morning and he has expressed a wish to say good-bye to ye. He says he is going to Ireland with his regiment, and he willna be back, mabbe ever." Alison's dark eyes were big at the thought of such a journey.

Major Litchfield was leaving, and saying good-bye was the least she could do, and yet . . . Almost reluctantly, but without the will to stop herself, Meg turned her head, and looked down at the man by her side.

He lay on his back, one arm flung above his head, the other curled over his stomach. The beard shadow on his cheek was dark, as dark as his eyebrows and his lashes. His lips were slightly apart, relaxed, the lines on his face smoothed out by sleep. He looked young, but innocent? There was nothing innocent in the breadth of his chest and shoulders, the swell of muscle in his upper arms, and the dark hair that furred his golden skin.

Meg felt her breath grow faster, shallower, as she remembered the night that had been. Her wedding night. He had done things, *they* had done things she had never imagined enjoying with any man. He had made her feel desire and passion; she could taste them still. Her fingers twitched to stroke him, her lips burned to kiss him, and to her amazed consternation she felt her body already preparing itself for his.

The sheer strength of her feelings frightened her.

When before had she ever contemplated, even for a moment, putting her own pleasure before her duty?

That was when Meg realized just how changed she was. And he had changed her. When he had taken her body with his, he had done much more than mark her flesh with his own. While he kissed her and touched her, he had reached into her chest. And taken her heart into his keeping.

Meg closed her eyes briefly, holding her breath, and clutched the knowledge to herself. Perhaps if she kept it secret, inside herself, then she could prevent it from affecting her.

He had taken her heart. He had turned lust into love. Meg loved a man who did not love her, a man she was not even sure she completely trusted. All her life she had been fighting against loving any man who would not feel the same for her. And she had lost.

From somewhere she found her voice, surprised that despite the turmoil inside her, it sounded quite normal.

"Very well, Alison, thank you. I will be down in a little while. Be sure the major breaks his fast—he has a long ride ahead of him."

"I'll leave your robe here, my lady." Alison gave Meg a knowing little smile, and closed the door softly behind her.

Reluctantly, stiffly, Meg climbed out of bed. There were marks on her body to go with the aches, and finding her robe, she covered herself so that she would not have to think about them. It was not safe here, in this room, with him. Her love swelled in her chest, wanting to escape: She felt as if she might blurt out her feelings to him. The thought made her cringe. What if she told him she loved him, and he looked at her in puzzlement, or amusement, or worst of all, with pity? She would curl up and die. No, it was better if she got dressed immediately and escaped this room of sweet, hot memories. After last night, she just didn't trust herself to be sensible. . . .

His strong arms came around her, squeezing just hard enough to make her catch her breath, and bringing her inexorably back against his chest. Meg thought she would actually melt as his warm breath stirred her hair.

"Where are you going, lady wife?" his teasing voice was deep and husky with sleep. He sounded nothing like the taciturn Captain Grant, or the self-contained man she had come to know on their journey from Clashennic.

"Major Litchfield is leaving and I must say farewell—"

"Och, why canna the man sleep late this once?"

His grumble made Meg smile despite herself. Now *that* was more like Captain Grant! She turned her head so that she could look up at him, and lifted a slim eyebrow. "Major Litchfield has work to do, as I do. And *you*, Captain Grant."

"They'll not expect us down till noon."

"I never sleep until noon," she said flatly.

"Sleep? Who spoke of sleep?"

He kissed her cheek, nuzzling against her, and then he turned her to face him. Meg's breasts were pressed to his chest, her nipples already tightening in anticipation. He knew it, too, because his mouth curved against her lips. He was arrogant, but she conceded that he had a right to be.

Now he kissed her, but very gently, promisingly, with nothing like the wild passion of last night. It didn't matter. Meg was certain that her legs were going to give way . . . again. His hands curved about her waist, sliding leisurely down to grasp her bottom. He drew her up, against his own hard hips, and into the rigid evidence of his arousal.

"Come back to bed," he whispered. His eyes were a hot,

molten gold, and again Meg was tempted to forget the major altogether. She was finding it very difficult to resist him, but she must. For her own sake, she must.

Meg took a deep and determined breath, and heard Gregor sigh as if he had read her mind. "Gregor, I owe the major a farewell. He has been a good friend to me and my father."

His eyes were sullen and sleepy beneath his dark lashes. " 'Tis very unfair."

"Well, I'm sorry, but it cannot be helped."

He kissed her gently, teasing her lips with his in a way that made her ache and tremble. "But you will make it up to me, later?"

Her lips clung to his despite herself, her fingers tangled in his hair. "Of course," she murmured. Their kiss deepened. For a moment Meg closed her eyes and let herself be swept away by this new and wonderful experience, by the fact of being in love with her husband, of loving him so much she never wanted to leave his side. It would be so simple to stay here and let him do all those things to her that she had already learned to enjoy. So simple to pretend the world outside this room did not exist.

Except that it did.

Meg had responsibilities and duties, and those, as well as a sudden need to preserve what was left of her independence from being swallowed up by her feelings for him, made Meg realize she could not stay here any longer.

She disentangled herself. "I must go and dress."

Gregor groaned and flung himself back upon the bed. "Verra well, Meg. I will follow you down in a moment. And Meg," he called as she reached the door. She turned reluctantly, trying not to think of what an enticing picture he made, lying there naked upon the rumpled bedding. "I will most definitely be claiming my reward. Later."

The color swept into her cheeks, and it was with a very warm face that Meg hurried down the corridor to her own room.

Despite the banquet of the night before, Major Litchfield appeared to have awoken with a hearty appetite.

Meg, feeling more herself again in her position as Lady of Glen Dhui, served him another helping of seethed fish, and poured more ale into his mug. Gregor, seated on her other side, had filled himself with coffee and oatcakes, and was now leaning back in his chair with half-closed eyes, taking little part in the conversation.

"You will write to let us know how you are?" Meg said, taking a sip of her precious tea.

Major Litchfield smiled, nodded, and spoke around his full mouth. "I will indeed, Lady Meg. I believe I will miss Scotland very much."

Was there something more to his words than could be seen on the surface? If there was, Meg had no wish to delve into it. Instead she smiled and assured him, "We will all miss you, too. And I am sorry, Major, that my father cannot be here to say good-bye. He is very tired after yesterday, and I thought it best to leave him sleep."

Major Litchfield made a sympathetic moue. "I understand. He was most pleased with your union, Lady Meg. A personal dream come true for him, eh?"

Yes, the general was pleased. He had played matchmaker for the second time, and finally made a success of it. His daughter was wed to a gentleman, and not just any gentleman, but a gentleman whom the general had always liked and admired. He must feel as though his world were full to overflowing. Completed.

Was that why he was letting go? Because he had done what he set out to do?

Meg chanced a glance at her new husband, and with a frisson of shock realized he in turn was watching her, his eyes alert beneath his dark lashes. When he caught her peeping, he gave a slow smile, as if she amused him, and then turned his attention to adding cream to his coffee.

Meg fiddled with her napkin, desperately wishing herself miles away. This man was her lover—last night he had initiated her into the pleasures of the flesh, and she loved him. Did he already guess how she felt about him? Had he realized she was completely and totally besotted with him?

She needed time to think, to consider her position.

Last night, for her at least, had been something remarkable, something almost beyond her understanding. If he were to know how she felt, it might spoil this remarkable thing that they had. If he knew she loved him, he may change toward her. And suddenly she was very anxious not to do or say anything that might spoil what had occurred between them.

Better to keep her distance, then, until she had decided upon her most sensible and practical course of action.

Pasting on a bright smile, Meg turned her attention back to Major Litchfield and began to ask him about his imminent journey, listening as if every detail were a fascinating revelation. By the time the meal was done and the major had set off down the yew tree avenue, she felt completely exhausted.

An awkward silence fell between Gregor and herself.

Meg felt his gaze upon her, but she could not look at him. She didn't trust herself.

"There is still work to be done with the men," Gregor said at last. "Mabbe I should get to it." But he sounded as if he were asking her a question, and his eyes were fixed on her, as if seeking some clue as to her possible answer.

"They will be sleeping off their whiskey from last night." His eyes lit up.

Meg had replied before she had thought, and now she wished she had said nothing. Clearly he had taken her remark as an invitation.

His gaze slid to her and seemed to fix upon her mouth. She shivered, turning away, tightening her shawl about her as if it would protect her from his attentions. He must not think she was desperate to be in his arms, Meg thought feverishly. He must not think that she did not want him to go out to the men because she . . . well, because she . . .

"Of course you must get to work with the men," she said quickly, with a falsely jovial note. "What a good idea!"

His mouth quirked up. "Is it? I have a better one, Meg."

But she was suddenly very busy, pretending to collect up some of the pewter plates that had been left out from last evening. "I must speak with Alison," she murmured. "So much to do."

Meg heard him sigh. "Then I'll leave you . . . if that is really what you want?"

She did not dare to look at him. She knew just how tempting he would appear—tall and strong, his face so handsome, so appealing. No, she could not look at him. In another moment she heard him stride to the door, and then the sound of it closing after him. Meg sank into a chair and put her head in her arms.

What must he be thinking? She was mortified by her own stupidity. How *could* she fall in love with Gregor Grant? It had been on the tip of her tongue to ask him to take her upstairs again, so that they could while away the afternoon in bed together. But she did not trust herself. She would blurt out the truth about how she felt, and then what? No, much better to wait, to collect up the pieces of her protective shield and fasten it about her once more. She must prepare herself well for her next encounter with her handsome husband.

I must treat him as he treats me, Meg told herself. Enjoy him, yes, delight in him, yes, but never let him realize I am in love with him.

"The men of Glen Dhui are quick learners."

Gregor nodded in agreement, and continued staring down the glen at nothing in particular, ignoring the line of men who stood eagerly awaiting his notice. Malcolm Bain was watching him—he could almost feel his friend's eyes crawling over his skin. Gregor was used to keeping his true feelings hidden, and with anyone else, he could feel certain that he showed nothing of his inner emotions on his face or in his manner.

But this was Malcolm Bain, and he knew Gregor very well. He probably knew that Gregor was thinking about Meg.

Because he was. He seemed to have thought of little else since he first saw her.

Gregor's new wife was a revelation to him. He had not known what to expect, although he had certainly been looking forward to taking her to his bed. He had planned to enjoy his wedding night, but still, the sheer glory of it had come as a shock. Each time he had taken her, each time he had planted his seed within her, the need to do so again simply increased. This morning he could hardly bear for her to leave the bedchamber, and just now, when she had pretended not to understand that he was asking her to come back to their bedchamber with him, he had been aching with frustration.

She was a new bride, he reminded himself. Maybe he had hurt her last night with his ardor and she was too shy to tell him so. No, Gregor smiled, Meg would have no qualms about telling him if he had hurt her. Probably she was just embarrassed at the thought of everyone in the household knowing they were in bed together again, after they had only just gotten up. It did not matter to Gregor if they knew—such things had never concerned him—but Meg was different. She liked to maintain a certain façade of purity and respectability: the Lady of Glen Dhui. He would not push her into a situation where she might turn against him.

But neither was Gregor fool enough to believe she did not want him anymore. He had been with enough women to be clear about how she felt. Meg was in the throes of a genuine passion for him—for what they had done together last night. She was as enraptured by their lovemaking as he.

Perhaps that was what had frightened her.

That losing control of herself, that insatiable hunger for another human being, that sense of being swept away.

Gregor didn't blame her for wanting to take a moment to catch her breath, because so did he. He had wed her for a tangle of reasons, one of them being his desire for her, and another Glen Dhui. But he had never expected her to creep inside him like this, to make a home for herself where no woman had ever been.

He would need to be vigilant.

Gregor had been hurt too many times, used too many times, to ever trust a woman easily. And Meg was no exception, for wasn't she using him, too? Using his strength and experience to protect Glen Dhui?

"There he is!"

Malcolm Bain's harsh whisper brought him back to the present. Gregor blinked, and obediently turned to follow Malcolm's pointing finger, over toward the stables. A lad was leaning against a mounting block, his fair hair bright against the gray stone wall, watching intently as the men drilled.

"Is that your lad?"

Malcolm Bain swallowed, as if his heart was too full for him to speak.

"What is his name again, Malcolm?"

Malcolm Bain clenched and unclenched his hands, fighting for control. When he spoke at last his voice was almost normal, except for the underlying angry tremor. "His name is Angus. Angus *Forbes*, they call him. By rights it should be Angus MacGregor."

"He looks like a fine, braw lad. I dinna see much of Alison in him."

"Aye, the stronger MacGregor blood has swallowed up the feeble Forbes strain," Malcolm declared with relish.

"How old is he?"

Malcolm Bain sighed, all pleasure leaving him. "He's twelve years old," he said, desolation in his voice, and a sense of waste. All those years gone, and he had not known he had a son.

"Give it time, Malcolm," Gregor advised. "She'll come 'round. She loved you once. She might again."

"She loved me, aye, Gregor, and I dinna treasure it as I should have. Instead I tossed her love aside, like a worn penny I dinna need."

Gregor could think of nothing to say to that. Besides, he felt a sense of guilt for being the cause of Malcolm Bain's leaving Glen Dhui. Perhaps for that reason he should be the one to do something about it. He did not particularly fancy facing up to Alison's famous temper, but maybe he owed it to them.

"One more time through with the pistols and muskets," he said brusquely, putting aside both his own and Malcolm Bain's emotional problems. "Then we'll send them all off home. I'm in urgent need of a dram, and you can keep me company."

Malcolm Bain gave a grim nod. "My head still hurts from last night, but I'll be glad to, lad. If I drink enough, mabbe I'll forget all about Alison and my son."

Gregor thought that was unlikely, but he didn't spoil his friend's delusion. In his experience, once a woman got under a man's skin, there was nothing could get her out, not even the finest whiskey in all of Scotland.

Chapter 21

Gregor had been drinking. Meg could smell the whiskey strong on him when he came in for his midday meal. She said nothing—what could she say? If he felt the need to drown his sorrows in drink, then that was his business. But she thought it was more likely that he was keeping Malcolm Bain company while *he* drowned *his* sorrows.

It had been clear from Alison's behavior that all was still very wrong between Angus's parents.

Surely, Meg thought, if all feeling was dead between them, they would be completely indifferent to each other, wouldn't they? Didn't this amount of ill feeling mean that some spark still existed? Although whether it was a spark of love or hate was debatable.

Meg had tried to speak to Alison while they and the other women were putting the Great Hall to rights, but Alison just shook her head. After a time Meg gave up, deciding it might be best to let them be. Eventually they might sort it out for themselves.

Perhaps Gregor had come to the same conclusion.

She didn't ask him, she barely spoke to him as they ate, and she left the table before he had finished, pleading a dozen excuses. He gave her a look that was both patient and resigned, both qualities most unlike the Gregor Meg knew.

Was he tired of her already? And was she so contrary as to want him to pursue her when she had already decided she needed space to think?

Meg went to sit with the general for an hour or so. The old man had been overjoyed with the manner in which things had turned out. As if, Meg thought wryly, he had planned it that way from the beginning.

"Now all we need to make the fairy tale complete is for the duke to be a gentleman and stand aside peacefully," she couldn't resist saying. "Do you really think that will happen, Father?"

The general's eyes were fixed on the window, as if he were not blind to the view outside. For a moment Meg thought he would not answer, but then he heaved a sigh and turned to her with a wistful smile.

"I don't know the answer, Meg. If we were speaking of an ordinary man, then I would say yes. If we were speaking of an ordinary man, then I would say that he would not want to appear foolish, so he would step aside. But we are speaking of the Duke of Abercauldy, and I have come to realize that the duke is no ordinary man. He frightens me, daughter, and I don't frighten easily. He is so determined to have you, Meg, that I don't know if there is anything we can do, apart from killing him, that will change his mind."

"Gregor released Lorenzo this morning."

Meg had not been present, but she had heard the details from Alison, who had heard them from Angus, and so on. How the duke's favorite servant had sworn a terrible revenge upon them.

"Lorenzo is not as important as he thinks he is," the general replied dryly. "Do not be afraid of Lorenzo; Gregor could crush him with his little finger." He smiled again, looking suddenly very tired and frail. "I am so glad you brought Gregor home. You have made me a very happy, old man, Meg, and I thank you for it."

"Then I am happy, too, Father," she whispered, feeling tears sting her eyes.

"I wish your mother were here to see you," he murmured, turning again to the window. "She's been gone so long. So very long. And I miss her."

It was not often the general spoke of his wife. Meg was not sure that his speaking of her now was a good sign.

Leaving the general to rest, Meg found her way to her retreat. But once there, alone at her desk, she found herself sitting, staring at her books. It wasn't that she had nothing to do. There were entries to be made, notes to be taken, figures to be tallied. Meg had often thought it a pity she had been born a woman, for she would have made a very efficient factor for some great lord. She would have run his estate at a profit, and kept all the tenants happy at the same time.

Why wasn't her life as simple as adding up a column of figures?

No, there was plenty to be done, but Meg did not feel like tallying profits or working on new crops she might bully her tenants into planting. This was the day after her wedding, and yet it was just like any other day. On the surface it was, anyway.

Underneath was a different matter.

She had fallen in love with Gregor Grant, the Laird of Glen Dhui. She had wed the boy of her girlhood dreams, and he was everything she had ever wanted. He was the man she had been waiting for, the man whom she had wanted to come and sweep her off her feet. Except that he didn't love her.

He was the sort of man who made all women feel quite wonderful, Meg was certain of it. If he turned that dazzling, golden gaze on a woman, then she was his. How could she not be? Meg knew that Gregor had not become such an accomplished lover by sleeping alone. There must have been other women, and plenty of them.

He was attractive and women wanted him. Beautiful women. With so many to choose from, how could he ever love Meg Mackintosh, plain and freckled? He might like her, in fact he seemed to delight in her sharp tongue and peculiar ways, but he could never, ever love her. Best she come to terms with that right now and learn to deal with it, before she was drawn into yearning for the unattainable.

Gregor had found some paper and charcoal, and secreting himself in a quiet corner of the Blue Saloon, set to work rediscovering his talent for drawing. At first his hands felt clumsy, more used to gripping a sword than making pictures, but gradually the lessons he had learned long ago returned to him. He had never really forgotten them. He didn't attempt anything too difficult—not at first—but was content to make images of familiar objects. Yet he couldn't resist a tiny, mocking sketch of Airdy Campbell as he had last seen him, wild-eyed upon his dun horse; and a reverent, rather melancholy sketch of the general, seated by his window, gazing at a world he could no longer see.

Satisfied he had not lost his ability to capture expressions and emotions with a few deft strokes, Gregor went to find Meg. Alison told him that she was working, and had asked not to be disturbed.

"Though I dinna see ye taking much notice of that, Captain . . . sir."

"Oh, and why not?"

Alison sniffed. "Ye have that look."

Gregor's eyebrows soared. "*That* look, Alison Forbes?"

"Ye know what I mean," was all she would reply.

That look? Gregor smiled as he climbed the stairs to Meg's hidey-hole. If he did have a look, then it was frustration. Lorenzo being set free meant that their time together may well be finite. They should enjoy themselves while they could.

Meg might be cautious, but Gregor wasn't about to deny himself any longer. If she would not come to him, then he would find her.

The memory of her, soft and warm, was already making his blood hot. Her breasts in his hands, the creamy flesh so plump and sweet, and the feel of her tongue on his cock. Her mouth opening delightfully to his, just as he pushed between her thighs. The dreamy, sensual look in her eyes, just as she shattered.

By the time Gregor reached her door, he was fully erect beneath his kilt, and burning with the need to quench his desire.

He didn't knock, just flung open the door. His strength was greater than he had thought, or he was more desperate. It slammed back against a chest of drawers, causing the window frames to rattle, a lamp to totter and several papers to flutter to the floor.

Meg was seated behind her solid, functional desk—nothing spindly and decorative for her. She held a pen in one hand, and the other was raised to her lips, while her blue eyes were big and anxious, and fixed on him.

"Gregor?" she demanded in a squeak. "What is it? What's wrong?"

He cursed himself for frightening her so. Of course, she would think he had come to give her bad news, that Abercauldy was at the door with a hundred of his men, or some such thing. In an attempt to make amends, he forced a smile that probably looked ghastly.

In contrast, she looked beautiful. Her remarkable coloring always struck him first, and then he noticed the other things. Her smile, her long lashes, her pert little nose, and that delightful gap between her teeth.

"Gregor? Can you answer me?"

"There's nothing wrong, *morvoren*. I wanted to see you. I'm sorry if I have broken anything."

Meg blinked, once, twice, clearly thinking him quite mad, and then she set down her pen. He noticed she had made a large blot on her nice clean page. She cleared her throat, and he could see by the color slowly climbing into her cheeks that she wasn't as happy to see him as he was to see her.

"I asked not to be disturbed."

"Och, but surely when you gave those orders you dinna mean *me*, Meg?" he said, with pretended surprise.

Her mouth opened, then closed again, in a thin, straight line. She gave him a sideways glance, trying to decide whether he was being serious. She might be cross, but she was also disturbed by him being here, where he had never been before. In her sanctuary. Perhaps this is a day, thought Gregor, for doing things they had never done before.

Gregor smiled and closed the door softly behind him.

Meg looked panicked. "Gregor, I don't—"

"You have a smudge of ink on your face."

She stared at him, frowned, and put her hand up to her cheek. "Have . . . have I?"

"Och, you have." He prowled closer still, rounding the end of her desk. He heard her catch her breath. She wasn't afraid of him, she was afraid of herself—he was almost sure of it. It was time he put a stop to this before she started running in the opposite direction whenever she saw him.

Gregor brushed his fingers through a curl of her hair, lying loose against her shoulder, and twirled it around. "I've missed you, Meg."

"I have my work," she said, but she did not move. She seemed frozen to the spot, her mouth unsmiling, her eyes fixed straight ahead. But Gregor could see the pulse in her throat, there under her fine skin, beating wildly. He stooped and set his lips against it.

She jumped as though he had threatened to cut her throat.

"Gregor!"

"Dinna ye like that?" he asked her softly, his mouth hovering over her collarbone, his tongue dipping in the hollow there. "What about this?"

"It's not a matter of whether or not I like it—"

"But it is, Meg. It's exactly that."

He tilted her chin up, turning her to face him. There was fear in her eyes, and something else. A desperate need to keep control, to disguise her passion for him beneath her role as the practical Lady of Glen Dhui. Well, Gregor thought determinedly, he'd soon topple that house of cards. And he bent his head and claimed her mouth.

This was no soft, teasing kiss. His mouth was hot and

moist, his tongue darting, his hands gripping her face, giving her no escape from his attentions. Not that she struggled. She gasped, yes, but more from surprise than a dislike of what he was doing. And then she gave a soft little moan, and slipped her arms about his neck and clung on.

He took advantage of the moment to unfasten a number of hooks at the back of her gown, so that he could slip it down and caress her breasts. He broke the kiss at last, bending to suck at her nipples.

More papers fluttered to the floor, the pen with them.

To his surprised delight, he felt her hand beneath his kilt, cautiously feeling its way up his thigh. He held his breath, as inch by inch her fingers drew closer. At first her touch was light, tentative, and then she took hold of him, gripped him firmly, and gently squeezed.

"Oh Meg, Meg," he groaned. "Ye'll kill me."

"I'm sorry," she squeaked, letting go. "I didn't realize I was hurting."

"Hurting?" he mocked. "Hurting! I mean ye'll kill me with pleasure, lass."

Meg stared, and then she smiled. Gregor found himself unable to look away from her, she was so gorgeous. Her blue, blue eyes alight with laughter, her luscious lips curling up at the corners and that sweet gap between her front teeth. He wanted to eat her up. He wanted to . . .

He lifted her up out of her chair and set her on her desk. Right on top of her book and her papers. The ink well tipped over and rolled off, thudding onto the rug, dripping ink everywhere. Meg tried to wriggle out of his grip, looking in horrified dismay at the mess he had made, but Gregor was in no mood to stop and wait for her to set things to rights. She'd run away from him. Instead he slid his hands under her skirts, running them up the soft length of her thighs. His finger found that moist, hot place and slipped within.

Meg forgot the ink and the figures to be tallied and everything else. She gazed into his amber eyes, and then her lashes swept down in an attempt to hide her own reaction. But he knew. He could feel her passion building, until it was as hot as his.

Savoring the moment and her eager response, Gregor claimed her mouth again. And this time when she kissed him back, her hands sought under his kilt, finding him, holding him. He gave a shaky laugh, and moved between her open thighs, feeling her stockinged legs wrap around him.

He wanted her, Meg, with a need that was beyond his ken. Never before had a woman had this effect on him.

Bewildered by his own reactions, trying to hold back, while the urge to thrust hard and deep inside her was savage, Gregor stilled. He took a breath, and slowly released it, regaining some sense of control.

Meg moaned, moving her hips, and digging her fingers into his hard buttocks beneath the kilt.

"Ye want me, Meg," he said, and there was no laughter in his voice now, no gentle teasing. It was a statement of fact.

Her lips trembled, tears filled her brilliant eyes. "Oh, I do, Gregor. I do, I do . . ."

"Hush," he murmured. " 'Tis all right, Meg. I just needed ye to say it. A vow, if ye like. I needed to hear it."

She managed a shaky smile, and then her eyes went dazed, as he entered her the first little way, stretching her, trying to ignore the tremor in his own hands. "Meg," he whispered. "Let me in, *morvoren*."

"Yes," she said in a husky voice. "Gregor, yes."

He thrust deep, and then adjusting the tilt of her hips, thrust deeper still. Meg gripped her legs tighter about him, holding him inside her. He felt the little quakes and shivers already beginning in her. He had never known a woman so quick to come to pleasure. Gregor was tempted to withdraw, to make her wait, but he was too hot himself. So he thrust again, deep as he could, scattering more papers to the floor and sending Meg's precious teacup after them.

Meg cried out in ecstasy, her head thrown back, her hair tumbling about her. Abruptly she went soft and limp in his arms, but Gregor had not finished with her yet. Lifting her, still joined to her, he sat himself down in her chair and settled her comfortably upon his lap. Her lashes lifted lazily, and she looked at him with glittering blue eyes.

"I can feel you," she said, moving a little, rubbing herself against the length of his erection, her hands resting upon his chest for leverage.

He groaned softly, planting his own hands firmly upon her bottom to hold her still. "Wait," he murmured. "Wait until I cool down a little, and then it will last longer."

Meg gave him a wickedly teasing smile. "I don't think so," she said, and began to move against him, watching his face as she did so.

Gregor felt himself dissolving inside her, lost in her tight heat. He resisted for a moment more, gritting his teeth, but she had his measure. She leaned forward and began to kiss him, not for a moment stopping her sensual up and down movement. Her tongue mated with his, doing a dance he found impossible to resist.

She won. He erupted forcefully within her, arching his back and crying out so loudly, Meg put her hand across his lips to smother the noise. But she was laughing. Doubled over with it, clinging to him, tears running down her cheeks. He held her in his arms, rocking her, content to wait.

"Do you think they know?" she asked at last, lying quiet and restful against him.

"Who knows what?" he murmured, kissing the top of her head.

"The servants. Do you think they know what we have been doing?"

"Och, Meg, who cares what they know or what they think?"

Meg tilted her head and gave him a look. "*You* may not care, but *I* do. You are very arrogant to speak like that, Gregor Grant."

Gregor lifted a lazy dark brow. "I *am* arrogant. Or I was. Now I am beyond caring. There is too little of pleasure in this world, Meg. Better to take what you can, when you can, and bugger what anyone else says to it."

She considered that unembellished advice a moment, and then she sighed and lay her head back against his shoulder. "Maybe you're right," she acceded.

Gregor smiled to himself. "Does that mean you have stopped running away from me and hiding?"

"I didn't run away from you, nor did I hide!"

"Dinna you, Meg? I think you did, and if you do it again, I'll just have to come and find you again."

He waited for her sharp response. But Meg had always had the power to surprise him. She did so now, as she smiled up at him and, with one finger, carefully traced the shape of his mouth. "Promise?" she murmured.

Gregor left her in no doubt as to his reply.

* * *

The general came downstairs and joined them for supper, but by the time the meal had finished he was weary and sagging in his chair. Gregor helped him back up to bed. Meg watched them go, the two men she loved most in all the world. When Gregor returned, he was thoughtful and a little melancholy.

"He told me that you are my responsibility now," he said, when Meg asked him what was wrong.

Meg frowned. "I am no one's responsibility but my own, Gregor. You know that."

"Och, I know it, my little hornet. But your father is of the old school, Meg. He believes it is a man's duty to care for the women in his household. I felt as if he were handing you over to me, and he was doing so in the belief and with the knowledge that I will take good care of you."

Meg's lip trembled. "Oh, Gregor! It's as if he's letting go, now that you have come."

He held her in his arms, comforting her as she wept. His heart was heavy, but it was far worse for Meg. She was losing her father, every day watching him sink deeper into old age and infirmity, every day watching him take another step toward death.

After a time she wiped her eyes and found a plain handkerchief on which to blow her nose. "What of *your* father, Gregor?" she asked curiously. "Do you still miss him?"

Gregor smiled. "I do. When he was alive we fought over most things, but he was my father and my laird. You can love someone, Meg, and still be at odds with them most of your life. Love is not a simple thing; it can make our lives more difficult."

She was quiet, her face pale in repose, his brave, beautiful Meg.

Gregor held out his hand to her. "Come to bed," he said, but there was no innuendo in what he said, only a wish to comfort in whatever way he could.

She stared at him a moment, as though trying to gauge the secret meaning behind those simple words, and then she put her hand in his.

Meg had been asleep for a little while, when she felt his hands on her body, touching her, learning her. He cupped her breasts, his thigh sliding between hers, and his tongue traced a journey down the arch of her throat. She pressed closer, tangling her fingers in his unbound hair, no longer caring what he thought of her. He was right. Life was uncertain, and one must take what pleasure one could.

"Meg," he whispered, "my *morvoren*."

Meg stilled him, holding his face close above her own. "What does that mean?" she asked softly. "That word you say? It sounds so beautiful."

"*Morvoren*?" He smiled. "Mermaid."

The word had puzzled her since he first used it, but she hadn't asked. How many other women had he call his "mermaid"? She had not wanted to be forced to face the fact that she was not special to him after all.

"My beautiful mermaid," he whispered into her hair. "Take me deep under the waves with you, Meg. Drown me in your kisses."

She gasped as he began kissing her, forgetting about the others as he branded her flesh with his lips, making his journey down, until he found the place that gave her most pleasure.

If he was drowning, then so was she. And she didn't care. Loving him was everything she had ever hoped it to be. And even if it lasted only a week, Meg was determined to be content with that. Her memories of him would just have to last her all her life.

Chapter 22

In fact, Meg had three weeks of perfect happiness. Long, dreamy days and hot, sultry nights. Always, there was the fear of danger hanging over them, but she and Gregor used their time fully and well. They rode out into the glen, visiting their larger tenants and the smaller crofters, bathing in the warm glow of their people's joy at their union.

Gregor, seated in one tiny cottage with an elderly, wizened couple, listened to Meg ask after the health of each of their relatives by name. She knew them all, he thought proudly, and clearly she cared about them all. She was their lady, and they belonged to her.

He had known Glen Dhui meant a great deal to her, but until now he had not understood the nature of her relationship with the glen and its people. She loved them—genuinely loved them—and she had dedicated her life to looking after them and making their lives easier—whether they liked it or not!

"I dinna know aboot these 'tatties, m'lady," the old man said, eyeing her from beneath his grizzled brows.

"What don't you know about the potatoes, Iain? Did you plant some as I told you?"

"Aye, I did."

"How did they taste?"

"They tasted fine, m'lady," Iain's wife interrupted, giving her husband a quelling look.

"I suppose they would be well enough, if a person was desperate," Iain went on, ignoring the look. "But they have no taste."

Gregor hid his smile, lowering his brows sternly. "They may have no taste, Iain, but they'll fill your belly in difficult times. Remember the last time the oat crop failed? It was in my father's day. People in Glen Dhui died."

Iain looked suitably chastened.

"Dinna worry," Gregor went on. "They taste better if you mix them with milk and butter, or mash them up with kale and fish and cook them on the griddle."

Iain and his wife exchanged wondering glances.

As they were leaving, the old woman took Meg aside. "'Tis fine that the laird likes to cook, m'lady, but ye shouldna encourage it. 'Tis no' proper for the Chief of the Grants of Glen Dhui to be holding a pan and doing women's work."

Meg nodded sagely, and it was not until they had ridden away that she burst out laughing. When she told him, Gregor laughed too, but he refuted the "women's work" claim.

"A soldier has to learn to cook for himself," he said, "or else he starves. And the Duke of Argyll has potatoes in his garden, too. And he is just as bossy as you, Lady Meg, in making his people eat them."

"If I am bossy, then it is for their own good," she retorted primly.

He grinned at her back, as she rode away.

As the days passed, their usual tasks were set aside, or given to others to complete. Malcolm Bain seemed happy enough to take over the forming of their little troop, and Alison the household chores. The general slept, rousing himself in the evening to greet Meg and Gregor when they came to take their supper with him.

On one warm, still day, Gregor took Meg swimming in Loch Dhui, holding her slippery body in his arms and kissing her cold lips until she burned. Then they lay upon the smooth stones and let the sun dry them.

"I used to come here as a boy," Gregor told her, lazily running his eyes over her naked back and the curve of her bottom. "I had my favorite places in the glen."

"I was fifteen when we came to Glen Dhui," Meg replied sleepily. "I spent my first summer riding, just riding. I had never been so happy. There was a cave, up on the side of Cragan Dhui. Sometimes I would sit there for hours and look down, over the glen. I still go there, now and again."

Gregor smiled. "To watch over your subjects, Queen Meg?"

Meg pulled a face at him, and then squealed as he reached for her, his intentions plain in the narrowing of his eyes.

On the ride home, Gregor pointed out the birds and plants and animals to her, naming them all, as if he had stored the information away in his head all the years he'd been gone. His eyes glowed with a deep, quiet joy.

Anyone could see, Meg told herself, that he belonged here. The glen was in his blood. No matter what happened between them, she would never ask him to leave.

It had been a perfect day.

The late summer continued to be kind to them, the rain stayed away, and the sun shone. And Meg was happy, happier than she had ever been in her life. She was in love; she glowed with love. But despite her happiness, there was almost a feeling of bitter-sweetness about loving Gregor. She knew it could not last. He was not the sort of man to live his life with a woman like Meg Mackintosh. Sooner or later he would glance away from her and see someone else, someone more beautiful, cleverer, more suitable for a man like him.

And then she would lose him.

Oh, not physically. He would still be here in Glen Dhui, for he was the laird now, and he loved this place and like her, he took his duties seriously. But, emotionally, he would remove himself from her. He would still be kind—Meg had come to the knowledge that Gregor was a kind man. He was the sort of man who picked up little children who had fallen over, or saved wounded birds from cats. He was *kind*. So he would be kind to Meg. But he could not love her; he could never love her.

Not as she loved him.

"My lady?"

Meg glanced up from the lavender bush she had been pruning. The spiky flowers had long since finished, and the woody stalks needed to be cut back. She had taken a moment, while Gregor was discussing some soldierly matters with Malcolm Bain, to visit the herb garden and make the most of her time alone.

Duncan Forbes was standing on the paved path, beside a sprawling mound of thyme, looking very much out of place.

"Duncan, what is it?"

She had seen little of her tacksman of late, but she had not thought of it until now, when he was back. Perhaps he had stayed away because Gregor was here to help her in the running of the estate. Or so Duncan would think. Duncan Forbes did not believe a woman was capable of such things; they were men's work.

The truth was, Meg needed no assistance in such matters; Gregor understood that and was not foolish enough to offer it.

"There is a thing that has been worrying me, my lady," Duncan went on slowly, looking down at his feet. "I dinna know what to do about it."

Something worrying Duncan? Meg had always believed him to be so sure of himself that nothing worried him. He infuriated her sometimes, with his black-and-white view of the world and everyone in it.

"Well, then, tell me what this problem is. Maybe I can help."

Duncan shuffled about, knocking against the thyme with his boot and sending the strong smell of the herb into the air about them. "Lady Meg, have ye ever done a thing because ye truly believed it was best for the person involved?"

"Do you mean, have I ever done a thing because I thought I knew best?" Meg smiled. "I think we have all done that, Duncan, at one time or another."

Duncan managed a sickly smile in return, and shuffled some more.

Meg sighed, and rose to her feet, the scent of the lavender on her hands. "Tell me what is worrying you, Duncan, please!" she cried in exasperation.

Her tacksman looked up from his boots, and his dark

eyes were bleak. "When Malcolm Bain left Glen Dhui that last time, my lady," he said, with the air of one making his last confession. "When he left with the laird, he gave me a letter for Alison. He had tried to speak to her, but she wouldna listen to him. She ran off. So he gave me a letter instead. He said it was to explain, and I was to give it safe into her hands."

Meg heaved a sigh, already knowing what he was about to say. "But you didn't give it to Alison, did you, Duncan?"

"No, I dinna do it," Duncan said with another sickly smile. "I had it in my head that it would be best if Alison thought he'd deserted her. Walked away without a backward glance. Then, I thought, she'd get over him the sooner. I was thinking of *her*, mind. She's a Forbes and my nearest kin, and it was my duty to see to her welfare. I thought I knew what would be best for her, Lady Meg."

"Oh, Duncan, you had no right to keep that letter from her! What did it say?"

"That he loved her with all his heart, but that he was bound by duty to go with the young laird. He said he would never forget her."

"So, no requests to wait, or promises to return," Meg murmured. But then Malcolm Bain was not a man to make promises he could not keep. He had made his choice, and left Alison behind, and if he now regretted it, 'twas too bad. "Well," she went on, shaking off her melancholy mood, "it was a romantic letter nonetheless. Alison would probably have kept it. Has she ever loved another man?"

"I used to hope, but no, there's never been anyone else."

"Then she may as well have had the letter all that time ago. It wouldn't have changed anything, would it? She must have loved Malcolm Bain very much, Duncan. You did her a disservice by keeping his good-bye from her, no matter that you believed you were doing what was best for her."

"Aye, I know that now." He scuffed his boots, hitting the thyme once again. "Do ye think I should tell her, Lady Meg?"

"Yes, I think you should. She has a right to know Malcolm Bain did leave her a letter when he went. He didn't just walk out on her without a word, and that is what she still believes. It's what you've allowed her to believe, Duncan. I do think it's up to you to set it right. If you like, I will tell Malcolm Bain, but I will order him not to intervene."

A flush had come into Duncan's tanned face, but he accepted her words without argument. "Verra well, Lady Meg."

"And Duncan," as he went to walk away, "thank you for telling me. I am sure Alison will be cross with you, but just remember, when she has calmed down she will understand."

Meg watched her tacksman leave, his head bowed, and hoped that was true. But if she was Alison, wouldn't she want to know about the letter? Even if it was twelve years too late? Clearly Alison and Malcolm Bain had been very close, but maybe it just wasn't meant to be. Sometimes circumstances were such that they drove people apart, or forced them to go their separate ways.

Life could be cruel and difficult.

Gregor was right, it was best to take from it what you could, when you could, while you could.

Meg shaded her eyes against the sun, watching Duncan's figure as it vanished around the side of the house. He was walking very upright and stiff, like a brave soldier going into battle. As Meg went to turn away, a movement caught

her gaze, a splash of color through the green yews, a flounce
of yellow on the gray stone bridge that spanned the burn.

A woman in a yellow dress.

One of her tenants, perhaps? But as Meg stared, she realized that there were two women and a man. They were approaching on foot, the man leading two horses. Meg soon
recognized the dark head of Shona and the lighter one of
Kenneth, her husband. But there was a second woman
walking beside them, a woman in a bright yellow gown that
swung and dipped to show her dainty ankles.

For some reason the sight of that yellow gown made
Meg's heart flutter.

Setting down her shears, Meg left the herb garden, closing the gate gently behind her. It was some time now since
Shona had come to visit Glen Dhui. Last time she had
come, she had brought lotions and potions, and her smile
had made everyone lighter of heart. The time before, she
had brought fear and consternation with her story of the
duke and his first wife, Isabella.

What would she bring this time? Meg asked herself
anxiously.

Despair or joy? Happiness or misery?

"Lady Meg!" Shona was waving her arm. She quickened
her steps, hurrying along in front of the others, her basket
banging against her side. Meg saw that her face was alight
with a smile, and she felt her shoulders sag in relief. Good
news, then!

"One of Major Litchfield's men stopped by our cottage,
and told us that ye were wed!" Shona was saying, breathless and beaming at Meg. The wind had whipped color into
her cheeks and the fine lines about her eyes creased as she

smiled. "Ye'll be verra happy. But then I knew that, from the first time I saw the two of ye together. I dinna need to have the sight to know that!"

Meg laughed, and accepted her strong embrace. "I did not expect you to come all this way to wish me well, Shona. Gregor and I intended to come and visit you, when it was . . . when we were able. It all happened so suddenly, I didn't have time to fetch you here before—"

"Och, I dinna mind that! I am happy for ye, my lady. I think ye and the laird are well matched."

"Do you?" Meg teased, but there was a genuine question in her eyes.

Shona sighed in exasperation. "Of course ye are! Ye with yer feet set firm on the ground, and he with his head adrift in the clouds. And he with his strong arm and brave heart to protect ye, and ye with yer caring ways and nurturing heart to wrap around him and hold him safe. Of course ye are well matched!"

Meg had never thought of it like that, and she wasn't sure now if it was the truth, but still she laughed as Shona squeezed her again, and finally released her.

Kenneth had reached them, and gave her a wink. "I'll not crush ye, too, Lady Meg, but ye have my good wishes. And Captain Grant, of course."

Meg thanked him, but her eyes strayed to the other woman, still dawdling along the avenue of yew trees. She was slim and pretty, with long, fair hair that straggled down her back and looked like it needed a good combing. The yellow gown, though limp and dusty, and grubby about the hem, nicely outlined her slim figure.

Shona followed Meg's gaze, shading her own eyes to watch the woman's approach. "We have a surprise for the captain," she announced evenly. "His cousin has come to visit. She happened upon us at the cottage a week ago, Lady Meg. Poor lassie. She is in desperate straits. Her husband has ill-treated her and she has run away from him, and now she is in need of some tender care."

Meg frowned. "Cousin? I do not think Gregor has any cousins. Apart from his mother and his sister, he is alone in the world."

Kenneth let out a snort of annoyance, and turned to Shona. "I told ye she wasna anything to do with Captain Grant!" he said, but his eyes twinkled. He knew his wife and her kind heart all too well. "Ye are far too soft, Shona. If King George of England came to yon door and told ye he was a Jacobite, ye would ask him in for a dram. I've told ye not to let yersel' be taken in, but still it happens."

Shona pulled a face at him, but the blue eyes she turned to Meg were anxious. "Despite what Kenneth thinks, I have had some doubts of my own. But she was so grief-stricken, so sad and alone. I couldna just turn her out. I hope I've not brought trouble upon ye."

Meg hoped so, too. There was something about the fair-haired woman that struck her with a sense of foreboding. Was this the dark shadow Alison had spoken of, that would blow up out of a clear sky to blight her happiness?

"I'm sure it is a misunderstanding," she began, "maybe she has the wrong Grant, do you think?"

"You dinna tell me it was so long away," the woman called out, in a soft, complaining voice. "My feet are all blisters."

"Well, ye are here now," Kenneth retorted unsympathetically.

The woman pretended not to hear him, giving a heartfelt

sigh, while her gaze was drawn to the façade of Glen Dhui Castle. Her eyes were a clear, guileless blue, but when she realized the size and grandeur of the dwelling, their expression became predatory—as if she saw an opportunity there. A moment later Meg told herself it had been her imagination, for the woman had turned to her with a sad little smile, and held out her hand.

"I am Barbara Campbell," she said prettily. "Is it true you have wed my Gregor?"

Chapter 23

For a brief moment, Meg found herself unable to move. Barbara's firm fingers closed on hers, so she must have held out her hand to the other woman, but she did not remember doing it. Up close, Barbara's face was an oval—smooth and perfect—and she had a tiny nose and full lips—and those big, blue eyes. Her fair hair was the color of butter, and its uncombed state did not detract at all from its thick and heavy beauty. It was Meg, rumpled from her pruning, wearing one of her oldest gowns, who felt out of place.

Barbara Campbell, the woman Gregor had fought for, the woman he had almost died for . . .

Meg heard Kenneth say something, but she could not distinguish the words, and then Shona's reply, but again the words were garbled and made no sense. If Gregor had fought a duel over this woman in Clashennic—if he had put his life at risk for this woman—then he must love her. He must love her desperately. And Barbara Campbell looked to be exactly the sort of girl whom Meg would imagine on Gregor's arm.

She had known this day would come, and that she would lose him. She just hadn't realized it would come so soon.

"Barbara Campbell? What are ye doing here?"

The voice behind her was so loud it made Meg jump. Malcolm Bain stepped up closer, breathing hard, as if he had run. Never the most handsome of men, he was frowning at Barbara in a truly hideous fashion. But Barbara did not seem to notice, as she gave him one of her sweet smiles.

"Malcolm Bain! 'Tis good to see you. I am run away from Airdy, did you know? I was looking for a place to hide from him, somewhere among friends, where I will be safe. And of course I thought of Gregor Grant."

"Of course ye did," was Malcolm Bain's grim retort. "Well, this woman is Gregor Grant's wife and she dinna want ye here in her house. So be on yer way, Barbara!"

Barbara blinked her big, blue eyes, her full lips trembled, and a single, perfect tear ran down her smooth cheek.

Shona's soft heart could take no more. She reached out a sympathetic hand to pat Barbara's shoulder, at the same time speaking firmly to Malcolm Bain. "That's enough. Lady Meg would no' be so cruel as to turn away a creature in distress." She looked at Meg as she said it, convinced that Meg would do everything in her power to comfort Barbara Campbell.

Meg found she could not disappoint her. "No, of course I wouldn't turn her away. You must come inside, Barbara, and rest your feet."

Malcolm Bain gave a groan of disgust, while Kenneth rolled his eyes at his wife.

But Shona was smiling. "There, my poor lassie!" she said. "I knew that Lady Meg would not let ye down." And she bustled ahead toward the castle, her arm around a delicately sniffling Barbara, with Kenneth trailing behind.

As Meg moved to follow, Malcolm Bain put out a hand to stop her.

"My lady, this isna a good plan," he said with a quiet urgency. "Barbara Campbell is no sweet lassie. She has an eye to what's best for Barbara, and she dinna care who gets hurt in the process."

Meg managed a grave smile. The emptiness inside her had given way to a tentative hopefulness. Perhaps Gregor would not cast Meg aside for Barbara, perhaps he would realize it was with Meg that his real future lay.

Either way, it was up to Gregor to make the choice.

"Thank you, Malcolm, I understand what you're saying," she said, her decision made. "But it is for Gregor to say whether Barbara stays or no." Yes, Gregor would decide his own future. And hers.

Malcolm heaved a sigh. "Aye, well . . . There's something ye should mabbe understand about the lad, Lady Meg." He looked uncomfortable. "He has a soft spot when it comes to the lassies. He canna bear to hurt a single one, however they might treat him in return. And Barbara Campbell is used to having her way with him; she'll not give up without a fight. Trust me, m'lady, he needs ye to stand firm *for* him."

Meg frowned. This did not sound like the Gregor she knew. Captain Gregor Grant of the Campbell Dragoons, shouting out orders, firing his pistol, waving his sword about? *A soft spot when it comes to the lassies?* Well, that was probably true, but why should he allow himself to be used if he did not wish it? After all, Meg reminded herself, stoking up her indignation, he had requested payment from *her*, when she asked for his help!

No, if Gregor allowed Barbara to have her way with him, then it must be because he wanted to. It was as simple as that. And if that was the case, it was best if Meg learn it as quickly as possible.

"Lady, dinna ye want him?" Malcolm Bain spluttered. "If ye want him, then ye need to send Barbara away. Now!"

Send Barbara away, when Gregor could very easily do it himself? Meg didn't think so!

"I have to go," Meg said, stepping around Malcolm Bain's wide bulk. But as she moved toward the house, Meg remembered Duncan and their conversation, what seemed ages ago, in the herb garden. "Malcolm Bain, there is something you should know. I have heard . . . that is, I believe that you left a letter for Alison, when you went from Glen Dhui all those years ago?"

His craggy face creased in confusion at the change of subject, and then as quickly cleared. His blue eyes turned bleak. "Aye, so I did. I'd forgotten."

"Well, for . . . for various reasons, the letter never reached Alison. She never received it."

He stared at her. "Never reached her? Then she must have thought . . . She must believe I left her without a word."

The pain in his voice struck a chord in Meg's own aching heart. She reached out to grasp his arm, giving it a compassionate squeeze. "Yes, I think that is what she must believe, Malcolm. Perhaps that partly explains why she is still so angry."

Anger pushed through the bleakness in his blue eyes. "Why did she no' get the letter, Lady Meg? I gave it to Duncan to give to her."

Meg tightened her grip on his arm, feeling the sudden rigidity of his muscles as the truth came to him. Rage and hurt burned in his eyes, and he was clearly longing to find Duncan and hurt him, too. But loyalty and obedience held him in place, rather than her feeble strength in comparison to his.

"I don't want a fight between you and Duncan," she ordered him firmly. "Do you hear me, Malcolm Bain? He loves his sister, he cares for her, he thought he was doing what was best for her. He is sorry now, and Alison will make him sorrier. Any words that need to be said about the letter should come from her."

Gradually he began to relax a little, and then, to Meg's surprise, he gave a hard laugh. "Aye, let Alison rip him up. She'll tear him to pieces with that tongue o' hers."

Meg allowed her hand to drop. "I don't envy him," she agreed.

Malcolm Bain smiled, and now there was real anticipation in it. "Nor do I."

"Well," Meg glanced at the gray stone house. Barbara was in there. Waiting. "I'd better go and see to Barbara Campbell's blisters."

She had turned away when she heard Malcolm say behind her, "If Barbara is here, my lady, then Airdy will follow. And ye know what *that* means, don't ye?"

"It is up to Gregor," she repeated, over her shoulder, and kept on walking.

"No, lady," Malcolm Bain called, "it is up to ye!"

So, what was she hoping for? Meg wondered as she walked. That Gregor would drive the poor unfortunate Barbara from his door? Remembering his wounds, remembering stitching the sword slash on his arm, Meg knew that secretly that was her hardhearted hope. That he would loudly declare his love for Meg, and tell Barbara to be gone. Well, that was all very well, if she were watching a melodrama upon the stage, but it was doubtful that could be true life.

He does not love Barbara, she assured herself as she walked. How could he, after she had turned from him, after he had won a duel for her? He must despise her. Or maybe he was just heartbroken? And now that she was returning to him, begging for his help again . . .

Meg had known her happiness would have a limited time—it was far too wonderful to be the forever kind. Would her role as Gregor's wife now go into its next phase—the helpmeet, the fellow ruler of Glen Dhui, the kind smile and sympathetic ear, and occasionally, the warm body in his bed? But the last would be a rare thing indeed, and would be restricted to procreation. Because they would need children, wouldn't they, to inherit Glen Dhui? So whenever Gregor came to her bed, she would know it was purely to make an heir. . . .

Something hot and wet trickled down Meg's cheek, and she put up her fingers to it, surprised to find she was crying. Meg never cried. For a moment she was too shocked to do anything, and then she wiped her face dry. A shaky laugh, and she shook her head at her own stupidity. She was not usually prone to flights of fancy, except where Gregor Grant was concerned.

"He won't turn to Barbara," she told herself firmly as she walked. "Of course he won't! He's your husband, you foolish lass!"

But her words sounded blighted. As if she were shouting them against a thunderstorm, with no hope of being heard.

Gregor had been upstairs to Meg's retreat, but it was empty. Only her perfume was there, to remind him of her. The smell of it was enough to make him twitch all over, thinking of her and the way she felt in his arms, the sounds she made when he did certain things to her.

Disappointed—he had been looking forward to another tryst on her desk—he wandered back to the head of the stairs. Voices in the Great Hall caught his attention. Curious, he looked over the banister and felt a jolt of recognition right down to his toes.

"I'm sorry I told you I was his kin," that familiar voice was saying. That sweet voice he had last heard on a cold, misty dawn, sobbing for forgiveness in Airdy's arms, while Gregor stood over them, dripping blood and wondering what the hell he was supposed to do now.

Barbara? Barbara Campbell, here?

"I was so frightened, Shona," she said, as high and clear and innocent as a child. "I dinna know what to do. I said the first thing that came into my head. I do that. Gregor will tell you, I am sadly scatterbrained."

Gregor flinched. She made it sound as if they were still . . . Abruptly, his eyes narrowed. Where was Meg?

Down in the Great Hall, Shona was making soothing noises, while Kenneth stood back and watched the scene with cool eyes. Alison Forbes was hovering in the doorway to the Blue Saloon, a little frown twitching between her dark brows, and her brother stood behind her. But no Meg.

Gregor all but groaned aloud. Barbara Campbell, here at Glen Dhui! That was all he needed! As if the Duke of Abercauldy and Lorenzo were not meal enough, he had to have the sly-tongued Barbara on his plate as well. He wished her and Airdy to farthest ends of Scotland, and felt inclined to tell her so.

At that moment she looked up. That blue gaze, so different from Meg's, fastened on him like a bird of prey. Predatory and selfish, that was Barbara, while Meg was warm and generous and good. He watched, appalled, as her eyes filled with tears, and then she was running, but in an elegant sort of way, up the stairs toward him, all the while making little gasping sounds. She was wearing a yellow gown he remembered that he had bought her when she claimed Airdy was too mean to do so. He could ill afford it, but he had thought at the time she looked damned pretty in it.

Now the sight of her left him cold.

"Barbara," he said in a flat voice, "what the blazes are you doing here?"

Instead of answering, she flung herself at him, almost knocking him on his back, and he had no choice but to catch her if he wasn't to tumble over the railing with her on top of him. As his arms went around her she burst into noisy sobs, clutching at his shirt with fingers that felt more like a hawk's talons. She was soft and her hair brushed his nose, and once he would have melted at the sight and touch of her.

Now the very feel of her repelled him.

This was Barbara Campbell, the woman who had humiliated him and left him to his fate. This was Barbara Campbell, who manipulated men for her own ends and pretended to be what she was not. And quite suddenly he realized he had had enough of her, and women like her. Give him Meg any day! A woman who spoke the truth and looked a man in the eye, who smiled when she was happy and cried when she was sad, and none of it was to get her own way.

Women like Barbara had too easily manipulated him, perhaps because of his mother, the queen of all manipulators. But no more. He would never again jeopardize his life for such a paltry reason, the life that Meg had given to him. . . .

Gregor opened his mouth to tell Barbara she had to go, and his gaze slid beyond her, down the stairs, and found Meg. The words died in his throat.

She was standing as if she had turned to ice, her hands at her sides, her head tilted up. But there was nothing icy about her expression. She looked as if someone had run her through with a sword, and it had hurt. It had torn her apart.

"Meg?" he cried, and then realizing that he still held Barbara Campbell in his arms, tried to set her aside. She clung even harder, sobbed even harder, and he struggled with her, cursing her under his breath. When he finally managed to get her away from him, and looked again to where Meg had been standing, he saw only empty space.

Meg had gone.

Bewildered, Gregor turned to look about the Great Hall from his vantage point on the top landing. The fact that Shona and Kenneth were there surprised him, and then Malcolm Bain, glaring up at him for some reason, Duncan looking pale beneath his tan, and Alison peering at him in open-mouthed astonishment.

Gregor came down the stairs, ignoring Barbara's wailing and floundering behind him. "Where's Meg?" he demanded an answer.

No one answered him. They looked embarrassed, except for Malcolm Bain, who looked angry.

"WHERE IS SHE?" he repeated, in his best Captain of Dragoon's roar. Were they deaf? Or did they somehow believe that he would betray Meg with that foolish woman?

"I think she's gone outside," Shona answered uneasily, avoiding his eyes.

"Ye great daft haddock," Malcolm Bain declared, glowering at him under his bushy eyebrows, and confirming Gregor's fears.

Gregor raised his own brows. "Say what you have to say, Malcolm. I can see you're bursting with it."

"Well, of course she's gone! What did ye expect her to do, after she's come upon ye and that piece there, clasped in each other's arms? Ye've broken her heart in twa, ye thick beastie. Och, ye dinna deserve her anyway!"

"Barbara threw herself at me," Gregor replied, fighting his anger, and wondering why he'd been adjudged guilty when he'd done nothing wrong.

"Oh, and ye couldna have held her off? Ye are a fool, Gregor Grant! If ye lose Lady Meg because of that baggage, then ye truly dinna deserve to be a happy man."

Gregor shot him a furious look, turned, and strode toward the door. From the corner of his eye he noticed Barbara hurrying to intercept him, but he ignored her and kept going.

Behind him, Alison's voice rose with temper. "A fool, is he? A fool, aye? I know who the fool is here, Malcolm Bain MacGregor!"

Duncan's murmur of, "Alison, hush, Alison, let me finish what I had to tell ye!" seemed to have little effect on her.

Gregor allowed himself one small, vengeful smile as he stepped out into the afternoon sunshine. And stopped, hearing the thud of a horse's hooves. A woman with red hair flew down the yew avenue and over the bridge, and turned up the glen.

She was gone.

He took to his heels, running to the stables. Angus was standing outside, and Gregor drew to a sliding halt in front of the boy.

"Dinna you know better than to let her go by herself?" he shouted, needing to vent his fear and frustration on someone.

The boy stared back at him, but there was no fright in his eyes, just a flicker of anger that reminded Gregor very much of Alison. "She ordered me to, sir. I didna have much of a choice, did I?"

"She should not be out alone. She could be in danger."

Angus frowned. "I asked to go with her, sir, but she said she wanted to be alone. I suppose I should have made her let me go, but Lady Meg is a stubborn one."

Gregor looked at twelve-year-old Angus and sighed. The boy had done his best, and Gregor had no right to chastise him. "You have my gratitude, Angus, for making the attempt."

Angus flushed, and looked pleased and worried at the same time.

"Go and get your fath— that is, Malcolm Bain for me, Angus. He's in the Great Hall, or he was a moment ago."

Gregor could have bitten off his tongue, but other than a puzzled look, the boy didn't seem to understand the error his laird had almost made. He took to his heels, hurrying toward the castle house and passing Barbara in her yellow dress, on her way to the stables.

Gregor groaned aloud. "Oh, no!"

"Gregor? Gregor, please . . ."

"Barbara, has it never occurred to you that I may not want you here? That I am tired of being used by you? I have a wife and I dinna want you in the same house as her."

That tear again, running down her cheek. How did she do that? Was it something she had learned, like reading and writing? Gregor shook his head in disgust.

"I am going after Meg. Stay here, Barbara. We will talk when I get back. Is Airdy somewhere behind you?"

Barbara's tears stopped as if by magic, and she pulled a sullen little moue. "How should I know? Probably. He follows me everywhere, Gregor. Wherever I go, he finds me. That is why I have come to you," her eyes brightened. "You are the only one who can make him go away."

Gregor laughed despite himself, but it was without any real humor. The woman was so self-centered, so focused on her own problems, that it was almost amusing. So different from Meg, sweet, practical, bossy Meg who prodded her tenants to grow potatoes so that they would have something to eat when the oat crop failed.

"I must go." He was already heading into the stables to find his horse. Barbara trailed after him, looking disconsolate.

"You've never spoken to me like this before," she said sadly, watching as he hurriedly saddled the animal. "You always cared what happened to me before, Gregor."

Gregor turned to look at her in amazement. "I fought a

duel for you, Barbara, and you went straight back to Airdy. Have you forgotten?"

"I'd hoped you'd kill him," she sighed, "and I'd be free."

Suddenly Gregor felt cold. He looked at her for a long, silent moment, and then he went back to saddling his horse. Behind him, Barbara was telling him how difficult it was to live with Airdy, how much she longed to be rid of him, but he was no longer listening. He was thinking about Meg and how he had to find her, how he had to explain to her that the sight of him and Barbara on the landing was not what she thought. That he had never loved Barbara, that he never could love a woman like Barbara.

It was Meg he wanted. Meg he couldn't live without.

Gregor swung his leg over the horse's back and rode it out into the yard. Malcolm Bain was running from the castle, Angus not far behind him. "Gregor!" he called. "Wait for me, lad!"

But Gregor did not wait.

"Gregor! Kenneth says he thinks they saw Lorenzo and his men, down in the glen. Do ye hear me?"

Gregor heard him. His stomach clenched, his hands tightened on the reins. Lorenzo was in the glen, and Meg was alone.

"Get as many men as you can!" he shouted over his shoulder. "We have to find her!"

He dug in his heels and his horse shot forward, away toward the bridge over the burn, and then up the glen in the direction Meg had gone.

Chapter 24

What if I canna find her?

W The words went through his head, over and over again. They were taken up by the thud of his horse's hooves on the ground. *What if I canna find her?* The thought left him feeling desolate, broken, a hollow man. If Meg was gone, then there would be nothing for him. He would have Glen Dhui, yes, he would be the laird again, and this he had longed for for twelve years, although he had not dared to speak his longings aloud.

But now . . .

Now all that was like rain on the wind, something that came and went and mattered not. It was Meg who mattered. Without Meg his life was nothing, he would be worse off even than he had been when he lost Glen Dhui. Meg was his future. He had not realized how much he had come to think of her as always being there, at his side. Until now, when he might very well have lost her.

As if to add to his anguish, the sky had clouded over, with mist hanging low over part of the glen, and a rainstorm sweeping down the slopes of Liath Mhor.

Where could Meg have gone?

He drew up his mount, wiping the rain from his eyes and tossing back his hair. *Think! Where would Meg go for shelter? Where would she go if she felt alone and threatened, abandoned and unwanted?*

Her retreat, of course. But if she could not go there, if she could not go home to Glen Dhui Castle, then where?

Another shower of rain swept over him, stinging his face, blinding him, but Gregor hardly noticed it. He was thinking back to the warm day by Loch Dhui, when Meg had lay upon the stones and told him how, when she first came here, she had ridden the glen upon her horse.

There had been a cave on Cragan Dhui, where sometimes she had sat for hours, looking down over the glen. Gregor had laughed, he remembered, and called her Queen Meg.

Of course, the cave! Gregor, too, had hidden there as a boy, playing games, drawing, or just enjoying his own company and that of the other boys of the glen. He knew the cave, and he had a strong feeling that was where Meg was now.

With a shout and a quick dig of his heels, Gregor set off at a gallop.

Smoke poured sullenly from cottage chimneys. Cattle and sheep stood, their heads bowed, beneath the driving rain. The linen shirt Gregor was wearing was soaked through, and his kilt dripped, but he hardly noticed, and if he had, he wouldn't have cared. He rode on, with only one clear thought. Meg was in the cave, and he had to find her.

At first he could not see the narrow opening in the lower slopes of Cragan Dhui at all. He could see the track, zigzagging across the side of it, but apart from that, the greenery appeared unbroken. There was an old rowan tree and bracken filling the hollows, and a hare went running, bounding through the grass. His eyes followed its path, and suddenly he spotted the cave. Like a thick, charcoal line, it cut through the green of the hillside.

With a smile, Gregor urged his horse forward.

As he moved farther to the left, the entrance to the cave opened up, becoming wide enough for a full-grown man to enter, if he stooped. He drew up his horse near the opening and stared, frowning. Was that a movement there, in the darkness? A flash of color? Or was he just seeing what he wanted to see? And if Meg was here, then where was her mare?

But he couldn't ride all this way and then not look inside. He couldn't leave without searching every inch of that dark cave. He turned his horse toward the rowan tree.

Gregor dismounted and tied his horse beneath the shelter of the tree. A protection against witches, he remembered, glancing up into the thick foliage. Perhaps it had acted as protection against Lorenzo, for Meg. Carefully— hopefully—he climbed back up the rough slope toward the cave. Everything was quiet, the only sound that of the rain falling softly and dripping from the foliage. Gregor heaved himself the last few feet to the cave and stood, panting a little, staring into the pitch blackness.

It was smaller than he had remembered. But that was part of getting older, wasn't it? He was a big man now, and he had been a boy when he played here all those years ago. It wasn't really a cave, just a fissure in the rocky side of the hill, with enough overhang and enough depth to make it a warm, dry place to hide out in bad weather.

Suddenly a memory came to him: himself, gangly and young, trying not to cry as he sat in the dank darkness and hugged his knees to his chest. He had drawn a picture of some primroses, especially for his mother's birthday. She had glanced at the meticulous rendering of the flowers with a critical eye.

"Very nice, darling," she had said, turning back to her own mirror, "but why didn't you draw roses? They are so much prettier."

Why had it upset him so? Gregor wondered now. It was not as if she hadn't done that before, dismissed his efforts as if they were nothing, belittled him through indifference. And yet he had continued to try and please her, endlessly, and all to no avail. Even when he had taken her to Edinburgh, after they lost Glen Dhui, he had walked the streets day and night to find the best lodgings that they could afford. For her.

Gregor closed his eyes. He had sat here, gazing down into the glen, and feeling that sense of hopelessness that always afflicted him when he had had a brush with his mother. She was beautiful, so beautiful on the outside that he had believed she must be just as beautiful on the inside. It was only with maturity that Gregor had realized that was not so. She was a manipulative and shallow woman, rather like Barbara Campbell.

And he was still trying to please her, or women like her.

Well, that was over. He had grown up and learned the value of a woman like Meg. He had no intention of allowing the Barbara Campbells of the world to ruin the wonderful life he had planned.

With new determination, Gregor pushed his wet hair out of his eyes, ignoring his sodden shirt and the way his kilt was dripping into his boots. "Meg?" he said.

The name echoed back from the cave, a soft hissing reverberation. There was a rattle of stones, as if he had disturbed an animal sheltering there. Or perhaps the
reverberation of his voice had shaken them loose.

"Meg?" he called again, moving forward, resting a hand
against the cold, damp stone and bending to peer into the
nothingness. If she wasn't here, then where was she? If she
wasn't here, what would he do? A bleak emptiness settled in
the pit of his stomach, a hollow ache that only she could fill.

"Meg, please . . . Meg!"

"What are you doing here?"

His heart nearly stopped. As he blinked hard against the
darkness and the dripping rain, she stepped forward, at first
a shadowy shape, and then her face a pale blur surrounded
by brilliant auburn.

"Go away," she said.

"Kenneth and Shona think they saw Lorenzo in the
glen," he said, ignoring her words, perhaps not believing
she meant them. "It isna safe out here alone, Meg. Come
home with me, where we can properly guard you."

"Lorenzo?" She took another step, and now he could see
how white her skin was, tinged blue with cold, and how her
long hair hung in damp straggles about her shoulders. She
looked only slightly less wet than him, and a great deal
more chilled.

"Och, Meg, ye'll catch yer death," he declared, and
reached out toward her.

She backed away, stumbling, nearly falling. The expression on her face had changed from anxiety to revulsion, and
Gregor went still.

She didn't want him.

On his ride here, he had thought only of losing her to

Lorenzo, or of how she was hurt when she saw Barbara clinging to him, of how he must explain to her and make all well again. He thought only of how he would feel without her, of how empty his life would be.

He had never once imagined that once he found her it could not be mended, that she would not want it mended.

If she turned from him now, he knew he would be far more abandoned and alone than he had been when he lost Glen Dhui.

"Oh Meg," he whispered, and pushed back his hair, twisting it at his nape. "She's a silly woman who thinks only of herself. I couldna love a woman like that, manipulating and selfish."

"And beautiful," Meg added quietly, her usually bright eyes dull. They were reddened, too, as if she had been crying. The thought of her here, alone in the dark cave, cold and unhappy, made his hands clench into fists with the need to hold her and comfort her.

"Beautiful?" he said in a carefully even voice. "Hmm, do you call her that? I don't call that beauty, Meg."

"Oh, and I suppose you'll tell me now that I am more beautiful than all the women you have ever known," she retorted, and some of the dullness in her eyes gave way to anger. Gregor felt relieved—at least she was showing some emotion. This was more like his Meg.

"But you are," he declared.

"Gregor, I am not a fool! I know that I was a means for you to regain Glen Dhui. I accept that. You will probably stay with me for that reason. But I do not expect you to be faithful to me. How could you?"

It was said so bitterly, but so acceptingly, that he was astonished. Is that what she really thought of him? What had she imagined he was doing, making passionate love to her over the past few weeks, since their wedding? Did she think it just a way for him to pass the time, until another partner came along? Was she so naïve?

But then he remembered. The only men she had known, other than tacksmen and tenants who were in awe of her, were those who sought her out for her father's wealth. Even if they had liked her for herself, how could she have known it or allowed herself to believe it? She had protected herself with a self-made shield and that shield was still there, held firmly in place, between herself and Gregor.

"There have been women," he said at last, the necessary words coming to him. Meg was honest, so he would be honest with her, and God help the two of them if she wanted lies. "Women to pass the time, or to stave off loneliness and sadness, women who look attractive when a man has taken a dram or two, but in the morning . . . Well, you see how it is for a man like me? I dinna look for someone to give me a home and children, what is the point? I have nothing to give in return—or I felt I didn't. Until now.

"I want you, Meg. More than any woman I've ever known or will know. I want you more than Glen Dhui, more than being the laird again. Did you know, that when you smile at me, you open me up inside? Until you, I'd been closed down, closed in, not allowing myself to feel anything because it hurt so much. Better not to feel, I thought, than to be in pain all the time. But now I'm alive again, and the pain is not so bad, because you are here with me. You've dragged me back into the world of living, Meg. For that I would give you all I have and am and ever will be."

There were tears shining in her eyes, but still she shook her head. "Very pretty, Gregor. You have a way with words,

I've noticed it before. But I am plain and practical Meg Mackintosh. I know what I am, Gregor. I accept it," she added bravely, but her mouth trembled. "Do not pretend I am other than I am."

"You dinna trust me," he breathed and sighed, a sigh from deep inside. "I knew it was so, but still it hurts. But I am used to hurt," he mocked himself. "I am used to giving presents, and having them rejected."

Tentatively he stepped closer, reaching out a hand to touch her cheek. She was watching him, listening to him, and as he stroked her cool, smooth skin, he thought about those presents he had made and had returned to him so ungraciously by his mother. That boyhood hurt had made him unwilling to try again. Even now he was tempted to shrug and let her believe what she wanted to.

Isna she worth fighting for? Malcolm Bain's gravelly voice filled his head. *Ye daft haddock, Gregor Grant! Say yer piece. Get on with't.*

"Gregor, I don't think—"

"Be quiet, Meg," he said quietly, firmly. "You have told me what *you* think you are, now let me tell you what *I* think you are."

She stepped away from his caressing hand, shivering a little. She looked grave and serious, a woman who did not joke often. If she let him stay with her, Gregor vowed, he would change that. He would make her laugh much more; he would bring joy into her days. It was the least he could do.

"Very well then, Gregor. Tell me what you think I am. I would be interested to hear it. And you must be honest with me. I prefer men to be honest."

He smiled, bowing his head to hide it. "Do you now, Meg Mackintosh? Then honest I will be. Firstly, I think of you as fire; fire, with your red hair and your burning blue eyes, so clear and true. You warm me just by looking. And you are strong, Meg, and generous, and kind. You want to help people, to make a difference, and even if it means hard work and a certain amount of . . . hmm . . . persuasion, Meg will do it."

There was a crease between her brows. "You make me sound very bossy," she said, but there was a tremble in her voice.

"Quiet now, or I'll lose my place. Now, strong and generous and kind? No, I've already mentioned that. Your people love you, Meg. If the priest would let them, I think they would worship you. Saint Meg, with the sun kisses on her nose. I would worship you, too, worship you with my body. When I think of your breasts, the way they fill my hands to overflowing, I get hard, Meg. When I think of you lying in my bed, smiling up at me, I get harder. I want to lie between your legs and feel you hold me as if you'll keep me forever. If you'll do that, if you'll keep me forever, then I don't need heaven. I will have found it already."

Meg gave a breathless laugh, but it turned into a sob. Before he could reach for her, she came into his arms, wrapping her own around him. She hadn't rejected him, she hadn't told him he could do better. Gregor felt the strength go out of his body, and he simply held her, rocking her, murmuring her name.

Meg felt as if she was the one who had found heaven. Heaven, in this dark, dank cave, her clothing wet and her hair like seaweed, in the arms of a man who felt wetter than herself. And yet she had never been happier.

She remembered how she had wept all the way down the glen, crying to the sky when the rain started, her heart breaking. She had been sure, so sure, that she had lost him. Lost her one, great love. But he had come after her, and he had found her, and suddenly all was not lost. He wanted her, he *needed* her, he could not go on without her.

Meg wondered, with some surprise, if Shona had been right after all. Perhaps she and Gregor did complement each other, she with her feet firmly on the ground and he with his handsome head adrift in the clouds . . .

"You must think me very shallow, to talk of beautiful faces and such," she began, needing to explain. "But when I saw you with Barbara Campbell . . ." But it hurt too much to go on. Instead she pressed her face to his damp shirt, and breathed in his scent. The cloth was so wet that she could see his skin through it, and feel his warmth and strength, seeping into her.

"She ran at me and hung on like a burr," he said, pressing his face to her hair. "Airdy is following her about and she believes I am fool enough to help her again. I think she wants me to kill him," he added evenly, as if the thought did not overly disturb him.

But Meg knew differently. "Oh, Gregor!" she whispered, and reaching up, stroked his cheek, comforting him.

He laughed shakily, turning to kiss her palm. "I am a soldier and I know it is my job to kill men," he said, "but I dinna do it for sport, Meg. I prefer to talk sense into a man, and only then do I resort to my sword. Even the duel was . . . unpleasant."

"I will never ask you to fight a duel for me."

His eyes narrowed, yellow through his dark lashes. "Never give me cause, *morvoren*. I dinna share women, especially not you."

Why did that make her quiver all over? Meg asked her-

self, between amusement at her own frailty and crossness
that he could toss her emotions about like a feather on a
strong breeze. The thought of him fighting for her, ordering
her about, was somehow romantic when he said it now.

"I dinna want Barbara Campbell at Glen Dhui," he said,
his eyes delving into hers, mesmerizing her. "In case you
were wondering, I told her so as soon as I laid eyes on her."

"Malcolm Bain said—"

"Och, Malcolm Bain has known me since I was a wee
lad. He knows my weaknesses and my strengths, but sometimes he forgets I'm grown."

"I thought—"

"Don't think, Meg. Kiss me."

Meg gazed up at him, her hair curling in wet tendrils
about her face. So he thought her strong and generous and
kind? He thought she was heaven, despite her freckles? Because of them! She knew she loved him with every part of
her, loved him for now and forever, and if he could not read
her love for him, aglow in her face, then he was a fool.

And Gregor was no fool.

With a groan, he closed his eyes, leaned down, and unerringly found her mouth with his.

His lips were cold, but inside he was hot. He placed his
hands on either side of her head so that he could plunder her
mouth like a starving man. Meg kissed him back, franti-
cally, ecstatically.

She ran her palms up over his chest, enjoying the hard
feel of him, and then slid them around his neck, tangling
her fingers in his damp hair. Glen Dhui Castle would be in
uproar. Everyone would be waiting. Meg's sense of duty
tapped her on the shoulder, and reluctantly she pulled away
from his mouth.

"Shouldn't we go back?"

Gregor didn't even take his eyes from hers. "It's still raining. It's more sensible to wait until it stops."

"Oh?" Meg looked into his eyes, reading the bright carnal glitter in them. He planned to make love to her, right now, right here in this cave. And she wanted him to. Suddenly duty to Glen Dhui wasn't as important as their duty to each other.

"You're all wet," she whispered.

"So are you."

"I fell off my mare."

He stopped, frowning, his eyes running over her. "Are you hurt, Meg?"

"No, the ground was soft." She smiled wryly. "Only my pride. My mare ran away, though. She will go home, when she is ready."

He stroked her face, her neck, running his finger down over the swell of her breasts. "I have an idea," he murmured, and turned her gently about, so that her back was to his chest. His fingers found her nipples through the cloth of her gown, and he spent some time rubbing them into peaks while Meg gasped and leaned her head back against his shoulder.

"What is your idea?" she asked at last, longing for him to make love to her.

He read her meaning, and she felt him smile against her cheek. "Our clothing, wet as it is, offers some warmth and covering. Much as I would like to, I willna strip you bare, Meg. Here."

She turned, and saw that he had pulled his shirt over his head, leaving him bare-chested in his kilt. Big and well muscled, his body was so fine she could look for hours. But he was already moving, laying the shirt upon the hard, damp ground.

Was she to lie upon that? Meg wondered. But before she could move, he was pressing her down, gently, easing her onto the soft linen so that she knelt, her back still to him.

"Lean forward onto your hands," he murmured, nuzzling at her neck, and suddenly he was hard up behind her. His hands reached down to find her breasts, gently squeezing her flesh, before he began to ease the hem of her skirt up, over the backs of her legs. His hands clasped her thighs, nudging them apart, and he slid a finger up into her.

Meg gasped and went still, afraid he might stop. But he didn't, pleasuring her with his hand and fingers, until she was moving against him, mindless with the need for him to continue. To her dismay, that was when he stopped.

"Gregor!" she groaned, turning her head to look back at him. He was kneeling behind her, a big dark shape against the light from outside the cave, but she couldn't see his face or his expression. He was lifting her skirts up over her bottom, and she shivered as her bare flesh was exposed to the cold. But in an instant he was there, pressed against her, his kilt covering them both. One strong arm came around her waist, drawing her back, back, while he eased his rod into her body.

Meg tried to push back, eager to regain her wave of pleasure, but he held her still and his hand crept over her belly, between her legs from the front, and found her favorite spot. He began to thrust into her, touching her at the same time, and Meg closed her eyes.

Her breath was loud in the half-darkness of the cave, and she was no longer cold. Gregor had seen to that. His thighs pounded against hers, and he went deep inside her. And then she was there, crashing to the shore with a keening cry. With a hard thrust, and then another, Gregor followed.

After a moment, when they had caught their breath, Gregor helped her to her feet, smoothing down her skirts and patting off any earth that might cling to the cloth. He shook out his shirt and pulled it back on.

"*Now* we will go home," he said with a smile.

He had exorcised some bad memories today; from now on, this place would hold nothing but pleasant ones for him. He looked at Meg, her cheeks still flushed from their lovemaking, her lips red and luscious, and wished he could do it again. But Lorenzo was loose in the glen, and it was safer to go.

She looked up at him, caught in the act of trying to tidy her hair, and sighed. "They will know," she said despairingly.

Gregor grinned. "Aye," he replied smugly, "so they will."

Chapter 25

Glen Dhui Castle was ablaze with light.

 That was the first thing Meg noticed, as they rode up through the yew trees. Every window glowed with candlelight or a lamp. And then she saw that there were men all about, and voices loud with excitement, or fear, or agitation. Or all three.

"Something has happened," Gregor said, at the same time as Meg thought it. His arms tightened about her, as she sat before him on his horse.

"Gregor!" Malcolm Bain came running, his hair wilder than ever from the rain and hard riding.

Gregor drew up, trying to read the other man's face in the evening light. When they had left the cave, the rain had gone and the sun was setting in streaks of gold and crimson in the darkening sky. Now the light was fading into mauves and grays, and Malcolm Bain was barely visible.

"Lady Meg's mare came back alone. We were fearing the worst, lad. Where have ye both been?"

"We found shelter out of the rain," Gregor said shortly. "What is happening here?"

"Lorenzo's men came to the house while we were out searching for Lady Meg."

Meg felt her heart flutter. "My father . . . ?"

"Is safe," Malcolm assured her, "but a little shaken. Shona is all right, and Kenneth was out with us. 'Tis Barbara Campbell who was taken."

Barbara Campbell? Gregor looked at Meg and saw the same confusion in her face that must be in his.

"Are you certain she just dinna go off somewhere?" he asked.

Malcolm Bain gave Gregor a grim smile. "It seems while we were all off searching, Barbara suddenly felt verra weary from her journey. She went upstairs to take a nap, and decided upon Lady Meg's room for her wee sleep. Lorenzo's men came creeping, and went straightaway to that room. It was dark. They bundled her into a cloak and were away before she could make them understand she wasna who they thought she was."

Gregor closed his eyes briefly. If Meg had been here, if she hadn't been with him in the cave . . .

Malcolm Bain went on. "The general heard her screams and tried to stop them. He thought they had ye, Lady Meg."

"Father!" Meg gasped, and Gregor heard the fear in her voice.

"Is the general hurt?" he asked. Best to know the bad news at once.

Malcolm Bain's expression was grave. "He's a braw man, lad, but I fear the experience hasna done him much good."

Swiftly Gregor dismounted and lifted Meg down after him. "I must see him," she said, and set off at a run for the door.

"I canna believe it," Gregor said flatly. "They came here, under our noses, and stole a woman from her room?"

"The house was all but empty, Gregor. Alison and Shona were in the kitchen, only Barbara Campbell and the general upstairs. 'Twas not such a feat for them to take her." Malcolm Bain paused, gave him a sideways look. "What do ye think Lorenzo'll do when he realizes his mistake?"

Kill her, Gregor thought, meeting his eyes in the half-dark.

"Aye," Malcolm Bain said with grim agreement, as if Gregor had spoken aloud. "That's what I thought, too."

Inside the house, people were standing about as if not sure what to do, their faces long and worried. Alison gave a cry of relief when she saw Meg, running to hug her. The cheek she pressed to Meg's was warm and wet with tears. "My lady, we thought ye taken for sure!"

"No, no, I am quite safe. Where is the general?" she asked, heading for the stairs.

Alison hurried after her. "In his room, my lady. He was verra shaken, poor man. But do ye know about Barbara Campbell? She was taken by Lorenzo's men! The silly creature was asleep in your room, thinking herself mistress of the house, no doubt! They thought she was ye!"

"Then I pray they do not hurt her when they discover she is not," Meg murmured hastily, all but running up the stairs. Her father had tried to stop the armed men; he had tried to save Barbara. If he was not badly hurt, then it would be a miracle.

The general's room was just as ablaze as the rest of the house. The old man sat up in his bed, thin beneath the quilt, his body tense as he heard his door open. "Meg?" His voice quavered.

"Oh, Father! You are not hurt?"

He shook his head, but he looked pale and the hands he held out to her trembled violently. There was a red mark on his jaw where someone had struck him. Meg felt her throat close up and had to swallow, grasping his hands, while she restrained her emotions.

"I tried to stop them," he was saying. "I heard the screams, and I found my old sword by the door there, and went to save you. . . . I thought they had you, Meg. Now they're saying it's some other lass I don't know. . . ." He shook his head in confusion.

"Barbara Campbell, Father. She was resting in my room."

"Well, when I heard this Barbara screaming, I went out onto the landing with my sword. I waved it about in the direction of their voices, so that they would think I could see them. For a time they believed me, but then I mistook the sounds they were making and they realized I am only an old, blind man." He looked as if he might cry. "If only I could *see* again. If only I were of some use to you all!"

"You are of use!" Meg cried fervently. "How can you say such a thing, Father? I have never heard of anything braver than what you did! One man against so many—and yes, a blind man. You are a hero—everyone in Glen Dhui will say so, and they will be right."

The general's gloomy expression lifted, and he managed a shaky smile. "So I am a hero, eh, Meg?"

"Yes, Father, you are."

"Oh, Meg, I thought it was you they had. . . ."

She went into his arms, and they were quiet, just relieved to be safe and together. After a time the general sighed and released her. "You are a good girl, Daughter. After I . . . after my act of heroism," he said wryly, "Alison told me you'd ridden off and they were all looking for you. Gregor found you, didn't he? You should always look to him when there is trouble—he will never let anything happen to you. You know that, Meg, don't you?"

Meg stared back into her father's blind, blue eyes, so very like her own. "I do, Father."

"Lady Meg?" Alison had come into the room behind her, dark eyes intent. "Some of the men who rode after Lorenzo have returned. They say that Lorenzo is taking Barbara Campbell south, onto the Duke of Abercauldy's estate."

Meg's heart sank. As much as she disliked Barbara Campbell, she had to feel sorry and concerned for the other woman. Barbara, whatever her shortcomings, didn't deserve this. She had come to Glen Dhui Castle for sanctuary, and instead had been kidnapped by strangers. And what would happen to her once Lorenzo and the Duke realized their mistake, if they hadn't already? Would they vent their anger and frustration upon her? Would they hurt her, or worse?

"What will we do?" she asked aloud.

The general's eyes were closed, and it was Alison who answered.

"I dinna know about that, my lady, but ye must be tired and hungry. I have supper ready."

Meg managed a smile. Heartless as it seemed, she realized she was ravenous. From long experience, Meg knew she would be able to think much better if she had something in her stomach.

"Will you eat with us, Father?" Meg turned to the general, but he shook his head.

"I will sleep, I think, Meg," he said in a fading voice. "Now that I know you are safe, I feel the need to sleep."

Meg kissed his cheek and followed Alison from the room. Gregor was standing in the Great Hall, several men gathered about him.

For a moment Meg paused, looking down, selfishly enjoying the sight of him. With his hair loose about his shoulders and his shirt barely disguising his muscular chest, while the faded kilt showed off his trim hips and long, strong legs, he was certainly a sight to behold. After their time in the cave, Meg knew she would never doubt him, or run from him, again.

There was a certain, quiet grimness about the group around him, and it made Meg pause in her pleasant thoughts, a terrible premonition coming to her.

He wouldn't!

But she knew he would. Because it wasn't really a premonition, it was a deep knowledge of the man, of Gregor Grant. Emptiness opened up inside Meg, and she felt suddenly so dizzy that she had to grip the wooden railing.

As if sensing her gaze, Gregor looked up and met her eyes. His expression told her what she already knew. He was not the sort of man who would let a woman be hurt if it was in his power to save her. Even a woman like Barbara Campbell.

"They are taking her to Abercauldy," Gregor said.

"Yes," she whispered.

"I must try to get her back, safely."

Of course he must. So Gregor would go to Abercauldy, who already hated him, and plead for the life of a woman he did not even like, who had betrayed him and manipulated him and hurt him. He may well die by Abercauldy's hand, or that of his men. It was possible that Meg may never see him again.

It was on the tip of her tongue to plead for him not to go, to beg him to think of himself, of her . . . but she didn't. Meg had learned enough of the Highlands and its proud men to understand that honor was prized very highly, sometimes more highly than life itself. And if Gregor did not go to Barbara Campbell's aid, if he stayed at home and let her die, then his honor as a laird and a man would be worth nothing.

"When will you go?" she asked quietly.

Her question made him smile, but there was no humor in it. "At dawn."

I will come with you.

The words were there in her mouth, but she knew there was no point in speaking them. Gregor would not allow it, and as Lady of Glen Dhui, her place was here in his absence. He needed her to be here. He would ride into danger and Meg, like so many women throughout the ages, would wait for him to come home.

We have tonight.

That single thought filled Meg as they sat down to eat, as Gregor huddled together with his men one last time, issuing instructions, offering advice, murmuring praise. Soon they would be gone, and she and Gregor would be alone.

We have tonight.

Of course he will come home again! she told herself,

but it was bravado. Deep in her heart, there was a terrible fear that maybe tonight was all they would have left of their life together. These memories would be all she would have to keep her warm after this night. It seemed very unfair. She had only just discovered love, and now she might lose it.

But we have tonight. . . .

At last they were alone, the door of the bedchamber closed behind them, the candle flame dipping and diving in Meg's shaking hand. As she set it down, his arm came around her, easing her back against his chest, his warm mouth nuzzling against the side of her neck.

"Do not be afraid for me," he murmured. "I have set myself tougher tasks and won through."

"Gregor—"

"I know what you are thinking, *morvoren.* You are thinking Abercauldy will take out his spite against me, but I am confident I can talk sense to him. He is an intelligent, educated man. He will listen to reason."

Would he? Meg doubted it, but she bit her lip and did not say so. She would not send him away with all her own fears weighing him down. She would not!

She turned in his arms, linking her fingers behind his neck and smiling up at him with serious blue eyes. "Come to bed with me, Husband."

His mouth curled at the corners. "Gladly, Wife."

It seemed to Meg that in so short a time she had grown to know Gregor so well, to love him so well. Perhaps she had always loved him, the sensitive boy and the tough man. She had been wrong to think of them as separate; they were one and the same. Wonderingly, Meg realized that she had in fact loved him most of her life.

And when at last he lay upon her, thrusting deep, so deep, it was as if he would claim every part of her. Perhaps this night they would make a child. Did he seek to console her with a baby if he did not return? Meg knew she would love a baby of his, a child to grow up here at Glen Dhui with Gregor's amber eyes. But it would not be the same if Gregor was not here to watch it happen. It could never be the same without Gregor.

"You will come back to me," she whispered, in the aftermath of their passion, her fingers stroking his hair, his head resting warm and heavy on her breast. "You will come back to me, Gregor."

It was not a request; it was a command.

"Meg—"

"Because if you don't, I warn you now, I will come and fetch you home again."

Gregor lifted himself up on one elbow, gazing down into her face with a look of deep tenderness. "Do ye remember, Meg, when ye came to the Black Dog and stood by my table in that terrible place and told me ye had come for me?"

Meg was entranced by his intensity, but she managed a yes.

"I thought you were an angel."

She laughed, but he put his fingers against her lips, warm and calloused and so gentle.

"I was more dead than alive before you came to me that evening, Meg. I was breathing, but my heart had stopped. Since I had lost Glen Dhui, I had existed, alone, a stranger in my own country. But you have brought me more joy in these past weeks than I have felt in all the years that went before. If I did not live another day past this moment, I would still be a fortunate man for what you have given me, Meg."

"I love you, Gregor," she whispered, her eyes blurred with tears.

"Och, Meg, my Meg. I want to give you a child," he murmured against her lips. "I want to make a child with you."

With a groan he slid over her, plundering her body with his, insatiable for her. And Meg gave herself up to him, felt her body melt into liquid fire in his arms, drowning in him and wishing this one night could last forever.

He was her own true love, the dream she had longed for. It was a truly bittersweet moment.

"Lady Meg is asleep?"

Shona was standing in the doorway to the kitchen, her lovely face tired and serious, and showing its age.

Alison nodded brusquely, moving about, preparing food for the morrow, keeping busy. The men would need to take something with them, and she meant to make certain they were well provisioned. Besides, she did not want to stop, because then she would have to think. She did not want to think.

"She must be worried," Shona went on. "Captain Grant is a braw man, but even the bravest can be hurt, and worse."

"He will be safe," Alison replied stubbornly.

"They say ye have the sight," Shona said. "Do ye see that then, Alison? Do ye see that he will be safe? Tell me what ye see."

Alison cast her an agonized look.

Shona went still and then sighed. "Aye, ye see something, don't ye, poor lassie. Tell me what it is; such things are easier to bear if ye share them."

Alison's hands stilled, and she stared into space. *I dinna want to know*, she thought. *Please, I dinna want to know.* But the words came anyway.

"There is a death. I've known it since the wedding, but I dinna know who will die. It might be the Laird, it might be another. I canna tell Lady Meg. How can I tell her that her man might die?"

"Dinna tell her," Shona advised, her eyes on Alison's pale, tense face. "What of ye? Does yer man ride to the duke's castle tomorrow?"

Slowly, Alison continued with her preparations. "I have no man, Shona."

"I thought," she began, but when Alison turned and glared at her, she changed her mind and shrugged instead. "Well, of course not. I'll leave ye to yer work. Good night, Alison."

After Shona had gone, Alison stood still and quiet. She should go to bed, she supposed. She should. But all she could think was that Malcolm Bain would be riding tomorrow to the Duke of Abercauldy's estate, and he might not come back. He had already left her once, and now he would do so again. The last time, she had grieved for twelve years, and when he had finally returned, she had done nothing but abuse him.

She put a hand to her eyes and rubbed them viciously.

He deserved to be treated badly! He had abandoned her, with Angus on the way, and . . . and . . . He had left a letter for her. Duncan had finally told her the truth about that. He had not walked out on her without a word, he had left a letter to tell her why he was going, begging her understanding, asking that she forgive him. Telling her he loved her.

It made a difference.

She had loved this man all her life, and even when she hated him it had been an all-consuming passion. He was a part of her, and Alison knew she could not let him go away again, not without making some sort of effort to reconcile their pasts.

With a soft, hissing curse, she flung down the bunch of kale she was holding and hurried from the kitchen.

He was in the stables. She had learned from Angus that that was where he slept. Running so that she could not slow down and think and maybe change her mind, Alison reached the dark building, entered it, and went straight to the ladder up to the loft. It rattled a little under her weight as she climbed, her mouth set in a straight, determined line. By the time she poked her head through the opening, he was wide awake.

He was sitting up, straw sticking to his hair, his eyes sleepy and blinking, his hand on his sword.

"Alison?" he said, and there was complete shock in his face. As he watched her climb off the ladder and step toward him, a mask of wariness hid all other feelings.

"I've come to say I *do* understand," Alison said, and her voice was breathless and wavering and strangely high. "I *do* understand why ye had to go with the laird, why ye couldna just leave him. Ye had a duty. Ye had to look to him, and put yer own feelings and wishes aside. If ye had not done that, then ye'd no' have been Malcolm Bain Mac-Gregor."

Malcolm Bain rose slowly to his feet. He was watching her intently.

"But ye put my feelings and my wishes aside also, Malcolm Bain. Ye sacrificed yer life to the laird, and that was yers to do, but ye sacrificed me and Angus, and that was no'. Ye should be sorry for that."

"I *am* sorry," he said quietly. "Ye canna know how sorry,

Alison. I look back, and I wish I could change what I did. I wish so much I could change it." His voice broke and he swallowed, bowing his head.

Alison blinked, and suddenly the spell was broken. His shoulders were shaking. Malcolm Bain was crying!

"Malcolm? *Mo nighean?*"

He didn't move, his face hidden from her, his wild hair hanging down to shield him. It was as if he had been stripped bare. "I have nothing," he said now, in a harsh, angry voice. "I left ye and now I have nothing. I will die alone, and my son will never know me."

"Malcolm," she whispered, and found that by taking one step, and then another, she was close enough to stroke his arm, and then close enough to place her hands, one either side of his bowed head, and raise it upward.

His craggy face was ravaged, his blue eyes swimming with pain and regret, and it was at that moment that Alison decided she would not hold on to her bitterness and anger any longer. She had justice on her side, perhaps, but what was the use of being right if it meant she was unhappy? She had loved this man, and she thought she just might love him still. He was Angus's father. And he was a good man, a fine man. Was it possible that they might make a life together, now, and put the past behind them?

If he came back to her from Abercauldy.

Alison kissed his rough cheek. And then kissed the other. He went still, staring at her in wonder, and she kissed one eye closed and then the other, and then she kissed his mouth. She had forgotten how soft his mouth was, how tender—an odd contradiction on such a rugged-looking man.

"Alison," he moaned, and his arms came around her, bringing her closer. "Oh, Alison."

"Malcolm Bain, my dearest, *mo nighean*, I've missed ye so much. Oh, so much."

And then she couldn't say anymore, because he was kissing her too desperately. And besides, what else was there to say?

Chapter 26

Meg woke abruptly.

Gregor was already up, dressing, buckling his belts about him, sliding his sword into its place. He looked at her, his expression grim in the dawn. Morning had crept through the window, stealing from them what might have been their last night together.

"Rest," he said softly, attempting a smile.

Meg sat up, pushing her hair out of her eyes. "There will be time enough to rest later," she told him evenly. "I will go and see to your food and drink." She swung her shawl about herself and, on bare feet, moved past him toward the door.

His arm slid around her, pulling her against him. His face was pressed to her hair, and she clung hard, feeling him breathe. With a sigh, he released her, and Meg hurried out of the room, her face streaked with tears, down the stairs to the kitchen.

Alison was already there, with a pot of porridge steam-

ing over the fire, meat and kale laid out on the table, and a
large jug of ale on a tray. She looked up, and Meg saw that
she was pale and tired, as if she, too, had had little or no
sleep. There was also a bruise upon her neck.

Concerned, Meg moved forward, but something in Alison's avoidance of her eyes, something in the way she became suddenly very busy, stopped her.

"The men are waiting," Alison said over her shoulder. "Is
the laird up?"

"He's just dressing now."

"I will see everyone is fed before they go."

"Thank you, Alison."

"At least we can do that for them, Lady Meg. And pray
that they come home safe."

They looked at each other in perfect understanding of
the travails of women who bind their lives to those of fighting men.

The bruise on her neck was from a man's kisses, Meg realized abruptly. Alison and Malcolm Bain had made their
peace with each other, and she gave thanks for it.

Gregor's step sounded behind her, and his hand rested
warm and heavy on her shoulder. "Alison," he said, with a
nod in the other woman's direction; then his gaze was on
Meg, and she found she could not look away. He was memorizing her, every feature of her, everything about her. As if
he would never see her again.

Meg's heart stammered and stuttered, but she forced her
fears away and made herself smile up at him. "You must
eat," she told him softly. "Who knows when you will get the
chance again?"

He nodded, and sat down at the kitchen table while Alison doled out spoonfuls of porridge. Then she carried out

the pot, with the help a sleepy-eyed Angus, to feed the rest of the men. When she returned, Malcolm Bain was with her. He glanced at Gregor, but his eyes soon returned to Alison, watching as she hurried about the familiar kitchen, absorbing her into his memory.

Gregor had finished; he rose to his feet. Meg followed, more slowly, realizing that this was the moment. He was going. It was real. And there was nothing she could do about it.

"I am leaving enough men here to keep you safe," he said. "If you are at all worried, then send to the military post for soldiers, or ride there yourself with a guard. They will protect you."

"Don't worry for me."

Gregor laughed shakily. "Och, Meg, how can I not?"

Meg put her arms about him and held him fiercely. "I will be fine, as long as you come home to me again."

He found her mouth, kissing her with a savage desperation that made her taste blood, and then he was setting her from him, calling for Malcolm Bain, who was cradling Alison in his arms. Malcolm Bain ruffled Angus's hair as he passed, making it as wild as his own.

"Watch out for yer mother," he said, with an intent look. "She couldna ask for a better son."

And then they were gone, and the kitchen seemed empty without them.

Meg ran after them, standing to watch as Gregor mounted his horse and called some last-minute instructions to the men he was leaving behind. He was not taking all of his special troop, she realized, only about half of them. She opened her mouth to tell him to take more, but she knew he was thinking of her safety as much as she was thinking of his. And then, with a last, quick look in her direction, he was gone, leading his men down the yew avenue, vanishing into the long, dawn shadows.

Meg stood watching until he was gone from her sight. She knew it was foolish, that she must go back inside and become again the practical, dependable Lady of Glen Dhui. That her people would be relying upon her and looking to her. But she could not seem to make that final move, to turn away. . . .

"Yer father is calling for ye."

Shona was there, her kind eyes full of understanding.

Gregor had spoken to the general last night and come away with his face like it used to be, his feelings hidden deep inside himself. Whatever was said between them was for Gregor, and Meg did not ask, but she feared that, after the old man had offered him what advice he could, Gregor had told him good-bye. . . .

Shona touched her arm. "Go and sit with him for a wee while, and then we will go to the herb garden, and I will show ye how to make a poultice for boils."

Meg laughed, close to tears. "I would do better with a poultice for a broken heart, Shona."

Shona smiled gently. "Och, Lady Meg, I dinna know how to cure a broken heart. I dinna think it is possible."

Probably not, thought Meg, as she turned away into the house. A heart, once broken, stayed that way. And the cruel thing was that, even with one's heart split asunder, one lived on. And on.

Gregor set his sights on the South, and the Duke of Abercauldy's lands. He dared not think about what he had left behind. He must think clearly, so that he could do what had to be done. Not only did he need to find and take care of Barbara Campbell, but he had to make peace with Abercauldy, so that he and Meg could live their lives without fear of reprisals.

And there was nothing he wanted more than to live the rest of his life with Meg.

He had told the general that, when he said his farewells. The old man had understood, and told him that he would do his best to care for her until Gregor returned. "But she needs you, lad," he had said. "We all do. Come home safe again to Glen Dhui."

Come home safe.

There was nothing he wanted more.

Gregor had about fifteen men with him. Ten were from the troop he and Malcolm Bain had been training, the other five were men simply willing to fight for their laird. It was not a great number, certainly not enough to win any decisive battles against Abercauldy, but Gregor knew he would not win a battle the duke was determined to win anyway. His plan had only ever been to hold Glen Dhui by harassing his enemy like a darting insect, cornering him and striking hard, and then going into hiding again. He did not have the men for an all-out confrontation.

Now his plan was to ride to Abercauldy Castle and meet the duke face to face. To reason with him. To make him understand that Meg should not be punished for a marriage that had never been her idea. And to sacrifice himself, if that was required. But Gregor sincerely hoped it would not come to that.

Despite his determination to focus on what lay ahead, Gregor couldn't help but remember the look on Meg's face as he prepared to ride away from her. She had been brave, hiding her pain at his going, but her eyes had given her away.

She had told him that she loved him, and Gregor knew it was true. And he loved her, loved her as he had never loved another woman, and had never expected to. Why had he not told her so? He should have told her, but he had never felt this way before—he had not known he could. Last night, as he took her again and again, he had thought only of giving her a child. His child. Then, if he died, there would be something of his living. His and Meg's. The future of Glen Dhui would be secure.

Gregor glanced sideways at Malcolm Bain. The older man had been very quiet since they left Glen Dhui Castle, lost in his own thoughts. Had he made his peace with Alison? Gregor thought, from what he had seen in the kitchen, that that might be the case. He hoped so, for Malcolm's sake.

The smooth, silver surface of the loch lay to their left. The stones rattled under the horses' hooves and wild ducks took to the sky with raucous squawks. Ahead, behind the craggy peaks of the hills that divided Grant land from Abercauldy's, was the man he sought. This way had come Lorenzo with the beautiful and troublesome Barbara Campbell.

Gregor wondered grimly if she was still alive.

Another day had come, each minute weighing upon Meg as if it were made of earth and stone. There was plenty to be done, but she had never realized how pointless it all seemed, how empty her life was, until Gregor had left it.

For the last three nights, Meg had lay in her bed, staring into darkness, longing for Gregor. She hurt all over. And she was desperate for something to do, something that would help him. Practical Meg Mackintosh could not bear to sit idly by while her husband might be in danger.

He had been gone now for three days and three nights, and she could only think that something must have happened to him. If all had been well, he should be home now, or at least well on his way. But there had been no word of a sighting of him from the men posted as lookouts to the South.

This morning she had decided to give up pretending everything was normal and that life must go on as always. Instead she planned to go and sit with the general. Perhaps a game of chess would help her concentrate her thoughts, and if he did not feel up to that, a quiet chat. But as she headed toward his room, Meg heard the shout of warning, and soon afterward the clatter of hooves on the gray stone bridge.

At first Meg thought the men with the red jackets must belong to Major Litchfield, that perhaps he had come for one last visit. She hurried outside, meaning to greet him. But as she shaded her eyes against the morning sun, she realized that the soldier in charge was not Major Litchfield. Whoever this man was, he rode upon a dun-colored horse and was bareheaded, his hair dark and wild, his face pale, and his eyes dark and staring.

Airdy Campbell.

"Oh, no," she gasped.

One of her men snatched at her arm and ran with her, all but dragging her back toward the door and safety. As they reached it, Airdy drew his horse to a rattling stop and slid to the ground.

"Barbara!" he shouted. "Come out, Wife! I know you are here, hiding like the cowardly baggage you are!"

Meg placed her hand on her man's arm to stay him, and turned to face Airdy. He was staring up at the windows, his head tipped back, and despite the lack of blood in his cheeks and the fact that he was relatively sober, he was still just as frightening as he had been outside the Clashennic Inn.

"Barbara isn't here," Meg said carefully. How would she tell him the truth? What would he do? A man like Airdy was capable of anything.

And then, in an instant, a plan blossomed in her mind, complete and perfect. Gregor would not be happy with her; he would probably be very angry. But Meg knew she couldn't stay here, waiting for his return . . . If he returned. It was not in her nature. She had been her own woman for too long, and she was used to making decisions and carrying them through.

Gregor needed her, and she must not fail him.

Airdy had lowered his black gaze to her and was frowning. "I've followed her trail," he explained, as if she should know what he was talking about. "My uncle the Duke of Argyll has given me the post of military commander at the pass, and when I came down to take over I heard she had been through there. She's here, now, I know it. You are lying!"

Airdy, taking over from Major Litchfield? Gregor would be horrified, and Meg was not much happier. Still, that was something to consider for later.

"No, Airdy, I'm not lying. She *was* here, but she was taken prisoner by the Duke of Abercauldy."

He looked at her as if she were the mad one, and Meg didn't blame him. It *sounded* mad. Airdy turned to the house, considered it, and then looked at her again. "Where has he taken her? I want her back. I willna rest until I have her back."

Meg hesitated a moment more, staring into those relentless black eyes. Airdy wasn't rational; was it fair to set him on this road? But then she remembered what he had done to Gregor. Yes, it was fair, and she would do it!

"Come inside, Airdy, and we will talk."

He came toward her, shooting a narrowed glance at the man by her side, as if to warn him not to try anything. "I know you," he said to Meg, as he reached her. "Ye were at the inn at Clashennic, with that bastard Gregor Grant. This is *his* house. Barbara came running to *him*, dinna she?"

"Yes, she did, and yes, I was. I am Gregor Grant's wife, Airdy. We are wed."

He looked shocked, his white face completely blank, and then he grinned, showing her several gaps where teeth used to be. "You are Gregor's wife?" His gaze slid down and up her again, and he opened his mouth as if to say something insulting.

"This is the Lady of Glen Dhui," the man at her side said warningly, his hand on his sword. Airdy's own men shifted closer, watchful.

"This is Airdy Campbell," Meg said, giving her man a long warning look. "He has come to help us, so we must treat him accordingly."

Airdy grinned at that, and then his smile faded. "Where is he?"

"Gregor? He's gone after Barbara and the Duke's men. He's gone to try and save her. But he needs help. Barbara's in danger, Airdy. That is why I want to speak to you. Barbara is in grave danger, and we have to save her."

"We?" he asked, a certain slyness creeping into his manner. Perhaps he was not quite so crazy after all.

"Yes, Airdy, you and me."

Doubt and questions flickered briefly in his black eyes, and then he seemed to make up his mind. Just like that, without any answers to his questions, without hearing her plan, without even knowing her other than through one brief meeting. Airdy Campbell was clearly a man of simple instincts and a single-minded determination to get his own way, and Meg thanked God for it.

"Tell me what to do," he said, and followed her into the house.

Chapter 27

The air was warm and calm. Beside them, Loch Dhui reflected the color of the sky, reminding Meg of the day she and Gregor had swum here and lay naked in the sun. Today the loch's shores were deserted, and the hills ahead looked ominous.

Where was Gregor? He must have reached Abercauldy's castle by now. Why was he not on his way home? Why had she heard nothing? Did he lie at night, wrapped in his plaid, thinking of her? Was he still able to think at all . . .

Please keep him safe, Meg offered a silent prayer. *Keep him safe until I can reach him.*

Airdy Campbell rode behind her, and seemed content to take second place. Meg didn't trust him. Even though he had agreed to her plan and seemed quite happy to do as she told him, she still did not trust him. There was something cunning about Airdy, something devious. And there was the memory of Clashennic, when he had seemed liable for any mischief. She could not help but wonder whether Airdy was quite mad.

But at least he was sober.

She had managed thus far to keep his mind from the silver flask he had fastened to his sword belt. She kept reminding him that the duke's men could come upon them at any time—a surprise attack. Airdy wanted to be ready to defend himself, didn't he? For sweet Barbara's sake?

"And you're sure she went unwillingly?" He had a way of staring intently into her eyes, as if he could read any lies. It was unnerving.

"She was kidnapped," Meg replied firmly.

"Och, well then!" But despite her reassurance there seemed to be a suspicion in his head that simply wouldn't go away. That was understandable, Meg thought, when your wife had an unfortunate tendency to use men for her own ends, and those ends revolved around plots to leave her husband.

Ahead of them, the dark hills cleaved the sky. Beyond was the Duke of Abercauldy and his fine castle and his fine things. And his simmering obsession with Meg. She had spurned him, made him look a fool, and not even the fact that she had not wanted to marry him, and had told him many times, had made a difference to him. He wanted her to pay, and Meg wondered if she was clever enough to escape her punishment.

It couldn't hurt to have Airdy Campbell at her side, deserted husband and nephew to the Duke of Argyll, who was arguably the most important man in Scotland.

"Will we camp this side of the hills?" One of her men had ridden up beside her and was eyeing her anxiously.

They had not wanted Meg to make this journey, but she had told them that if they did not wish to accompany her, then she would go alone. They came, but they were not pleased, and Meg guessed it was Gregor's anger they feared, if anything should happen to her.

But she could not stay at Glen Dhui—it was impossible. She was a woman used to doing what needed to be done, not one who relied upon a man to do it for her. She should have made this journey months ago, cleared the air once and for all, instead of skulking on her own lands, hoping it would all blow away. Already she felt better, as if she could breathe properly again.

"No, we ride as far as we can today," she ordered. "There is plenty of light left, and we need to make up time. The laird has a head start."

"Verra well, m'lady."

"The *laird.*" Airdy sneered. "Aye, I can see Gregor as the laird, mincing about, aping his betters. I hope this Abercauldy cuts him down to size."

Meg bit her lip. She had a cutting retort of her own in mind, but it was best not to upset Airdy. Not when she planned to use him. He was going to save Gregor for her; he just didn't know it.

The duke's dungeons were far more extensive, and far grimmer, than the single cell at Glen Dhui Castle. There was no light here, apart from a single flaring torch in a wall sconce outside the door, and that barely penetrated the corners of this damp, slimy place, where Gregor and his men were being held.

Above them, far above, was Abercauldy Castle. Gregor remembered his first sight of it. All crenelated towers and pink granite stone walls, it had loomed upon the hill before them, looking as if it were the creation of a madman. Gregor had ridden forward, at the head of his troop, ignoring his niggle of doubt.

"Bloody hell," Malcolm Bain had muttered at his side.

At least Abercauldy was at home, Gregor had thought, seeing the flag flying atop one of the towers. He remembered wondering if that was the tower from which the duke's wife, Isabella Mackenzie, had fallen to her death. Fallen with Abercauldy's help, according to Shona. Gregor remembered hoping that he would find the duke in a more reasonable mood.

The gates of the castle had opened, and as he expected, a couple of dozen men with uncompromising expressions had ridden out to meet them. Gregor and his troop were subsequently accompanied into the castle yard. It had seemed very quiet for such a large place, no servants bustling about, no blacksmiths or carpenters at work, not even the ubiquitous castle hounds barking at their entry.

That *had* been odd, but Gregor did not have a chance to give it much thought. For at that moment, Lorenzo had appeared, seated upon a pretty white horse, directly in his path. And so their fateful conversation had taken place.

"You are very brave to come here, Captain Grant," Lorenzo had said, smiling, his eyes spitting hatred.

"You have taken something that does not belong to you, Lorenzo. I want it back."

"The fair-haired one?" Lorenzo had retorted. "She does not belong to you, either. She does not even want to return to Glen Dhui. She is happy here with His Grace. Ask her!"

Gregor had felt a slow anger ignite inside him. Had he come all this way on a wild goose chase? It would be just like Barbara Campbell to land on her feet and make herself at home in a duke's castle. But he must make certain. Lorenzo was a cunning liar, and he could be lying now.

"Let me speak with her."

"Oh, you will speak to her," Lorenzo had said, still with his sneering smile. "In a little while. She is not ready for you yet, Captain. You will have to wait."

He had jerked his head at the duke's men, and they had promptly drawn their swords, although the sergeant in charge had looked a little apologetic. The slither of steel had been loud in the quiet of the yard. Gregor's men had moved swiftly to retaliate, but Gregor called for them to hold. They were already outnumbered, and there were probably many more armed men close by.

"We have not come here to fight," Gregor had said evenly. "We have come to talk sense."

"Very wise," Lorenzo had said mockingly, when Gregor didn't resist. "I would not wish to kill you before you have 'talked sense' to His Grace. If he decides to see you. Now come, this way. I have some very comfortable quarters for you to wait in. I'm sure you will find them just as comfortable as I did, when I stayed at your little house."

"I need to see the Duke of Abercauldy," Gregor had said, a little desperately now.

"All in good time," Lorenzo had replied, with an airy wave as he turned away. "All in good time, Captain Grant."

Now Gregor looked about him at the cramped, pungent cell. This was Lorenzo's revenge, the revenge he had promised. But Lorenzo had been locked up under far different conditions than this, and he had been promptly released following the wedding. Gregor was beginning to lose track of how long they had been down here.

Did Lorenzo intend to take them to see the duke? And, of more concern, did the duke even know they were here? Lorenzo was quite capable of keeping this as his own little secret for weeks. Or even months . . .

"That wee man isna from Italy," Malcolm Bain mumbled from the shadows. "Who does he think to fool with that monstrous accent?"

"The Duke of Abercauldy," Gregor replied. "No one else's opinion matters to Lorenzo."

Malcolm Bain grumbled more insults, but Gregor didn't pay much heed. Instead, he leaned his head back against the wall, uncaring of what might be creeping upon it, and closed his eyes. He was weary of prisons, they were all the same: Dark, dank, and evil-smelling.

Why couldn't he and Abercauldy sit down like sensible men and talk this thing through? Why did everything have to come down to a bloody fight? He had asked his father that, when they were riding toward Preston during the 1715 Rebellion. His father had looked at him as if he wasn't quite sure what he meant. Gregor had realized then that, to his father, there was glory in battle, in shedding blood for one's cause, in dying for futility.

Gregor had never understood the point of dying for a lost cause.

Fighting for those in one's care, for those one loved, that was different. He would fight to the death for Meg and Glen Dhui.

How he longed for Meg now. What was she doing at this moment? Was she thinking of him? He tried to imagine her, to put himself there with her, as he had once imagined himself home in Glen Dhui when he had been imprisoned after the Battle of Preston.

The ability had not left him.

He could see himself, walking up the stairs from the Great Hall, hear the ring of his boots. And there she was, smiling as she looked up from her desk, surrounded by her books and papers and pens.

"Gregor!" she would cry, her mouth curling up in a smile of pure joy. Her blue eyes, so blue they hurt him sometimes, and her flame hair loose about her creamy shoulders. She would smile at him, so that he could see that little gap in her teeth that pleased him so much, and he would lift her into his arms, and kiss that lush mouth, and lose himself in her.

He groaned, softly, and covered his face with his hands. "Meg, oh, Meg, I love ye," he murmured. "Let me only be free of this place, and I will come home to tell ye so. I have had enough of prisons and pain."

She was there, in his head. He smelled her, heard her voice, touched her skin. And suddenly the cell could no longer hold him—he felt his spirit soar. Out of the darkness and up into the light.

Airdy wasn't cooperating.

"I am not here on my uncle's business," he said for the third time, "so why should I say I am?"

"Because if you say you are come on your uncle's orders to fetch Barbara home, the duke will be obliged to let her go," Meg answered him for the third time. "Your uncle, the Duke of Argyll, is an important man here in Scotland. The Duke of Abercauldy will not want to displease him, will he? So he will release Barbara, and then Gregor can come home, too."

Where was Gregor? Was he being looked after properly

by Abercauldy? Meg feared it was not the case. She feared he might be locked up or hurt. Not dead, though. She was certain that if he were dead, she would feel the loss of him, in her heart.

Last night she had heard him call her name. His voice on the wind, soft with longing. And then he was gone again, and she was left, sitting up in the darkness, gazing at the stars, more alone than she had ever been.

"Gregor Grant is nothing to me," Airdy was saying. "He can rot in the dungeons for all I care. Aye, I'd like him to rot. He deserves to rot."

"Then your wife will rot, too," Meg said sharply, losing patience with him. "Do you want Barbara to rot?"

Airdy shook his head, slowly, frowning. "I love Barbara," he said, and to Meg's horror his eyes filled with tears. "Why does she no' love me?"

Meg could have given him several good reasons, but thought it prudent not to. "Fetch her home," she said instead, "and then maybe she will love you, Airdy."

He sniffed and wiped his hands over his face. "Och, verra well! You go on and on, woman, until a man can take no more. I dinna know how Gregor puts up with you."

Meg bit her lip on a smile. Gregor found her sharp tongue a delight, and that was another reason why she loved him. And then all urge to laugh was taken from her, as they reached the top of the hill and looked across at Abercauldy Castle.

She had never been here before in her life, and although she had known it to be large, this seemed even bigger than her imaginings. As for the castle's appearance . . . it looked grotesque, like a madman's nightmare.

Please, she thought, *let Abercauldy be sensible for once. Let him listen to reason, and agree to leave us be.*

"Come on then, woman!" Airdy called impatiently, pushing ahead. "What are you waiting for?"

Meg stabbed him with her eyes, and, with a kick of her heels, she followed him down.

"Captain Grant?"

The voice was lowered, but clear enough in the silence of the dungeon. Most of his men were sleeping, although Malcolm Bain stirred and half sat up. Gregor shook the sleep from himself and stood—or stooped beneath the low ceiling—to move toward the heavy wooden door, with its single, barred window.

The face that peered through, in the half-light of the torch, was one he found vaguely familiar.

"Captain Grant, I am Sergeant Calum Anderson. I am in the duke's private army."

Gregor wondered what Sergeant Calum Anderson was doing here at the dungeon door, but he forbore to ask him. He remembered him now. He was the soldier who had thrown Gregor an apologetic look as he drew his sword on him.

"Things are no' right here at the castle," Calum Anderson went on. "I dinna like the way Lorenzo is giving us orders in the duke's name. We havena even seen the duke himself for three weeks now. Lorenzo has sent off most of the servants and the castlefolk; there are hardly any left. It just dinna feel right."

Three weeks. Gregor tried to clear his head, rubbing a hand over his eyes. Three weeks? It sounded ominous, but maybe the duke was simply sulking over the fact that Meg had wed someone else. Though why send away his household to sulk? Apart from Lorenzo . . .

"Lorenzo gives you all your orders?" he demanded.

"Aye, all of them. We are used to that, but usually the duke will make an appearance, off and on. This is the longest we have ever gone without seeing him."

"So when you locked me and my men in this place . . . ?"

"Lorenzo told us he was following the duke's orders. But it was only on his say so, we never heard anything from the duke himsel'."

Sergeant Anderson leaned in closer, and Gregor smelled the whiskey on his breath. The question was, had the man drunk a dram to gain the courage to come down here, or was he simply a drunkard with an axe to grind against the duke's favorite servant?

"That is very strange, Sergeant."

"Aye, sir. We all think so. We dinna like taking our orders from Lorenzo, but he says he speaks for the duke, and what if he does? What if it's true? And yet . . . it has come to the point where there is talk of us going up to the Duke's rooms ourselves, and taking a wee peek. If ye ken?"

"I ken, Sergeant." He fixed the man with a straight look. "What do you want me to do?"

Calum Anderson shifted his feet, uncertain in his mind, and then took a deep breath. "We've been talking, sir, me and the others. We want to let ye out. The duke would never have left ye here so long. He'd have wanted to see ye straightaway, talk with ye, play a game or two of chess with ye and beat ye soundly. It is his way. This," he waved his hand at the cell, "is more like Lorenzo. So we want to let ye out, so that ye can go and talk with the duke yersel'. Then we'll all know."

And my going will save you from being reprimanded, if what Lorenzo says is the truth, Gregor thought to himself. But he held his tongue. This was their chance to be free.

And if it meant solving the mystery of the duke and Lorenzo at the same time, so be it. Gregor wasn't at all adverse to a wee confrontation with Lorenzo.

"I would be verra happy to speak with His Grace for you, Sergeant. Have you a key?"

Calum gave him a grin, and held up the ancient dungeon key with a flourish.

"Then let us out, ye daft bugger!" Malcolm Bain growled from behind Gregor. "Let us out, and we'll do the rest."

Calum eyed Malcolm Bain askance, but Gregor reassured him: "If there is something amiss, Sergeant, 'tis best if we waste no more time."

A moment later, Gregor heard the metal key in the lock. It was the sweetest sound he had heard in a long time, but he remained calm and steady. There was much to be done yet—no time to celebrate. If what Calum said was true, there was a mystery to be solved, and Lorenzo to be dealt with, before Gregor could go home.

The door swung open. It felt as if a cool breeze swept in, though in reality they were far underground. Time to move. Gregor took a deep breath of that imaginary air and turned to his men, calling for them to wake, while Malcolm Bain went about rousing the laggards. Calum, helpful man that he was, showed them to the armory, and they were able to reclaim their weapons.

"Do any of your men favor Lorenzo?" Gregor asked, tucking his pistols back into his belt.

Calum gave him a scornful look. "He isna even an Italian, sir. We reckon he's from the south, Hawick or somewhere close. One o' my men was in Rome for a time, and he set him some traps—questions, do ye ken? Lorenzo, as he calls himsel', couldna answer a single one."

"Gregor?" Malcolm Bain was back at his side, questions in his eyes.

"We find the duke," Gregor said. "We find Barbara Campbell. Then we find Lorenzo. And after that, we go home."

Malcolm grinned. "That sounds bonny to me, lad. Let's do't."

Chapter 28

Outside it was day. Why had Gregor thought it was night? He supposed he had become disorientated in the dungeons, where it was always night. How many hours had passed, how many days and nights? He did not know. Not many, he thought, for though he was hungry, it was not the gut-clenching sort of hunger he had felt in the gaol after Preston.

Meg would be worrying.

"There, sir." Calum pointed up a huge staircase, where wood gleamed and gold leaf glowed and silver fittings shone. Candelabra were heavy with candle stubs—no one had thought to replace them. There was no sound from above, no laughter, no shouts of merriment. Only a thick, unbroken silence.

Gregor frowned. The whole castle was silent, empty. Calum was telling the truth when he said Lorenzo had dismissed most of the servants. But how could a place like this run without sufficient staff? And, from all Gregor had heard, the Duke of Abercauldy liked his luxury. He certainly would never live in an empty, echoing castle with only Lorenzo as company. Not if he had a choice.

He began to climb the grand staircase, and then paused with his boot on the bottom step, turning to Calum. "Are you coming?"

Calum looked uneasy, glancing up into the still shadows as if he expected to see the duke peering down at him. "I shall wait here," he said firmly.

Gregor nodded at Malcolm Bain, and then they and their men, began to climb, attempting to be as quick and quiet as possible. At the top of the stairs an open door led into a flamboyant room, its ceiling painted in rich, jeweled colors, and its grand silver chandelier reflected in the numerous mirrors. Several doors opened on this room, and Gregor went first to one and then another, but the rooms were empty. When he reached the last door, he found it led into a small sitting room, made comfortable with damask-covered chairs and burning candles, and a fire alight in the hearth.

A man sat in one of the chairs.

He was before the fire, staring into it. He did not look up as Gregor stepped into the room, nor did he speak. His gaze was fixed upon the flames, and either he was lost in his own thoughts or he had no intention of acknowledging his unwelcome guests.

"Your Grace!" Calum Anderson had followed them after all. He stood staring at the silent, still shape in the chair as if he expected it to stand up and order him away. But the duke did nothing.

"Your Grace?" Gregor said, loud enough to be heard, and entered the room cautiously.

But the man in the chair did not turn. He wore a brocade coat with a stiffened skirt, the cloth weighed down with decoration. There was a sparkle of jewels at his throat and on his fingers, and his shoe buckles were sprinkled with diamonds. His curled wig was a little crooked upon his head, but other than that he looked normal.

Gregor took a step to one side, examining the duke's face, although Abercauldy never once looked at him. The man's eyes were dreamy, as if his mind had long ago left the confines of his body. In his hands he held a decorated silver locket, which he stroked and ran between his fingers lovingly, as if it were a living thing rather than made of cold metal.

"What has that devil done to him?" Calum whispered, shocked. "Can he hear us?"

"I dinna know." Gregor bent and, very gently, took the locket from the duke's hands. The man whimpered and clutched at it, like a child who has been deprived of a favorite toy. But Gregor was firm, straightening with the locket in his own hands. He clicked it open.

Meg! But no . . . it was a face *like* Meg's. A woman with a cloud of auburn hair, creamy skin and blue eyes. She even had a sprinkling of golden freckles. When Gregor's heartbeat had slowed again, he realized it wasn't Meg at all. The face was narrower, the nose longer, the eyes harder. Clearly this must be the Duke's first wife, the famous Isabella Mackenzie.

Shona had been correct when she said Isabella and Meg could have been sisters. No wonder Abercauldy, when he saw her, had determined to marry Meg. Isabella, according to Shona, had died when she fell from the north tower. He had lost her forever.

But then he saw Meg.

Malcolm Bain came up to Gregor's shoulder and also looked down at the portrait. "Did he murder her, do ye think?" he whispered loudly.

"I dinna know. Mabbe. Whatever happened in that tower, though, it sowed the seeds of his destruction."

"His mind's gone, then?"

Gregor didn't answer him, turning instead to the duke. "Your Grace?" he called, but still the man in the chair did not turn. He was at least twice as old as Meg, and not handsome, although his features were aristocratic. Only his chin, which was receding, spoiled his looks, making what might have been a strong face into a weak one.

The Duke of Abercauldy was not a man who was in control of his emotions; they were controlling him.

Something had happened. Had his mind always been weak? Gregor suspected so. From the rumors about him, the duke had always controlled women, used them. And then he had wed Isabella, a woman who sought to control him. He had loved her to madness—she had made his life hell, but still he had loved her. Some people *did* love like that. When Isabella died, whatever the means of that death, the duke had felt lost. And then he had found Meg, fixed upon Meg—but it was not Meg he had wanted, it was Isabella. He had seen Meg as another Isabella. And he had meant to reclaim her, whether she wished it or not. He had worked upon the general in his devious fashion, tricking him into signing the marriage papers, thinking he had won. But he had reckoned without stubborn Meg.

And he had reckoned without Gregor Grant.

Gently, Gregor returned the locket to Abercauldy's hands. The narrow fingers clenched hard about it, and he made keening sounds as he lifted it to his lips, kissing the cold silver and whispering to himself, words that made no sense nor had any meaning, except to him.

"He is mad," Malcolm Bain said with disgust. "For three weeks he has been like this? So Lorenzo has ruled in his stead."

"Who was it dressed the duke, cared for him?" Gregor asked, looking over his shoulder at Calum Anderson, who still appeared dazed by what he saw.

"Lorenzo. He guarded his privileges like a rabid dog."

"Then he's still playing valet, even though his master is beyond knowing, or caring, what he looks like."

"Where *is* Lorenzo?" Malcolm Bain asked, looking about, as if he expected to see the black-clothed servant appear in a puff of smoke.

"Where, indeed." Gregor moved towards the door. "And where is Barbara Campbell? Perhaps it is time we found them."

"I wish to see the duke! My uncle is the Duke of Argyll and he has sent me to fetch home Barbara Campbell. Do you not understand plain Scots, you fool!" Airdy was growing frustrated. They had been waiting at the gate for some sign that they were to be allowed in, but as yet none had come. The single soldier on guard above them simply ignored them, after calling out that they would be allowed in when the Duke of Abercauldy said so.

Meg wondered what they could do if the gate was not opened to them. How could she find Gregor then? The thought that he was inside there, somewhere, was awfully frustrating. Would she and Airdy storm the walls? It seemed a mite unlikely, although since she had been in his company, she had come to believe that Airdy Campbell was capable of anything.

He was muttering insults now. Words Meg had never imagined could be strung together. What on earth was a yellow-livered bullyhuff?

"Ah!"

Airdy moved forward expectantly, as the gates began to open. Meg hurried to follow, determined not to let Airdy take charge. Gregor was in here somewhere, she knew it in her heart. He needed her, and she would not leave without finding him. . . .

"Lady Meg."

That familiar sneering voice! It was the black-clothed Lorenzo, resplendent in his frilly cuffs and lacy shirtfront, and his gleaming black boots. He was standing slim and straight on one side of the curling double staircase that led to the grand front doors.

"Lorenzo," Meg said, trying to be calm. "I have come to discuss my wedding plans with the duke, just as you asked me to. Will you take me to him?"

But Lorenzo smiled and very gently shook his head. "The duke is indisposed," he told her smoothly. "I am afraid he cannot see anyone."

"How can he be indisposed?" Meg retorted, trying not to let her desperation show. "I have come all the way from Glen Dhui to see him! Take me to him now, Lorenzo. He will want to see me, and he will be angry with you if you send me away."

Lorenzo's smile did not waver—it was as if it were painted onto his face—but his eyes grew bleak. "The duke loves me, lady. He will not be angry with me for protecting him from a woman who is unworthy of him. He wanted to wed you, to raise you up higher than you could possibly imagine, but instead you turned to another. A soldier," he spat. "No, he will not see you. Go home now. Go home to your soldier, you are nothing but a soldier's whore."

He had never been so openly insulting. This was not a good sign. And yet she could not give up, she would not. She would not leave without Gregor, and if she could not find him . . . What was the point in going home at all?

"There is nothing common about the Laird of Glen Dhui," Meg replied with dangerous quiet, "and there is certainly nothing common about me. Take me to the duke, Lorenzo, or you will regret it. Believe me. I will not leave until I have seen him."

Lorenzo laughed, opening his mouth for more insults.

"Shut up!"

Meg had forgotten about Airdy, and clearly Airdy had had enough of this conversation. For once she was glad of the interruption and watched with interest as Airdy pushed forward on his dun horse, his voice rising dangerously.

"I dinna give a bugger about your duke, you stupid man. I want my wife! Where is Barbara? Take me to her, you wee bastard. Now!"

Lorenzo looked surprised to be the target of such aggression, from a man he didn't even know. His eyes narrowed. "Your Barbara is happy here. She and the duke have become very close. I don't think she will be going home with you, whoever you are."

"You ill-favored cur!" Airdy dug his heels in, and was suddenly riding at a hard gallop. Meg squealed as he sent his dun horse up the curling stairs, straight at Lorenzo.

The servant spun about and ran, with Airdy close after him. Meg turned a wide-eyed look on her men, where they had formed a protective half-circle about her, and found them similarly astounded. For a brief moment she considered following Airdy, on horseback, into the Duke's house. But it would not do.

Hurriedly she dismounted and ran up the staircase, into the castle. Ahead she could hear Lorenzo screaming, a high-pitched sound that rang throughout the many rooms. There were other voices, too, calling out in confusion. Airdy was furiously cursing and, as Meg stopped and watched in amazed wonder, he sent his horse up the magnificent inner staircase and started firing his pistol.

Plaster fell from the ceiling. A glass jar shattered.

"Barbara!" Airdy bellowed. "Barbara, come to me!"

Above the sound of the horse and the screams and the pistol, there was a thudding, as if someone were battering down a door, and above it Meg could hear Barbara Campbell's shrill squeals for help.

Airdy forgot all about Lorenzo. He turned the dun horse down a corridor, shouting Barbara's name. Lorenzo, taking his chance, made his escape up a second, much less grand staircase, and reached another landing just as a man stepped out. Lorenzo ran straight into his arms.

The man was Gregor Grant.

With a low moan, Lorenzo promptly fainted, leaving Gregor holding a lifeless, dangling puppet.

Behind him, Malcolm Bain gave a snort of disgust. "He is yellow-livered after all," he said, and removed the offending article from his laird's arms.

Gregor looked over the banister to where Meg now stood on the lower landing.

"Was it you who brought Airdy, *morvoren*?"

"I'm afraid so," she said, with a breathless laugh, her eyes brilliant at the sight of him. She wondered she could speak at all. She was trembling with happiness and relief.

"Och, well, he came in useful."

She gazed up at him, wondering when it was that she had last seen anything so wonderful. His clothes might be grubby, and he might be pale and tired, with the beginnings of a fine beard, but he was her beloved husband. Her beloved Highlander.

"Oh, Gregor . . ."

"Wait there, Meg. I'll come down to you."

And he did, taking the stairs two and three at a time, straight into her arms. He promptly picked her up, and whirled her around until she laughed and cried, and then he simply held her.

"You should not have come, Meg," he scolded her softly, tenderly. "You should not have left the safety of our home."

"Home isn't home without you in it," she snapped, and then wished she could cut out her sharp tongue. How could she speak so to him, at such a time as this?

But Gregor gazed down into her eyes and smiled his delight and his agreement. "No," he said. "It isna."

"I thought you were locked up," she whispered, tears spilling down her cheeks, as she remembered that mournful, lonely call in the forest. "I thought you were in prison. I could not leave you like that, Gregor. I had to come and save you."

"You have saved me," he said, kissing away the tears. "And I love you for it, Meg. I love you."

Meg pressed her face against his chest, breathing him in.

He loved her. Gregor loved her. Could her heart get any more full?

"Next time you go to fight a duke," she said, struggling for equilibrium, "then I am coming with you, Gregor Grant."

He smiled, his handsome mouth curling at the edges. "Och, Meg," he murmured, "I wouldna have it any other way."

"It was truly a bedlam," Malcolm Bain told his son Angus, the day after he returned home. "Airdy Campbell found his wife locked in one of the salons. It seems that when Lorenzo realized he had kidnapped the wrong lassie he was furious, but he was too stubborn to let her go. Probably embarrassed, too. But with all the servants gone, he was lonely, and he began to treat her as a guest rather than a prisoner. He and Barbara spent many an evening together, sipping the duke's wine and sharing their troubles."

Angus chuckled, glancing up at his father shyly. "And what of Airdy? What of him?"

"Well, Airdy saved Barbara, in a manner of speaking, so she flung herself at him and climbed atop his horse, and they rode back down the stairs together. We dinna see them again. I dinna know if Airdy's still taking up his post at the pass. I suppose the pair of them will be happy enough, until the next big argument, eh?"

"And the Duke of Abercauldy was truly insane, was he?"

"Aye, something had happened to him. When he came out of his faint, Lorenzo told us that the duke truly had loved his wife, Isabella. It had been like a madness with him, as if he wanted to own her body and soul. There had

been other women in the past who did not like the duke so
well, and when he was weary of them he . . ." Malcolm
Bain cleared his throat, "Well, that is not for yer ears, Angus. He was an evil man. I can tell ye, though, that Isabella
must have been crazy herself, to stay with him. They were
two of a kind, the Duke of Abercauldy and his wife.
Lorenzo told us that they liked nothing better than to tie
each other up and . . ." He cleared his throat again. "Well,
anyway, they spent their time trying to best each other, until Isabella fell . . . jumped . . . was pushed to her death.
Who knows the truth?"

"I dinna suppose the duke will tell us?"

"No, Angus, he canna say. If he pushed her, then she has
had her revenge on him, because without her he is a shell of
a man. He thought with Lady Meg he could relive his life
with Isabella, make it turn out differently, but when
Lorenzo told him that she'd wed another, he realized at last
that it could never be, and he sank into his madness.
Lorenzo tried to pretend he was all right. He was afraid that
if the servants found out, they would tell the world that the
duke was mad. Lorenzo couldn't have that—he would lose
his own position, his own power. It was all he lived for. So
he played pretend. And now the duke is put away in a bedlam of his own. Poor Lorenzo."

"Poor Lorenzo!" Angus cried indignantly. "He locked ye
up in the dungeon, Father!"

The word *Father* stilled Malcolm Bain for a heartbeat.
Shocking and yet wonderful, the name hung in the air between them. Realizing what he had said, Angus went red
faced, making Malcolm aware that it would be a long journey before they could truly be comfortable with each other

and their relationship. But it would be a journey that was very worthwhile, every moment of it.

"Aye, he did lock me up," Malcolm went on evenly. "He dinna want us finding out about the duke. And I think, too, he wanted his wee bit of revenge upon the laird, for locking *him* up."

"So now what will happen to him?"

"I dinna know, Angus. The laird said mabbe he would send him to prison, but I dinna think Gregor Grant would do that to any man, not even Lorenzo. Mabbe he'll go home, to whatever place he comes from. Not Italy, I know that for sure!" he muttered to himself.

"Aye, let him go home." Angus nodded his head, preferring that ending. "And what of the laird and the lady," he added, with another bashful glance.

"They are verra happy, and all is well."

"And what of my mother and . . . and . . ."

"Your mother and I will be happy, too, Angus. We are happy now, but with every year we will grow happier. And I will grow uglier, and she will grow rounder."

"Enough of that, Malcolm Bain!" Alison's hand tapped him on the shoulder, but it did not hurt, and a smile lurked in her angry Forbes eyes. "I think we have all had enough of fairy tales for one night."

"Whatever ye say, my little oatcake," Malcolm Bain replied blandly, and winked at his son.

Angus chuckled, and glanced from his father to his mother. And it was clear, that for him, the fairy tale had just begun.

Epilogue

One year later

Meg looked out upon Glen Dhui, watching the sun sinking over it. *All was well.*

The past year had been a good one, the crops had been bountiful, and there had been no great sickness in the glen. The people were happy and content.

There had been one sadness: The general was no longer with them. Meg thought of him every day and mourned his loss, but she knew he had lived his life and had left her in the clear knowledge that she was well protected and well loved. Alison had foreseen his passing.

And Gregor, her husband the laird, had reclaimed his position as if he had never left it. No, that was not quite true. Gregor treated his position as laird with a genuine joy and gratitude that he probably would never have felt if he had not lost it for twelve years.

The baby stirred in Meg's arms, and she stroked the soft,

velvet cheek. Her son, hers and Gregor's. His fine hair was darker than his father's, but she had the feeling it would end up like Gregor's—certainly there was no fire in it. But his eyes were definitely hers, blue and clear, and she had a feeling that they would stay so.

"They'll change to gold," Gregor had insisted.

"Maybe the next one."

"Och, Meg, how can you speak of another so soon after this?" Gregor asked, genuinely shocked. He had been anguished at the birth, suffering more, Meg suspected, than had she. That had been four months ago, and he hadn't seemed to want to touch her since, as if he were afraid to . . .

Meg rocked the baby in her arms, singing a soft lullaby.

A warm arm slipped about her, and a warm voice murmured, "My bonny wife, keeping her sharp eye on the glen."

"Someone has to watch out for the people of Glen Dhui," she replied evenly, and turned her head to smile at him.

He smiled back, his eyes moving over her face, memorizing each feature with an intensity she would never grow used to. An artist's eye, she supposed, for Gregor was always drawing her. He saw her in a way that she had never seen herself; when he sketched her, Meg was beautiful.

His gaze dropped to the sleeping baby, and his smile softened into a mixture of love and pride.

"His eyes are still blue," Meg murmured.

Gregor frowned. "Aye." He glanced at her and away, as if there were words he had to speak and yet did not quite know how to. "Meg, it has been four months now, since the baby."

"Och, Gregor, are ye wanting another already? Just so that ye can have a babe with golden eyes?" she teased.

He laughed at her imitation of his accent, but his eyes held doubt. "No, Meg, 'tis not that I want another, although

I do, when you are ready. I am thinking of . . ." He sighed, impatient with himself. "Och, Meg, I want ye! I am burning up for ye. 'Tis been four months, six if we count the two before, when ye were unwell. I have been hard as a sword for weeks now. I dinna know if I can go on much longer without ye in my bed again."

Meg stared at him, feeling the color slowly heat her cheeks. He wanted her. He had wanted her for six months, and she had thought . . . How could she have been so foolish? He had been giving her time to recover, probably waiting for her to make the first move.

Gregor rubbed a hand over his eyes. "Mabbe I've spoken too soon," he said, but there was disappointment in every line of him.

Meg's heart overflowed with love. Carefully, she chose her words, making each one special.

"Gregor, I have been lying in my bed thinking of you every night since our son was born. Sometimes I get out of my bed and go to the door and stand there, thinking of you. I have been afraid to go to you. I thought, well, I am a fool. I thought maybe you did not want me any more. So I waited. We have both been waiting, and wasting time."

He was watching her with that same intensity, reading her expression, searching her eyes. And now whatever he saw there made him give his beautiful smile. "Meg, my Meg, how could I no' want ye? I will always want ye; my body hurts for yours. Without ye I am nothing."

"Does it?" she whispered. "Does it hurt for mine?"

He moved closer, his mouth brushing hers and then deepening into a long and passionate kiss. They both groaned when it ended, trembling with need.

"Gregor, come to me tonight," she sounded breathless.

"I will, *morvoren*."

"After supper, Gregor."

"Aye, Meg."

"Immediately after supper."

He kissed her again, tracing the shape of her lips with his tongue, until Meg clung to him. She had been waking in the night dreaming of him, dreaming of the things he did to her, and now, at last, she could make those dreams come true.

Reluctantly, Gregor put her aside. He stepped away from her, paused, and then turned back. His golden eyes glinted beneath their dark lashes in a way that made her legs weak with desire.

"Meg," he said, his voice soft with longing, "do we really need supper?"

Romance is always better with Avon Books . . . look for these crowd pleasers in November

THE PLEASURE OF HER KISS by Linda Needham
An Avon Romantic Treasure

The Earl of Hawkesly exchanged wedding vows with a woman he barely knew, then left her to play the spy for his country. Now two years later, he's ready to perform his much neglected husbandly duties . . . except Kate doesn't recognize him! He may have met his match in this spirited woman, and it will take a special seduction to win her heart.

A THOROUGHLY MODERN PRINCESS by Wendy Corsi Staub
An Avon Contemporary Romance

Her Highness, Emmaline of Verdunia, would have wed her suitable prince and be done with it—if she hadn't been swept off her feet by Granger Lockwood IV, "America's Sexiest Single Man." Now she's hurtling across the Atlantic in the private jet of the surprised playboy . . . and falling in love with the last man she could ever marry!

TO TEMPT A BRIDE by Edith Layton
An Avon Romance

From the moment she first saw tall, dashing Eric Ford, Camille's heart was lost. But Eric seems content to be no more than her unofficial protector, watching over the younger sister of his dear friend. When danger and betrayal threaten, will it destroy a secret love . . . or bind two hearts for all eternity?

WICKEDLY YOURS by Brenda Hiatt
An Avon Romance

The *ton* is abuzz over the arrival of Sarah Killian, a stunning stranger who shrouds her past in mystery. And no one is more intrigued than Lord Peter Northrup. The handsome rake wants to know *everything* about this beauty who has so enflamed his desire. But the enchantress guards her secrets well, even as she pulls him into a world of danger any self-respecting gentleman would be well advised to avoid.

REL 1003

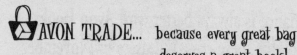

AVON TRADE... because every great bag
deserves a great book!

Paperback $13.95
ISBN 0-06-056277-3

Paperback $13.95
ISBN 0-06-053214-9
Audio $18.95
ISBN 0-06-055710-9

Paperback $13.95
($21.95 Can.)
ISBN 0-06-093841-2

Paperback $13.95
($21.95 Can.)
ISBN 0-06-051237-7

Paperback $13.95
($21.95 Can.)
ISBN 0-380-81936-8

Paperback $13.95
($21.95 Can.)
ISBN 0-06-008166-X

Don't miss the next book by your favorite author.
Sign up for AuthorTracker by visiting *www.AuthorTracker.com*.

Available wherever books are sold, or call 1-800-331-3761 to order.

ATP 1003